Voices of My Fathers

Voices of My Fathers

A Five-Hundred-Year Journey

David Scoboria

DAGMAR
MIURA
LOS ANGELES

Published by Dagmar Miura
Los Angeles
www.dagmarmiura.com

Voices of My Fathers: A Five-Hundred-Year Journey

This is a work of fiction and a memoir. Names, characters, businesses, places, events, and incidents are either the products of the author's imagination or used in a fictitious manner. Any resemblance to actual persons, living or dead, or actual events is purely coincidental.

First published 2025

ISBN: 979-8-89195-082-5

Contents

Prologue ix

My Fathers xi

1. The Boat 1
   Ramon Escobar, 1502–1542

2. Building the Barns 23
   Ewan Skiburio, 1531–1597

3. Fighting for the King 57
   Robert Skyburriowe, 1613–1645

4. Trafalgar 99
   John Lower, 1782–1847

5. The Crossing 141
   John Scabora, 1802–1867

6. Finishing the Brass 165
   Joseph Scoboria, 1832–1905

7. Night Train to Calais, Maine 183
   Clarence Preston Scoboria, 1882–1960

8. Darling Girl 213
   C. Preston Scoboria, Jr., 1912–1993

9. State Line 249
   David Scoboria, 1950–

   Final Notes 267

   Appendix: Evolution of a Name 270

   Acknowledgments 272

   Notes 273

   Bibliography 275

Prologue

Every person has a story to tell. Most of our stories disappear when we die, lingering for a short while in the memories of our children and grandchildren. Only the stories of famous people live on in the public sphere. My great grandparents are known to me only through a few anecdotes told by my parents. Ancestors before that are a blank slate, only names and dates in a book.

For years I have thought about my forefathers, the men who were my direct ancestors. There is little that I know about most of them other than their dates of birth, marriage, and death. What they did during their lives and what they thought about, those details are unknown.

When I was a small boy, family stories were told at the dinner table. They happened before I was born and were important enough to be remembered and recounted years later. My father served aboard a ship in the Pacific Ocean during World War II. What was his life really like during the war? My grandfather lost a famous track race when one of his shoes came off. Could he have won the race? A distant ancestor was said to have been a ship's pilot in Falmouth, England, and rowed across Falmouth Harbor to court the young woman who became his wife. Were these stories true? Could the real stories be uncovered?

The Internet provides enormous research possibilities from old books and records which have been scanned and are now available online. If a person has an odd name like mine, it is possible to find clues about the men and women who came before us. The spellings of the names may be different, for until about 1800, most people did not read or write, and information was taken down verbally by a scribe or a curate in the local parish. The clues may only be a line here or there, a name on a list.

The clues I found provided background information for a series of stories about some of the men who preceded me, my fathers. Each was born and raised, had dreams and disappointments, experienced success and tragedy. They were farmers and sailors, shoemakers and builders.

There are no heroes or villains in this book. Each story is a work of fiction, but each contains a particle of truth. Some historical characters appear in the stories, although their portrayal is fictional. All mistakes in historical facts, dates, or places are solely my responsibility.

These are the voices of my fathers.

My Fathers

Ramon Escobar
1502–1542
teacher

Ewan Skiburio
1531–1597
farmer

two generations

Robert Skyburriowe
1613–1645
farmer, soldier

John Lower
1782–1847
farmer

six generations

John Scabora
1802–1867
laborer, cobbler

Eden Lower
1800–1883

Joseph Scoboria
1832–1905
brass finisher

Joseph Lower Scoboria
1855–1945
minister, machinist

Clarence Preston Scoboria
1882–1960
teacher and track coach

Clarence Preston Scoboria Jr. "Scibby"
1912–1993
teacher, coach, builder, owner of
numerous small businesses

David Scoboria
born 1950
carpenter, building contractor

CHAPTER ONE

The Boat

The Spanish Inquisition officially began in 1478 with a decree issued by Pope Sixtus IV that authorized King Ferdinand of Aragon and Queen Isabella of Castile to appoint an inquisitor to investigate persons suspected of having heretical beliefs. The Inquisition functioned mainly to investigate Jews and Muslims who had converted to Catholicism, but also investigated Catholics who were suspected of various nonreligious crimes, including disrespect to the crown. Persons were chosen based on anonymous accusations and were imprisoned, tortured, and in extreme cases, put to death. The Inquisition was highly active from 1478 until 1530, but continued until its abolition in 1834. Persons who were denounced could lose their liberty, their property, and ultimately their lives.

Excerpt from Foxe's *Book of Martyrs*, published in 1563:

The Persecution of Dr. Constantine

Dr. Constantine, — was a medical man of uncommon natural abilities and profound learning; inclusive of several modern tongues, he was acquainted with the Latin, Greek, and Hebrew languages and perfectly well knew not only the sciences called abstruse, but those arts which come under the denomination of polite literature. — A worthy gentleman named Scobaria, having erected a school for divinity lectures, appointed Dr. Constantine to be reader therein. He immediately undertook the task, and read lectures, by portions, on the Proverbs, Ecclesiastes, and Canticles; and was beginning to expound the Book of Job, when he was seized by the inquisitors.[1]

Ramon Escobar, 1502–1542

October 1530

The man was on a boat. The boat was on the ocean, a gray, waving sea that dipped and swelled, splashed over the bow of the boat, and went on forever. There was nothing in sight except the sea. There were no birds or sea creatures, just the sea. The man hung on to the rail of the boat. He was seasick, had been seasick since the first choppy rollers tossed the boat about as it left the shelter of the harbor. He had forgotten what it was like to be on land and could not remember how long he had been on the boat. Each moment was endless.

He was not alone on the boat, just alone in his misery. The sailors who worked the boat, raised the sails and furled them, climbed the masts and tightened the lines; they laughed at him at first, chuckled at the plight of this landsman, who had fled his native land, but now found himself in such misery. After several days had passed, they were no longer interested in him. They knew that when they came up from their foul-smelling quarters below deck, they would see him crouched at the rail. During the night, he had tied himself to the rail for fear that he would fall asleep and be washed overboard by the rough seas. But he had never come close to sleep, and drowning didn't seem like a bad alternative to this endless nausea.

———◆———

Ramon Escobar, for that was the name of the man on the boat, had heard about seasickness and had imagined it as a distant problem, one that would never bother him. After all, he lived in Leon, a city far from the coast, and he taught in a school for young men. But a short time ago, one of his students had quietly whispered that he was implicated in the heresies associated with his good friend, Dr. Constantine. He found it hard to believe. He had been dismayed when Dr. Constantine had been accused of heresy. How could anyone believe that this mild and gentle man could dishonor the words of Jesus? When he heard of the charges against Dr. Constantine, he wondered how anyone could believe evil thoughts about a doctor who taught poor men about the Bible. How could anyone believe that treating the illnesses of the poor children of the barrio was a threatening act, especially when he taught them about a God who loved them and who sent his only son to die for them? But when the officers of the Inquisition came to his school and asked for Dr. Constantine, Ramon looked into their eyes and realized there was no laughter in them. These were men who knew that if the Officer of the Inquisition had made the charge, then it had justice and reason behind it. They arrested Dr. Constantine, and he was taken to prison.

Ramon had gone to the court and urged the release of the doctor. At first, he had been dismissed without being heard. But after a week, he was allowed to come inside and talk with the prosecutor, a man who seemed at first interested, then curious about the doctor's beliefs. Ramon defended Dr. Constantine's actions as those of a man trying to help poor people who could least help themselves, those with little learning and less money. Ramon talked on. He praised the doctor, telling of the times he had sat with old men who were near death and afraid and had given medicines to mothers with sick children. These mothers came to him later and blessed him for saving the lives of their children and for describing the love God had for them. The prosecutor listened, and Ramon began to think he was making an impression, so he talked more, telling of the times he had seen the doctor set the bones of injured workmen without getting paid and had taught small children to read the Bible. The prosecutor listened, then abruptly waved his hand and said, "There is much this man has done, too much to hear in one sitting."

Ramon was ushered suddenly out of the office. He realized that what he had said in the doctor's defense could be used in other ways when twisted around in the mouth of someone who was trying to damage him. He was ashamed of having possibly hurt his dear friend. Then he realized that perhaps he had hurt himself the most. Maybe the prosecutor had already judged the doctor and found him guilty, but Ramon, who had innocently gone to help a friend, was now under suspicion.

Days passed, and nothing happened. Ramon began to think that it had been a dream, that his fears were groundless, and one day, news would come that the charges against the doctor had been dropped, that he was to be released and could resume his teachings at the school and his good works among the poor. But that did not happen. Each day, Ramon went to his school and taught his classes. Each evening, he went to the café for his supper. He met his friends there, drank a glass of wine, and ate a light meal. He and his friends laughed a little and discussed the events of the day. Rarely was the doctor's name mentioned, and then only in passing. It was as if he had gone away on a trip or moved to another city instead of being held in prison a few streets away. After supper, Ramon walked to his home, spoke politely with his neighbors when he met them, and greeted the priest when they passed on the road. He went to Mass every Sunday and made his confession, just as before. Life was the same.

Then one day, Ramon arrived at school and found that one student was missing from class. A servant waited with an elegantly written note. It stated that Bartholemew would not be coming to class at the school any longer. His father felt the boy needed to attend a school where his religious training would be pursued with more firmness. That was all. No criticism or accusation, just one student missing. Two weeks later, another student came to Ramon to say that his parents were sending him to an academy in the capital, and he would leave the next day. Two students, only two out of nine, yet it seemed uncanny that in the seven years Ramon had been a teacher, never had two students left in such close succession. Students had grown too old for the classes or had left to pursue specialized studies, but never had students left in the circumstances of these two. This would not have worried Ramon, except times were different now. In the past, he and his friends had laughed about the day's events, but those days were no more. Now, people talked carefully, as if someone might be listening, as if it might be wrong to laugh at what happened at the royal court.

———◆———

A strong wave washed against the boat and broke over the bow. Ramon, hunched down along the rail on the lee side of the boat, felt a splash as the spray hit him. He was so wet that a little more water didn't matter, except that he had not felt a wave hit him before. He peered out into the mist, hoping to see something on which his eyes could focus. The sea stretched into the distance, wave upon wave, as far as he could see. Sometimes, the boat rode high atop a wave, and Ramon could see a long distance across the sea. Then the wave passed, the boat lay in a trough, and the horizon was only a few feet away. The wind blew ceaselessly. The guy ropes, which stayed the masts, made a peculiar whine that varied slightly as wind gusts hit the boat. There was no visible sign the boat was moving forward through the water. For all Ramon knew, it could be bobbing in place and not traveling at all. He knew they had left port three days before, and it was at least four more days to their destination, the Spanish colony of the Netherlands. The boat was not fast, only able to sail at six knots in a favorable wind. It had made the trip to Antwerp many times. But to Ramon, it was a trip into a fearful, strange place. He couldn't believe anyone could tell where they were. For all he knew, the boat might be just outside the harbor of Gijon with the officers of the Inquisition nearby.

———◆———

When Ramon crossed the mountains to Gijon, he knew the officers were close behind him. He fled from Leon at night, sensing that his arrest was only hours away, and the urgency allayed his fear. He was not a traveler and had been across the mountains only two other times, both in midsummer, when he went to Gijon to escape the heat in Leon and to spend a few days at the small coastal city. He associated the trip with pleasure and relaxation. This time was different. Ramon had never been a good horseman and seldom rode for fun. The mare he found had an uneven stride, and he was sore after traveling only a few miles. In the darkness, he misjudged the turns, and twice he turned the horse into the rough at the side of the road. This jarred him badly. He realized the horse could find her way with little guidance from him, so he let the reins loose and clung to her like a flour sack, only reacting when she slackened her pace or tried to pull up. The night was endless. The trip usually

Expected route of the boat

took a full day with a fresh horse, and he was not making good time. He knew the officers who pursued him would travel much faster. They were accomplished horsemen, strong and confident. He was a man of letters, hesitant at physical trials.

Ramon would not have left Leon at all but for the warning given him by Jaime, one of his students. Jaime was the son of an officer of the Inquisition, a young man who had been sent to his school because so many other schools had closed in the past few years. Teachers were often under suspicion by the Church, and many of them had been arrested. Some had been executed, and others remained in prison. Jaime's father brought him to the school on the first day, then stayed and listened to the lessons for most of the day, waiting for Señor Escobar, as Ramon was known, to criticize or comment on the actions of the Church or the crown. But Ramon never felt that his role was to criticize the king or his ministers, and he refrained from political talk. His role was to educate young minds with the knowledge that had been passed down for a thousand years. He continued to speak of the teachings of Saint Ignatius of Loyola. This was followed by hours of drills in Latin verbs and phrases.

The father must have been satisfied, for after lunch and siesta, when the heat of the afternoon deadened the lessons, he dropped off to sleep in the back of the classroom. He only woke when the drone of the students reciting the declension of third series verbs ended, and there was a moment of silence. It must have been the silence that woke him, for he stirred and looked about, startled at finding himself in a room with eight young men sitting on stools around Ramon. One of the boys may have snickered a little. The father snorted and shook, drew himself up and stood, then turned and left the room. Ramon wondered if he had been offended, but nothing was said, and the son continued to attend class. It had been eight months since that first day, and there had not been any sign of disapproval from the father. Monthly fees appeared regularly at the start of each month. But yesterday, at the end of class, Jaime waited until the rest of the students had left the room, then approached Ramon. "You must leave now," he whispered. Ramon was startled and began to protest, but Jaime spoke again. "You must go, sir." Then he turned and left the room.

———◆———

Ramon had seen ships in the harbor at Gijon, and they were foreign to his world. He had passed sailors in the streets of the town, small men in tattered clothing who smelled of *orujo,* the local liquor. They wore ragged scarves wrapped about their heads. But Ramon had never been aboard a ship. He had seen them making their way across the harbor on sunny days, and the sight was tranquil and carefree. He imagined that the life of a sailor was to be envied, that they spread the sails and then did little while the wind conveyed them to their destination.

Now, he had been on a ship for three days, and he saw that a sailor's life was far from easy. This was not July, but October. The weather was not sunny, but wet, cold, and windy. The sailors toiled constantly, shifting sails, tightening and then loosening lines at the command of their captain, a small man with a stern look. One time, a sailor failed to carry out his orders, and the captain leaped down from the quarterdeck and screamed at the sailor, threatening him with punishment if the man did not carry out the orders immediately. It had been a simple misunderstanding; the sailor had been busy and had not heard the orders, and he was shocked that he had become the focus of the captain's rage. But Ramon saw that inattention was no excuse on the boat, and he compared it to his own classroom, where he expected his pupils to pay attention through even the most tedious lectures.

Ramon could see that all the sailors were afraid of the captain. They were simple men who owned almost nothing besides their clothes. They wore no shoes, and the soles of their feet were blackened from the tar on the deck and cracked from the constant exposure to seawater. Several of the men had no teeth that he could see, and the rest had blackened and diseased teeth, which Ramon attributed to their terrible diet, mostly salt pork and biscuits with no vegetables or fresh meat. Yet they were cheerful, sometimes singing as they worked. They displayed a rude form of camaraderie. Often, he saw one sailor slap another on the back or whisper in his ear, and both erupted in laughter. Ramon knew they laughed at him and at how seasick he was. Several times, he looked up and saw two sailors laughing and looking his way. He heard one of them talking to another about the "ailing gentleman," then both of them laughed. Ramon knew they enjoyed the sight of his discomfort.

But after two days had passed, first one of the sailors, then another, began to sympathize with him. The first was an old man, his body twisted from some past accident. He didn't climb the masts with the others, but spent his time on deck or below, doing odd jobs that required no great agility. At the end of the second day, when Ramon was at the depth of his agony and thought that dying might be a relief, the old man approached him with a cup of water. "Ye need to drink something," he said, holding out the cup. Ramon took it and tried to drink, although the liquid came back up almost as fast as he swallowed. "Slowly, slowly," said the old man. "Just sip on it. Or ye will begin to swallow salt water from the waves that splash on you, and it will kill ye." Ramon looked up in thanks, and the man smiled slightly. The man's face was covered with grime, and coarse whiskers nearly covered his mouth. What few teeth he had were jagged and rotting, and his breath was foul. But his voice was kind, and Ramon thanked him. Ramon kept the cup and drank a little at a time as the old man had advised. He was able to keep it down, although he felt no better. That night, a few stars appeared, and the waves quieted slightly, giving Ramon hope the next day would have calmer seas. He drifted off to sleep late in the night, crouched at the rail, and slept for a few hours.

Ramon woke at early dawn and found that the wind, rather than quieting down, had grown stronger and was blowing from the southwest. The captain was pacing back and forth on the quarterdeck, the raised platform at the stern of the boat. From time to time, he spoke to the man at the tiller. Each time the captain spoke, the man moved the tiller slightly. Ramon was curious why the captain was on deck at this early hour, and why he was so concerned about the boat's heading. Ramon had read about ships that sank. Once, a friend of his had been aboard a vessel traveling from Bilbao to Gijon. Just outside the harbor of Gijon, the pilot made an error, and the boat hit a rock. The impact made a hole in the hull, and the vessel foundered. Ramon did not understand why men would go to sea if there was a high chance of death, and when he boarded the ship, he had taken for granted he would reach the Netherlands safely, as long as seasickness didn't kill him first. But now, through his nausea, he began to sense that even the captain, a man who had spent most of his life at sea, might not be fully in control of their fate.

The day passed. The crew now acknowledged Ramon as part of the deck, even nodding in recognition when they passed by him. He marveled at how three days before, they had never seen him, while now they accepted him as part of the fabric of the vessel. He supposed it was the nature of their lives. The ship had a constantly changing group of passengers, and the sailors accepted new people quickly, while his world remained the same, and it took a long time for him to accept change.

It was a shock to Ramon that he might have something to learn from the sailors. Yet, as they worked, and he listened to their speech, crude to his ears but well suited to their tasks, he realized he had been arrogant toward them. In the three days he had been aboard the vessel, he had scarcely seen one action that he understood or could have accomplished without someone showing him. Even the sailors' language was filled with terms he had never heard before, words referring to lines that held the sails, others referring to protrusions on the deck to which the lines were fastened. The sails themselves had names strange to him. Often, he heard the captain utter two or three commands, and he had no idea what the sailors were told to do. But the sailors knew, and they obeyed immediately, moving with great agility up the masts and out onto the horizontal poles that held the sails. It terrified him to see them up there, clinging by their legs while untying ropes with both hands. Once, he saw a man clench a rope tightly with his teeth to steady himself, and Ramon was fearful for the man's safety until his hands were free. But he came to realize this work was routine for the sailors; sometimes they joked as they worked, and they called out from one mast to another.

But this morning, Ramon noticed signs that all was not right. The men were less cheerful and held their mouths more tightly than before. As the morning passed, Ramon expected the captain to leave the quarterdeck and for the mate to take command, as had happened every other morning. But on this day, the captain stayed on the quarterdeck, peering sometimes at the swell of the sails, sometimes at the waves in front of the ship, as if his gaze could penetrate the murky weather. The rain continued; the waves remained high and broke around the ship on all sides. There was no sign the weather was going to clear. Ramon didn't know how far the ship had already traveled, whether they had four or five more days of sailing until they reached their destination. The rest of the passengers stayed below deck, although how they could bear the stench of the cramped quarters that passed as cabins was beyond Ramon. He knew that if he was going to die on this boat, he wanted to meet the sea outside, not trapped in a box.

At midday, Ramon saw the old sailor approach, holding out a cup. Ramon saw that it contained soup and took a small sip. He retched a little at the smell of food, but he was able to swallow. When he looked up to thank the sailor, he noticed the man was not at ease. The old sailor leaned forward toward him, close enough that Ramon could smell the stink from his clothing. "He fears the rocks," the old sailor said, and he nodded toward the quarterdeck where the captain was still pacing. Thinking back to an atlas he kept in his classroom in Leon, Ramon remembered that at the tip of Brittany, where the ocean met the waters of the channel, there were a dozen or more tiny islands with the name Îles du Diable, the "Devil Isles." He had always seen maps as instruments of learning, suitable for hanging in a classroom to teach students. But now, he appreciated that the shapes and lines on those maps were real places with real hazards. He realized that the name for the rocks likely derived from the fate of many real ships that had smashed into them and had been wrecked in weather much like this.

The old sailor spoke again. "He fears the wind from the west; he is holding into it to clear the devils." That was all that he said, for the captain called out to him to help secure one of the lines, and he scurried off. Ramon now understood what was happening, and he watched with more interest and growing dread. Once or twice, Ramon saw other passengers climb to the top of the hatchway. Several even stepped onto the deck momentarily, but the wind and rain repelled them, and they quickly returned down the ladder. How they could tolerate the cabins below deck was a mystery to Ramon. He had gone below deck when the rain began to fall, but was overwhelmed by the stink of vomit, shit, and unwashed bodies. The air was thick with strong tobacco smoke. He barely made it back to the rail before he retched again, and after that, he didn't try to go below again, preferring to bear the cold and wet as long as it came with clean air.

The wind grew stronger in the afternoon. The waves, instead of rising to a peak and breaking in a froth around the ship, now seemed like a flat sheet of water, because the wind was blowing the tops off the waves. More seawater was sloshing onto the deck. It was colder than Ramon remembered from the day before, and his hands became numb. He flexed his fingers constantly, trying to keep the circulation flowing. His ankles were becoming raw where the blanket rubbed against them. He was grateful for his layer of fat, and that his blanket was made of good wool, for though he shivered with the cold and wet, the fabric retained some body heat around him. He marveled at the sailors and their skimpy clothing, ragged cotton pants with rips that showed their buttocks, and guessed that the constant exertion of their work kept them warm. No sooner did they finish changing the sails and go below to keep out of the wind, than the captain called them back to adjust the sails again and cursed fiercely if they didn't move quickly enough for his liking. The ship shuddered each time it struck a wave, but Ramon saw that as long as the sails caught some wind, the ship maintained a steady direction. How did it go the way they wanted, he wondered, and how did the captain know which direction to steer in this gray world?

Ramon was not clear as to when the day ended and the night began. The gray deepened, and he realized that he could see little beyond the bow of the vessel. The wind was steady and strong, the waves choppy and broken, and the sound made by the hull against the sea shifted noticeably. The captain was back on the quarterdeck, pacing and looking into the murky night ahead of the ship. He was subdued and gave no orders to the man at the tiller. Ramon watched him pace, saw the cast of his shoulders, and wondered if he was resigned to what the night would bring. The captain must have been awake for many hours without rest, but he stayed on the quarterdeck, peering into the night.

It was not clear what happened first. Ramon felt a slight shudder pass through the boat, then he heard a scream from the man at the tiller. Ramon was very aware of what happened next. The boat stopped being a creature of the sea, gracefully rising and falling with the waves. Instead, it became an obstacle that the waves beat against and tried to push aside. The boat slewed to one side, and Ramon felt it tip sharply, followed by cries from below deck and a crash as a boom swung across the deck and hammered against a spar. He sensed rather than saw the men on deck run to the lines that held the sails in position, although their efforts made no sense to Ramon. Waves that minutes ago had slipped alongside and left only spray and an occasional crest to fall upon the deck, now beat heavily all about him. He feared he might be washed overboard.

Ramon was still tied to the rail to keep from falling overboard, and he wondered if his freezing hands had the strength to untie the knots that secured him. He realized they were so numb he could scarcely even feel the knots. He cursed himself for not carrying a knife as did the sailors, and he thought what a foolish way this was to die, tied to the rail of a sinking ship because he had been too seasick to go below. But strangely, now that his fate was settled, he felt calmer and stopped struggling.

He wondered about the sailors and passengers who had been below deck, and as he saw the size of the waves that swept across the boat, he knew many of them would never make it up the narrow ladder from the cabins. He heard another scream from the stern of the vessel, where the man had been at the tiller. After a while, it became silent, and the only noise was the crash of the waves against the ship and the wind beating against the sails. The waves swept across Ramon, and several times his mouth filled with seawater, but each time, as he grew desperate for air, the water passed over, and he coughed and spit and breathed again. Several times during the night, he felt the boat shift. Each time, he expected the vessel to capsize and submerge him for good. But to his relief, it remained upright.

The darkness was endless. Ramon alternately shivered, then stopped shivering and felt curiously warm. He reasoned that he could not be getting warmer, so he must be getting colder. But then another wave washed over him, and he began to shiver again. How strange, he thought, the water was making him miserable when it was warmer than the air, which was cold and biting. He could not bear this much longer without losing consciousness, but there was no choice but to endure.

In the deepest part of the night, Ramon looked out across the waves and saw a distant light. It flickered and momentarily disappeared, only to reappear moments later. Ramon could not imagine that this light was aboard another ship. He guessed he was near a shore and looking at a fire, which sometimes shone through the rain and other times was obscured by the spray passing over the ship. He wondered about the men who had lit the fire. Were they warm? Did they know a ship had struck a rock so near to them?

Eventually, Ramon passed out. When he came back to consciousness, it was dawn, and he shivered violently. The boat was still rocking in the heavy seas, and he was hit by waves from time to time. The wind did not seem as strong as it had been during the night, but the waves remained violent. He was still tied to the rail, as the ropes had held despite the battering from the waves. The boat was a wreck. The masts had fallen, and one had washed overboard, held to the boat only by lines. It lay bobbing in the waves and banging into the now submerged deck. The top of the mast was under the waves. Pieces of sail clung to the lines and occasionally billowed in the wind, futilely trying to move a vessel that would never sail again. Just above the line of waves, Ramon saw two men clinging to the shrouds wrapped around the mast. Their faces were buried in the ropes, and they did not move. There had been sailors on deck, and he guessed these were two who had been able to cling onto the lines through the night. Ramon saw no one else alive. He called out, but his voice was lost in the noise of the wind and the banging of the floating mast against the hull. The boat lay on its side, and everything that had lain on the deck was gone.

Ramon looked around as best he could, twisting in the ropes that bound him, but no one else was visible in the wreckage. He raised his head and saw rocks which extended out of the water near the boat. Lifting his head farther, he looked about. The boat lay tilted at an angle so that the deck sloped down into the water. As the waves washed against the deck, Ramon could see the hatchway appear momentarily, then disappear beneath the waves. He wondered if any of the other passengers had escaped when the ship had run aground. The hatchway was full of water, so he knew that anyone still below deck must be dead.

Ramon looked past the wreckage, past the heaving sea, and in the distance he saw a headland with waves battering against it, spray thrown high into the air. The headland narrowed to a point nearest the boat, and the jagged tops of rocks showed above the sea between the boat and the shore. He could not see the land to the left of the point, but the roiling waves and spray indicated that it was a cliff face on that side. To the right of the point was a small cove with a rocky shingle, too small and rough to be called a beach. Perhaps this was where the light had come from during the night, but he could see no sign of life or remnants of a fire. A steep slope continued to the right of the beach, and there the seas were flatter, sheltered from the driving wind. Trees clung to the steep slope, growing right to the shoreline, and trunks of fallen trees lay in the water. The land curved back out of sight, and Ramon could not be sure if he was looking at an island, but far off, there was a line of darkness, possibly a distant shoreline. All of this he saw while holding his head up and turning to the side. It took great effort, and a brief look was all he could manage before lowering his head to rest.

How could he be alive at all? There seemed to be no other survivors except the two sailors clinging to the shrouds of the mast in the water, if they still lived. Could everyone else have been washed overboard in the night? Didn't any of the men make it up the narrow ladder to the deck before the waves filled the cabins with water? What about the captain, whom Ramon had last seen pacing the quarterdeck? What of the sailors, who had seemed so sure of themselves, who had spent their lives at sea? How could it be that none of them survived, and yet Ramon had lived to see this day? Ramon had no idea what to do. He could scarcely move and was numb with cold, intermittently shivering when the waves hit him, colder still when they did not, and the wind dried out the blanket that was wrapped around him and stole what meager warmth his body generated. He could scarcely feel his hands, let alone untie the rope that was holding him fast. The knots were soaking wet, impossible to untie even if he had the strength. Ramon could only lie there and hope that someone else was left alive and would cut the lines that held him. He was in the hands of God, and this made him content. Whatever was to be his end, he would accept it. It was only after realizing he was alive for another day, after his visual search for other survivors, after he realized that he could not free himself, and there was no one on the ship who could loose his bonds, and after he had resigned himself to his fate, did he notice one thing had changed. He was not seasick any longer.

Sometime later, Ramon was aroused from his stupor by voices. In his exhaustion and cold, he couldn't understand what they were saying. They should be speaking French, and that language was close enough to his native Spanish that he should recognize many of the words. But even the cadence of their speech was wrong, it was too choppy and harsh for French. He was too numb to move, and so he simply listened for a while, trying to make sense of what he heard. He could make out three or four voices and several conversations from the sound of it. Meanwhile, he heard and felt several bumps, as if a boat had been rowed to the wreck and was being made fast to it. There was a confusion of sounds for a while, and then, unmistakably, he heard someone climb onto the deck and move across it. The noise stopped, and the voices resumed, closer than before. He again tried to understand what was being said but could not, although it seemed that he was the subject. When he heard a laugh, even though he could not understand the words, it was clear they were talking about him.

"There's another one of them, up there at the rail, hanging on for dear life," came a voice. "Scared shitless, I imagine, to hang on upside down so long. The waves must have beat on him all night."

Ramon did not move, waiting to find out if these men were hostile.

The same voice spoke again, "No, he's not hanging on. He's tied there, trussed up like a chicken on a spit."

Another man spoke up, "How the hell did he do that when this old boat met Sweet Nellie here. Sweet Nell takes you in her arms and holds you fast. Then we come along and take what Nell has brought in for us."

There was a murmur of noise among the men below Ramon, and he just hung there in silence, anxious, but helpless and resigned to his fate.

The first voice sounded out, "Hey you, Spaniard, what do you think of Nell? Has she treated you well? She takes good care of us, does Nell. But what the Hell are you doing up there, you dirty bastard Spaniard? Maybe we let you hang there and see what the bonxies leave when they find out you can't move. Take your eyes first, they will, home to their nest as a treat for the little chicks. Then they'll pick the rest of you clean and leave only the big bones."

This was followed by laughter in half a dozen tones, and Ramon could tell the group was larger than he had first thought. He could hear clumping as they clambered across the wreckage to see this odd sight of a dead Spaniard tied to the rail of a wrecked ship. With great effort, he raised his head and opened his eyes to see the men who had climbed aboard. The men were startled, and Ramon heard them talk among themselves when they noticed his movement. Their voices became a little more respectful toward a live Spaniard than toward a dead one. The man closest to him was short with a reddish face, dressed in dark cloth, and wearing a broad cap on his head. His clothes were ragged, but he looked well fed and stood firmly on the deck. He was wearing leather boots, which helped explain the sounds Ramon heard when the men first came aboard the wreck. He studied the rest of the men and saw they were all wearing boots, and their clothing, while plain and worn, covered them from head to foot, not like the bare feet and cotton pants of the Spanish sailors.

The group stood on the steeply sloping deck, clutching the rail to support themselves. They were twenty feet or so beneath Ramon, and he wondered how they could reach him. For a moment, he stared at the men, and they stared back but made no move to assist him. He wondered if they intended to help. But then the man who had first spoken turned to one of the others, a much smaller figure, scarcely more than a boy, and motioned for him to climb up to the rail to reach Ramon.

"Cadan, go up there and cut that bastard loose. Quick now, climb up on that rail and work your way along until you reach him. Get your knife out. If he tries to do anything to you, stick him with it, you hear."

The boy looked at the distance to the rail and called back, "Da, I can't reach it. The rail is way above my head. Let's leave him and let the next storm take him."

"No," the first man shouted. "He might have something of value on him, even though it doesn't look like it. We can always dump him over the side, like the two dead ones on the mast there. Dirty buggers, how can they stand the cold with so little clothing on, nearly naked? Not a damned thing of value on them. The crabs will love them though, won't they? Good for something, at least. Little crabs eat them, big crabs eat the little ones, and we eat the big ones. Boy, think of this as part of your dinner; just run through a crab first. Now get up there and cut him free."

The boy tried to scramble up the deck to reach the rail, but it lay at too steep an angle. Finally, two of the men cupped their hands and lifted him as high as they could reach, and he was able to take hold of a line that was lying on the deck. Climbing hand over hand, he reached the upper rail and pulled himself up to sit on it. Ramon could not see him after that, but he could feel scuffling as the boy worked his way along the rail, spurred on by calls from the men below.

"Hey, Cadan, why don't you stand up and walk to him?" called out one of the men. Don't hang on like a little girl. Then stick that Spaniard with your knife just to see if he can feel it."

The leader spoke again, and Ramon wondered if he was the boy's father. "Don't listen to these sons of bitches, Cadan," he said. You hang on tight and don't fall off the other side, or you will be the one feeding the crabs. Go slowly now and take your time."

Ramon felt the scuffling get closer as the boy worked his way along the railing. When the boy was directly above him, the noise stopped, and Ramon heard no sounds for a few seconds, as if the boy was trying to decide what to do. Then the boy called out, "Da, if I cut the ropes, he will fall down the deck into the water. I can't hold him."

"Just cut the lines, Cadan," the man replied. "If he dies, it won't hurt him any. If he lives, we will see if he can swim."

The boy began to saw at the lines that held Ramon to the rail, and after a moment, Ramon felt the first one cut through. His head and upper body began to swing toward the water. He hung there, completely helpless, and he knew from the laughter of the men down below that they were enjoying the sight of this stranger about to get a bath. The boy moved along the rail until he reached the second line, which secured Ramon's legs, and he began to saw away at it. All of Ramon's weight was hanging on this line, and the boy had only cut halfway through when the line parted with a snap.

Ramon tumbled down the deck and hit the water headfirst. He flung his arms wildly to try to right himself. His arms had been motionless for so long that he felt a rush of blood through them as he thrashed about. When he yelled with pain, he got a mouthful of water, and he struggled and thrashed about, coughing and spitting to clear his lungs. Somehow, he turned himself around, and his foot contacted one of the cleats that were fastened to the deck, got a purchase on that cleat, lifted himself out of the water, and spread his arms wide on the deck to avoid slipping back in. Ramon coughed and sputtered, sucked in air, and coughed some more. He choked and spat up water until he finally got a full breath of air. Only then did he hear the laughter of the men who were watching him. They were roaring with laughter; one was pointing while another, a scrawny one who seemed a little simple-minded, was imitating Ramon's arms thrashing about. From above, Ramon could hear the high-pitched laughter of the boy. This lasted for a few minutes until the leader yelled out to them, and the laughter died out. The leader spoke again.

"Well, he has shown us he is alive, although for what I don't know.

Cadan, you come back now, and don't fall while you are at it. James and Thomas, go out there somehow and get the Spaniard. Don't let him pull you in."

The two men told to get Ramon edged out on the deck, stepping carefully from point to point, holding onto the lines, which were strewn every which way. One of the men reached for a line that wasn't secured, and he slipped, going up to his knees in the water before catching himself by grabbing another rope. He cursed loudly, and the other men laughed, giving him suggestions about what to hold onto to avoid a full dunking. He yelled back, telling them to shut up and let him be. Seeing the difficulty they were having, the leader directed two other men to go back to the rowboat and bring it around to the near side. Meanwhile, Ramon held on. He was breathing more easily now, and he was no longer shivering, as the thrashing about had warmed him up. But he didn't know what to do and so he waited while the men slowly worked their way across the deck.

The men on deck reached Ramon at about the same time as the rowboat arrived alongside, and in the end, it was the men in the rowboat who rescued him, hauling him in over the side. He collapsed into the bottom of the boat. The man who had hauled him in yelled out, "This bastard stinks like the devil, Colin! He went and shat himself."

"Well, you would too if you were hanging from that rail all night while the storm was raging. Take him to shore and tell Emma to clean him up. But tie him up first. Make sure he can't get away. He has good clothes on him, and he might be worth something to us yet."

The man sat down in the rowboat, took hold of one oar, and began to row with his partner, and the boat slowly moved toward the shore. The sea was quiet at first, but as the rowboat left the shelter of the wreck, it was tossed and thrown about by the waves, and the men worked hard to keep the bow pointed toward shore. They appeared to be heading toward the little section of shingle near the point that Ramon had seen earlier. At the bottom of the boat, he had no intention of trying to escape. He knew he was still alive, had no idea where he was, and had no idea where he was being taken. But it didn't matter, because a more urgent problem arose. As soon as the boat began to toss about on the waves, nausea engulfed him. He tried to fight it, but the sensation overwhelmed him, rising in his throat until he lifted his head and retched out what little was in his stomach. He heard one of the men curse in disgust. Ramon let himself sink back into oblivion. He was seasick again.

Ramon woke to strange smells. They were not the smells that he knew from Leon, familiar scents of hot sun on stone, warm leaves, spices. These were damp, heavy, earthy smells. They reminded him of the wine cellar he had played in as a boy. There was the smell of bodies, food with strange flavors, damp wood. He lay without moving for a while and took inventory of his body. All of it was there, although his arms and shoulders ached. He wiggled his toes and felt a heavy layer covering him, perhaps a quilt. The lumps beneath him rustled as he moved and made him think he was lying on a straw pallet. His fingers flexed with some effort. Content that he was alive and whole, he opened his eyes and looked around. He lay on the floor of a small log building with a low ceiling.

It was daylight outside, although it appeared the sun wasn't shining. Ramon was alone in the hut. A woman was singing in a low tone outside the hut. Her voice rose and fell, but with no melody Ramon had heard before. He listened for a while, but heard no other voices, even in the distance. It was enough to lie on his back and listen to the singing while he pondered where he was and what had brought him here. He was the only survivor from the boat through none of his own doing, merely dumb luck that he had been tied to the rail on the side of the boat that ended up high in the air. If he had been tied to the other rail, he would have drowned, as had the rest of the passengers and crew. Ramon thought about the laughter of the men who had rescued him. They could have killed him, but they didn't. They could have left him on the wreck, but instead, they cut him loose, brought him to shore, and kept him alive. Perhaps they thought they could obtain a ransom from his family. If so, they would be disappointed, because his family was small and unimportant. His parents were dead, and his brothers and sisters earned only enough money to support their families. Ramon was not married and had no children who wished for his return. To his country, he was not a loss, except for the privilege of trying him for heresy and perhaps burning him at the stake. Would this make a difference to his captors? Would they kill him as soon as they found out he was not worth anything? They did not seem like cruel men, but they were not rich; he could tell that by their clothing.

Ramon put his hands down and lifted himself up, but the effort made his head throb. He groaned but remained sitting. Every muscle in his body was sore and stiff, and he wondered how long he had been lying on the pallet. A wave of dizziness hit him, and he steadied himself so that he didn't fall over. When it passed, he noticed he could no longer hear the woman's voice. It was quiet outside. He had the feeling there was someone close by, although he couldn't tell where. He suspected a figure stood next to the hut, and a face was pressed close to one of the cracks between the logs, watching him.

"Ho," he called out with a croak, his voice stiff from disuse. There was no answer, but the figure moved slightly. "Ho," he repeated, louder. The figure moved away from the hut, and he heard light footsteps receding. It was quiet again. He waited, but no one came back, and his dizziness returned. He lay back on the pallet and slept again.

When next he woke, there was a torch burning in the hut, and it cast shadows on the thatched roof. A voice called out in a language he did not understand.

"Spaniard, wake up. You have slept enough." Ramon opened his eyes and saw the man who had first mocked him on the boat, the one he assumed was the leader, standing at the foot of his pallet. Behind him was the boy, Cadan, and off to one side was a woman. She was not a young woman, though she was not a crone either. In the dim light of the torch, he could see some gray in her dark hair, but she stood straight and still. He guessed she was the woman who had been singing, and he nodded to her slightly. The man's voice rang out again, calling him back.

"Who are you, my friend, and what brought you here?" the man asked. "Are you worth money to us?"

Ramon shook his head, not understanding anything the man said, although he knew the words were not threats.

Seeing that his words were not understood, the man shifted to a tongue so strange and convoluted that Ramon could only wonder at the sound of it. It flowed like water in a brook, running on and on with little pause until the wonder in his eyes brought the man short.

"So, you don't know the language of the Saxon curs, and I can see you are unfamiliar with the true tongue of men. Are you only versed in your damned Spanish jargon?"

At this, Ramon tried to answer, speaking first in his native Castilian, then in Basque, the language of the mountain men who lived to the north of his home, but neither of these brought any recognition to the man's eyes. He shifted to Italian and even tried a little French, but the man scowled at the sound of it, and his manner became so fierce that Ramon quickly stopped. At a loss to know what to do, Ramon spoke softly an *Ave Maria,* a prayer to protect himself from harm. At this, the woman started and called out, "Colin, that is the holy tongue that he speaks; perhaps Father Thomas could talk with him?"

"I'll not have that damned priest here yowling at me about why I don't bury the dead bodies from the wrecks," the man said. "Not when the weather is howling, and my men and I risk our lives just to get the little salvage we can from these filthy Spanish crafts."

The man spoke with anger, and the woman was quiet, but the boy spoke up, "Da, I'll get the father," he said. "You do not have to be here."

"All right, then," the man said. "But I'll have none of his entreaties about saving the souls of the poor buggers that we find out there. They came into our waters at their own risk, came to Sweet Nellie's arms, and found that her charms were not what they had sought. The sea brings them here; the sea takes them away again." With that, he turned and left the hut.

The boy looked to the woman, who motioned to him. "Go then, fetch the holy father, Cadan, and bring him quickly," she said. "But warn him that Colin is in a foul mood tonight. He spent two days wrecking that craft and got precious little for his trouble. The poor souls aboard her were dead when he got there, and he did what he could to save this one at least. Now run."

The boy darted out the door, and Ramon heard his footsteps recede. He turned his face back to the woman and found her watching him. He realized she was saying a prayer in Latin. Listening closely, he heard it was a prayer to Saint Christopher, the patron saint of travelers, often recited to help ward off danger. "Si, Saint Christopher," he said, and finished the last phrase with her. Her eyes widened slightly, then she turned and left the hut, barring the door firmly behind her.

CHAPTER TWO

Building the Barns

1485–1603

Tudor England

The reign of the Tudor kings in England began at the Battle of Bosworth in 1485 when an army led by Henry Tudor of Wales defeated an army led by King Richard III. Richard was killed during the battle, and Henry became the King of England, reigning as Henry VII. At his death in 1509, he was succeeded by his son, who reigned as Henry VIII.

The Tudors ruled England for 118 years, and much of this time was marked by unrest. In 1485, England was a Catholic country with hundreds of monasteries, friaries, and nunneries. Historians estimate that one-quarter of the nation's wealth was held by groups associated with the Catholic Church, headed by the Pope in Rome. Starting in 1530, Parliament passed laws that disenfranchised the monasteries, friaries, and nunneries. Many buildings were destroyed or converted to other uses. Church lands became property of the British crown, which sold many into private hands. Meanwhile, the Church of England was established with the King of England as the Supreme Head of the Church.

When Henry VIII died in 1547, his nine-year-old son, Edward, became king and was crowned Edward VI. He continued the reforms in the Church his father had begun. The Act of Uniformity, passed by the English Parliament in 1549, required that all churches use the 1549 *Book of Common Prayer* for services, and it would be recited in English rather than Latin. These actions caused a great uproar in Devon and Cornwall, where many people did not understand English. The Prayer Book Rebellion of 1549 was a reaction to these changes.

King Edward VI died in 1553 at the age of fifteen after reigning only five years. Upon his death, his half-sister Mary was crowned Queen Mary I. Mary was 37 years old when she became queen and a devout Catholic who married Phillip II, the Catholic King of Spain. She attempted to reverse the transformations her father and brother had made and return England to the Catholic faith with the pope as its head. During her reign, many Protestant clergy were burned to death for refusing to follow her edicts. Mary was Queen for only five years and died in 1558 without bearing any children.

Mary was succeeded by her half-sister Elizabeth, who ruled as Queen Elizabeth I for forty-five years until her death in 1603. She did not marry and bore no children. Elizabeth followed a more moderate religious path than her predecessors, continuing the transition to the Church of England but with less oppression of the country's Catholic minority. However, her actions angered King Philip II of Spain, who wanted England to return to the Catholic faith. In 1588, he sent a vast armada of ships to conquer England. The war with Spain continued intermittently for the last fifteen years of Elizabeth's rule.

During the 118 years of Tudor rule, the people of England had to follow the edicts decreed by the crown and the laws passed by Parliament regarding religion. It was a time of great anxiety. England had been a predominantly Catholic country for centuries, and its people held strong religious beliefs. These were now expected to change overnight. By the end of the reign of the Tudors, the Church of England had become the official church, and attendance at Sunday services was required of every English man and woman.

During the sixteenth century, English citizens tried to survive the great changes in their society, care for their families, and live as well as possible. This was especially true for those who lived far from London. In southern Cornwall, three hundred miles from London, many people spoke Cornish rather than English, and this made the changes in church services especially difficult. On a small farm in South Cornwall, near the end of the Lizard Peninsula, a man named Ewan Skiburio navigated this challenging time, doing his best to make sense of how he fit into it.

Barn on Skiburio (Skyburriowe) Farm[2]

Ewan Skiburio, 1531–1597

Summer 1566

The Eighth Year of the Reign of Queen Elizabeth I (Good Queen Eliza)

As he worked on the walls of the barn, Ewan often thought about his father. In fact, he sometimes thought of the barn as a memorial to his father, a tribute to the stories his father had told him as a young boy, combined with Ewan's visions of the places in Spain his father had described: quiet afternoons in Leon, hot sun on stone plazas, people resting and waiting for the day to cool as evening approached. Ewan had never been to Spain, and he could only imagine how the buildings looked, and how it might feel to live there. However, he created an imaginary place in his mind and he often returned to it as he labored slowly and carefully, building the walls of the barn.

The nature of the work helped to recall the memories. Building a stone wall was a slow process, and the placement of each stone took all of Ewan's concentration to ensure that the completed work remained strong. Each stone was a different size and had irregular facets. The placement of each stone created a space for the next one. Ewan considered how each stone would look in place, how it would rest on those below, and how the wall would appear from the outside. Sometimes, his placement of a stone left a space where no stone in the pile would fit well. Then he broke a stone until it more closely fit the space, searched the pile for a replacement stone, or in the worst case, brought more stones from the quarry. If none of these efforts produced a suitable stone, he removed the last stone placed and found a new one. This was something that he tried to avoid doing. If he started removing stones he had already laid, the process might not end until he took the wall entirely apart and started again. It was better to accept some imperfections, make the placement of each stone just good enough, and know there would be some flaws. When Ewan looked back on the completed walls of the barn, he saw a few places that bothered him, where the mortar joints were too large or a stone knob projected outside the wall surface. He forced himself to accept these imperfections. The walls were solid and straight, two stones thick, carefully mortared to prevent water from entering the joints. The uppermost layer of stones in each wall was covered with bundles of thatch to prevent water from entering the voids between the stones until the roof was in place.

As Ewan surveyed the barn, he could distinguish his newer work from the portions he had finished the previous summer and the summer before that. At the present rate, the walls would be finished in a few more summers, and it would be time to build the roof trusses. Meanwhile, he had more feet of wall to complete and many decisions about stones to place. It was good not to look too far into the future, or he might get discouraged and never complete his project.

Ewan's wife, Mary, was patient about the barn project. She realized the barn was something Ewan had set his mind to. As long as the farmwork was done, he was not neglecting her and their two boys. This was Ewan's way to relax, much as one man might dedicate a day to fishing and another spend his day in the pub. Ewan spent his spare time working on the barn walls, mixing small batches of mortar and choosing a few more stones. Gradually, the barn took shape.

As Ewan worked on the barn, he often thought about his father. He remembered countless long winter evenings in the small cabin when he was a young boy, sitting on the fireplace hearth and listening as his father told stories of his life in Spain. His father spoke in broken Cornish, occasionally lapsing into Spanish or even Latin if he didn't know the words in the Cornish language. His mother, Emma, was always nearby, working on her knitting or sewing a patch onto his father's pants. She occasionally leaned toward the fire to illuminate the stitches. The firelight reflected off her hair, which had been streaked with gray for as long as Ewan could remember. He asked her about it once, why did she have gray strands in her hair, as she was not an old woman.

"Perhaps I am an old woman," she said, laughing gently and reaching out to softly tousle his hair.

Ewan knew her reply wasn't strictly true. She was not old like his grandmother, but then she was not young like the mothers of the boys he played with in the village. She was somewhere in between, neither young nor old, but always the person he turned to when he had a problem. She could be abrupt, even severe if she thought he had failed to wash himself thoroughly in his weekly bath. She was always near the house, her house really, for she had lived there alone before his father came and before Ewan was born. The house had only one room with a hard-packed dirt floor and a fireplace in the middle of one wall. It was simply furnished, with a single bed in one corner and a table with two benches where they sat to eat their meals. Occasionally, when visitors came, most often Ewan's uncle Colin, Ewan would move to sit on his bed, a pallet on the floor with a bundle of dried rushes beneath it to protect him from the damp. From this point of view, he could watch the three adults.

Ewan's uncle Colin was a small man with a big voice and a loud laugh. He was older than Ewan's mother, and his hair was gray, pulled back into a loose braid. He sat on a bench and talked with Ewan's father, their hands resting on the rough table, each man holding a mug of ale. Ewan knew his father preferred wine and sometimes said how good the wine was in Leon. But in rural Cornwall, wine was only used for the mass at church. Here, the drink was ale, and occasionally, Ewan's mother put down her knitting and brought the jug to refill the mugs of the two men.

Ewan liked to watch his uncle as he sat at the table, the firelight reflecting off his face and the dull pewter mug in his hands. He did most of the talking and waved his arms as he spoke to Ewan's father. He laughed as he spoke, and his laughter filled the room.

"Ramon," he said, "after more of this ale, I will forget myself and call you Raymond, as I do when we are on the boat with the men."

"It doesn't matter," said Ewan's father. "I know who you mean."

"Yes, I know that you do, but I should call you by your real name in your house when I come and drink your ale. Out on the boat, with the rest of the crew within hearing distance, it is better for you to have an English name. In this house, with just you and me and my sister and the boy," and at this comment, he waved his arm toward Ewan to include him in the conversation, "Here, we can do what we like."

Ewan's mother Emma broke in with a chuckle. "As if you don't do what you like all of the time, Colin! The men on your crew are scared rabbits who would jump into the bay if you commanded them to do it."

Colin threw up his hands in mock alarm and shook his head. "Ah, Ramon, you see what I have to put up with. Even my little sister pokes fun at me, her big brother, who looked after her when she was small and got her this fine house."

"Abandoned wreck of a hut, you mean," Emma responded with a laugh. "I remember when old Grannie Miles died, the place sat empty, and the roof was so bad there were not many folks eager to move in. It took me one entire summer to repair the thatch on the roof, and there were still a few leaks during the first winter I lived here."

Colin snorted. "Well, now you have a fine man here in your house. He can fix the roof, and the boy is big enough to bring in wood for the fire. That gives you plenty of time to brew more of this good ale!" With that last remark, he lifted the mug to his mouth, took a long draught, and smacked his lips with pleasure.

She answered him and laughed. "The more ale I brew, the more often I see you over here at my table drinking it. Why, I can hardly brew it fast enough." With this last exchange, Ewan saw his mother shake her finger at her older brother. The words might be sharp, but Ewan knew the two loved each other dearly. Meanwhile, Ewan's father sat with a gentle smile on his face as he watched the two siblings in their sparring. Ewan knew that once they finished, his mother would return to her knitting, and his uncle would sit and talk with Ramon for the rest of the evening.

"It is a strange thing that I hear in the village," Colin spoke one evening, after several mugs of ale had been drunk, and the two men sat across from each other. "Ever since King Henry broke away from Rome and made a new church, people have not been happy. The folks around here are faithful to the Church. They know it, and it sustains them through hard times. Most of them don't even know what the priest is saying when he says the mass in Latin, but they believe what he stands for. I have heard rumors that the King is going to marry again. There are some men who say that all of the religious changes have been only to satisfy the king's desires. I fear that a dark time will come to us if the rumors are true."

Ramon sat quietly for a few minutes before he answered. "I believe the king's desires will take precedence over the beliefs of the people. The king is determined to marry another woman. That can be a strong impulse in any man. He sounds like a man who must have things his way, even if it is harmful to others. I have been a teacher of religion all my adult life, and I see many faults in the Church. In Spain, it has been decreed that the Church has no faults, and anyone who expresses doubt in Church doctrine is an enemy of the king and must be suppressed. Here it is different. Some doubts are allowed, but the nation will have to follow the wishes of King Henry in the end."

"Perhaps so," replied Colin. "But the people have followed this faith for many years. They cannot change to new beliefs overnight. I am concerned there will be deep discord and tragedy with these changes." With this comment, Colin relapsed into silence and took a long draught of the ale.

This talk was strange to Ewan. His world consisted of his mother and father, the cabin, a few animals, and his friends in the village. The mention of the king meant little to him. He had heard of London and knew that it was many times bigger than the village, even bigger than Falmouth, where he had gone with his uncle to get a load of supplies. But he could not conceive of a town that large. Still, he loved his father and his uncle, and if these things mattered to them, he would listen and try to understand what they were talking about.

Colin often came to their house in the evening, always claiming it was the fine ale that drew him, but Ewan suspected the real reason was to talk with his father. Ramon was not from the village. He had arrived ten years earlier, a passenger on a small ship heading toward the Spanish Netherlands. Ewan did not exactly understand why his father was on the boat, but he knew it had foundered on the rocks at the headland, and Ramon was the only survivor.

From the stories his father told, Ewan knew he had been terribly seasick and had tied himself to a railing to keep from falling overboard. When the ship crashed upon the rocks, the captain and crew launched the rowboat, but they were never seen again. Two crew members climbed one of the masts, thinking they would be safe from the storm. But during the night, the mast toppled, and the men drowned. When the storm quieted the next day, Colin and his crew came to the wreck to see if there was anything to be salvaged. They found Ramon still tied to the railing, more dead than alive. Some wreckers would have cut the ropes holding him to the rail and let him drown in the bay, but Colin had his crew bring Ramon ashore. They locked him in a shed and asked Colin's sister Emma to see if she could dry him out and nurse him back to life. It was several weeks before Ramon was strong enough to leave the shed, and by that time, it was clear to Colin that he was not a wealthy man. He knew not a word of Cornish nor English, and neither Colin nor Emma knew any Spanish. But Ramon had taught his students Latin in Spain, and the local priest knew a little Latin, though he spoke it with a terrible accent. And so, haltingly, Ramon was able to tell his story.

Ramon had been a teacher in Leon, a small city in northern Spain. One of his friends and fellow teachers, Dr. Constantine, had been accused of heresy by officers of the Inquisition. When Ramon spoke on behalf of his friend, he too was suspected of heresy, and he fled Leon at night and traveled to Gijon, the nearest ocean port. There, he took passage on a small trading vessel heading to Antwerp in the Spanish Netherlands.

Upon hearing Ramon's story, Colin threw up his hands in dismay. "I have saved a poor Spaniard!" he exclaimed. "What am I to do with him?"

The priest spoke up: "Maybe it is not hopeless. This man learns quickly. He has already learned a few words of our language, and he can talk a little with your sister. Perhaps when he learns a little more of our language, he can teach the children of the village. His knowledge of Latin and the Bible is much better than mine."

At this remark, Colin shook his head, rolled his eyes, and said, "Now I know that this will not make me any money. A hungry Spaniard is living in my shed, and my sister is probably getting sweet on him."

A dozen years had passed since that time, and much had happened. Ramon lived in the shed for a while, and then, as the weather grew cold, Emma gently suggested he could move to her hut. Ramon was agreeable, but before this could take place, Colin insisted that the priest preside over a simple marriage ceremony. Ewan was born in the autumn of the following year.

The following years flowed in a stream that seemed unchanging to Ewan. There was his mother and father, his uncle visiting in the evenings, the light of the fire, the warmth of the small hut on cold nights. Ewan learned his letters and recited the chants in Latin at the church. His mother cared for the house and the small garden, raised a few chickens, spun wool for thread, and mended his clothes when they tore. His father helped the local men with house raising, thatching roofs, and other building projects. He was not accepted as part of the community, but he was accepted as Emma's husband, and an extra hand was always welcome at the work. On winter nights when the west wind howled around the cabin, sometimes Colin sent a message that a ship had foundered on the rocks, and Ramon was needed to help salvage the wreckage.

Ewan's mother worried when a message came, for it was always during cold, wet weather, and Ramon never seemed to get used to the cold. "I miss the hot sun of Leon. It warmed my bones," he said when he went off with Colin. When he returned, usually soaking wet and exhausted, Ewan's mother made him change into dry clothes and threw extra wood on the fire to keep him warm.

It was on one such night, when Ewan was ten years old, a message came from Colin for Ramon to meet him and the rest of his crew at the beach. A ship had been seen struggling against the seas, and it might founder in the night. Emma shook her head as she looked outside the hut and tried to persuade Ramon not to go. One more person would not make a difference in the salvage efforts, she said, but Ramon would not listen.

"I am only here because of the kindness of your brother," he said. "Another man might have left me on that wreck to die of exposure or be eaten by the crabs. If he says I am needed, I will do whatever I can to help." Ewan strode off into the darkness, protected a little from rain by the oilcloth over his shoulders.

The next morning dawned, still wet and cold, with no news from the beach. Ewan watched his mother fret all day. She kept busy with her regular chores, but she was preoccupied. Several times when Ewan spoke to her, she did not respond. Darkness came early, for it was wintertime, and the days were short. The house seemed empty without Ramon, and Ewan thought about his father out on a wrecked ship as he listened to the wind blow across the thatch on the roof.

Early the next morning, two of Colin's crew brought Ramon to the hut wrapped in a sodden blanket, carried him inside, and laid him on the bed. The men explained that a ship had indeed foundered on the rocks, but there was a reason for the wreck. When they reached the wreck in the morning, they found that most of the ship's crew were sick, some already dead. There was no one to man the sails to control the ship as it neared the rocks the night before. Ramon had tended to some of the sick, while the dead were put overboard. But it was no use. The rest of the crew had died on the second night, and Ramon had collapsed shortly afterward.

Ewan's mother listened to this explanation, turned to Ewan, and spoke sharply, "Ewan, I want you to go to your Aunt Catherine's house right now and stay there. Tell her I will send a message when you can return home." Ewan knew better than to argue with her, so he gathered a few of his belongings and left the house, while his mother removed Ramon's sopping wet clothes and began to warm him up.

Ewan often visited his Aunt Catherine. Her house was in the village, and her sons were his playmates. She welcomed him at the doorway, and her boys shouted happily when they heard that Ewan would be staying for a few days. However, his stay turned out to be longer than a few days. One of Emma's neighbors brought a message later in the week that Ramon was ill and asking if Ewan could stay until the fever broke. Days passed, and Ewan missed his home and his mother and father. After two weeks, another message arrived. Ewan and his Aunt Catherine walked to the family's little cabin, and Ewan's mother met them at the door. She seemed exhausted, and Ewan thought her hair looked grayer than he remembered. She hugged Ewan tightly and held him against her for a long time. "It will be just you and me now," she said. "We have to look after each other."

Ewan clearly remembered the funeral of his father, the men standing at the graveside, his mother in her black veil with his Uncle Colin beside her. In the years that followed, he never saw his mother cry, but she did not laugh as much as before. When Ewan left to marry and start his own life, she lived on by herself in the little cabin near the bay. Ewan offered many times for her to come and live at the farm with him and his wife Mary. She would see her grandsons more often, he said, but she always smiled and turned him down.

"I wouldn't know what to do if I left this place," she said. "Living here lets me think of your father and of you when you were a little lad. That keeps me going." Emma had not changed much over the years. Her hair was mostly gray, but with still a hint of brown that reminded Ewan of how she looked when he was young.

The Cornish Prayer Book Rebellion broke out in 1549, eight years after Ramon's death. Ewan was a young man, barely eighteen years old, still living at the cabin with his mother. The rebellion started with a bad harvest in the fall, the first in many years. Then news filtered into the village that great changes were coming. Old King Henry had died a few years earlier, and his young son Edward was now on the throne. Still in his teens, Edward was determined to complete the changes his father had begun, strengthening the Church of England and ridding it of the traditions that had been the bulwark of the Catholic faith. All images of saints were to be removed from churches, and the service was to be recited in English instead of Latin. These changes were bad news to the village, but worse was yet to come. A tax would be imposed on each head of sheep. The people's grumbling turned to anger. Talk in the village pub was of nothing else. Word spread that farmers and miners from all over Cornwall and Devon were gathering to protest the new laws.

At first, Ewan's uncle Colin said little about the discord. He came to the hut to talk with his sister, and Ewan sat at the table with them. The religious changes did not mean much to Colin.

"The bastards will always argue about one thing or another," he said, "and it has little effect upon me. I will still get up in the morning and go to bed at night." But after a few weeks, he spoke more seriously. "The lads have asked me to lead the group from the village. It seems that they are used to listening to me telling them what to do."

"But this is not your fight, Colin," said Ewan's mother with concern. "Do you need to go?"

"It sticks in my craw that some arrogant prick in London can decide how we are to live our lives here in Cornwall. I guess this is the best time to make a stand and show them how we feel."

A few weeks later, the men from the village marched off with Colin at the head of the crowd. A few carried bows and arrows, but most of the men held pitchforks and scythes. They were cocky enough, but Ewan's mother shook her head when she watched them pass. "Don't even think about following them, Ewan," she said. "Those men think they will be heroes, but many of them will not come home again."

As the weeks passed, news filtered back to the village. Men from all over Cornwall and Devon had marched and defied the authorities and the hated edicts. Led by Sir Humphrey Arundel, the army of farmers and miners had swollen to two thousand men, and they besieged the city of Exeter. News came that a royal army led by Lord Russell was sent against them from London with thousands of German soldiers and Italian crossbowmen. Pitched battle brought deaths on both sides. It was quiet for a time, and the village wondered if a settlement had been reached. But then rumors came, news so shocking it could scarcely be believed. The Royal army had defeated the Cornish and Devon men, and the city of Exeter had been relieved of the siege. During the battle, nine hundred men from Cornwall had been taken prisoner under a flag of truce, but after the battle was ended, all had been slaughtered, their throats slit in minutes.

The village waited for more news, but only after weeks had passed, a few men quietly returned to the area. All the rest were dead. Colin had died in the front of the battle, fighting next to his men. But the rest of the village men were among those slaughtered after the fighting ended. Not even their bodies were returned to be buried, for their corpses had been thrown into a mass grave. There was mourning at every house. It was a dark time, and Ewan recalled that his mother seldom smiled.

The old priest from the village church was the last of the familiar figures in Ewan's life to leave. He came to the cabin to see Emma one last time after the end of the rebellion. "It is too much of a change for me to see the church become something I cannot recognize," he said. "A boat sails from Falmouth to the low countries next week, and I will be on it. Perhaps in the Netherlands I can find a congregation that needs a priest who speaks poor Latin." A week later, he was gone, and the new priest who came had no qualms about reciting the service in

English, though to many of the Cornish-speaking parishioners, this was as foreign a language as the Latin that had preceded it.

Many local families lost young men during the rebellion, and that is how Ewan came to the farm a few miles from the coast, where he now lived with his wife, Mary, and their two sons. Ewan knew Mary from their church. She and her parents lived on a farm half a dozen miles from the bay, just north of the rocky wasteland called Goonhilly Downs. Her two elder brothers had gone with the Cornish troops and had not returned from the slaughter in Exeter. Mary's father grew despondent at the loss of his sons, and the farm went to ruin. Finally, Mary's mother suggested that Ewan marry their daughter and try to make a go of the farm. Ewan moved out of the little cabin near the bay and came to the uplands where the farm was located.

That was years ago, and the farm was doing well. Mary had borne two sons, and they were growing fast. Thomas, the older boy, was named after Mary's father, who died of grief a few years after the rebellion. The younger boy was named Colin after Ewan's uncle. Mary's mother lived on and helped with the boys. Her grief at the loss of her sons would never fade, but the hard work of raising the boys and keeping the farm going each day pushed it out of her mind most of the time.

The years passed. Some were joyful, as Ewan and Mary watched their boys grow into young men. Some were sad, like the winter Mary's mother weakened and died, mourning her lost sons until her final breath. The work at the farm was endless. Every day Ewan toiled in the fields to raise the grain and vegetables they harvested for their own use, to care for a small flock of sheep and goats that provided wool and meat, and to maintain the small herd of cows that gave milk for making cheese.

Ewan's mother, Emma, lived on through all this time, growing a little grayer each year, but otherwise she did not seem to change. Ewan took time away from the farm each week and rode Brutus, the old farm horse, down to see her, sometimes bringing a loaf of bread or a pot of stew. She welcomed him, and they sat at the trestle table that Ewan remembered from when he was a boy. The little cabin still had a hard-packed dirt floor, which Emma swept every day, and the thatched roof still kept out the winter rains. When Ewan's sons were little, he often brought one of them with him, carrying the boy in front of him on the broad back of Brutus. Now that the boys were grown, he visited by himself and sat with his mother for an hour or two. Sometimes, he split some firewood if the pile was low, then returned to the farm before dark.

It was a bitterly cold day in January when Ewan visited his mother for the last time. She moved more slowly than he remembered, but she sat with him at the table and shared the stew he brought. He asked how she was feeling, and she responded that she was fine, the same thing she always said. He asked if she would come to the farm to stay with them for a while until the weather warmed up, but she said no, she preferred her own home. It was warm here, she said, and she felt as though his father, Ramon, was always near.

Ewan felt some misgivings about leaving his mother alone that day, but the cabin was warm, and she had plenty of wood for the fireplace. At the farm, he talked with Mary about his visit and his concerns for his mother. Mary listened, and when he was finished, she spoke softly: "Ewan, don't wait a week to visit your mother again. Go soon so that you won't worry about her."

Two days later, Ewan saddled Brutus and slowly rode the half dozen miles to the patch of woodland near the coast where the cabin was located. As he approached the hut, no smoke rose from the chimney. He knocked on the door but there was no answer. Anxiously, he pushed open the door, felt the cold of the house, and saw his mother lying in her bed, swathed in quilts. Ewan sat at the edge of the bed and looked at her lying so still. He reached out to touch her face. Her skin was ice cold, and he knew she had died quietly, possibly dreaming of her husband Ramon and the years they had spent together.

Ewan sat on the bed for a while, keeping his mother's body company for the last time. Then he lit the fire to warm the house. Once it was well started, he set off for the village to notify the priest of Emma's death and to get help to prepare the body for the funeral.

Emma was buried a few days later, laid to rest next to Ramon and near the gravestone that had been placed in honor of her brother Colin in the modest village graveyard. Ewan was surprised by the number of people who attended the funeral, but as he listened to the minister's eulogy, he thought how his mother had been born and raised in this village and had lived in the simple cabin most of her life. She had been part of the lives of everyone in the area, and had mourned with them, whether it was for a dead newborn or for a gray-haired elder. She had lived through the tumultuous years of transformation from the Roman Catholic Church to the Church of England, and watched as the monasteries and chantries were seized by the crown, emptied, and destroyed. She saw the icons of the saints removed from the church and shattered into bits. During the rebellion, she had watched as her brother led the men of the village to protest the decree that services be spoken in English rather than Latin, and she had mourned alongside the other village families when he and the other men had not returned from the battlefield.

During the brief reign of Queen Mary, Emma had watched the Queen's attempts to return the country to the Catholic faith. In Cornwall, there had been no burning of local priests who defied royal orders, but there had been great anguish and anxiety among the people of the village. It was a time when people kept their beliefs private. When Queen Mary died after only five years on the throne, succeeded by Queen Elizabeth, Good Queen Eliza, as she was commonly called, there was a sigh of relief when it became clear that the people could accept each other and be more tolerant of different religious beliefs. Through all this uproar, Ewan's mother quietly attended church services, cared for her husband and son, and lived her life. All this Ewan thought as he stood at the graveside next to Mary and his sons, Thomas and Colin, and surrounded by the people of the village. Finally, the priest finished his prayer, and Ewan made his last goodbye to his mother.

After Emma's death, Ewan had little reason to ride to the coast. He occasionally spent an evening at the quiet pub a mile up the road from the farm, but most evenings he stayed at the farm with Mary and his sons. His boys were young men, and soon they found partners among the young women of the village. Their weddings occurred close together. The house at the farm was too small for even two more people, especially with the promise of babies to follow soon, so Ewan stopped working on the barn and began building a small addition to the farmhouse, a bedroom for him and Mary to live in. Then, with the help of the boys, he built a separate house down the lane from the farmhouse.

Along with the endless work at the farm, these projects took years to complete, and by the time they were done, babies had been born to both families. One was a beautiful baby girl, and Ewan saw the delight on Mary's face as she cared for the precious little one, named Mary after her. Ewan's hair was now streaked with gray, much as his mother's had been. His sons now did the plowing and harvesting, and Ewan duties were reduced to driving a wagon during the harvest and making sure the tools were sharp and in good condition. He and Mary had more time to spend together, and occasionally he went into the house for a mug of ale in the afternoon. When Ewan finally finished the houses and the farmwork was well in hand, he returned to work on the barn.

Years had passed since Ewan stopped working on his project, and the partially built walls were overgrown with weeds. He cleared away the weeds and spread out the pile of rocks that had sat while he had been busy with other things. As he mixed up the first batch of mortar and began to lay new stones on the barn walls, he thought about how many years had elapsed since he moved to the farm. He had been a young man then, with the energy to work long hours every day. Now he was fifty years old, and he grew tired easily. He could not move as fast as he did when he was a young man, but he had more time. In three years, he completed building the remainder of the stone walls, cut and assembled timbers into trusses for the roof, then carefully thatched the building to shed the winter rains. The barn became a winter shelter for the animals.

The next year, Ewan began to build a second barn, this one to store hay in the winter. With the additional time he had to work on the project, after only three years, the walls were completed except for a section on the rear of the barn. Ewan built trusses and roofed the front half of the second barn. He then cut the timbers for the rest of the trusses and stacked them to season while he completed building the stone walls.

During one of Ewan's occasional visits to the local pub, he heard rumors of new trouble coming to England. This was with Spain, the powerful nation that had colonies in the New World, and which for the past decades had ruled the Low Countries, the "Netherlands," which lay across the English Channel. A rebellion had begun, led by Protestant forces struggling to make the Netherlands into an independent nation. The Spanish army and the Protestant rebels fought bitter battles. Queen Elizabeth sent an army to support the rebels, and the

Spanish King Phillip II vowed to avenge this intrusion.

The execution of the Scottish Queen Mary triggered the final break between the two nations. Many years earlier, Mary had been given refuge in England by Queen Elizabeth when Scottish nobles drove her out of Scotland. Recently, it was discovered that she had plotted with the King of Spain to overthrow Queen Elizabeth and return England to the Catholic faith. Mary was tried by the English Parliament, convicted of treason, and condemned to death. A few months later, her head was severed from her body. When the news of her execution reached Spain, King Phillip II assembled a huge armada of ships to carry an army to invade England and seize the crown from the English queen. Cornwall was the closest part of England to Spain, and there was talk in the local pub that the Spaniard army might land at Falmouth or Plymouth and march overland to London. Ewan listened to the talk and said little, although he wondered how this would affect his family. The news was widespread, and an invasion was expected. How soon and where it would happen was unknown. But nothing happened for months, and Ewan gradually forgot about the rumors of invasion.

Another year passed, and it was midsummer again. Ewan was standing on a scaffold, installing stones on the upper wall of the barn, when he saw a horse and rider walking in the lane. Visitors to the farm were rare, but this was even more unusual because the rider was the sheriff of Cornwall, John Rashleigh. Ewan assumed he had come to talk with Thomas, Ewan's older son, but instead of going to the house, Rashleigh rode to the back of the barn where Ewan was working and dismounted.

Ewan climbed down from the scaffold, and they exchanged greetings. The sheriff was a tall man, dressed simply but well. Ewan had only seen him a few times at village meetings. The sheriff asked how Ewan was doing, and then there was silence. Finally, Ewan asked, "What brings you here today, John?"

"Well, Ewan," he said, "it is like this. You may have heard that the Spaniards are coming with a fleet of ships and an army of men to attack England. We know they will arrive soon, but we don't know when. We don't know where they will land, but their ships will first be seen here at the tip of the Lizard Peninsula in Cornwall as they make their way up the Channel. When we see the ships, we must get the news to London as soon as possible. In the past, we have lit bonfires along the coast to signal that invaders are approaching. This time, we plan to set up a line of alarm fires from the peninsula straight to London to get the news there quickly. Ewan, if there were a bonfire at the high point of Goonhilly Downs, about a mile south from here, it might be seen all the way to Hensbarrow Downs, twenty miles to the north. We need someone to build that bonfire alarm. Would you do it?"

Ewan was startled by the request. He had never been a member of the local militia, nor had he been much involved in village business. "Why me?" he asked.

"Well, I thought your sons might spare you from the work at the farm for a little while so you could help with the bonfire. Frankly, the last thing we want is a bunch of the village men drinking and partying out on the downs when they should be watching for the bonfire alert down at the coast." That made sense to Ewan. Many community activities consisted of a group of men drinking, sometimes forgetting what purpose had brought them together.

Ewan asked, "How long do you suppose the wait might be before the Spanish ships are seen?"

"We think less than two weeks," the sheriff said. "The bonfires can only be seen after dark and before dawn. During the day, we will make smoky fires, but they can't be seen as well as nighttime blazes. Some-one will need to be at Goonhilly Downs during the day, but night is the most crucial time."

Ewan thought for a moment. "I have timbers ready to build the trusses for the roof of this barn," he said. "I could take four of them and some shorter timbers and build a simple platform twelve feet high. That would ensure the bonfire could be seen all the way to Hensbarrow Downs."

"That sounds good," said John. "We'll build another bonfire on the hill above Penryn, ten miles north of here, but we want each location to be able to see at least two bonfires in case one gets missed. We want the fires ready to light in two days. Could you get the tower ready by then?"

"Yes," responded Ewan. "Thomas can help me haul the timbers out to the downs tomorrow and set up the platform. The next day, I will get the bonfire ready. It can be ready to light in the evening, two days from now."

John doffed his cap. "Thank you, Ewan." The sheriff mounted his horse and turned away.

The next two days were exhausting ones. Ewan picked out four timbers about twelve feet long and four shorter ones to bind the posts together at the top and provide a base for the bonfire platform. The platform would consist of round poles lashed to the crosspieces in two layers. The whole business would be tied together with rope so it could be easily taken apart when the tower was no longer needed. By noon of the first day, Ewan and Thomas finished loading the farm wagon with timbers and poles, rope, a few tools, and the ladder that usually rested against the barn where Ewan was working. Thomas hitched up the two plow horses, the offspring of old Brutus, and they set off. It was a mile across the fields to the high point of Goonhilly Downs, an hour of travel before they reached the spot where Ewan planned to erect the tower. Once there, Ewan surveyed the area. The downs were covered with low shrubby bushes and scant grass with a few low trees, and there was good visibility in all directions. Ewan could see the coast in the distance to the south. Far to the north, a dark line of hills could be seen, Hensbarrow Downs, where another bonfire would be lit.

The evening looked to be clear, and Ewan planned to work until dark. He picked an open spot on top of the knoll, and he and Thomas dug four small pits for the upright posts to sit in. Next, they lashed a crosspiece across the top of two of the posts to hold them four feet apart. Two thin poles tied to the uprights to form an X made sure the assembly would be steady from side to side. They tied a rope to the crosspiece and hitched it to the horses, then gradually pulled the top of the assembly upright. Ewan attached a straight pole to the center of the diagonals where the poles crossed to act as a brace. As the horses pulled the assembly into a vertical position, Thomas held onto the brace. When the assembly was standing, with the base of the two posts sitting in  the small pits and the top leaning slightly more than vertical, Ewan left the horses and came to help. He pounded a short pole into the ground and lashed the brace to it to hold the assembly in place. Then Thomas leaned the ladder against the posts, climbed up, and untied the rope. The men joined the other two posts, crosspiece, and diagonal poles to form the second half of the tower. Then they pulled it upright with the horses, tying a brace to the diagonals and lashing it to a pole hammered into the ground. Ewan leaned the ladder against one of the posts, carefully carried up the other two short timbers, and lashed them across the tops of the ones already attached to the vertical posts. They added diagonal braces, and the tower was solid and secure, with the crosspieces sticking out a foot on either side of the posts at the top. Ewan stayed on the ladder, and Thomas handed up bundles of poles. Ewan laid them across the crosspieces to form the platform and tied them together with rope, creating two layers crosswise to each other. This created a solid platform, and the poles were close enough to hold the layer of dirt that would protect the wood from burning when the bonfire was lit.

Ewan sat on the platform and lowered a rope to Thomas, who filled a wooden bucket with loose dirt, tied the handle to the rope, and helped lift it up the ladder as Ewan pulled from the top. Ewan dumped the dirt on top of the poles and sent the bucket down for another load. It took almost two hours to pull up enough buckets of dirt to make a thick layer on top of the poles, and both men were exhausted by the time the platform was finished. The sun had set, and the light was beginning to fade, so they returned to the farm in semidarkness walking alongside the horses which were pulling the empty cart.

The next day, Ewan started off alone to the tower site on foot. Once there, he cut dead branches to use as fuel for the bonfire. He hauled the branches up the ladder and built a pyramid-shaped stack on top of the platform, laying small branches and kindling in the center, with larger sticks and a few timber cutoffs on the outside. Ewan had brought sections of tarred rope to add to the fire, to produce smoke if it had to be lit during daytime. Then he stacked an extra pile of cut branches and poles on the ground near the base of the  tower in case the fire needed more fuel once it was lit.

Ewan finished setting up the bonfire by early afternoon and walked back to the farm, hoping to get a few hours of sleep before returning to the tower for the night. He sat and talked with Mary and assured her that he would not fall off the tower in the darkness. She made up a basket with bread and cheese, with a goatskin bag of cider to drink when he got thirsty. Ewan lay down on the bed to rest. It was hopeless for him to sleep at such an odd hour, but he lay there quietly until dusk.

As daylight faded, Ewan walked back to the downs. At the base of the tower, he dug a small pit in the ground, added kindling, and built a small fire, lighting it with hot coals he had brought from the kitchen fire at the farm. This fire would be kept going night and day, so when the bonfire signal was sighted on the coast, it would be a quick matter to take burning material from the small fire up the ladder and light the bonfire alarm. Finally, he made a seat out of branches at the base of the ladder in a spot where he could see to the southwest, from where a bonfire signal would come. He leaned back against the ladder and waited.

The evening grew dark, and stars appeared. The wind whistled gently through the poles of the tower. It was often windy on the downs. Ewan heard night noises: the call of a nightjar, the distant scream of a fox, even the harsh, unmusical screech of a small owl. The stars above him were bright, and Ewan realized it had been a long time since he had spent a night outside. It was a restless night. He was tired from the two days of hard work preparing the tower and bonfire, but he did not want to miss a signal. He drifted off to sleep a few times but stayed awake most of the night. As dawn began to light up the sky, he stayed vigilant in case the sails of Spanish ships were seen at first light. But no signs of a bonfire at the coast appeared, and Ewan relaxed.

It was still early morning when Thomas appeared, walking across the field and up to the tower. He had agreed to take a shift each morning until noon, and his younger brother Colin would watch during the afternoon. Ewan planned to arrive each day in the late afternoon and watch through the night. His sons were not pleased to miss parts of each workday, but they agreed to help for at least one week.

Ewan walked back to the farm, and in the kitchen, Mary poured a mug of ale for him. "You look tired, Ewan," she said. "Are you going to do this every night? Will you get any sleep?"

"I will get a little sleep in the middle of the night. There is almost no chance a bonfire signal will be lit then," he said, adding after a moment, "It's beautiful out on the downs in the darkness, and the stars are bright."

"Wrap that blanket around you well," she said. "I don't want you to catch a chill."

Ewan paused for a moment, then said, "Mary, do you remember when we first got together, before I moved here to the farm? Sometimes, I walked up from the coast, and you met me at the edge of the fields. We watched the sunset and the sky grow dark, and the stars shone brightly in the sky. We never stayed out late, but the night was beautiful. That is what it is like on the downs at night. You might not want to spend a whole night there, but I will be safe."

Ewan ate a bowl of pottage Mary dished out for him, made from early vegetables in the garden mixed with barley and cooked into a rich stew. Then he went into their bedroom and lay down on the straw-filled mattress. This time, he had no trouble falling asleep, and even the voices of his grandchildren did not wake him until the afternoon. After he rose, he sat with Mary for a while and watched the little ones play together. As the day ended, he took the basket of food she had prepared for him and headed back to the downs.

It was early evening when Ewan arrived, and Colin could return to the farm for dinner and spend time with his family. It had been a quiet day for both of his sons. They were not accustomed to having hours during the day with no pressing chores at the farm. Colin was glad to be done with his shift, but he promised to take the same shift each day for the rest of the week. Ewan made sure he had good coals in the little fire at the base of the tower, then sat down to watch night fall. Because he had slept so well during the day, it was easier for him to stay awake this night than the night before. He looked frequently toward the coast, but each time saw only blackness. The stars shone above, and the Milky Way was a bright band crossing the sky from north to south. He listened to the same noises he had heard the night before.

As Ewan sat and watched, he thought about other times he had stayed awake all night. He remembered when he and Mary were a young couple. Mary had two miscarriages early in their marriage, and they wondered if they would be able to have a family of their own. But then Thomas was born, a healthy boy named after Mary's father. Colin's birth followed a little more than a year later. Mary would have loved to have had a little girl in their family, but this was not to be. The two boys were the extent of their children, and she loved them nonetheless. On the nights when his sons were born, Ewan sat anxiously at the table in the kitchen while Mary's mother and the midwife stayed by Mary's bedside. Those nights were filled with screams that filled Ewan with fear that the birth would not go well. These worries only eased when he heard the faint cry of a baby in the early morning hours. He felt huge relief at the sound, the promise of new life in their family.

Now, those babies were grown men with wives and children of their own. He had sat in the kitchen with his sons at the birth of each of their children. They had been mostly joyous times when the new baby arrived, and the mother was all right, but there had been tragic times as well. One night, Ewan sat in the kitchen with his older son, Thomas, and there were no cries from a newborn because the baby had been stillborn, and the mother died shortly after the birth. It was a terrible night, and Thomas had cried aloud, not knowing what he would do. But the next morning, Thomas left his two year old son with Mary and went back to his work in the fields. He did not smile for many months. Finally, three years later, Thomas met and married a young woman from the village. When she gave birth to a healthy baby girl, he began to smile again.

When the boys married, Mary welcomed the young women into the family. The farm was a busy place now, with a half dozen youngsters running about. Ewan was rarely in the house during the day, and he was surprised at the amount of noise coming from the children, although he slept through much of it. Several of the little ones wondered why Grandpa was asleep during the daytime, and they had come into the bedroom to check that he was all right, waking him each time. He returned to sleep as soon as Mary gently shooed the children out of the bedroom, and Ewan got enough sleep that he felt rested and was confident he could stay awake during the long hours of darkness.

As the night progressed, Ewan added wood to the fire at the base of the tower to keep hot coals ready. He opened the basket Mary had sent with him, ate some of the bread and cheese, and sipped cider from the goatskin bag, eating sparingly so he would not grow sleepy. The wind rose to a gale in the middle of the night, and Ewan wrapped his cloak tightly around his shoulders to stay warm. He frequently looked toward the coast, but no lights appeared. It was unlikely anything would happen during the middle of the night, but he checked anyway.

Finally, as he started to tire, the sky in the East grew pale. Dawn was near. As the minutes passed, the dark shapes around him resolved into individual bushes. The horizon became a defined line, and a glimmer of color tinted the sky. The day was not going to be clear, but patches of sky were visible through the clouds. This was the time when he thought a bonfire alarm might be lit at the coast, a time when the sails of the Spanish fleet might be visible from the cliffs. But there was no fire and no alarm. The Spaniards had not arrived yet.

Ewan felt some confusion about his feelings toward the Spanish fleet. His father, Ramon, had been Spanish, and Ewan often thought about the gentle man who had told him stories about living in Spain, about lovely stone buildings and warm sun on balconies, of friends sitting in little cafés and drinking wine during the long evenings. Ewan realized that the men on the ships were soldiers, far different from his father, yet he felt no hatred against them, only concern about what might happen to his family. If the Spanish ships landed at Falmouth or Plymouth, he would fight alongside his sons, but he hoped it would not come to that.

When the night finally gave way to dawn, it was mostly gray. Ewan fed the fire one more time and ate the rest of his food from the basket. Thomas would arrive after a while, and Ewan could go to the house and rest. If this waiting went on for many more nights, he would have to get good sleep during the day to stay awake each night. Ewan looked toward the farm and saw Thomas approaching across the fields. When he reached the tower, the two men greeted each other. Thomas was not happy about taking a shift at the tower instead of doing his chores at the farm. He was a hardworking man and hated to let things go that needed to be done. But Ewan joked with him and reminded him this might be the only time in his life that he would have a whole morning to do nothing but sit and watch for an alarm.

Ewan took his empty basket and headed home, where Mary was waiting for him to arrive. She took the basket, poured him a mug of ale, and sat with him while he drank it. "How was the night out there, Ewan?" she asked.

"It was a long night, Mary. I thought about you and the boys, about the nights when they were born, and how anxious I was about you."

Mary took one of his hands in hers. "You have been a good father to our sons," she said, "and they will be good fathers to their children.

I watch how Thomas spends time with his little ones. They love to be held in his arms."

"It is wonderful to see them together," said Ewan, "and I hope this affair with Spain won't ruin our lives. It is hard to imagine the Spanish would land at this far corner of England, but who knows what they are thinking."

"We cannot know, Ewan, and all we can do is the little bit that is our part. I am glad Thomas and Colin are not aboard one of the English ships anchored in Plymouth Harbor. The ships are packed with men, and when there are many men crowded so close together, there will surely be diseases."

Ewan heard what Mary was saying, but it only registered a little. The warmth of the kitchen and the mild ale he was drinking let him feel the fatigue he had put off during the night. Mary saw that he was fading and encouraged him to lie down in the bedroom.

"It will be a few hours before the little ones are up and making noise," she said. "Try to get some sleep before they start playing."

Ewan fell asleep quickly and only awakened a few hours later when a small voice called out in his ear, "Grandpa, are you awake?" It was Honour, Thomas's younger daughter, who came to make sure he was okay. He roused a little, smiled at her, and gave her a gentle hug when she came close.

"Grandpa is sleeping today," he said, "maybe you could go and play with your brothers."

"Yes, Grandpa," she said and ran out of the room, only to return quickly.

"Grandpa, will you always sleep during the day?"

"No, dear, just for a few days."

"Okay then," she said, then off she went.

Ewan slept for a while, then lay on the bed, not sleeping but trying to rest. It was midafternoon when he finally got up, feeling rested but with another long night ahead. He ate dinner with Mary, walked in the yard, and looked at the barn project, now put aside for the past few days.

The front of the second barn looked complete, and the thatched roof on half of the structure would protect the hay from the coming winter weather. The back wall had a large section that was not completed.

Ewan looked at the pile of stones waiting there and wondered whether he could finish the back wall with them. He was not as concerned about the look of the back wall since it faced the fields, and he could be less careful about the stone placement. He hoped the watch for the bonfire alarm would not go on for many more nights, so he could get back to the stonework before harvest time. Everything else stopped during the harvest, and Ewan worked with his sons from dawn to dusk each day. He drove one of the wagons and was available to do anything else that was needed. By the end of the harvest, all of them were exhausted.

Ewan went back to the house and sat with Mary for a while, then picked up the basket with the provisions she had packed for him and walked across the fields toward the Downs. The sun was getting low on the horizon, and he estimated it was about one hour until sunset. He wanted to relieve Colin at the tower early enough that his son would have time to spend with his wife and children before it grew dark.

Ewan reached the tower, and Colin headed for the farm. Ewan checked the fire at the base of the tower and added wood to make sure there would be hot coals all night. He climbed up the ladder and looked out toward the coast and the Channel beyond. There were no sails in sight and no bonfire alarm, so he returned to the ground, sat down, and faced the southwest. It would be another long night, he guessed, a night of watching and waiting. This felt familiar now, unlike the first night when he was anxious about missing the alarm. He was flattered that the sheriff had called upon him and that he was seen as a trusted man in the community.

Almost no one knew that Ewan's father had come from Spain. It was forty years since Ramon died, still a man in his middle years, and thirty years since Ewan had moved to the farm. He rarely had to write his name for any reason, but since he moved to the farm, he had changed the spelling from Escobar to Skiburio so it would sound more like a local name. One word for "barn" in the Cornish language was *skibborow,* and people assumed his name came from that word. So the farm became not only the home for the Skiburio family, but since Ewan had built the barns, most people assumed the farm was named for the barns. Ewan did not tell them anything different.

Thinking about the name, Ewan thought again of his father, long gone but often in his mind. Ramon had taught him how to read and spell, and though Ewan had little use for those skills at the farm, he had taught his sons what he knew. For many years, the only book in their home was a copy of the Bible, written in Latin, with some sections translated into English, and that is what Ewan taught from. He knew that most books now were not hand-copied by a scribe lettering each word but were printed using tiny metal shapes for the letters mounted into a frame, carefully inked, and then pressed onto vellum.

A few years earlier, a traveling peddler had stopped at the farm. Among his stock of pots and pans and other practical household items, he had a few books. They were each printed on vellum and bound in leather. It had been a good year at the farm, and after the rent payment to the Duchy of Cornwall, which owned the property, Ewan and Mary were left with a little extra money. Ewan asked the man about the books. "I carry them for the lords and the gentry," said the man. "Few others can read or write more than their own names." Ewan carefully paged through the books and decided that, for once, he would be spendthrift. The book that interested him was a copy of *The Canterbury Tales* by a man named Geoffrey Chaucer. He bought the book, surprising the peddler with his purchase. He read it through carefully, and now in the evenings, he read parts of it to his grandchildren, making sure the subject was appropriate for their young ears. After each reading, he carefully wrapped the book in oiled paper to protect it from dampness. Ewan imagined that when his grandsons grew into manhood, reading books like these would become a common occurrence for them too. Already, his oldest grandson, Thomas Junior, liked to sit beside Ewan and follow along with him as he read. Perhaps his sons' homes might have a few books like these one day.

Ewan's father had known how to speak Spanish and Latin, and when he landed in Cornwall, he learned English quickly. He never became fluent in Cornish, but Ewan had grown up with it. He spoke English and Cornish with equal ease. Cornish was the language spoken in the village pub, but when the sheriff came to the farm the other day, he spoke English. English was the language used in church services each Sunday and the language spoken by the local gentry, so it was growing increasingly more familiar to the people of the area.

Ewan came to with a start and realized his thoughts had drifted off. He looked toward the coast, but there was no sign of a bonfire. It was still early dusk, although the sun had set. He relaxed and leaned back against the post of the tower, thinking about what he was going to do when the alarm finally came. If the Spanish did not land in Falmouth, the ships passing by in the Channel would have little impact on the area, and he could return to working on the barns, get ready to help his sons with the hay harvest, and continue reading to his grandchildren in the evenings. It was many miles to London, farther than Ewan had ever traveled in his life, and he doubted his life would change much, even if the Spanish army attacked the city. The farthest Ewan had traveled was to Plymouth, a town that seemed huge to him, but according to men who had been to London, was not even a fraction of the size of that city.

Something caught Ewan's eye as he glanced out toward the coast again. A pinprick of light was visible, so tiny that Ewan wondered if he actually was seeing anything. As he watched, the light grew larger and brighter until he clearly saw that it was a flame soaring into the sky.

This was the alarm! It had to be. There was no sign of any other light but the single flame. Ewan rushed to the fire he had kept burning at the base of the tower and chose a stick with hot coals at the end. He carefully climbed the ladder and thrust the stick under the dry shavings he had placed three days earlier. The shavings began to turn black, and a tiny flame appeared. He blew gently on the shavings, and the fire spread. He added more kindling gradually to the flame so as not to suffocate it. Ewan watched as the flame grew, caught fire to the kindling, and began to lap at the larger sticks arranged in a pyramid on the tower platform. The fire grew steadily, and Ewan descended the ladder to watch that sparks did not ignite the surrounding bushes.

There was little or no wind this early in the evening. The fire burned freely, and most of the sparks went skyward and disappeared in the darkness. Now that the fire was lit, Ewan worried whether the alarm had been picked up at the next station to the north. He watched intently, and after a short while, a tiny light appeared at the alarm tower on the hill above Penryn. The light grew steadily until Ewan could see that it was burning brightly. A little while later, far off in the distance, at the summit of Hensbarrow Downs, another light appeared and grew, very tiny in the distance but reassuring to Ewan that the alarm was received. He looked back toward the coast, where the first bonfire alarm burned brightly, and when he looked to the northeast, he saw another bonfire burning out on the coast toward Falmouth. The bonfire alarms were working, the news was being sent across England, and people would come to defend their land. Ewan's part was nearly finished, but he had helped ignite a larger fire, one that might protect England from invasion.

Now that the bonfire was blazing brightly on the tower, and the alarm had been passed along to other stations, Ewan was exhausted. He had been anxious for five days, and his part was nearly done. He found a spot where he could see the fire on the tower, and he sat down to watch. The fire burned brightly for a while, then died down until only a few sparks were flying. Ewan watched until the fire burned low, then wrapped the cloak around his shoulders and let himself relax. He fell asleep for a few hours.

It was early dawn when Ewan woke again. He looked to the south and to the north, but none of the bonfire alarms were visible. It was cold, and Ewan shivered a little as he stood up. He climbed the ladder to the tower. The fire had burned down completely, and only a few coals still glowed. Ewan carefully ladled dirt over the coals to make sure they would not reignite. Then he climbed down the ladder, picked up his basket, and started walking back to the farm. There was just enough light to see where he was walking. He was pleased that his part was finished. It was up to others now, men aboard English ships and men from the trained bands who waited on the shore to defend England against the Spanish army.

As Ewan neared the house, he saw a flickering light in the kitchen. Mary was in there with one candle burning beside her. The table was covered with flour, and she was kneading bread dough. She looked up when she heard Ewan enter and said, "Ewan, I was thinking about you out there in the darkness, and I could not sleep any longer, so I decided to start the bread for this week. You are back early. Is everything all right?"

"It's done, Mary," he said. "The alarm came, and I lit the bonfire. It is passed along. The Spanish fleet has been sighted. Our part is finished, and now it is time for others to do their part."

Mary stopped kneading the bread dough and looked at him. "Ewan, I am glad it is finished. I worried about you this week, and whatever happens now, we have done what we could. The boys will be glad to return to the farm work and prepare for the harvest. And what about you, Ewan?"

"I will get some sleep, Mary, then Thomas and I will take the horses and bring back the materials used to build the tower. It is time for me to go back to work on the barn."

Epilogue

The Spanish armada, 130 huge ships sailing in a crescent formation miles across, was sighted near the Scilly Islands on July 19, 1588. When the bonfire alerts were lit on the mainland of Cornwall near the tip of the Lizard Peninsula, it took only a short time for the news to travel 300 miles to London.

The armada proceeded slowly up the English Channel, pursued by a fleet of English ships, larger in number but smaller in size and armament. The two fleets were different in many ways. The Spanish intended to attack the English ships by attaching grapples to them and boarding them with the soldiers carried on the Spanish ships. However, the English ships were faster and more maneuverable than the Spanish vessels, and they managed to elude capture. The English plan of attack was to damage the Spanish ships with cannon fire. But they had to stay at a distance to avoid being boarded, and the English cannon fire had little effect on the massive Spanish galleons.

For nine days, the two fleets slowly drifted up the English Channel, fighting sporadic and inconclusive battles. The Spanish fleet anchored in the Channel outside the French port of Calais to await the arrival of twenty thousand additional soldiers sent from the Spanish army stationed in the Spanish Netherlands. However, these soldiers were prevented from arriving because Dutch rebels controlled the shallow waters off the Netherlands' coast. The Spanish and English fleets waited, anchored about a mile apart from each other.

During the night of July 28, 1588, the English launched eight small ships that had been turned into fire ships, loaded with flammable material and with their cannons loaded. These drifted into the Spanish fleet and caused terror among the ship captains, who feared the fire ships might be "hellburners" loaded with tons of explosives. Many Spanish ships cut their anchor cables and drifted away, disrupting the tight formation that had been maintained until then. During the next two days, English ships attacked Spanish ships one at a time, sinking several of them and causing others to run aground.

Meanwhile, the two fleets continued to drift north, away from the proposed invasion landing sites of the Spanish army in England. The Spanish ships could not sail back against the prevailing westerly winds, and the Spanish admiral decided to abort the invasion and return to Spain. The ships followed the prevailing winds on a long journey north around Scotland and into the Atlantic Ocean west of Ireland. During this journey, they encountered fierce storms, and many ships were wrecked on the west coast of Ireland. The crews that made it to shore were massacred. Only half of the Spanish ships made it safely back to Spain.

No English ships were sunk during the battles, but the overcrowding and poor food aboard them spread disease, killing approximately three thousand of the sailors. The rest were discharged without being paid for their services.

This unsuccessful attack did not end Spain's attempts to conquer England. Two more armadas were sent in 1596 and 1597. Both were unsuccessful due to bad weather and did not reach the English Coast. Finally, in 1604, after the deaths of Queen Elizabeth of England and King Philip II of Spain, a peace treaty was agreed upon between their successors, King James I of England and King Phillip III of Spain. In 1607, a truce was agreed upon between Spain and the provinces of the Netherlands, which had remained under rebel control. These provinces became the independent country of the Netherlands.

Bonfire alerts were used for the next two centuries to alert the English people that enemies were approaching.

The stone barns still stand in South Cornwall.

CHAPTER THREE

Fighting for the King

1603–1649

England

Queen Elizabeth died in 1603 after ruling England for forty-four years, succeeded by King James VI of Scotland, her first cousin and the son of Mary, Queen of Scots. He ruled England for twenty-two years as King James I. James was a devout Protestant who believed in the divine right of kings, the doctrine that a king's authority came from God and freed him from earthly controls such as Parliament. This resulted in disagreements between the king and Parliament throughout his reign. During the years that he was king, England established the first successful colonies in the New World. These included colonies in Jamestown, Virginia, in 1607, Plymouth and later the Boston Colony in Massachusetts in 1620, and a colony on the island of Barbados in the Caribbean in 1625.

At James's death in 1625, he was succeeded by his son Charles, who ruled as King Charles I. Charles attempted to impose new taxes on the English people without the approval of Parliament, and this led to a confrontation. Charles dissolved Parliament in 1629 and ruled without it until 1640. In 1641, with the Crown nearing bankruptcy, Charles requested that Parliament reassemble, but the conflict between the two only intensified. He attempted to have Parliamentary leaders arrested, and in return, they called out the London militia, the "trained bands," to take over the government. Charles fled London and called upon his supporters to come to his aid.

Both the king and Parliament requested that settlers return from the American colonies to England to join their ranks. The Massachusetts colonies largely supported the Parliament, while the Virginia and Barbados colonies supported the king. Armies were formed, and fighting broke out in 1642. It lasted without a break for five years and intermittently for another decade. All of England, Ireland, and Scotland were involved in this struggle. It is estimated that close to two hundred thousand people died during the British Civil War.

Robert Skyburriowe, 1613–1645

Autumn 1641

The letter from his older brother, Edward, persuaded Robert to leave Barbados and return to Cornwall in the year 1641. The dull yellow parchment was carefully folded and secured with a plain wax seal, unusually formal for the rare letters Robert received from his family. The previous letter had arrived three years earlier and informed him that his father had died. The funeral was long finished by the time Robert received the letter telling him about it. This one was different. Written by his older brother, Edward, it was only a few sentences on one side of the sheet. "Robert, come home," the letter read. "The king has left London and has called upon those who support him to come to his aid. Sir Bevil Grenville is putting together a regiment of Cornishmen. You could be one of his men. The king needs you here." It did not take much to persuade Robert to leave Barbados. The poor price for his tobacco crop this year left his small plantation in serious debt. Several neighbors had already sold their land and left the island. Most were going to a new settlement in South Carolina, where land was plentiful and cheap, but Robert was finished with farming.

Robert had grown up on a farm near the southern coast of Cornwall at the end of the Lizard Peninsula. As a small boy, he ran about in the fields and played with his older brothers. The years passed, and he spent his time minding the small herd of sheep, fixing the fences through which they were constantly escaping, and helping with the hay harvest in the fall. It was a good life for a boy. He had two brothers and a sister to play with, cousins in the house at the end of the lane, and plenty of things to do. Sometimes, twenty people sat together at dinner on Sunday. The foods they ate were mostly grown on the farm: vegetables from the garden, mutton from the sheep, even ale brewed from the barley. It was a happy life. But as Robert grew into his teens, he realized that life at the farm was not quite as he had imagined it. His oldest brother wanted to marry and start a family of his own, but where on the farm was there room to bring a new bride? The house was full. Robert's sister had married a local boy whose family held a farm nearby. She moved there, but it too was crowded, and the young couple was unsure what they should do.

Robert waited and watched, worked each day at his chores on the farm, and sat with his father reading most evenings. His father insisted that Robert learn to read, although the boy could not see the sense of it. There was little need for reading on the farm, and the vicar at the church kept the family history by recording the births, deaths, and marriages, writing them out carefully in the parish record. But Robert's father insisted, so every night they sat together to read by the light of a single flickering candle. There were a few books at the farm, among them an old Bible, handwritten in Latin with sections translated into English. There was a worn copy of *The Canterbury Tales,* which dated to the time of Robert's great-grandfather, and a few newer books that Robert's father or grandfather had acquired. Each was carefully wrapped in oiled paper to protect it from dampness, and they were stored in a small cupboard in the kitchen. From time to time, Robert's mother suggested the cupboard could be used to store more useful things than old books. But Robert's father insisted the books be kept in a safe, dry place, so they remained in the cupboard.

Recently, during a rare trip to Falmouth for supplies that were not produced on the farm, Robert realized his reading skills had some practical use. He read the labels on the packages at the store. He noticed a wall where handbills of varied types were posted. One printed sheet described events taking place at Parliament in London. Robert read the title and opening sentences but did not find them interesting. On the wall were scraps of paper with handwritten notices that advertised lost farm animals and items for sale. One printed handbill attracted Robert's attention. It began with the heading FREE LAND! How could this be, he wondered, when every place in Cornwall was already owned? The following few lines were written in smaller text but still in a bold-face style. "Fertile Soil! Salubrious Climate! Great Opportunities on the Island of Barbados!" The rest of the poster was printed in a smaller typeface and listed many details. Robert didn't understand what was being offered, so he asked his father. His father responded gruffly, "It is a way to lure young men who don't realize that nothing is free. A person who answers that advertisement will be taken advantage of."

Despite his father's warning, the words of the advertisement stuck in Robert's mind. On the farm, as he walked behind the horse pulling the plow in the fields, he thought about free land in Barbados, and it sounded good to him. Some day, the farm would be passed to his older brother, and there would be room for only one other family member to stay and work the farm. Robert's middle brother would fill that role. What was Robert to do? He could hire out to one of the other farmers in the area, but it would never help him to own his own land.

When Robert turned seventeen, he decided it was time to leave. He knew his parents would not approve of his plans, so he talked instead with his older sister Margaret, or Meg, as he called her. She had looked after him when he was little, and he trusted her with his plans. He walked to the farm where she had moved after she married. Her husband, John, was working in the fields, and she was in the cottage with their one-year-old baby. She was surprised to see Robert during the daytime, but she welcomed him, and they sat at the trestle table in the center of the room.

She gave him a questioning look and asked, "What brings you here, Robert?"

"Meg, I need to leave Cornwall," he said. "There is nothing for me at the farm, and I need to find a place of my own. There is work for indentured men on the island of Barbados."

"Do you have to go so far away?" Meg responded. "An ocean lies between England and Barbados. How do you know what you will find there?"

"I will learn," he said. "I will work five years as an indentured man, but after that, I will be free. I will buy land with my earnings. It will be up to me to make it work. Life will be hard, but that is all right."

"Oh, Robert, I will miss you. We will all miss you. Couldn't you work for one of the farmers around here for a few years first?"

"No, Meg, I want to get started now so I can get on with my life."

"We will miss you so," she said. They spoke a few minutes longer, then he rose to leave. Meg put her arms around her younger brother and held onto him for a few moments.

Much had changed in the twelve years since Robert talked with Meg in Cornwall. When he told his parents he was leaving the farm, his mother cried. His father did not approve, but he did not forbid Robert from going. In fact, Robert thought his father may have expected something like that to happen. When the fall harvest was completed, it was time for Robert to leave. The hay was stored each year in one of the old stone barns on the farm. As Robert piled hay, stacking it to the rafters with a pitchfork, he glanced around the old building. A family story recounted that his great-grandfather built this barn by himself, along with the larger barn where the animals were stabled through the winter. Robert could not imagine how one man could have built both barns unless he worked on them for most of his life. Why would a man spend so much time on one project? Hadn't he been eager to go places and see things, to get away from the endless routine of farm chores? It didn't matter. The barns were there, and every autumn, they were filled with hay and safely housed the animals.

On the day harvest was completed, the family sat down for dinner. Robert looked around the table and realized it might be the last time they would all sit together. His sister, Meg, and her husband, John, had come, bringing their one-year-old toddler. Robert's two brothers and his parents were there. His older brother, Edward, was a quiet man in his mid-twenties. His middle brother, Joseph, was talkative and laughed a lot. Joseph was always busy with a project and could hardly wait for the meal to end before he raced off to finish it. Robert's mother was quiet, like her oldest son, but she carefully listened to every part of the conversation. If a discussion became heated, she spoke softly but firmly to calm people down, and her husband and sons followed her direction.

Robert's father sat at the head of the table. He kept the conversation going, asked the boys about how their work was that day, and checked in with his daughter to find out about his grandson. He recited a short prayer before the meal and included a phrase asking God to keep Robert safe on his journeys.

A few days later, Robert sat next to his father on the seat of the wagon as they traveled along the rutted dirt road that led to Falmouth.

As they neared the docks, he saw the masts of the brig that would carry him to Barbados. Robert and his father had a brief leave-taking at the dock, and his father held onto him for a few moments. "God be with you, son," he said in a broken voice. Then it was up the ramp and onto the deck of the ship.

Everything aboard ship was new to Robert. The deck was a bustle of activity, with men rolling barrels toward an open hatchway where a davit slung them down into the hold of the ship. There were wooden crates of live chickens and rabbits, a mixed herd of horses and cows stabled in small box stalls, and a flock of sheep and goats penned up against the rail. The noise was deafening; chickens clucking, sheep and goats bleating, and men giving orders in loud voices. Robert stood on the deck, not sure what to do.

"Get out of the way, youngster," came a gruff voice close behind him. Startled, Robert turned and saw a heavyset man, his arms wrapped around a chest. "You are in the path. Now move."

"But where?" Robert stammered.

"To the devil for all that I care, but if you are one of the lucky ones going to Barbados, then get yourself into the forecastle. That is a lovely place for you to stay on your pleasure trip to the island." He motioned to an open hatchway.

Robert walked over to it and looked down. He saw something that was a cross between a ladder and stairs, with treads like stairs but as steep as a ladder. He was looking into the opening when the same gruff voice sounded out. "That's your home, all right, and remember to face the ladderway when you go down. Otherwise, you might have a long drop."

Obediently, Robert turned so that he faced the ladder and started down. He carried a blanket with extra clothes wrapped inside, and he balanced it on his shoulder as he descended. There were not many steps before his foot hit a solid deck. Turning around, he found himself in a room about twenty feet long and fourteen feet wide, with the ceiling about a foot above his head. It was filled with what looked like narrow shelves stretching from the floor to the underside of the deck above. As he stood there, wondering what to do next, he heard a voice call out.

"Grab yourself a bunk, laddie. The top ones will be warmer, but there may be drips through the deck above. The bottom ones are easy to get into, but you may get stepped upon by someone climbing into an upper bunk." The voice came from the other side of the room. Robert, squinting through the dim light, saw a young man sitting on one of the shelves, hunched over because the shelf above him was so close that there was only room to lie down.

Robert looked around the room and saw men lying on most of the shelves, or bunks, as that is what they were. Some of the men were sleeping; others looked at him with curiosity.

"Welcome to our humble home for the next six weeks," came another voice.

"Soft beds, good food, what more could a man ask for?"

"Well, you aren't going to get it anyway," came a third voice.

Robert looked around the space and saw that the lower bunks were occupied, as were those near the ladder that led to the deck above. There seemed to be an unoccupied top bunk near the back of the space. He started to walk between the tiers of bunks, but the space between the rows was too tight, and he had to turn sideways to fit through. Holding his blanket above his head, he sidestepped awkwardly until he reached the tier of bunks where there was an empty one. Careful not to step on the man lying on the lower bunk, he lifted himself past the middle bunks, slipped his blanket onto the upper bunk, and pulled himself up. Once there, he found that the deck above his head was too low to allow him to sit up, so he turned sideways, undid the cord that was wrapped around his blanket, and by a series of small motions, spread it out on the rough boards of his new bed, leaving enough bunched at the side to pull over him.

He lay on the blanket and looked up at the underside of the deck, barely a foot from his face. His bunk was up against the hull of the ship, so there was solid planking on one side. Peering across the room, he saw four rows of bunks, each four layers high. End to end, there were three bunks in each row. Forty-eight bunks in all. How was it possible to house forty-eight men in this small space? He looked across the room. Most of the bunks were full. A few heads turned his way to see who the newcomer was. The man who had called out when he first entered the space nodded at him and spoke up. "Welcome, friend. Settle in. It is a long trip to Barbados."

Robert looked at him in wonder. "How is there room for all of us in here?"

"Oh, once the ship is sailing, we will be allowed on deck most days, and we will have to go up there to do the work that is assigned to us. It may be working the pumps, tarring the lines, or taking care of the animals. There will be plenty to do. You wait and see."

This prediction was accurate. The next day, as soon as the sails were spread and the ship cast off from the dock, the first mate came down the ladder and yelled, "All right now, it's time for you to start earning your keep. Which of you are experienced in caring for the stock we have aboard?" Robert raised his hand, as did three or four other men.

"Come with me," shouted the mate. They followed him up onto the deck and were introduced to the animals, a mixed herd of sheep and goats, a dozen horses and as many milk cows, along with crates of chickens and rabbits. "These are your responsibility until we reach Barbados," the mate said. "Heaven help you if any die from neglect. You have to feed and water them, clean their pens, milk the cows and the ewes, and gather the eggs. There will be chickens to kill and pluck, and rabbits to skin. The meat will all go to the captain's table, not to you lot. It will be salt pork and biscuits for you. Now choose among yourselves who is to handle which animals."

Robert was the youngest of the men, and he said nothing. He waited as other men chose the horses, cows, sheep, and goats, leaving the chickens and rabbits. The next man to choose took the rabbits, so for the duration of the voyage, Robert fed and watered the chickens, gathered the eggs, selected chickens for the captain's table, and killed and plucked them. It was not the most enjoyable part of the trip, but it was something he had often done on the farm.

Each day on the ship was much the same as the one before. At first, the weather was cold, and sometimes there were storms. The ship rocked from side to side, and everyone in the forecastle was seasick. Robert was sick along with the others, but he had to look after the chickens, and this task got him up onto the deck, where he felt better. At least he wasn't down in the hold, manning one of the bilge pumps.

The winds grew calm after a couple of weeks, and the weather became warm. Robert stayed on deck each day as long as possible and took on extra jobs to stay out of the cramped bunk area. Land was not in sight until almost a month had passed. Then a mountainous island appeared in the distance, and the sailors identified it as Flores, one of the Azores Islands. The captain intended to stop there to obtain fresh water for the rest of the voyage. Robert hoped he could leave the ship and see a little of the island, but his only time ashore was spent rolling barrels of fresh water to the ship and up the ramp. But once he stopped and smelled a sweet fragrance wafting off the hills and noticed masses of blue flowers on the slopes above the port. An old sailor told Robert they were called hydrangeas, and the island was named after them, Flores, the island of flowers.

Then the anchor was hauled up, and the ship set sail on the final leg of the journey, crossing the Atlantic Ocean. Robert found this part of the trip a pleasure. Each day, he enjoyed the gentle winds and warm sun. He watched the sailors climb the rigging to adjust the sails, and he longed to see what it was like to be so high above the ship. Robert got his chance one day when he was finished with his work, and one of the young sailors was about to climb the rigging up the main mast. Robert nodded to him and pointed upward. The sailor shrugged and said, "Why not?" The sailor started up the shrouds, and Robert followed, but he was not as agile and quickly fell behind. He was halfway to the crow's nest when a bellow from the deck below startled him. It was the mate yelling, "Landsman, get down off those shrouds and back to the deck where you belong!"

Robert reluctantly climbed back down to the deck, where he got a severe tongue lashing from the mate. "What were you doing? If you fall from up there, we lose some valuable cargo. Every one of you is worth money to this ship, but only if you arrive in Barbados in good shape, ready to work hard in the fields." Robert looked down at his feet, red-faced, but he glanced up as the mate finished scolding him. There was a hint of a smile on the man's face, and Robert thought perhaps he sympathized a little with this boy who just wanted to see what the ocean looked like from a hundred feet above the ship. Robert stayed on the deck after that, killing and plucking the chickens, until a few weeks later, a cry came from the lookout: "Land ho!"

Robert rushed to the rail and looked to the west. No island was in sight, but a cloud indicated where land might be. He waited by the rail and watched until slowly the top of a line of hills appeared and the outline of an island gradually took shape below.

That was twelve years ago, and Robert remembered his excitement at reaching Barbados. He worked five years in the tobacco fields of a large plantation, then spent seven more of endless toil, clearing the scrub from the few acres of land he had been able to buy, trying to raise a crop of tobacco. As his father had predicted, there was no free land for the taking. He did most of the work on his acres by himself, built a small shack to live in, and by the third year, had a few bales of tobacco to ship to England. Since then, the harvest had been one good year, two fair years, and the rest were terrible. One year looked to be a good harvest until a storm fell upon the island with savage winds and driving rain. The entire crop was destroyed. After that, he was in debt with little chance of paying it off. He saw endless years of work ahead, scraping to raise a crop of tobacco each year that would barely earn enough to pay the interest on his debt.

Meanwhile, Robert noticed a change occurring on the island. Fewer indentured men arrived from England each year. Instead, shiploads of black slaves from Africa were unloaded at the port, men chained together. They worked at the large plantations, where they tore out the tobacco plants and replaced them with sugarcane. Robert did not have the money to buy slaves and convert his small acreage to sugarcane. Besides, he didn't like what he saw in the sugarcane fields. The slaves were forced to work endless hours, and many died soon after they became field workers, replaced by new arrivals. One of the plantation owners approached Robert and asked if he would come to work as a slave overseer. But this had no appeal for him. He finished harvesting his tobacco crop and got it ready to sell. It was a good harvest. However, months later, when the ship returned from England, he learned that the price paid for the tobacco was much lower than the year before. He did not know what to do, but he realized he could no longer make a living farming tobacco on his few acres and could not afford to convert the farm to sugarcane.

When the letter on yellow parchment arrived from his brother, Robert thought it might be the answer. He approached the plantation owner who had offered him a job and proposed to sell the man his acreage. The money he received for the land was enough to pay off his debts and leave a small amount for the cost of the ship passage back to England and his expenses when he reached there. This late in the season, the choice of ships was limited. A brig had recently arrived from New England with a load of salt cod and lumber, and it was being unloaded at the port in Bridgetown, the main town on Barbados. Barrels of sugar and molasses would be loaded into the hold, and the ship would sail to

England. Robert spoke to the captain, who confirmed there was room for another passenger. Robert agreed to bunk with the sailors, help load cargo, and take on menial tasks while the ship was at sea.

A few days later, Robert was helping load barrels of provisions for the return trip when he noticed a man wearing dark clothing and a broad dark hat hanging around the dock. When Robert took a break from work, the man approached and sat down on a crate near him.

"Hello, friend," he began. "My name is Vincent Potter, and I am a Puritan from New England. I see that you are hardworking and fit. Is this a job that will lead to something better for you?"

Robert bristled a little at the man's tone of voice and what seemed like an impertinent question. "No," he answered. "The work is just work."

"Well, then," continued the man, "I have an offer for you. I am traveling back to England on this ship. Once I reach there, I will fight for the rights of Englishmen against an unjust king. Will you join me? Your passage will be fully paid, and I guarantee you a place in the Parliamentary army. You will have good comrades and a banner to follow."

"I am not interested," said Robert, unwilling to reveal that he had already booked passage on this ship. At this response, the man tightened his mouth, rose, and walked away. Later that day, Robert saw him talking to other men working on the dock and he realized the man had come to Barbados for the very purpose of recruiting soldiers to fight on the side of the English Parliament.

Two days later, the ship was fully loaded with barrels of sugar and molasses destined to be sold in England. Barrels of fresh water, kegs of salt pork, and biscuits for the sailors lined the cargo hold. Alongside stood a host of animals: goats for milk and crates of rabbits and chickens for the captain's table, for the captain and for the passengers who had paid full fare and would dine with him.

When the sails were spread and the ship eased out of the harbor at Bridgetown, Robert stood at the stern and looked out at the town. It was twelve years since he had first seen Barbados, twelve years of struggle with not a lot to show for it. He had a little silver in his pocket, and he was a bit wiser about the world. The ship slowly made its way through the water, and he watched the island grow smaller. When Robert turned away from the rail, he noticed Vincent Potter standing on the quarterdeck with the other passengers. Robert pulled his hat low over his face so the man would not recognize him. They would cross paths on this voyage because the ship was not very large. But for today at least, Robert felt strong emotions about leaving the land that had been his home for over a decade, and he did not want to talk with anyone.

It would be a long trip to England. The ship would sail north on the east side of the Caribbean Islands, then enter the Gulf Stream current. This would carry it quickly up the coast of America, a wild and unsettled country except for the scattered British colonies and the Dutch colony of New Amsterdam at the mouth of the New York River. This ship would not stop at any of these settlements but would stay in the current, which turned to the east and flowed toward England. It would be six to seven weeks of sailing if the winds held and the ship did not meet any storms. Robert let the captain know he came from a farm background, and once again, he had a flock of chickens to feed, rabbits to care for, and a few goats to milk each day.

On the fourth day of the voyage, Robert was plucking two chickens for the captain's table, standing near the rail on the lee side of the ship so the feathers fluttered over the side and into the water. He heard someone walk up behind him, and a voice called out: "Rolling barrels and now plucking chickens. What other honorable tasks are yours to carry out that are more important than fighting for the rights of the English people?" It was Vincent Potter, dressed as usual in his dark suit.

Robert nearly exploded in anger at the man, but restrained himself and answered calmly, "I am sure there will be other tasks for me on this ship."

"Well, keep my offer in mind, young man," Potter replied. "There is a higher calling waiting for you if you accept it."

Robert kept his mouth shut, aware he might lose control and strike the man at any moment. He kept plucking the chickens. A voice called down to Potter from the quarterdeck, and the man walked away.

The days passed, each one much like the one before. Robert had a hammock in the forecastle with the sailors, but he did not have to stand watch. Instead, he was assigned to other tasks that needed to be done on the ship. He spent hours working the pumps that carried foul water out of the bilge, and he occasionally helped the ship's carpenter when a repair needed an extra hand. Most of the time, he took care of the goats, rabbits, and chickens.

Midway through the voyage, the mate came looking for Robert. The captain's boy had taken ill, and someone was needed to serve dinner at the captain's table. The mate was apologetic about his request. "It is a stiff-necked bunch, that group of Puritans from New England who eat with the captain," he said. "I feel bad asking you to serve them, but it should only be for a day or two until the boy is back on his feet."

This was not a task Robert looked forward to. Taking care of animals was all right, serving meals felt like a menial chore. But he had agreed to do the tasks assigned to him, and the voyage had gone well up to this point. He put on his cleanest shirt, washed his hands with salt water, and went to see the cook.

The main course at dinner that night consisted of two chickens Robert had killed and plucked earlier that day. When he carried the platter into the captain's cabin, piled high with juicy pieces of roast chicken, it was met with cries of approval from the half dozen passengers who dined with the captain. But as Robert placed the platter on the table, he heard the familiar voice of Vincent Potter call out, "Not only does he kill and pluck the chickens, but he serves them also. He would rather serve chicken than fight for the rights of Englishmen."

At this remark, Robert could hold back no longer. Softly but firmly, he said, "I return to England to fight for our anointed king against the Parliamentary rebels."

This brought an uproar from the men sitting at the table. One stood up and reached for his sword. A sharp bang on the table silenced the noise, and the men turned to the head of the table where the captain sat. He roared out at the group.

"Gentlemen, on land, you can kill each other for all that I care, but on this ship, there is only one law, and I am that law! Anything that disrupts the order I keep on this ship is strictly forbidden. If I hear of any altercations amongst you, I will put you both in one of the ship's longboats and set you adrift in the ocean. Whether you kill each other or row to England matters not to me."

This outburst silenced the room. The captain returned to eating while the Puritans muttered to each other. Robert returned to the galley to get the next course of the meal.

Robert heard no openly hostile remarks for the rest of the voyage, although several of the Puritans frowned when they passed him on the deck. He kept his head down, milked the nanny goats, plucked the chickens, and skinned the rabbits. Gradually, the ship neared England. It would have helped Robert if the ship had stopped at Falmouth or Plymouth in Cornwall, where he could have disembarked, but the ship was headed to London. Robert could only stand at the rail and watch as they passed by familiar landmarks on the coast of Cornwall. A few days later, the ship arrived at the mouth of the Thames River and dropped anchor to wait for a rising tide to carry it upriver to the London docks. Robert was finished with his tasks and stood at the rail of the ship, looking at the shore. He had never been to London and was curious about it. But most of all, he wanted to be home in Cornwall. Suddenly, these thoughts were interrupted by footsteps behind him as Vincent Potter appeared at his side. Potter spoke softly, "That is our home, England. Ten years since I saw it last, and I never thought I would see it again."

Robert was quiet, waiting for an insult or a challenge. But Potter continued, "Friend, this is a sad time in our country when two Englishmen return across the ocean to fight against each other. I wish you were joining us in this struggle, but I know you have other plans. I respect your choice, though it is different from my own." He turned and held out his hand to Robert, who grasped Vincent Potter's hand in his. They stood there silently for a moment before releasing their grip and turning back to the rail.

London was everything Robert imagined and much more: incredible amounts of noise and dirt, crowds of people on the streets, horses and carriages everywhere. He found a cheap inn near the docks and paid for a meal and a place to sleep. The bed was only a straw pallet on the dirt floor in the common room, but he wrapped his cloak around himself and fell asleep. His money was safe inside his shirt, and he paid the innkeeper a few pence to hold the bag with his few belongings. The first night back in England passed without event. After months at sea, it was strange to lie on a bed that was not moving. But the snoring and coughs emanating from the men sleeping on pallets around him reminded him of the nights in the forecastle, and he slept soundly.

It was early morning when Robert woke, not yet light outside. He heard a rooster crow in the yard behind the inn, and a few of the men were already up. He paid for a bowl of hot porridge, retrieved his bag from the innkeeper, and set off down the docks to search for a vessel that would take him to Cornwall.

Robert spent a long day walking along the docks, stopping at each vessel to inquire about their destination and then moving on to the next dock. Finally, late in the day, Robert stopped at a dock where a small coastal freighter was tied up. It was being loaded with an assortment of crates and bales, wooden boxes holding jugs of wine, furniture, and assorted other items. He went aboard and found the captain, who confirmed that, yes, Falmouth was one of the stops the ship would make, but only after stopping at numerous ports along the south coast of England. The ship had room for a passenger, although he would have to sleep on the floor. And yes, he could help with loading and unloading to pay part of his passage. Robert put his bag where directed, returned to the dock, and reported to the ship's mate who was in charge of loading the cargo.

Two days of hard work loaded the vessel. At ebb tide and with minimal sails set, the ship eased away from the dock and drifted down the river. The trip to Falmouth was a slow passage as the boat stopped at many small ports along the way. It had to beat into the prevailing westerly winds most of the time, and each stop took a time to unload and take on cargo. But Robert enjoyed the trip and got along well with the crew. Each day brought him a little closer to Cornwall. His only problem was that he was always cold. After twelve years in Barbados, he had grown used to the hot weather, but now every day was cold and windy with intermittent rain showers. At one of the ports, he purchased an oilskin to keep himself dry on the days when it was raining. The rest of the crew were used to the weather, and they laughed at Robert in a good-natured way. In exchange, he told them what it was like to live in Barbados, about the tropical birds and fish and the fierce storms that sometimes blew across the island in the fall. The young men listened to his stories in wonder. The farthest any of them had traveled was to Dublin on the east coast of Ireland, where the boat delivered goods.

Meanwhile, days passed, and the boat slowly worked its way along the south coast, stopping at Southampton, Bournemouth, Weymouth, and Exmouth. At each port, they unloaded barrels and crates and took on cargo destined for the ports to the west. When the ship sailed into the harbor at Plymouth, Robert felt as though he was nearly home.

The next port would be Falmouth, and then it was only a twelve-mile walk to the farm. The coast began to look familiar, and he felt the wind blowing out of the Atlantic Ocean, something he had felt all his life until he left Cornwall. The arrival at Falmouth was almost a letdown. The trip was finished. The captain shook Robert's hand and offered him a place on the boat should he ever lack for work. Robert helped unload the cargo that was coming to Falmouth, then picked up his bag and began the walk to the farm.

The route passed through the village of Mawnan and crossed the Helford River at the ferry crossing. When Robert paid the fare for the ferry, he heard in the ferryman's response the familiar accent of a Cornishman. He thanked the man in Cornish and was rewarded with a string of Cornish oaths about Englishmen who crossed the river and did not appreciate the effort it took to operate the ferry in a river with strong tidal currents. Robert smiled to himself; yes, he was home.

The village of Helford looked much the same as he remembered it, and he stopped at the inn for a midday meal and glass of ale. He had only another six miles to walk. From Helford to the farm, the road sloped gradually upward through the village of Manaccan and met the main road just east of Goonhilly Downs. At this point, Robert took a side road past Trevasack Lake, where he and his brothers had learned to swim when they were young. He cut across the fields on a footpath to the lane. When he caught sight of the house, his pace quickened a little. The house looked the same, with the two old barns in the background. Smoke drifted upward out of the chimney. Robert paused a moment at the door, then pushed it open and entered the open room. A slight, womanly figure was stirring a pot suspended from a hook at the fireplace. She turned and looked at Robert without recognition.

"Hello, Mother," he said.

"Robert, is that you? I would not have known you, so grown up, and it has been so long." She came closer as if to check that it was actually her son. Then, recognizing him, she put her arms around him and held him close. After a long embrace, she stepped back, saying, "I did not know if I would see you again. When your father died three years ago, his last words were to ask about you."

"Mother, Barbados was all that I hoped for and then some. It was a good place for me to go, but now it was time for me to leave. Edward's letter came at the right time. I am happy to see you."

She held his hand and drew him to the table in the center of the room, bade him sit on one of the benches, brought a mug of ale and sat down across from him. Robert told her about the trip to Barbados, his life as an indentured man on the plantation, and the years he spent trying to make his life a success as a planter with a few acres of land.

"Now, Mother, it is back to where I came from and perhaps life as a soldier."

"It is a disturbing time," his mother said, "when one Englishman will fight another."

They sat together and talked as the afternoon passed, until with a sudden interruption, Robert's two brothers, Edward and Joseph, pushed open the door and entered the room. Both were dusty from work in the fields. They were overjoyed on recognizing Robert, and he retold the stories he had just shared with their mother. They sat together drinking mugs of ale as the afternoon passed into evening, and there was always more to say. Robert told stories of Barbados, about the sun and the storms, while his brothers spoke of their lives at the farm, the good harvest years when the barns were filled with hay for the animals, and the poor years of hail or blight and the hungry times that followed. Both of Robert's brothers had married and had families. Their children were growing quickly. The middle brother, Joseph, lived in the house at the end of the lane with his wife and two children. Edward's wife, Mary, had gone there to visit early in the day, taking their six children, including a new baby. They would arrive back soon, and the house would be filled with the noise of many small footsteps.

The men discussed the troubles between the king and the Parliament. One of the Cornish gentry, Sir Bevil Grenville, had left Parliament and was raising a regiment of Cornishmen to fight for the king. Edward thought this would be the best place for Robert to volunteer. "Sir Bevil is said to be a devil of a fighter, as brave as a lion, and he treats his men well," he said. "Both pike men and musketeers will be needed for his company."

"Well, I know just as little about both skills," said Robert.

"It matters little. Few of the men have soldiering experience. Bevil will provide the pike or musket. You will need your clothing and a sword if you can afford one."

The men's conversation paused when the door opened and a cluster of children erupted into the room. Their sizes varied from that of a silent little boy with his fist held mostly in his mouth to a boy of ten who earnestly shook Robert's hand. The children were followed by Edward's wife, Mary, a quiet woman, who bustled about and served bowls of pottage to the children while carrying a new baby in one arm. Only when the children were all served and sitting at the table did she come to Robert, give him her hand, and welcome him back to Cornwall. Joseph excused himself and left to spend the rest of the evening with his family. Robert was a bit overwhelmed by the activity in the house. Edward remained at the table with one child on his lap and one snuggled up to his side. One of the little girls sat beside Robert and kept looking up at him with questioning glances while she ate spoonfuls of her dinner. Robert looked at his brother and asked, "Are these really all yours?"

"Yes, there are six that I know of," Edward said with a laugh, "including the little one in Mary's arms. They keep us busy every day. It is the part of the farm that has never been bad. When Joseph and his family are here for a holiday dinner, the house practically shakes with all the noise."

It had been a busy day for the children, playing with their cousins. After dinner, they headed off to bed in the loft while Mary took the baby into a corner and sat on a stool to nurse him. The room grew quiet, and Edward and Robert sat finishing their ale. Edward spoke up. "It is good to have you home, Robert, and it is good for the farm. You will represent us well, and we will keep the farm going while you are away. It would be very hard if Joseph or I had to join up to fight."

"I am still not sure what I will need to bring with me when I go to join Grenville's regiment," Robert replied.

"A blanket, certainly, and an oilcloth for protection against the rain. You have a dagger, I presume. A sword would be a good thing to have, but that would cost money. Most of the men do not have any armor, so it will not be strange if you arrive without any."

Mary chimed in, "Perhaps you should visit my father, Henery. He has some items left to him by his father, who fought in the wars in the low countries during the time of the queen. I have not seen what he has, but I believe it would be useful to you."

"I will visit him tomorrow, and thank you for your suggestion,"

Robert replied. "I have never been part of a fighting force, but I will learn."

The evening ended with Mary and Edward going off to bed while Robert lay on a pallet on the floor of the main room. The fire threw flickers of light on the underside of the rough planks that made up the ceiling. The house felt familiar to Robert despite his long absence, and he quickly fell asleep with his blanket wrapped around him.

Robert woke at early dawn to the sound of someone stoking the fire. It turned out to be his mother, who got the fire burning well, then hung a pot of water from one of the hooks. Hearing the rustle as Robert sat up, she turned to speak: "I start a pot of porridge early so the others can sleep a little longer. Their days are busy, what with the work in the fields and the animals, and Mary has the children to mind."

"I have thought about this house many times during my travels," replied Robert. "It is good to be here, even if only for a little while."

"I know this is only a brief stay for you," his mother said. "But thank you for returning to Cornwall. After you join up, there will be less pressure for your brothers to go to fight, and heaven knows there is an endless amount of work here at the farm. Even if there is a war, the crown will expect the rent payment come harvest time."

Robert rose and washed his face at the well, then sat with his mother at the table while the porridge bubbled in the pot over the fire. Once it was cooked, he ate a bowlful and washed it down with a mug of whey left over from the butter churn. Rustling sounds from the loft above them made it clear the children had woken up. His mother spoke softly. "They all sleep together on a pallet of rushes covered with blankets, and when the first one wakes in the morning, it disturbs the rest of them. They all get up together. In a few minutes, it will be a madhouse down here. It might be good to roll up your things, or you may find them strewn all about the house."

Robert rolled his few belongings into his blanket and secured the bundle with a cord. No sooner was this done than five children raced into the room with a great deal of commotion. He stood back and watched. The younger children clustered about their grandmother, curious about what there was to eat. The two older boys noticed Robert standing in the corner and came over to him. They wanted to know if he was staying long and if he would tell them stories about his adventures. He sat down at the table and told them about the sky in Barbados, how there were different stars from the ones they saw in Cornwall, and how the sun looked when it rose out of the sea. It was two hours before he was able to break away from his eager audience. Edward and Mary appeared shortly after the children, ate a bowl of porridge, and then left to start their chores.

Midmorning had come and gone by the time Robert walked down the long lane and turned toward the village. The two older boys wanted to stay with him, but he sent them home when he reached the end of the lane. It was a walk of half an hour to the edge of the village, where Mary's father, Henery, lived alone in a small hut. Robert had met Mary's father a few times before he left for Barbados, and he remembered him as a small, good-natured man always ready to laugh at a joke. When Robert knocked on the cottage door, Henery opened it and stared for a few moments before recognizing him. "Oh, lad," he said. "Ye have changed much since I saw you last. You left here as a stripling, but you return as a man, while I have not done much except grow a little grayer and shrink a bit. Come in now and tell me about yourself and where you have been."

Robert followed him to the table in the middle of the room and sat on one of the benches. He talked about his life in Barbados and the circumstances that brought him back to Cornwall. Henery sat and listened, a little old man hunched over from years of toil in the fields. After a bit, he spoke up: "That is quite an adventure you had, and the warm days in Barbados sound good. But I think it would be hard for an old man like me to get used to them. The winters are cold here, but my working days are finished, and it is good to sit before the fire. But lad, I suspect that you didn't come here just to hear an old man talk. What is on your mind, and what are your plans now that you have returned to this troubled land?"

"Well," said Robert, "I plan to join the regiment that is being formed by Sir Bevil Grenville and fight on the side of our rightful king. All that I own are my clothes and a blanket, but Mary said you might have had something left to you by your father from when he served in the war in the low countries."

"Aye," said Henery. "He served under the Earl of Leicester for two years back in the time of the queen. He told me that he had never seen country as flat and wet as the Netherlands, and he and the rest of the troops spent as much time trying to stay dry as they did fighting. Glad to get back to the West Country he was, and he never left it again. And aye, he left me a few things picked up when he was over there, and I have cared for them ever since he died. I never had the need for them, but I kept them safe. Lad, you seem to be getting yourself into a spot where they might be useful, and I would be pleased to pass them along to you."

Henery rose from his bench and walked over to the narrow bed that sat in the corner of the cottage. He reached underneath and pulled out a parcel wrapped in rough cloth and tied with a cord. As he untied and unrolled the parcel, several items came into view. The first thing Robert saw was a sword scabbard with a hilt projecting from one end. He picked it up and withdrew the sword. The steel gleamed in the dim light of the cottage.

"I have rubbed it with a little grease from time to time to keep away the rust," Henery said. "My father told me that he took it off a dead Spaniard after the attack on Zutphen in the year 1591. He figured the man would not need the sword any longer since he had the shaft of an arrow sticking out of his neck. Good Spanish steel it is, not the sword of a nobleman, but it is a strong blade and can give you many years of good service."

"Henery, I don't know how I can thank you enough for this," Robert said. "I despaired at purchasing a sword, and this exceeds anything I could afford."

"Lad, it is a pleasure to pass it along to you," Henery said. The other item here doesn't look as good, but it may be just as important to you." He picked up what appeared to be a vest, but made of several layers of leather. It looked to be very stiff. "This is a leather buff coat, protection for your upper body. My father told me that no sword blade or lead shot from an arquebus could penetrate the boiled leather. It has sat here for many years, and the leather is as hard as a board. It will take a good deal of rubbing with grease to soften it up. But if you do that, you will have protection almost as good as a steel breastplate and much easier to wear. There is a surprise hidden in the folds of leather." The old man fumbled with the vest for a few moments, then to Robert's amazement, he pulled out a sheet of plate steel from one corner. "There are six pieces of steel plate hidden in pockets," Henery said.

Robert took the vest and inspected it. The outer layer of leather was as hard as a board and shaped to fit a man's torso. Inside were several softer layers, each containing pockets that held the pieces of steel plate. The vest wrapped around the body and fastened in the back, making the front a nearly impervious barrier. He tried on the vest and found that it molded to his upper body well and was heavy but not uncomfortable. Swinging his arms about, he found their motion was not restricted. "This is quite a garment, and it fits me well," he told Henery. "I will feel safer in a fight if I am wearing it."

"If you wear it under your cloak, no one will know you have it on," said the old man. "It is much lighter than a steel breastplate."

Robert thanked Henery for the items and prepared to leave, but Henery put his hand on Robert's arm and said, "Nay lad, don't go yet. I get few visitors here except for my youngest daughter, who comes by every few days to make sure I am eating enough. She does some of my washing also, so I don't live in squalor. Sit with me a while and tell me more of your travels. I have never been outside of Cornwall, and I have heard strange things about the rest of the world."

They sat back down at the table, and Robert recounted his trip to Barbados a dozen years ago. The old man laughed at his stories of plucking the chickens and getting scolded by the mate when he tried to climb up to the crow's nest. But Henery let out a whistle of surprise when Robert described the forecastle, with forty-eight men crowded into a room no bigger than the hut they were sitting in. The old man shook his head, saying, "Tight quarters that, especially if one of the men near you had a bad case of the farts. I suspect that was common enough, eating that poor food for two months." But the descriptions of the colorful birds and fish in Barbados brought a smile to his face. "It sounds a bit like paradise, son, warm weather and strange creatures. But I suspect there were downsides, or you would not have come back to Cornwall."

"I might never have left Barbados," said Robert. "But I could not see a way to pay off my debts. The only future was to work on a plantation as a slave overseer. That did not sit right with me. The blacks are men also, and their lives are very hard. I suppose one more thing brought me back here. A man grows lonely when he lives by himself for years. There are not many women on Barbados except the wives of plantation owners. Back here, I might meet a young woman who is looking for a partner, although I don't have much to offer her."

Henery shook his head, "You are a good man, and a woman can

see that," he said. "The money part matters, but most of us don't have much of it anyway. I worked my whole life, and now that my son has taken over the farm, all I have is this little hut. But it suits me fine."

A knock on the door interrupted their talk, and Henery called out: "Come in." A young woman opened the door and entered the cottage carrying a jug and a bundle of clothes. She hesitated a little when she saw Robert sitting at the table, but then stepped in and addressed Henery. "Father, I brought you a jug of milk," she said, setting the jug on the table, "and here are your clothes that I took the other day."

"The girl even wants me to change my socks," Henery said to Robert, loud enough that the girl could hear him.

"That does seem a little extreme," Robert replied as he glanced at the young woman and smiled. She kept her head down for a moment but raised it and smiled slightly when she realized he was saying this in fun.

"Catherine," Henery said, addressing the young woman. "This is Robert, Edward's brother. He arrived back from Barbados just yesterday and is going to join up and fight for our king."

"Oh," she said, unsure how to respond. As Robert looked at Catherine, he remembered her from before he left Cornwall twelve years ago. She was a little girl then with braids in her hair and bare feet. When Henery came to the farm to talk with Robert's father, she had accompanied him a few times. In the dozen years since, she had grown into a comely young woman with dark brown hair and hazel-colored eyes. When Catherine saw Robert looking at her, she blushed and blurted out, "I remember you."

"Yes," said her father. "You saw him at Skyburriowe Farm back when you were a lass. Now sit with us for a few minutes and keep us company." But she shook her head, bustled about the hut for a few minutes, then slipped out the door, professing to have more chores to do.

"She lives with my boy and his family at our farm," Henery said. "Helps out with the children and the animals for her keep. She is still single, though a few lads have approached her. They must not have been right for her, for she never gave them any encouragement."

Robert sat holding his mug, enjoying his time with the old man. "Did you see my father before he died?" he asked.

"Aye, and he talked about you, lad, told me a few things you had written about in your letters. He died quickly that winter, just worn out, without much pain. He was at peace, knowing that the farm was in good hands with your two brothers, and that your mother would have a place to live when he was gone."

The two men sat together a little longer before Robert said good-bye and walked back toward the farm, wearing the buff coat and with the sword strapped to his belt. That evening, he proudly displayed his new possessions to his brothers. The children were fascinated by the sword. Robert had to restrain the oldest boy from pulling it from the scabbard and waving it about, fearing it might nip off a finger or worse. Robert and his brothers talked long into the evening. At one point, Joseph reached into his pack and produced a leather hat with a broad brim. "This might keep a bit of the rain off the back of your neck. A long stretch of cold weather lies ahead before spring arrives. You may be sleeping outside much of the time, and you will need more than your cloak."

Robert sat and listened to his brothers, enjoying their company. Before he left Cornwall, they had seemed much older than he was. But now, after his experiences in Barbados, they all seemed about the same age. Both brothers had hair streaked with gray, much like Robert's father. Joseph's beard was partly gray, and there was a white tuft in the center beneath his chin. They were grateful that Robert had returned to Cornwall. The sheriff had been traveling around the rural areas looking for young men to recruit for the king's army, and it was only a matter of time before the encouragement to enlist would become a demand. The farm was land owned by the crown, and it was important that they show support for the king.

Edward spoke up, saying to Robert, "Sir Bevil Grenville is at his manor at Stowe, and that is a five day walk from here. On horseback, it would not be so long a trip, perhaps three days. Old Nell is getting too old to pull a plow, but she would carry you easily. She is not very fast, mind you, but she is very steady. Take her with you when you go. It is our way of thanking you for coming this long way from Barbados. I don't know if the horse could make a cavalry charge. A slow walk on a country road is more her style, but she is good company and will do whatever you ask of her."

This was a long speech for Robert's quiet older brother, and Robert thanked him profusely for the gift of the horse.

Over the next few days, Robert took care of last-minute details.

He spent time playing with the children each day, remembering his time as a young boy growing up at the farm. He rubbed the leather of the buff coat with grease until the inner layers softened and became flexible. Each day, he brushed and fed Old Nell. She was a placid animal, a little swaybacked from endless years of pulling a plow. Robert brought her a few roots from the root cellar, and after three days, she nickered a little when she saw him approach her stall.

The day to leave finally arrived. Robert rolled his few possessions in his blanket and tied it behind the saddle on Old Nell. He strapped on his sword, donned his buff coat, cloak, and hat, and made his farewells to the family. He tousled the hair of the little children and shook the hand of the serious oldest boy. He put his arms around his mother, kissed her forehead, and saw tears in her eyes. Mary hugged him, smiled, and told him to return safely. "My sister mentioned she saw you at Father's cottage," she said. "You should stop in and see her again when you return."

Robert grasped the hands of his two brothers and thanked them for everything, then mounted up on Old Nell and rode out the lane.

It was a long ride to Stowe, where Sir Bevil Grenville lived, but Old Nell walked steadily along and the miles passed. At first, the roads were familiar to Robert, but after he passed through Truro, the landscape was new to him. He passed fertile fields filled with young shoots of grain and herds of sheep and goats. Next, he crossed long stretches of barren land in the downs, the rugged country that filled the center of Cornwall. In the evening, he stopped at an inn a few miles north of the town of Bodmin. The inn had a stable for Old Nell, and Robert made sure she got a pail of water and plenty of hay. Inside the inn, he sat at one of the trestle tables and ate a bowl of mutton stew while listening to the banter of the local men. The inn had gone silent when Robert first entered wearing his sword, but after he explained he was from the Lizard Peninsula and was on his way to join the regiment of Bevil Grenville, several of the men nodded and one called out, "Good for you, lad. Show those Parliamentary bastards that Cornishmen support our king." Soon, the place was buzzing with gossip and rumors, and Robert sat quietly, lifting the wooden mug and taking a drink of ale from time to time.

Bed was only a straw pallet on the floor of the common room, but it was a quiet inn and Robert had the room nearly to himself. The second day, he rode on for miles and grew sore from sitting in the saddle. A few times, he dismounted and walked beside Old Nell, holding the reins in his hand. The horse did not seem overly tired, and Robert thought the break from farm work was probably good for her. He stopped again at a rural inn for the night and continued on the next morning.

It was late afternoon on the third day when Robert neared Stowe, and he wondered if he should wait until morning to talk with Sir Bevil Grenville. But he got directions to the manor house and decided to push on. He had come this far, and it was time to carry out the mission that brought him across the ocean.

The manor house of Sir Bevil Grenville was a two-story stone structure with wings on both sides. Robert stopped at the gates to the front drive, and there he was asked about his business and told to wait by the entrance. "The Master may be at dinner," the gatekeeper said, and he sent a boy to the house to find him. After a few minutes, a smartly dressed, middle-aged man appeared at the gate and approached Robert.

"Well now, young man," he said. "I see by your sword that you have come prepared to fight, but I sense that soldiering is not your trade."

"Indeed, my Lord," responded Robert, "I have worn this sword only two days, and it is more likely to trip me than to protect me."

The man laughed and said, "Well, your honesty is perhaps your best defense. The swordplay will come in time. Where are you from that you are arriving at the end of the day?"

"My family works a farm south of Truro, near the end of the Lizard Peninsula," said Robert. It has been a three-day walk from there."

"A long way to come on your warhorse," answered Sir Bevil, with a hint of humor in his tone as he looked at his new recruit and the old farm horse who stood quietly beside him.

Robert replied, "I think that Old Nell is grateful that she is not hitched to a plow. She may not be a charger, but she walked steadily these past three days and brought me here."

"That speaks well of her," said Grenville. "I suspect that a little hay would appeal to her right now." With this last remark, he motioned to the gatekeeper's boy and said, "Take this fine steed to the stable and make sure she has hay and water in a good stall." Then, looking at

Robert, he said, "My fair wife and I are soon to sit down for an evening meal with some of my men. There is plenty there for you to join us, and you will meet some of those who will be your companions on our little adventure. Come." Grenville turned and walked toward the house. Robert followed, somewhat bewildered by this turn of events.

The massive entry doors of the house opened onto a lavish hallway, with doors on both sides and a grand curved stairway in the center leading to the upper level. Robert followed Grenville through the first door on the right and into a large open room. A fire burned brightly in the massive fireplace on the far wall. In the center of the room was a long table filled with trays of food. A dozen chairs sat on each side of the table, most filled with men eating and drinking. The noise was considerable, but it subsided when Sir Bevil stood at the head of the table and raised his hand.

"Friends," he said, "we have a new companion here who just arrived from the Lizard Peninsula on his warhorse." At this remark, Grenville glanced at Robert and winked. "Accept him as one of us and make him feel comfortable. Anthony, perhaps tomorrow you could introduce him to some of the finer points of sword play." This last remark was addressed to a man sitting in a chair near the center of the table. Robert followed his glance and saw sitting there the largest man he had ever seen. He took up the space of three men and towered above all who sat near him. "This is Anthony Payne," continued Sir Bevil. "He is my right-hand man and will give you direction in the morning. Otherwise, all of these men are equals. We are all as one here." He pointed to an empty chair at the other end of the table. "Now, seat yourself and eat. Any of the men can show you to the common room, where there are sleeping pallets enough for all."

Robert sat down at the table and filled his plate with meat and vegetables from the tray in front of him. The man sitting beside him passed a pitcher of ale, and Robert filled the flagon that sat at his place. He ate and drank, hungry after the long journey. Before the meal was finished, he met several of the other men. Most of them farmed on Sir Bevil's land, but a few had come from other parts of Cornwall, much like Robert.

This opened a new life for Robert. He became one of Sir Bevil's men, accepted by the others, with meals every day and a straw pallet to sleep on at night. Anthony Payne had one of the experienced soldiers introduce him to the use of a sword. He sparred with the other men using blunt wooden swords until he felt sure that he would not harm himself. The men rode out on horseback regularly, and during these outings, it became clear that Old Nell was not cut out to be a warhorse. She would start out gamely enough and try to keep up with the other horses. But before long, she would begin to pant heavily and eventually stop and stand, her sides heaving. When that happened, Robert would walk the old horse back to the stable. He felt embarrassed about not keeping up with the other men. They chaffed him about it a little, but their jibes were in good fun.

A month passed, and spring was well underway. Trees were flowering, and the nights were warmer. Robert was in the yard sparring with one of the men when he noticed Sir Bevil watching him from the sidelines. Beside him stood a younger man, scarcely more than a boy, also smartly dressed. When there was a break in the sparring, the two of them approached Robert.

"Robert," spoke Sir Bevil, "This is my son, John. He will command a troop of cavalry during our little engagements. You will be in his company as a dragoon. Your company will travel with the cavalry and act as a support force to guard our supply line, bridges, and camps, and also act as mounted infantrymen to provide musketry when needed. John is young, but brave and smart. He will need mature men to accompany him and provide advice."

"I will do my best, my lord," responded Robert, "but my horse?"

"Yes," continued Sir Bevil, "the old mare is not strong enough for this duty. We have another horse for you. I suspect you want to return the old girl to her barn. You can take several weeks and return to the Lizard, then return to us here. This will give you time to get to know your new mount, and it will give you a chance to see your family. We may get busy in a month or so, and there is no telling when you will see them again."

The next day, Robert mounted the young horse Grenville had provided and put a lead on Old Nell, who would follow them back to the old barn. "This horse is not a charger," Grenville said, "but she is young and strong and will keep up with the others." The ride home was a pleasant trip, and the road was familiar to Robert. He stopped at inns for meals and a place to sleep. At the inn near Bodmin, some of the men he had talked with before were sitting at the trestle tables. They remembered Robert and asked about Sir Bevil and about his activities over the past months.

On the afternoon of the third day, Robert rode up the lane to the farm, and the children raced out of the house to meet him. They marveled at the young horse he rode and led him to the house. Edward and Mary came out to greet him, noticing how straight he sat in the saddle. It was clear he was now a fighting man, not a farmer. Robert led Old Nell to a stall in the barn. She had the adventure of her life in the past months, and Robert's new horse was stabled in the stall next to her.

That evening was a family gathering, and Joseph and his wife and two children walked up the lane carrying their contributions to the meal. The family was sitting down to eat when there was a knock on the door, and Mary's sister Catherine appeared. She greeted Robert shyly and sat among the children at the far end of the table, but Robert caught her glancing at him occasionally as he talked with his brothers. It was a happy occasion and lasted past dark. Finally, Joseph picked up his youngest boy, who had fallen asleep on the floor. He and his wife left for home with their little ones, and Catherine began to collect her things. "Stay here, Catherine," urged Mary. "It is dark out tonight. We will make up a pallet in our room where you can sleep."

"Thank you, but no, Mary," Catherine said. "My brother will worry if I don't return home." Robert spoke up and offered to walk with her to her brother's house. She accepted, and they set off in the darkness. The walk was no more than twenty minutes, but Robert was aware of each step. The night was dark, their way lit only by the stars. They walked side by side, and he told her of his life in Barbados: the beauty of the sun when it set over the ocean, the brilliant colors of the tropical birds, and the fragrance of the flowers. Catherine walked quietly beside him and listened intently to his stories. They reached her brother's house too soon for both of them, so they sat on a stone wall and talked a while longer. Finally, they walked to the front door, and Robert met Catherine's brother. On the walk back to the farm, Robert heard the noises of the night creatures and the whistling of the wind. He watched the shapes of trees appear out of the darkness as he walked along the lane. That evening, he lay on his pallet and thought about Catherine for a long time before he fell asleep.

Robert stayed at the farm for a week, helped his brothers with spring chores in the fields, and enjoyed the meals Mary and his mother prepared. Each evening, he walked over to meet Catherine at her brother's house. They sat and talked, either at the table in the main room or on the stone wall outside the house, where they watched the stars.

Then, it was time for the ride back to Stowe and to learn the skills of soldiering, which included daily sword practice. The assignment to become a dragoon marked a change in Robert's training. No longer was he just a member of Sir Bevil's company; he was a dragoon. He was given a flintlock musket and instructions how to load, prime, and fire it. He learned how to mold bullets and clean the musket after each use. John Grenville often came to talk with Robert. He wanted to find out how the training was going, and he shared his anxiety about the position in which he had been placed. Robert found the boy to be smart and thoughtful, cautious about making a decision but willing to stand behind it. He listened and offered advice when asked, and the two of them became friends. John was desperate to not let down his father, but he had never been in a battle before and worried that he would make a mistake. Robert told him of his travel to Barbados when he was a boy, not much different in age than John was now. The boy listened and was comforted.

As the summer progressed, more men came to the manor each day, and the yard filled with tents and campfires at night. Many talked of coming battles, but summer passed and the country remained peaceful. As autumn arrived, the regiment finally left Stowe and traveled south, mustering new troops in Bodmin and Truro. Then it turned north and east, crossing out of Cornwall into Devon. As summer changed to autumn, then winter, the force joined other supporters of the King and besieged the city of Exeter. The siege was not successful, and their forces were repulsed. The regiment returned to Cornwall, pursued by a Parliamentary army.

A month later in January in the year 1643, the king's army and the Parliamentary army tangled at Braddock Downs, on a ridge outside Liskeard. This was the first

Oliver Cromwell at Marston Moor[3]

action Robert took part in, and he was amazed by the noise and confusion. The battlefield was nearly obscured by smoke from the muskets. His company of dragoons was assigned to form a barrier at the edge of the battlefield, where they had to stop the enemy from passing around the side of the Royalist lines. Several times, their position was assaulted by infantry, whom they fought off with gunfire and hand-to-hand combat. The dragoons were stationed behind a hedge, which the infantry tried to penetrate. Robert fought against several men, stabbing with his sword through the hedge. He heard men cry out when the sharp blade entered their bodies. It was not something he wanted to do, but he knew they would kill him if given the opportunity. He was so involved in the fighting around him that only when the attacks stopped did he realize the King's forces had pushed their foes back until they fled, leaving several hundred men dead or severely wounded on the field. More than twelve hundred were taken prisoner, and it became the duty of the dragoons to guard the prisoners.

Winter continued, and the dragoons were assigned to guard the bridges over the River Tamar, the boundary between Cornwall and Devon. The army made several forays into Devon, but they were unsuccessful. The Cornish troops fought fiercely inside of Cornwall, but they were reluctant to go beyond the borders of their county. In May, a new threat approached. Robert was with his company at Stratton, not far from the Grenville estate in Stowe, when a Parliamentary army crossed into Cornwall and took a position on Stamford Hill above the town. The armies skirmished inconclusively until the Cornish infantry stormed the hill and routed the Parliamentary troops. The victory was decisive, and Cornwall was safe from attack for a time. After the battle, John Grenville came to Robert and said, "It has been nearly a year since you last saw your family. Why don't you go home now and return here in a month?"

The trip from Stowe to the farm was familiar to Robert now. He stopped at the inn north of Bodmin and told the men there of the battles he had seen. When he reached the farm after his year-long absence, his brothers were glad to see him and to hear of his experiences. Mary was quiet until the talk slowed down. She then told Robert, "My father, Henery, died last winter. After the Yuletide holidays, he grew tired, then one day he stopped getting out of bed. He died a few weeks later. Catherine lives in the little cottage now, and she would like to see you soon."

Robert rode to the village the next day and dismounted in front of the cottage. The last time he was there, Henery gave him the sword that was now strapped to his belt. A great many things had happened since then. Catherine met him at the door. She wore a simple brown petticoat of homespun fabric, with a bit of white lace at the neck, her long hair wrapped in a scarf. She smiled when she saw Robert, took his hand, and led him to the table. I hoped that you would come," she said. "It has been quiet here since father died. I have thought about you during the past months."

Robert looked at the lovely young woman and realized they shared the same emotions. "You know I could be killed in the next battle," he said.

"Yes," she answered softly, "But that only makes the days when you are here more important. It is time we get on with our lives together despite the fighting between the king and the Parliament."

Robert and Catherine announced their engagement to their families, and two weeks passed while the traditional banns were read three times. They wed at the small church in the village with both families present. Neither the bride nor groom had special wedding outfits, but Catherine laced flowers into her hair and Robert wore the sword strapped to his side. A feast followed the wedding, lit by a roaring bonfire, while family and friends danced to music played by a neighbor on his old fiddle. After the wedding, Robert had only two weeks before he was due to return to the regiment. He and Catherine spent as much of that time as they could together making plans for their future.

Robert reluctantly traveled north again, and he learned the Grenville regiment had moved into Devon now that Cornwall was secure for the king. He followed their path and caught up with the army near the town of Bath. They were preparing to attack the Parliamentary army, which had taken a defensive position on Lansdowne Hill. The attack failed. Toward the end of the

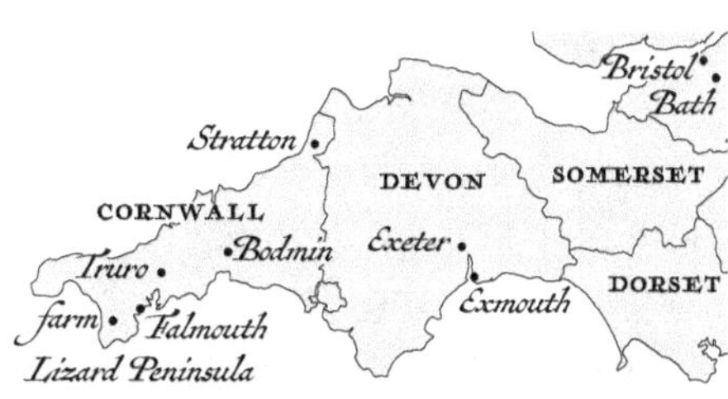

Southwestern England

battle, Sir Bevil Grenville led his men in a charge against the enemy infantry. During the struggle, he was struck on the head with a poleax and severely injured. He was carried from the battlefield by his enormous bodyguard, Anthony Payne. Sir Bevil died the next day, and his death was deeply mourned by his men.

Richard Grenville, Sir Bevil's brother, took command of the regiment. He was a harsh, outspoken man, not much liked by the troops. John Grenville was removed from the cavalry troop and assigned to assist his uncle. From then on he had little time to spend with Robert. The Royalist army had a series of battlefield triumphs, including a resounding victory at Roundaway Down and the successful storming of the defenses at the city of Bristol. After the capture of Bristol, young John Grenville was knighted by the king. But through it all, the death of Sir Bevil Grenville left a great hole in the morale of the regiment.

With Sir Bevil dead and Richard Grenville in command, army life was different for Robert. He traveled with the rest of the dragoons and slept in barns, under supply wagons, or in the open air if there was no shelter. The pay was often late, which provoked much grumbling. The regiment was fighting outside of Cornwall, which did not sit well with many of the troops. Finally, with little action on the horizon, Robert was permitted to return to the farm in December of 1643.

When he arrived at the little cottage in the village, Catherine met him at the door. She was big with child, and when he held her in his arms, he felt life stir within her womb. A baby boy was born in February, and they named him Henery, after Catherine's father. Robert felt as though his life was now complete. He spent his days working on the cottage or helping his brothers at the farm. Six months passed, and in early summer he received a message from Sir John Grenville, wishing him well and summoning him to return to the regiment.

That summer was filled with danger. The Earl of Essex had brought a Parliamentary army to retake Cornwall, and King Charles I was coming from Oxford with a Royalist army to oppose him. The Parliamentary army occupied Launceston and Bodmin, and the enemy troops looted and despoiled the Cornwall towns. The Grenville regiment hovered nearby, too small to attack the much larger force. Only after the king arrived did the Royalist forces, now eighteen thousand men, substantially outnumber the twelve thousand man army led by Essex. Weeks of maneuvering and skirmishes followed. Finally, the Parliamentary army was surrounded and surrendered along with all their weapons. The Earl of Essex fled by ship. Cornwall was again safe for the king.

After the surrender was complete, Sir John Grenville came to Robert. "Prince Rupert, who commands the King's forces, has asked if we could spare our dragoons to join the king's army. You will be away from Cornwall and your family, but this is the most important part of the struggle we are involved in."

This request was not something Robert welcomed, but he agreed to go. He spent autumn and winter in parts of England he had never seen. Robert was unable to return to the farm that winter, and it was a bleak, cold time spent in a strange country, following commanders in whom he had little trust. He saw the king several times, but that meant nothing to him. Several of his dragoon companions deserted and returned to Cornwall. The men were told little about what was happening, but they heard endless rumors. One was that the Parliamentary armies were being reorganized, and the men would wear matching uniforms. This was astonishing to the Royalist dragoons. After several years of living outdoors, their clothes were mismatched and ragged. Their pay arrived only occasionally. When it did come, Robert sent most of his pay back to Cornwall, hoping it would arrive safely. The marching and fighting went on and on.

An incident in early winter tested Robert's resolve. He and his company were following the cavalry through a forested area north of Newbury when they were surprised by a force of Parliamentary infantry. The dragoons dismounted, formed a line, and gave the enemy a round of musket fire, which made them scatter and flee into the woods. The dragoons followed on foot. Robert chased two men until suddenly he felt a tremendous blow to his chest and collapsed on the ground. He lost consciousness for a few moments. When he came to, he heard the men talking.

"That was a good shot, dead on," said one voice, "that bastard will never fight again."

"Let's see what he has on him," said the other voice, "I will check his pockets while you make sure we are not disturbed."

Robert lay on his left side with his hand beneath him. He could feel his dagger, and he slowly moved his hand to grasp the hilt. A man approached and began to rummage in Robert's pockets, looking for coins. Then he grasped Robert's shoulder and started turning him over to check the pockets on the left side. As he did so, Robert pulled out the dagger and buried it in the man's side. As the man gasped and collapsed, Robert struggled to his feet to face the second infantryman. The man was standing, his eyes wide in surprise that this apparently dead man had killed his partner and risen to fight him too. He turned and ran. Robert retrieved his dagger, wiped off the blood, then took stock of his condition. His chest was terribly sore, but he could walk, so he rejoined the company and mounted his horse.

When Robert took off his leather buff coat that night, he saw what had happened when he was struck. The infantryman was right; it had been a shot square to his chest. But the powder charge must have been weak. The steel plates in his coat had stopped the bullet and saved his life. The plate that took the brunt of the shot was badly bent. Robert hammered it flat with a rock and slipped it back into the pocket of the vest. In his mind he thanked old Henery for giving the coat to him years before. For weeks afterward, Robert was in severe pain with a livid black bruise on his chest.

Winter passed into spring and then summer. June found the army in the center of England, where they stormed the city of Leicester. Afterward, news came that the main Parliamentary army, under the command of Sir Thomas Fairfax, was approaching from the south. The two armies drew near each other, and it appeared a battle would occur on a hill called Naseby Ridge. Robert could tell from the sharp commands he was given that something important was about to happen. His company of dragoons was assigned to guard the Royalist camp, where the king's tent stood. Several hundred women were there. Some were wives of the officers, others were prostitutes who accompanied the army. When fighting began between the two armies a mile away, noise and smoke from the battle drifted overhead. It was unclear for several hours what was happening until Royalist soldiers appeared, running away from the battle. "Flee, flee for

your lives!" they yelled. Some of Robert's men fled, but most of the company remained on guard to protect the camp. They did not see the tidal wave of Parliamentary cavalry approaching them until it was too late.

———•———

Several months later, on a cool, sunny day in September, a lone horseman approached the farm in Cornwall. He was a well-dressed young man, and the sword at his side proclaimed him to be a soldier. It had taken him a while to locate the Skyburriowe farm. The first man he asked for directions scowled and responded in Cornish. A second man pointed up the road and gestured wildly with his arms. Finally, the young soldier approached a lane that appeared promising. It led to a cluster of buildings with a house on the right side and two long stone barns on the left. He pulled up in front of the house and dismounted. At his knock, an attractive woman holding a baby opened the door, dressed in homespun fabric. She looked anxiously at the sight of a strange man carrying a sword.

"Hello," he said. "I am Sir John Grenville of Stowe. Is this the home of Robert Skyburriowe?"

The woman reacted with surprise at the introduction and curtsied slightly. "Yes, my lord. He was born here. He moved to the village when he married two years ago. He is not there now. He is with the king's army."

"No," the young man said. "The king's army is no more, I fear. Robert was killed after the battle of Naseby when he and his men were guarding the king's camp. They and the women they were protecting were all killed by the Parliamentary cavalry."

The woman gasped softly, then said. "Robert was a good man. He returned from Barbados to fight for our king, and two years ago, he married my younger sister. Our family will mourn for him.

"I will go to your sister's house if you tell me the way," the soldier said. "I have the rest of Robert's pay for her."

Grenville rode on to the little cottage in the village. A small garden lay on one side of the path, and a few flowers blossomed next to the door. At the sound of his knock, a young woman came to the door, a toddler clinging to her skirt.

"Ma'am, is Robert Skyburriowe your husband?" he asked.

"Yes, he is. I am his wife, Catherine," she said. "Would you come in and tell me how he is? It has been over a year since he was here."

Grenville followed the young woman into the cottage. It was plain inside but spotless, with a hard-packed dirt floor. Several pots hung from hooks at the fireplace. The only furniture besides the trestle table and benches was a small bed in one corner of the room. The two of them sat at the table and talked while little Henery fussed about and held onto his mother. Grenville told Catherine about meeting Robert and about the many times they had talked before John's father was killed.

"He was a good friend to me and told me about his life here and about the years he spent in Barbados. The last time I saw him was almost a year ago. He was very happy about marrying you and about his baby son. He fought bravely until his death."

The young woman answered softly, "We knew he might die in one of the battles, and we tried to make the time we had together as good as possible. He saw his son when he was born, and I will tell the boy about his father when he grows older."

John took out his purse and began counting out the money that was due to Robert for his pay. It seemed like such a small sum, only a few pounds, and he realized that after this money was used up, there would be little or nothing to support Robert's wife and child. He looked at what remained of his own funds, removed several more pound coins, and gave them to Catherine. She seemed so grateful that it embarrassed John, who moved to rise and leave.

Catherine looked up at him, her face filled with grief, but holding her emotions in check. "Thank you for coming all this way to tell me about Robert," she said. "He told me your father was a good man, and I can see you also are one. God bless you."

On the road heading back north, Grenville reflected on the events of this morning. The war would continue, although Cornwall and the West Country were the only large areas of England still held by the king's forces. John suspected one more year would see the last of the battles. The king hoped his cause would be salvaged by an army from Scotland, but John suspected this was a false hope. John wondered about the future of families who farmed land owned by the crown, such as the Skyburriowe Farm. Crown land had been confiscated in areas now controlled by the Parliamentary troops, and it was only a matter of time before this would occur in Cornwall. He did not know if the tenant farmers would get to remain on their land.

His thoughts turned to where he would stay that night. He had enough money left in his purse to pay for lodging and supper at a rural inn. Robert had told him of one just north of Bodmin. If he hurried, he would arrive there before dark. John urged his horse into a trot and quickly passed through the forest. The trees were beginning to take on fall colors, and the breeze carried a faint tang of the ocean. He had come a long way to tell Robert's family about his death, and now that sad duty was finished, so he could move on. It was a beautiful day.

Epilogue

The battle of Naseby in June of 1645 nearly destroyed the main Royalist army. The following year, a series of smaller battles completed the defeat of the king's troops, and the Royalist forces surrendered in late 1646. King Charles I fled to Scotland but was surrendered to Parliament, brought to trial, convicted of tyranny and treason, and executed in 1649. His son Charles II became king in exile for the next dozen years, living in France and the Netherlands. Oliver Cromwell, a Parliamentary general, ruled England during that time with the assistance of Parliament for a while and later as a military dictator. Cromwell died in 1658, and a year later, negotiations began with Charles II, resulting in his return to England and restoration as king. The messenger who handled the negotiations for Charles II was Sir John Grenville. He had fled England for a time, returned and was imprisoned, then freed and allowed to live in England. Charles II returned to England and was crowned king in April 1661. Sir John Grenville was named Earl of Bath for his services to the Crown.

After the restoration of the king, a new Parliament was elected, and all participants in the Civil War were pardoned, except the men who had been involved in the trial and execution of the king. Vincent Potter, who had returned from Massachusetts at the start of the war, had risen to be a commissioner for the Parliamentary army under Oliver Cromwell and was one of the men who participated in the trial of King Charles and voted for his conviction. He was imprisoned, tried, and scheduled to be hung, drawn, and quartered as a regicide, but he died in prison before his execution.

During the British Civil War much land owned by the crown was sold to pay the war debts incurred by the Parliamentary army. Many tenant farmers who had worked their farms for generations were forcibly removed from their land.

———•———

When a family lost their farm as may have happened to the Skyburriowe family, what could they do? The economy in Cornwall was based upon three occupations: farming, mining, and fishing. Fishing boats left every winter from ports on the west side of Cornwall, heading for the Grand Banks off Newfoundland. It was said that the cod were so plentiful there, a man could lower a bucket into the sea and pull it up filled with fish. But the fishing life had its drawbacks. Men were away from home for months at a time, and a man's pay depended on how many fish he pulled in with a baited line. The weather was miserable and cold, and a man was wet much of the time. Back home in the village of St. Columb Minor on the west side of Cornwall, the Skyburriowe family had to scrabble for work to buy food until the man returned home.

As the decades of the sixteenth and seventeenth centuries passed, in London, one king gave way to the next. Men spent their lives striving for fame and fortune, but only a few achieved success. Styles of hats and dresses changed regularly, and the life of the rich was spent in lavish ballrooms and counting houses. In rural Cornwall, very little changed from one decade to the next. Each December, fishing boats left to cross the stormy Atlantic Ocean to reach the fishing grounds. Sometimes they returned with holds full of salted fish, but every year some boats failed to return to port and families mourned for their lost husbands and sons. Some years the mines prospered, but other years the price of ore fell and miners suffered. There were years when a poor family had enough to eat, and years of epidemics, when children died of smallpox or cholera. When a child died, it was a common practice to name a new baby with the same name, so there are records of families with two or more children named Joseph or James.

Child mortality was high, but some children lived to become

adults. Somewhere along the line, one of the sons in the Skyburriowe family became apprenticed to a cordwainer, a man who made shoes from new leather, as opposed to a cobbler, who repaired shoes. When he grew old, the man passed his trade and his foot molds, known as lasts, to his son, who in turn passed them along to his son. In this way, a hundred and fifty years passed, while the Skyburriowe family eked out a living, fishing, making shoes, and working at menial jobs. The young women in the family married men who were miners or farmers. The young men married women from working-class families in nearby neighborhoods. Each family had its own customs, its strengths and weaknesses. This stability was interrupted in the last decade of the eighteenth century, when a man came along who threatened the peaceful nature of British life. His name was Napoleon Bonaparte.

CHAPTER FOUR

Trafalgar

October 21, 1805

England was at war with France from the early days of the French Revolution in 1792 until Napoleon's defeat at the Battle of Waterloo in 1815. Napoleon proclaimed himself Emperor of France in 1803 and planned an invasion of England. He stationed a French army of 300,000 men on the French coast in 1804. However, the British Navy dominated the English Channel and trying to cross it would have been disastrous for Napoleon's army. Attempts to defeat or divert the British ships from the invasion route were unsuccessful.

In August 1805, Napoleon shelved the plans for invasion. He sent his armies toward Austria and Prussia and ordered the French fleet away from England toward Italy. This required the ships to pass through the Straits of Gibraltar into the Mediterranean Sea. En route to the Straits, they were intercepted by a British fleet led by Admiral Lord Nelson near a cape on the Spanish coast called Trafalgar. Twenty-seven British ships engaged thirty-three French and Spanish ships with devastating results for the French fleet. Never again during the Napoleonic Wars did French ships confront a British fleet in a major sea battle, and the invasion of England was not a serious threat after the Battle of Trafalgar.

The British ships involved in the Battle of Trafalgar were man-of-war vessels, each carrying 74 to 110 cannons. The hulls were built of British oak, the masts and yards of pine and spruce. It required two thousand oak trees to construct one man-of-war. The hulls were sheathed in copper to retard damage from wood-eating teredo worms. Many men were needed to handle the cannons during a sea battle, and eight hundred or more lived aboard each ship. The British Navy grew from 14,000 to 120,000 sailors during the Napoleonic Wars. In order to maintain the navy with sufficient crew members for the ships, press gangs seized able-bodied sailors and other healthy men from seaports and placed them aboard ships, sometimes for years. This could change a man's life.

John Lower, 1782–1847

1832

Falmouth, Cornwall

"Grandpa, tell us about the battle!" called three-year-old John. Not to be outdone by her younger sibling, four-year-old Annie echoed, "Yes, pop-pop, tell us a story." Their mother, Eden, looked over at me, shrugged her shoulders, and gave a half smile. I had promised a story last night, and now the promise was due. I had to tell enough to make the story interesting, but without the details that would keep the little ones awake at night.

"Let me have one more cup of tea, and I will tell you a story about how I fought alongside the great Lord Nelson in his final battle," I said.

The little ones drew up close. John sat on the floor in front of the bench while Mary climbed up beside me and leaned her face into my vest. The story was not important to her, but it mattered that she was a part of whatever was going to happen. John, on the other hand, wanted every detail, and he interrupted and bickered if the details of a story varied from a previous telling. Each time I told them a story, memories flooded into my mind. The truth of the story was less important than the telling of it, so I started at the beginning.

"It was a sunny day in Falmouth, and the harbor was filled with the sails of mighty ships. The fleet was in the harbor, and criers were in the town, calling for men to come aboard and join the fight against Napoleon. I was young then, and I answered the call and headed down to the quay. I came aboard one of the great ships and signed up for the duration of the voyage. It was a dangerous time, and we all feared that Napoleon would bring an army to invade England. I wanted to do my part to protect our land."

———•———

If only it had happened that way. I cannot bring myself to tell these little ones the truth of the matter. I had come to town to deliver a wagonload of rations to the quartermaster for the fleet in Plymouth. Afterward, I stopped in the Dog and Whistle Pub near the docks to enjoy a few pints of ale before returning home. It was foolish to stay in town longer than necessary, but no press gangs had been seen for several days, and then only at night when the pubs were filled with young men, and the pickings were easy. During the day, the pub was quiet, containing only a few old men, all past their working years. I was talking with Betsy the barmaid, almost finished with my second pint, when the door burst open and a file of marines from a press gang entered. I started for the side door, but two marines blocked the way. They hustled me out onto the street despite my protests that I had more rations to bring from the farm to the harbor. "Rations, is it?" said one of the marines. "We have plenty of rations. What we need is strong young sailors like yourself, ready and willing to fight for the king."

I hadn't known that ships were coming out of the Plymouth drydock short of crew and needing sailors. It turned out that press gangs had been sent to all the ports in Cornwall to gather up young men. I was caught in the sweep.

"I need to let my wife know where our wagon sits," I called out.

"When you don't come home, she will figure out that you have chosen to serve your country," came the reply. "You can come willingly or come in chains, but come with us you will."

Betsy came to the door of the pub and called out, "John Lower, I will send the stable boy to tell your wife you've been taken. The wagon will be safe in the back of the pub." I waved my thanks to her. Libby might not have me for the next few months, but at least she would not lose the horse and wagon.

Further protest was hopeless, and a marine with a pistol stood at my side ready to use it if I made a move. A line of young men filled the street, some chained together, others standing sullen but without complaint. Most were dressed in workman's garb like me. Two were barefoot and in nightclothes, while another wore a waistcoat and silk shirt marking him as a clerk or bank teller. It was not a happy group of men. The press gang proceeded along the street, stopping at any establishment where they might find likely victims. One young man was dragged out of a shop, yelling that his master would stop them. The marines just laughed. Most of the men caught were resigned to their fate.

The marines marched us to the docks, where a small schooner awaited. We were ordered to file onto the vessel and pushed into a room on the main deck. The door was barred behind us. This was not our final destination, only a holding vessel that would take us to our assigned ship. Portholes adorned the outer walls, but they were far too small for anyone to squeeze through. A bucket sat in the corner, and this was the extent of the toilet facilities. The men's reactions to their new quarters varied. Some cursed, some complained this wasn't right, and a few sobbed. I didn't see much that could be done about our predicament, so I found a spot near the wall and sat. The second pint of ale from the pub was making me tired, so I closed my eyes and promptly fell asleep. A few men started yelling about the treatment, and a marine came to the door. He yelled back that if the bucket was not good enough for us, he would remove it and let us piss on the floor. That shut up the complainers. After a few hours, the press gang returned with another group of men and crammed them into the room with us.

As the room grew dark, it became clear we would be on the ship overnight. There were no sleeping pallets in the room, only the wooden floors. Each man sought the best place to sleep, some settling against a wall, some near a porthole, but all avoiding the bucket in the corner, which was starting to reek. I had slept on hard floors many times over the years, but all around me this night, men coughed and hacked, and the time stretched on forever. Gradually, the sky became light, and dawn was near. The door opened, and several marines appeared. They directed one of the men to remove the bucket and dump it over the side of the ship. The marines brought a pot of porridge and a pile of wooden bowls and spoons. We passed them out and ate. We were prisoners, but at least we were fed.

After a while, the door opened again. Outside was a line of marines carrying loaded muskets to ensure none of the men tried to escape. An officer called for some of us to come out onto the deck. I joined the first group. We walked out of the room, and the door was closed and barred behind us. The officer sat at a table with an open register in front of him. One at a time, we approached the table and gave our names, places of residence, and names of our closest relatives, be they father or mother, wife or sister. The officer asked whether we had served aboard ship before. None of the men admitted to having worked as a sailor. Most listed their occupation as laborer or warehouseman. I was one of the two who were farmers. A young man in a waistcoat listed his occupation as clerk and protested that he should not be in this group. The officer listened to him for a sentence or two, then cut him off and barked, "So you think the Navy doesn't need clerks also?" When the young man kept protesting, the officer nodded at two of the marines, and they seized the troublemaker and dragged him to join the men who were already registered.

After all the men were registered, the officer stood and addressed the group. "Today, you men have the honor of joining His Majesty's Navy and helping to protect England from the tyrant Napoleon. England needs many young men to come to her aid, and you have been chosen. This honor will only be available to men who are strong and healthy. To make sure that no man brings disease to our fleet, you will be examined by a medical expert. Take off your clothes and stand by the rail." There was a muttering of protest, but it was quieted by an order from the officer: "Silence! If you do not undress on your own, these soldiers will help you."

I took off my clothes, and the breeze made my teeth chatter, as it was a brisk day in February. The naked men formed a line at the rail. Once the group was assembled, two soldiers started working the handle of a pump, which sprayed frigid saltwater out of the end of a canvas hose. Another soldier swept the stream across the shivering crowd of men, ordering us to turn around and get the full benefit of the shower. This went on for at least five minutes until all of us were drenched.

We were told to stay in formation as a gray-haired man stepped out from behind the marines. He started at one end of the line and began examining the men, paying particular attention to each recruit's chest and privates. Meanwhile, we stood in place, still naked and shivering. He pulled two men out of the line and directed them to another part of the main deck. One of them was visibly filthy, so much so that his smell was offensive from even a few feet away. The other man had an intermittent cough. The rest of us must have met the doctor's approval, for when he reached the end of the line, he turned to the officer and said, "A sorry lot, this group. But healthy enough to haul on ropes and scrub a deck." "Except for these two," he added, nodding toward the men he had pulled out.

The officer ordered us to dress and then directed us to stand in a line again before the officer, who announced, "Men, you have a choice to make. You are going to serve on one of His Majesty's ships. Each of you will be rated as a landsman because you have no prior experience as a sailor, but you do have one opportunity. You can sign up to serve as a volunteer and receive a bonus of two pounds, six shillings. This can be paid to your closest kin. If you do not volunteer, you will still serve aboard ship, but you will not receive a bonus." Some of the men grumbled about this, but to me, there was no choice. I signed as a volunteer. The bonus was small, but if my wife Libby received the money, it would help her feed the children.

We were herded into another room and locked inside. A few small portholes provided some light. The reality of the situation sank in, and the grumbling ceased. A couple of the men protested that they should not have to serve since they were not sailors. This had been the standard procedure in the past. But another man told a story he had heard, that ships were coming out of the Plymouth drydocks were short of crew. All men were liable to be pressed, whether or not they had been sailors before. It was likely we would be at sea within a few days. Upon hearing this sobering statement, the group fell silent.

As the day passed, the door opened from time to time and another group of men were shoved into the room. By late afternoon, the whole group had been examined, unsuitable men had been culled out, and the rest had signed into the Royal Navy. A large vat of oatmeal was brought in along with wooden plates and spoons, so we were fed, although it was a plain meal. Eventually, we heard orders to weigh anchor and make sail. Within minutes, the rocking of the ship indicated it was moving, and we saw it was leaving the harbor at Falmouth and sailing east in the Channel.

Outside the portholes, we saw daylight fade, and the ship sailed on into the night. It was nearly dawn when we heard orders from the deck to furl sails and lower the anchor. I guessed the vessel was in Plymouth Harbor. When morning arrived, I looked through the portholes and saw Drake's Island off to the north with the town of Plymouth in the background. The marines unbarred the door and ordered all of us onto the deck. They had anchored the schooner midway between two enormous ships whose hulls extended high over our heads. Their masts seemed to reach the sky. A black stripe was painted on the hull around each vessel at the waterline, and we recognized the square doors in each hull as gunports for cannons. I had never been this close to a man-of-war before, and I stood dumbfounded. Other men were as much in awe as I was, for they stared with open mouths. What had we gotten ourselves into?

The answer came soon. We were separated into two groups. One was directed to the left side of the schooner while the other, of which I was a member, was sent to the right side, which faced the larger of the two ships. On the hull at the front of the man-of-war was painted the name *Temeraire.*

Shortly, a ship's boat set off from *Temeraire* and headed toward us. We were taken aboard the boat and told to sit on benches in the middle, while it started back toward the larger ship. As we approached, I saw a net was attached to the ship's railing and hung down to the water. When the boat reached the hull, we were ordered to grab the ropes of the net and climb up to the railing. The boat rose and fell in the waves, bouncing against the side of the ship then pushed away. I waited, saw my chance, and grabbed the net. Its ropes formed a grid with each segment about twelve inches square. I climbed up the side of the ship, past the closed gunports, and up to the railing. Some of the men were not comfortable with heights, and I heard groans and cries of dismay from those who climbed halfway to the deck, looked down, and were paralyzed with fear. When I reached the railing, two men pulled me over onto the deck of the ship.

Temeraire was as impressive up close as it had appeared from a distance. The mast nearest me was the size of an enormous tree trunk. Looking up, I saw upper sections of mast attached to the main mast with heavy bands of iron. The deck stretched off to my left and right, and everywhere, there were ropes of different sizes attached to cleats on the deck and stretching high into the air, fastened to the mast and to the horizontal spars. As I stood gaping, other men climbed up the net and were pulled over the railing onto the ship. Off to one side stood a naval officer, apparently waiting for all the men to reach the deck. Behind him was a row of soldiers dressed in red uniforms, all carrying muskets. When the last man came over the rail, we were ordered to form a line. The officer stepped forward until he stood in front of us and spoke these words:

"Men, you are now part of the crew of His Majesty's Ship *Temeraire*. You are not sailors because you know nothing about the workings of this ship. But there is plenty of work that you can do: haul on lines, scrub the deck, and work on gun crews. You will learn to be a sailor. This is a fine ship on which to serve as long as you follow the rules. If you break the rules, you will suffer punishment. You will sign the ship's register and then be shown to your stations. Your work begins today. *Temeraire* is due on the blockade of Brest, and we leave immediately."

The new men signed their names in the muster book, while those of us who could not read or write made our mark. We were ordered to form a line on the deck. Each man was told to call out a number starting with one. The men with odd numbers were assigned to the starboard watch, while those with even numbers went to the larboard watch. My number was five, so I became a member of the starboard watch. We were ordered to follow a petty officer, who I learned was a bosun's mate. He led us down two ladders to a large area called the lower gun deck. It was dark, lit only by a few hanging lanterns with small candles inside. A row of enormous cannons lay on each side of the ship, their muzzles pointing at the closed gun ports. Each cannon rested on a heavy wooden gun carriage. What I noticed about this area was the smell. On the main deck of the ship, the air was fresh and clear, but as we descended to the lower gun deck, it grew increasingly stuffy and odorous. The smell reminded me of the cattle barn at the farm, except that men were the cattle here and the odor was much more pungent.

The bosun's mate led us across the deck and assigned each man to a location. Mine was at gun number 4 on the starboard side of the ship. The mate explained that each of us would receive a hammock and blanket and that this was where we would hang them to sleep when we were not on watch. The other men at this position would be our messmates for the three daily meals. We were taken to the purser's stores and issued our hammocks and blankets. This was also the place where a man could buy clothing, or "slops" as they were called aboard ship. The cost of these items would be deducted from our first two months' pay. After being shown where to store our hammocks and bedding when not in use, we were ordered to return to the deck. Most of the eight hundred men on the crew of the ship were assembled near the quarterdeck. Besides the sailors, there were squads of marines in red coats, a variety of officers, a group of men dressed like clerks, and a surprising number of lads, some as young as ten years. A middle-aged officer, who I learned was the captain, addressed us, emphasizing that we were on this ship to protect England, to be part of the "wooden walls" that prevented Napoleon's armies from invading.

When the captain finished speaking, the first lieutenant announced it was time for the ship to get underway. The first duty was raising the anchor. Landsmen were directed to the lower gun deck, and I followed the crowd down the ladders. On this deck, the men clustered around the capstan, a large, round, wooden drum with a heavy rope coiled around it. The drum had large square holes in its side. Long wooden poles were inserted into the holes, resembling spokes of a giant wagon wheel, and we all lined up behind the poles. At a signal from the bosun's mate, we pushed hard, and the drum rotated. Noises from the deck above indicated that the ordinary seamen were performing the same operation on the upper gun deck. It took two hundred men working together to raise the enormous

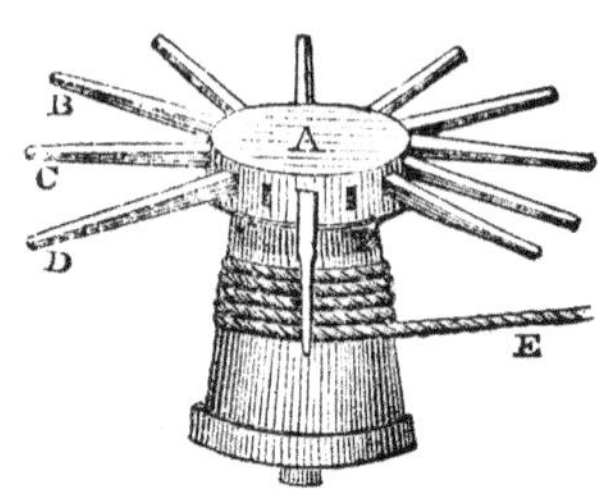

A capstan[4]

anchor that held the *Temeraire* fast against the wind and the tides. This work became tiresome quickly. An older sailor with a fiddle began to play, and the men broke out into a rough sea chantey. I did not know the words, but the chant had a simple refrain. Soon I sang along with the rest of the men, and the work went easier.

At intervals, the bosun's mate gave an order to stop pushing, and we rested. A cog assembly prevented the capstan drum from turning backward when we let go. During one of the breaks, I walked forward to find out how our efforts at the capstan caused the anchor to rise. A three-inch-diameter rope wrapped around the capstan led forward through a series of rollers to meet the anchor rope. There, sailors tied the two ropes together with short pieces of cord. As the capstan turned, it reeled in the three-inch rope, bringing the anchor rope along with it. The ropes slid along the deck, and a group of the ship's boys followed and untied the wraps just before the anchor rope descended through a hole to the deck below. There, sailors laid out the anchor rope in large coils.

Raising the anchor seemed an endless task, but eventually the bosun's mate called out "Avast!" and we stopped pushing. The anchor rope had been pulled in, and we heard the clanking of a heavy chain against the hull. This was pulled up along with the anchor, and both were secured near the bow of the ship.

After the anchor was secured, sails were spread, and the vessel moved slowly out into the Channel. Once underway, it began to rock from side to side in the waves, and some of the new men became ill. The motion didn't bother me. When I was a boy, I loved to climb trees at the farm and hang on as the wind blew them back and forth. The motion of the ship reminded me of hanging on to the branches of a tall tree in a strong wind. We were ordered to go to supper, so I searched for the location where I was to eat and sleep. The gun deck was dark, and the ceiling was low, barely above my head. Hanging from the underside of the deck above were lanterns, each containing a single candle. This created a small pool of light and illuminated a group of men clustered around a plank table. These were crew messes, and I searched for the one I was ordered to join. At each mess, the plank formed the dinner table, and on it were square wooden plates, each one piled with a mound of food. Most of the men sat on wooden chests, sea chests, which contained their extra clothes and the few other possessions a sailor might accumulate. There did not seem to be enough chests to use as seats, for a few men sat on overturned wooden buckets, and others lazed against the sides of the wooden gun carriages that supported the cannons.

As I crossed the deck, voices called out to me through the gloom. "Hey landsman, looking for your home?" came one cry.

Another answered, "Here's another recruit for the bilge pump." Both sallies were followed by laughter, although I didn't find the comments amusing.

Finally, I reached the mess to which I was assigned. Beneath the lantern at the end of the table sat a remarkably large man. He was not tall, but his girth was that of a bull, and his upper arms were the size of my thighs. He was spooning out food from a large pail onto a square plate, which was then passed down the table of waiting seamen. He talked as he worked. "Here is your lobscouse, Charlie," he said. "Make sure you eat it all so you'll have the energy to haul lines tomorrow. Today, it felt as though Big John was the only man pushing at the capstan, and the rest of you laggards could have sat and watched me as I raised that anchor by myself." This remark brought voices of protest from the other crew members, but the big man kept talking: "Then, after raising the anchor by myself, I had to go and fetch dinner for you while you sat here and jawed with each other. There's no justice in it, no there ain't."

I stopped just outside the circle of men. After a while, the big man looked up and noticed me. "Landsman, what are you looking at?" he called out.

"Is this gun number 4 mess?" I asked.

"What does that matter to you?" he replied. "Although it should rightly be called Big John's mess since I do most of the work around here."

"The man said I was to join this mess."

"Was this some man you found while you were wandering around the ship, or do you mean bosun's mate Evans?" the big man asked.

"I suppose it was bosun's mate, sir, as I did not catch his name," I replied.

The big man snorted, "Sir, he called me. Now lads, you heard that. Maybe you should all call me sir when we are down here. But don't do it up on deck, or someone might think I was a bleedin' officer."

I remained standing, unsure of what to do. Finally, the big man stopped dishing out food, looked over at me, and barked, "Well, don't just stand there. Get yourself a plate and find a place to sit. There's a bucket up against the wall. Pass your plate down to me. I don't want to dish out food all night since I am half-starved as it is."

I went where he pointed and found an open chest that contained a stack of square wooden plates, some worn spoons, and a few mugs. Taking one of each, I upended an empty bucket at the end of the table and used it as a seat. The bucket was shorter than the sea chests the other men were sitting on, and only my head and neck showed above the tabletop. I felt like a child sitting at the adult table.

Big John addressed me, "Newcomer, pass your slab this way and I will load on some salt horse."

I had not heard that expression before, and I turned to the man sitting next to me, a compact fellow with a blue cap.

"Is this really horse meat?" I asked.

"Well, it could be, for all we can tell," he said. "But no, that there is beef because it is Tuesday. If it be Thursday, then it would be pork. Not that you can tell much difference between them. You see, the meat is salted and stored in barrels, and it might be six months or a year before a barrel gets opened. The cook soaks the meat overnight to get the salt out, changing the water two or three times. Then, into the pot it goes and gets boiled for hours. The fat rises to the surface and cookie, he skims it off. That's slush, you see, and it belongs to the cook. He sells it to the mess cooks for the men to spread on their biscuit."

My plate soon returned, piled with a mound of mush. I saw that oats were the main ingredient, with bits of carrots and onions and what looked like chunks of meat. I paused before taking a spoonful, and there came a bark from Big John: "Don't look at your food, landsman, eat it. It doesn't matter what it is. What matters is that you can haul tomorrow, not like the rest of this sorry bunch." There were a few grimaces from around the table but no outcries, and he continued: "Landsman, what are you called, so we have a name to go with your worthless carcass?"

"John is my name," I replied.

"That won't do," he growled. "We have too many Johns here already. I am Big John, and that one is Little John," he continued, pointing his spoon at a scrawny man sitting near the middle of the table. "Then there's Bristol John there beside you, though we mostly call him Bristol." At that remark, the man sitting nearest me at the table raised his head, turned to me, and nodded in recognition. "And we got our Bible thumper over here, John the Baptist," said Big John as he pointed to an older man, who turned to me, grinned, and called out, "Praise the Lord."

"Praise the Lord, my foot," said Big John. "Thank him for setting us here on this miserable tub to freeze in the winter and swelter in the summer, to take orders from fools and get whipped if we complain. No thank you, I say. Newcomer, the name John is taken; it will have to be something else. Where do you come from?"

"St. Just, a village in Cornwall," I answered.

"St. Just, huh. That don't ring well," he said. "What did you do in the pitiful village of St. Just?"

"My wife and I have a small farm," I replied.

"A farmer, now that is more like it. Farmer John is your name now, although few will get around to the John part. Now Farmer, eat up." At this he stopped talking long enough to take up a huge spoonful of his meal. I surveyed the pile in front of me and took a mouthful. It was bland and salty, mostly oats. The shreds of meat were tough and taste-less but recognizable as beef. A few bites left me craving a drink to quench my thirst, and I looked around to see what was there. One of the men noticed my search, lifted a bucket from the deck, and passed it down the line to me. It was half full of foamy liquid, so I poured a mugful and tasted it. It was beer. Not the good ale from the Dog and Whistle, but a weak brew with little flavor. Nevertheless, it quenched my thirst, so I drank down the mugful in one gulp. Then I abruptly set down my mug, wondering if it was acceptable here to drink so much. The man beside me, Bristol John, noticed my uncertainty. He paused from eating, looked up at me, and said, "Drink as much as you like. We each are allotted a gallon of beer every day, although few drink their full ration."

Meanwhile, Big John was focusing on his meal amid a murmur of general conversation around the table. The mess numbered ten men now that I was a part of it, and it was a mixed bag. Sitting along-side John the Baptist were an old man and two lads who looked to be scarcely more than boys. The rest appeared to be in their twenties and thirties, all clean-shaven or with short stubble, indicating they shaved regularly. The man to my right, opposite Bristol John, was a wiry fellow of less than medium height. He wore a blue and white striped shirt and sported a cap. He noticed me observing him, turned slightly to nod at me, then returned to his supper. By this time, Big John had consumed a huge plateful of dinner. He looked at me and spoke loudly: "Farmer, you get the pleasure of being mess cook next week. Make sure they don't short you on the cheese and butter. And bring back two buckets of beer for each meal!"

That was my first meal with the mess. I would spend the next two years with them, eating together three times a day and sleeping in a hammock slung from the beams of the deck above. Usually, only half the men slept at one time at our mess, since it was split between the starboard and larboard watches. Every four hours, men rose from their hammocks, rolled them tight with the bedding inside, and carried them up to store at the deck rail. On their way up the ladders, they met the men from the other watch descending, carrying their hammocks, ready to hang them up and go to sleep. But when the ship was in port for repairs or taking on stores, sea watches were suspended, and all of us slept at the same time. Those nights, we were packed together like herrings in a tin. The men whose hammocks were next to Big John were practically engulfed in his enormity. If he rolled over, it was like an earthquake shaking their hammocks.

That was in the future. Meanwhile, the first night on *Temeraire,* I did not sleep well. More than two hundred men were sleeping on the lower gun deck, and it was never free of coughing or murmuring. A few men cried out during the night. It was pitch black, as the candles were blown out at the start of the night watch. Only a faint glimmer of light came from a lantern hanging near the ladder, where a marine stood guard. It took almost no time to get used to the hammock, which molded to my body. But I had hardly gone to sleep when a gruff voice yelled out, "Show a leg. Get up now, or the hammock comes down." It was time for the midnight watch. We had a few minutes to get out of our hammocks, roll them into a tight roll with the blanket inside, and report to the main deck. There, we stowed our hammocks at the railing, where they were covered by a canvas sheet to keep off the rain.

All around the deck was activity that I could hear but barely see. The bosun's mate called out orders to haul on one line or another, accompanied by toots on his whistle. In the darkness, I had no idea what his orders meant. Some men seemed to know what to do, so I followed them, hauling on a line when they did, then waiting with the others for the next order. This happened numerous times during the four-hour watch. The ship's bell rang out every half hour. I learned that the first half-hour period was followed by one ring of the bell, the second by two rings, and so on. When the bell rang eight times, it was the end of the watch. We retrieved our hammocks and went below, passing on the ladder the men coming back on duty. After I hung up my hammock and crawled into it, I fell asleep immediately and only woke up when the call to breakfast sounded at seven in the morning.

This was a taste of life aboard ship. There was an assigned task for every moment of each watch. Only at meals was the time our own, as we sat around the plank table under the dim candle lantern. I grew accustomed to sleeping in three-hour periods, rising quickly and rolling my hammock, surrounded in the darkness by hundreds of other men rising to go on watch. We ascended the ladderway to the main deck, where we inhaled the fresh air of the sea instead of the stale smell of the lower gun deck. The tasks were endless. Sometimes, we tore apart old lines and picked out the fibers, which were mixed with tar and used to caulk the deck. Other days, I was sent below with a dozen others to pump the foul water from the bilge, an endlessly monotonous task. Six of us pushed a rotating crank attached to the pump, which lifted a series of buckets filled with bilge water and dumped them into a wooden sluice. The sluice funneled the water to the outside of the ship. Turning the crank in the near darkness while smelling the foul odor of bilge water made for a long watch. But when it finally ended, I joined my messmates at a meal or lay in my hammock.

Sunday routine was different from the other days of the week. Sailors shaved and washed in cold seawater, then dressed in their cleanest clothes. The crew mustered on the deck, where the captain read a Sunday service. They sang a few hymns and heard announcements from the officers. Afterward were several hours of leisure, when a man could patch his clothes, carve on a piece of scrap wood, or just sit on the deck and yarn with his mates. It sounds good, but the ship was on blockade duty off the coast of France, where the weather was cold and the wind brisk. Most of the men retreated to their berths on the gun decks.

I came to know the men in the mess. At each meal, we sat around the plank table in the near darkness, with the candle lantern shining a narrow cone of light down upon us. There was a little talk, some complaints, a few jokes, but mostly banter about how the day was going. We were not friends exactly, but we had to get along, and we became used to each other. Sometimes there were arguments, but never was there a fight.

The two lads in the mess were just lads, from families with little more than a roof over their heads. When the boys went off to sea, each family had one less mouth to feed. They didn't say much at meals; just sat and listened while the older men talked.

The two old-timers were as different from each other as the two lads were similar. John the Baptist, or "Bap" as everyone called him, had spent his life at sea. Somewhere along the way, he had picked up religion, and now he spent his time reading the Bible if he wasn't working or sleeping. He was a gentle soul and did whatever was asked of him. His sentences were sprinkled with "God bless you" and "Praise the Lord." The other old-timer, Little John, was the most foul-mouthed man I ever heard. He didn't say much at meals, but when he did, it was a string of curses. No one knew where he came from, perhaps pressed off a merchant ship, but he harbored a grudge against the British Navy. Most of his talk was how bad was the food, how stupid were the officers and mates, and how cheap were the Navy goods we were issued. Almost no one talked with him, and at meals he sat and glowered most of the time.

The other four men were a varied sort. Bristol John had been on one ship or another most of his life. He was a talkative man and told stories about the ships on which he had served. He had been at Spithead in 1797 when the great mutiny occurred, a time when all the sailors on Navy ships in the harbor outside of Portsmouth stopped work to protest the low pay and poor living conditions. The strike lasted a month and in the end was successful. Sailors' pay was increased, and some living conditions were improved. Bristol never said what part he played in the strike, but he knew so much about it that he may have been one of the leaders. He was an able-bodied seaman and worked as a topman on the foremast. At meals, he often talked with Billy, the man who sat on my right and worked as a topman on the main mast. Their talk was usually about the spreading or furling of sails. It was filled with jargon that left me wondering what they were talking about. They spoke of "stunsails," "clewlines," and other terms I had never heard before. They discussed details of shipboard tasks I didn't understand and rattled off names of countless kinds of knots they tied in the ropes.

On one of my first days on *Temeraire,* I learned that ropes were called lines aboard ship. It happened this way: The bosun's mate ordered me to coil one of the lines lying on the deck. When I asked him what rope he was talking about, he exploded at me. "Landsman, there are no *ropes* aboard this ship. There are only *lines.* You had better learn that unless you want to feel one of them across your back."

When Bristol and Billy spoke, it was clear they understood each other. Billy was quiet and always neatly dressed, although how he managed the latter was beyond me, as he worked outside in the weather and the lines he handled were impregnated with tar to preserve them. At meals, he said little, instead focusing on his food. Rarely was anything left on his plate when he finished eating.

The other two men in the mess sat farther down the table, and I did not know them well. One was a Scot with a heavy accent, originally from Aberdeen but at sea for many years. He was called Scotty, of course, but there were several dozen Scots at other messes, and when someone called out "Scotty," numerous men answered. Our messmate's given name was Angus, and so we used that name to get his attention. The tenth man in our mess was another landsman like me, pressed a few months earlier in Plymouth, where he lived with his wife and five children. Like me, he worked on deck as a waister as I did, hauled on lines, scrubbed the deck, and attended to the many other jobs that kept the ship running. Waisters manned the bilge pumps, rowed the ship's boats, and turned the capstan to raise the anchor. Sometimes they raised the largest anchor, the "best bower," which required two hundred men to raise. Other times it was one of the smaller anchors, which took only fifty men to turn the capstan. The tenth man's name was Charles, but everyone called him Charlie. He did not seem upset to be aboard the ship and said that the noise and disruption of living with eight hundred men was peaceful compared to life in his house in Plymouth when his wife was unhappy and the children were yelling.

In any group of men, there is one who dominates the conversation, and in our mess, it was Big John. He was always complaining about something, whether it was the attitude of the bosun's mate in charge of the deck at the main mast or the quality of the salt beef or biscuit we were issued. He often harassed his shipmates about how hard he worked and how little they did. It was so wearisome to hear him that one night at dinner I told Billy I could hardly bear to hear any more of Big John's tirades. Billy stopped eating and looked at me for a long moment before answering.

"John is a little hard to listen to sometimes," he said. "On the other hand, look at his life. He cannot climb the shrouds, so he will be a waister as long as he is aboard this ship. He went to sea as a boy ten years old and worked as a servant and helper for many years. He has no wife on shore, and this will be his life until he is too old or crippled to work aboard ship any longer. Then he will be put ashore with little or no way to earn a living." He paused a moment, then said, "But aboard ship, no man hauls a line or pushes on a capstan pole any harder than does John. Since he has no family of his own, he looks after the two lads in our mess. Notice how one of them sits next to him at meals, and he never singles them out during his tirades. They look up to him and he looks after them." This was the longest speech I had heard Billy make, and when he finished, he returned to his dinner. After that, I looked at John differently, and I learned to tune out his bellows at meals.

Other groups of men sat near us, though enormous cannons separated their mess from ours. We heard them talk, laugh, and occasionally erupt in angry words, but we didn't pay much mind. Beyond them on both sides were other messes of ten men or so each, about forty groups in all on the lower gun deck. These were not always fixed groups. If a man grew unhappy with his mess, he could request a transfer to another. Sometimes a mess found that a man was intolerable to live with, too profane or foul in his habits. If so, they could request that he be moved to another mess. Men constantly shifted from one mess to another. Sometimes men who no regular mess could tolerate were thrown together into a remnant mess of three or four sailors. But our mess didn't change. It wasn't perfect, with Big John pontificating at every meal and Little John griping and glowering, but at least they were known quantities. A stranger might be intolerable in a different way, so we got along as best as we could.

Big John announced when I joined the mess that I would be mess cook for the next week. Mess cook was just the name of the job, as I did not cook anything. Instead, I fetched food that was boiled in vats on the enormous iron stove in the galley on the upper gun deck. As mealtime approached, I lowered the table from its hooks and laid out the plates and mugs. A few men had their own pewter spoons, but most used the worn wooden ones. The mess cook had many chores. I had to fetch two buckets of beer from the beer locker at each meal, get the meat for the meal from the cook's helper, encase it in a cloth bag with a metal tag to indicate our mess, stand in line to return it to the cook, then return to retrieve it after it was boiled. The same process occurred with the oats, the dried peas, and the occasional fresh meat we were issued when animals housed on the upper gun deck were slaughtered. Occasionally, the mess cook assembled the food into a concoction. Such was lobscouse, a mixture of oats, onions, carrots, and bits of meat. These ingredients were issued separately and had to be combined, bagged up, and returned to the cook to be boiled in one of the huge vats. The cook then retrieved the finished product and served it to the mess. After each meal, I cleaned the area, washed the plates and spoons with cold salt water, and hauled any scraps to feed the pigs. A daily inspection was conducted every day to see that the mess was clean and orderly. Afterward, I got ready for the next meal.

Breakfast was always the same: oats, soaked but not cooked, sometimes mixed with molasses. Dinner at 11:30 a.m. (seven bells of the forenoon watch) was the main meal of the day. Four times a week, we ate salt beef or salt pork. The pieces were pulled from a barrel, soaked for hours to remove most of the salt, then boiled in huge pots on the stove. On days when meat was not served, we received either oatmeal or cooked dried peas mixed with carrots and onions. Occasionally, we had a fish soup based on dried cod. Every day we also got a biscuit, which was a hard, dry cracker. Twice a week, we were issued rations of cheese and butter. Onions and sauerkraut were provided to help prevent scurvy.

My time was mostly spent standing in a long line of mess cooks waiting to get the food while holding two buckets. When we finally reached the vats, a clerk stood by to check off each mess from his list. The clerk informed the cook's helper how much food was allowed for each mess, and the helper spooned it into the buckets with a great ladle. When I had our ration in hand, I raced back to the lower gun deck, trying not to drop the buckets as I descended the ladder. Once there, I hurried to the table where the men waited for their meal. I dished out the food in large or small servings depending on each man's preference. Lastly I served myself and hurried to finish my meal before it was time to clean up. It was stressful, and by the end of the week, I was exhausted. I learned how to do each step, got yelled at a few times, and nearly dropped the meat bucket one day when it rained and the ladder steps were slippery. But the men got their meals, and the following week I went back to my regular duty.

My regular duty was to be a waister at the main mast. When I emerged onto the deck in the dim light of early morning on that first day, I saw thirty other men standing near the mast, and I wondered what work took so many men to do. Then came a yell from the bosun's mate: "Swab the deck!" Men began strewing sand over the deck, even into the corners. Others dragged a large stone from its storage location and started pulling it back and forth across the sand-covered deck. It was as big as a small cask, but with ropes attached to it. Sailors opened a chest nearby, revealing a pile of smaller stones, each about the size of a large book. One of these was handed to me, and the petty officer ordered me to "scrub the corners at the larboard rail." When I gave a blank look to this order, the old tar gave me a withering glance, pointed to the left side of the deck, and said, "On your knees now and be quick about it!" I knelt and began to scrub the wood with the stone. Looking around, I saw other men doing the same thing, so I moved along down the rail, scrubbing the places that could not be reached with the larger stone.

This went on until I reached a spot that had been cleaned by another man. Seeing no reason to go over it again, I stood up. Immediately, the bosun's mate yelled at me, "Landsman, to the pump," and nodded toward a group gathered at the rail. They were setting up a water pump to fill buckets with seawater. I was given two buckets and told to "Look sharp!" so I joined a line of men carrying water to wash the dirt and sand from the deck. We carried the buckets to the center of the deck and dumped the water while men with brooms pushed the water and sand toward the side of the ship, where it passed out through the scuppers. Finally, the sand was washed off the deck, leaving it newly cleaned. I glanced toward the stern of the ship and saw other men cleaning their area much the same as we had done.

This activity occurred nearly every morning. Once a week, we cleaned the upper and lower gun decks. Those decks had no scuppers, so the dirty water and sand ran into the bilge and had to be pumped out to sea. This seemed like a lot of cleaning, but it was part of being aboard one of His Majesty's ships. While we scrubbed the decks, another group polished the brass handles, hinges, and other metal fittings. Some days, the morning watch was spent applying blacking to the cannons on the gun decks with a mixture of soot and grease, and our hands were stained black.

The most important task aboard *Temeraire* was tending the enormous sails that caught the wind and propelled the ship through the sea. No matter what else we were doing, if the sails needed adjusting, the bosun's mate blew his whistle and we ran to perform the task. This might happen numerous times during a watch. Spreading a sail had many steps. The topmen spread out along the yard with their feet on the footrope, and untied the canvas gaskets that held the sail to the yard. Below on the deck, a group of waisters hauled on lines attached to the lower corners of the sail. This spread the sail, making it billow loosely. Another group of waisters hauled on lines attached to the yard and raised it until the sail was taut. Finally, the yard and sail were turned to catch the most wind. Each of these steps required numerous adjustments. As the bosun's mate blew his whistle to give orders, we scrambled to follow them as quickly as possible.

When the lines for one sail were secured and cleated off, we moved to another sail, and the process was repeated. Sometimes, no sooner were the sails spread than an order might come to furl them. The ship was constantly reversing course and sailing back and forth to blockade the port of Brest. Each change of direction required many steps, with the topmen climbing up and down the shrouds and the waisters hauling on lines. Each mast had three sails plus studding sails, which hung from spar extensions. Numerous sails hung between the masts, as did a massive jib, a sail that hung between the foremast and the bowsprit. When a change of direction was ordered, several hundred men worked to adjust the sails, and with all the sails spread, the ship was a glorious sight.

After three weeks on *Temeraire,* I was starting to settle in. I had grown used to sleeping in three-hour naps. The food was bland, but there was plenty of it. Mealtimes were a trial with Big John dominating the conversation, but I was growing used to life aboard ship. But two things bothered me. My clothes were always dirty and ragged, and the razor I shaved with left my face looking scruffy. One day at dinner, we had a quiet moment while Big John was eating. He consumed an enormous amount of food, but he was a huge man and probably needed to eat that much. I turned to Billy, who was eating steadily as usual. He ate a plateful of food at every meal and never complained. Billy was neatly dressed in a striped blouse and canvas vest, wearing a cap on his head.

"Billy, how do you keep your clothes looking decent all the time?" I asked. "I have been here only three weeks, and I feel dirty and ragged."

He looked up from his dinner and seemed surprised at the

question. "Lad, there is no magic to it," he said. "Betty looks after my clothes every week. She washes and hangs them to dry and mends the rips. I have two spare blouses in my sea chest and an extra trouser, so there is usually something fairly clean to put on after a rainy watch. I hang my wet clothes on the line here and put on a dry outfit before I eat. It makes things go better."

"Who is Betty?" I asked.

"Cor, lad, you have seen some of the gals on this ship," he said. "They stay out of sight most of the time, but on a clear night you might see one of them on deck by the rail, enjoying the fresh air. Betty has lived aboard ship for many years. When she was young, she went with the men, married one of the sailors, and lived ashore for a few years. When she returned, she said married life was not for her. Her man drank up most of the money she earned, and she had to do for free what she got paid for aboard ship. She has been on one ship or another ever since. She mostly does laundry for sailors now, although a few of the old tars still visit her from time to time. But for me, it is just my laundry."

"How does she get her water for washing?" I asked. "And how does she get paid, since we don't receive any money while we are aboard ship?"

"She gets a pail or two of hot water from the cook, heated on his stove during slow times," Billy said. "In exchange, she likely does his laundry. As for accounts, there are seven clerks who work for the purser, keeping track of the men's pay. One of them likely has a column that notes how a man gets his laundry done. I pay Betty sixpence a month to take care of my few things, keep them clean and presentable, and it gets taken out of my wages each month. The clerk takes a cut for keeping the records, and Betty gets paid in cash every few months. She has a sack full of shillings stashed in the hold somewhere, and she is probably richer than most of the sailors. She told me she has the money to live ashore, but she likes this life."

"What about the captain?" I asked. "Does he know she is aboard?"

"The captain knows there are women aboard this ship, but as long as there are no fights, he is wise to ignore them," Billy said. "Most captains want their ships to be in good shape and the crew to be content. If the men turn out on Sunday with clean clothes, does he care how that comes about? One of the secrets of life on a ship is to find ways to make it as regular as possible. For me, that includes having Betty take care of my slops and going to Isaac for a shave once a week. I never see my wages anyhow. They get sent to my old mother up in Manchester every six months."

I had noticed that Billy was closely shaved every week and wondered how he did it.

"Where is Isaac who shaves you?" I asked.

"I wondered when you would ask me," Billy said. "I saw you trying to shave yourself, and I noticed the poor results. Isaac is at gun crew 8. He spends most of his time shaving men, although he has other duties as well."

"How does he manage that?" I asked.

"He gets a pail of hot water from the cook at the start of the watch, along with a little slush to make the shaving go easier. The men schedule a time during their watch to get a shave, and they slip away for the little time it takes. The bosun's mate, who is Isaac's boss, makes sure that Isaac's time is free. In exchange, he likely gets a free shave once or twice a week, the same as the cook. One of the purser's mates keeps the accounts of Isaac's customers, takes a cut out of his earnings, and likely gets a free shave each week in the bargain. There isn't a lot of money left for Isaac, but it keeps him off the deck and out of the weather. The captain is happy to have the men clean-shaven. And for me, the thruppence that comes off my wages is a small amount to pay. Besides, he does a better job than I could ever do myself."

"So when a man leaves the deck during watch, he might be going for a shave?" I asked.

"Well, he might be going to see Isaac, or going to the head, or even going to see one of the girls," Billy replied. "He doesn't leave until he gets a nod from the bosun's mate. That is the man you must please. As long as the work is going well and there are plenty of men to do the tasks, almost anything can be worked out. But it all comes with a price."

"But I have no money to pay anything," I said.

"No, but accounts are kept for each man," Billy said. "There are thirty clerks on this ship, and all of them spend their days writing in ledgers. Right now, you are behind because you had to pay for your hammock and bedding. After a month or two, your wages will start to build up. Almost anything can be purchased through the purser. I suggest you go to him and purchase more slops, a blouse or two, and extra trousers. That way, you will have clothes to wear while yours are being washed. Talk to Betty and Isaac and see if they can take care of what you need. If Isaac is too busy, I know of three other barbers on this ship. And watch for ship auctions. When a man dies aboard ship, his clothes and possessions are auctioned off to the highest bidder. That is how I got this vest. It came from a fellow who died of scurvy a few years ago. He was about my size, and it looked like it would shed the rain well. I paid four shillings for it. Betty washed and rubbed slush on the outside to waterproof it. Best investment I ever made. Lad, there are plenty of ways to make life on this ship easier. It's a lot better life than that of the poor sods who go into the mines before daylight and don't come out until after the sun sets."

While Billy was talking, he kept eating, only pausing a little as he chewed. I was interested in what he said, so most of my dinner still sat on my trencher. Billy looked down and noticed this. "Now, lad, finish your dinner," he said. "The bell for the afternoon watch will ring soon, and you need the strength that food gives you."

The next time the purser's store was open, I bought two blouses and a pair of trousers. The purser's mate wrote in the register the amount that would be deducted from my pay, and I made my mark on the chit he held out to me. Then I went in search of Betty. I found her on the orlop deck, the lowest deck on the ship, where cannon balls and barrels of water were stored. She was in a small alcove outside the shot locker. Betty was a sturdy woman with tinges of gray in her hair. She looked at me with some wariness when I approached. But when I said I was a messmate of Billy's and he had suggested I talk with her about doing my laundry, she brightened up quickly.

"I can take care of your slops for you," Betty said. "Leave the dirty ones with Billy's on Thursday, the day I take in his laundry. I will put in a few stitches to indicate your initials so your clothes won't get mixed up with other laundry. You need to let the purser's mate know about our arrangement. The washing will cost sixpence a month, with simple mending included. If you tear your slops to pieces like some I know, I will have to charge you a bit extra." I confirmed this arrangement sounded good, and she gave me a hearty smile when I left.

When I approached Isaac about shaving, he hemmed and hawed for a minute. "It's not that I be trying to avoid the work, you see, it's just that my days have gotten so full," he finally said. "The time spent shaving is not so bad, but Evans—he's the bosun's mate of my crew—wants to see me on deck from time to time so the lieutenant doesn't think I have died." After calculating in his head for a bit, Isaac said, "I might be able to work you in on Tuesday about six bells in the afternoon watch. The water is cold by that time, but your beard ain't too heavy, and I think it will do fine. If this works out, I will try to fit you in earlier in the watch when the water is hot."

I thanked Isaac and went to find the purser's mate to tell him of the arrangements I had made with Betty and Isaac. "A good choice, young man," he said. "The captain likes to see a crew that is clean-shaven and looks good." I sensed he was mostly happy to get another man in his books so he could extract a cut of what I would pay Betty and Isaac.

After that, life on the ship was better for me. My clothes were clean and presentable, and Isaac was a master with a cut-throat razor. Each time he shaved me, he spread a small amount of slush on the shaved area "to close the pores, you know," he said. I walked away with smooth cheeks, smelling a little like salt beef.

Over the months I worked as a waister at the main mast, the tangle of lines gradually began to make sense. Each was attached to a sail or spar on one end and to a specific cleat on the deck. Eventually, I thought I had mastered the lines and their locations. Then one day, the bosun's mate yelled out to haul in on the clew line for the starboard topsail. I went to the line I thought was the right one and began to take it off the cleat. Suddenly, I felt a vicious crack across my back from the rattan cane the bosun's mate carried. "Idiot landsman!" he bellowed at me. "That is the clew line for the t'galant sail, not the tops'l. Get your lines sorted out, or you will taste more of the cat than just this cane." This was no mean jest, for every few days one or more of the crew would suffer flogging with a cat-o'-nine-tails while the rest of us stood and watched. The most common reason was drunkenness, usually when a man obtained some of the grog allotted to his mates. But men were flogged for other offenses: backtalk, disobedience, failure to touch your cap when given an order by an officer, or sometimes just doing something stupid, as I had been about to do. After that incident, I thought carefully before untying a line.

I saw sad times aboard the ship as well. During the cold, wet winter months, men came down with sickness, and at least one died each week. When a man died, his body was wrapped in canvas and laid on a plank on the quarterdeck for a day, so the crew could pay their respects to his body. Then after a short service read by the captain, the body was slid off the plank over the side of the ship with two cannonballs strapped to his feet to keep it from floating to the surface.

Afterward, there was an auction of the man's belongings. These could be as little as a few worn clothes, but might include a pewter spoon or cup, a knife, a carving the man had been working on, or maybe a sewing kit. The proceeds from these auctions were sent to the man's family along with any wages he was owed. At one such auction, Billy nudged me and pointed to the items about to be sold. "Farmer," he said, "there's an oilcloth vest in that lot, and the man was about your size and build. It would come in useful in wet weather." When the vest came up for sale, I raised my hand and found myself the owner of a vest in worn but usable condition, the five shillings to be deducted from my wages. Betty washed it and rubbed some slush in the fabric to waterproof it. The vest helped me stay warm on wet days.

Gradually, ship life became my life, and a year passed. I was promoted from landsman to ordinary seaman, which came with a small increase in my wages. A few times during the year, the ship returned to Plymouth to stock up on fresh water and food. Men were not allowed to go ashore during the time in port, but wives of sailors were allowed to come aboard for the duration of the stay. Night watches were suspended during these times, and the gun decks became crowded with hammocks serving double, sometimes noisy, occupancy. There was no way to let my wife, Libby, know the ship was in Plymouth and little chance she could make the trip there from Falmouth, so I remained alone.

The press gangs were active across England, and new hands arrived on deck from receiving ships. Some men were sullen and resigned, but others were wide-eyed and terrified to find themselves in such a strange place. I remembered how I had felt a year earlier when I arrived on the ship, as lost and anxious as these men were. But each were assigned to a mess and a watch, and gradually, they fit into the life of the ship, as I had done. After the ship was stocked with casks of fresh water and salt beef, along with fresh vegetables and an assortment of animals kept in a pen on the upper gun deck, the wives were taken ashore in the ship's boat. Then we raised the main anchor, spread the sails, and *Temeraire* slowly made its way out of Plymouth harbor and into the Channel again. I was glad to get to sea and back to the routine that ruled our lives there.

After I was made an ordinary seaman, I began talking with Billy about working as a topman. He put me off at first, saying the crew was filled, and I had it pretty good working as a waister. It was hard work up on the yards, he said. But I kept after it, and after a while, Billy said he would watch for an opening on his crew. When that finally occurred, it was in the middle of winter, when the weather was terrible. Two men on his crew came down with fever, and a replacement was needed. I could fill in, he said, but only until the two men recovered. "You need to dress warmly," Billy said. "The wind has been fierce lately, and the rain beats down upon us. There is no protection." I listened and said nothing as I considered what to do. Only a few hours remained before the start of the next watch. I bought some slush from the cook and rubbed it into my vest and over the tops of my shoes. Billy had told me that the most important part of the topman's job was keeping warm. It was all right for a man's arms and legs to get wet as long as his chest remained dry, he said. I did not get much sleep before my first watch as a topman, but my slops were as ready as I could make them. I lay in the hammock, and when midnight came around, I dressed quickly to be ready for work.

The bell rang for the start of the watch. Billy went straight to the shrouds and started climbing. I followed him. It was a long climb to the fighting top, the small deck at the top of the mainmast where it connected to the topmast. I still remember the coarse texture of the ratlines I clung to as I climbed. Billy climbed up the futtock shrouds, the lines that ran from the mast around the flat platform called the fighting top, and continued up to guy the topmast. At one place, a man had to hang nearly upside down as he climbed. When I reached that point, Billy yelled down to me, "Use the lubber's hole." This was the hole in the platform used by officers to reach the small deck. But I ignored his direction, grabbed hold of the futtock shrouds, and climbed up, digging my feet into the lines to keep from falling to the deck a hundred feet below. It was only a short climb before the shrouds turned vertical and continued up to stay the topmast. At that point, I jumped down onto the deck of the fighting top, where Billy and the rest of the crew stood waiting. Billy looked at me and said, "Up here, you won't be known as Farmer John. Here it will be Futtock

John." I never felt so good in my life.

A whistle from the deck below signaled we had work to do. Billy turned to me and said, "Follow me, lad," as he started out on the starboard yard, his feet on the footrope and one arm wrapped around the yard to keep his balance. I followed him, and the footrope swayed as other men stepped on it behind me, but it remained secure. Billy reached the end of the yard with me about six feet behind him. "Untie the gaskets," he yelled out. These were canvas wraps that held the furled sail tight to the yard. I untied the gaskets but held onto the bunched sail as Billy did. The bosun's mate watched until all the gaskets were loose. Then came a blast from his whistle, and the topmen let go all at once while the waisters hauled on the lines to pull the sail down and spread it. The sail billowed out loosely. The yard began to move upward as another group of waisters hauled on lines to raise it until the sail was taut. As soon as the lines were cleated off, the sail and yard were turned and braced up so the sail caught the most wind.

"Now up to the tops'l," Billy called out to me. I carefully walked the footrope back to the mast and followed Billy as he climbed the shrouds to the topsail yard, where we repeated the operations. When the topsail was taut, a whistle came from below. "No topgallant today," Billy said to me. "Too much breeze." Indeed, the sails were straining with the wind, and the ship was moving well through the water. The sails on the foremast and mizzenmast had been spread, so from where I stood on the topsail yard, I saw sails before and behind me.

The ship rolled from side to side as it cut through the waves. It was rough enough that a man needed to hold on with one hand, but the topmen were as comfortable with the swaying as if they were standing on the deck. The fresh air blew in my face, the mast swayed, and I felt more free than at any time since my feet first landed on the deck of the ship. Billly saw my exhilaration, for he turned to me and spoke. "Not a bad place to be on a fine day like this!" Fine it was, because the ocean stretched out on all sides and white caps dotted the surface of the water. No other sails were in sight, so our ship was alone on the ocean.

"What are we doing out here?" I asked Billy.

"They say that we are blockading the Frenchies in the port of Brest," he said. "But I've not seen a French ship or even the coast of France. It is just back and forth out here in the waves. In a few hours, we will furl sails and the ship will come about and head back on the course we are following now. Once in a while, another of our ships comes into sight, but most days, *Temeraire* sails alone."

A sharp blast from the whistle interrupted our talk. "He wants us down now. Hop to it," Billy said. We clambered down the shrouds to the deck, where we were each given a bucket of tar and a rag for tarring the shrouds to keep them from rotting. We took our buckets up the shrouds to the top and began working our way down, rubbing tar into the lines as we went. It was impossible to do the work without getting tar on our hands, and after a while, they were as black as the lines we were working on. Around us were topmen tarring the larboard shrouds and others doing the same on the foremast and mizzenmast. This went on for the rest of the watch, except for a short break when we were whistled to shorten the sails we had set earlier. Finally, eight bells rang out, and the watch was over. I cleaned the tar off my hands as best as I could, picked up my hammock, and headed down to the lower gun deck with Billy ahead of me. After we were in our hammocks, he leaned across and whispered, "So now you have had a taste of the life of a topman, do you fancy it?"

Setting a sail

"It's grand," I said. "I would like to be there full time." On that note, I instantly fell asleep.

A topman was to be my lot. One of the two sick men recovered and returned to work as a topman on the mainmast, but the other man lingered sick for a while, then died, and his body was put over the side. I remained a topman, climbed the shrouds with the others, learned to distinguish the different tones of the bosun mate's whistle, and began to know the flow of the job. It was hard work, as Billy had warned. Sometimes, we spread and furled sails numerous times during a watch. At other times, the wind remained steady, and the sails required little attention. On those watches, we tarred lines or reeved new lines to replace worn ones. Sometimes, when there was nothing to do aloft, we were sent below to man the bilge pumps or spread blacking on the cannons. But there were a few times when the bosun's mate was occupied on the deck far below, and we were left to ourselves. During those times, we sat on a yard and yarned with each other or just looked out upon the sea. Winter passed into spring and summer. Those were great times to be a topman, for the winds were light and the sails were soft in the warm air. Sometimes, I thought about my wife Libby and our children back in St. Just. I missed them, but this life aboard ship was good. I was used to it and would scarcely trade it for another.

It was mid-autumn when everything changed. We had just left Plymouth, after taking aboard fresh water, casks of beef, crates of onions, and kegs of sauerkraut. The ship put out to sea, but when we reached the area where we had been part of the blockade of Brest for the past year and a half, the ship continued to sail south. For four days, we sailed out of sight of land or other ships. The weather grew warmer, and when the sun shone, it was hot.

On the morning of the fifth day, I came on watch and was amazed by what I saw. *Temeraire* was sailing in a fleet of huge ships similar to ours, ships as far as I could see, all with sails spread, looking like white clouds on the horizon. That day, after adjusting the sails, we were put over the side of the ship on bosun's chairs, each with a bucket of black paint and a brush. Our task was to paint the outside of the gunports black. This gave the ship an odd checkerboard appearance. When the watch was finished and we were at dinner, I asked Billy about it. "This is Lord Nelson's fleet," he said, "and that is his distinctive mark. All the ships have that look."

Lord Nelson. I had heard his name, and there was much talk of his exploits. He had led the fleet that crushed the French ships in Alexandria at the Battle of the Nile and later destroyed the Danish fleet in Copenhagen in 1801. A few of the men had served under him on other ships, and they talked of his bravery. He was an insignificant looking man, but sometimes he joined the boarding crew when attacking another ship. "He fought like a right demon, thrusting and hacking with his sword," said one man. That ended when he lost his right arm in one encounter.

He had been made a Lord after the Battle of Copenhagen, and as Admiral of this fleet, he had overall command of the array of ships. Billy pointed to a vessel ahead of *Temeraire,* saying, "His flag is on the *Victory,* the three-decker off to starboard at the bow." I looked and saw a ship of the line, much like the one we were on. Below the union jack flying on the main mast was a white flag. Billy continued, "He is admiral of the white, so we know he is on that ship." I looked at the *Victory,* curious if I could see Lord Nelson on the quarterdeck, but it was too far away to see clearly. "Now we will see some action," Billy said. "Lord Nelson likes a scrap, he does, and he will do whatever he can to get us to fight the French fleet."

But for three days, our ship sailed peacefully among the others in this huge array of ships. I tried to count how many ships of the line were there, but it was hard to know because the sails stretched into the distance behind us. We were always near the front of the fleet within sight of *Victory.* Meanwhile, the skies remained clear, the wind light, and the watches were spent cleaning the ship and making sure everything was in working order.

It was the middle of the third day when a British frigate approached from the east under full sail. It altered course to match *Victory* and set out a ship's boat to carry an officer to the larger ship. Not long afterward, *Victory* raised a series of signal flags. Immediately, a whistle sounded from below us, and the order came to put out the studding sails, the "stuns'ls" as the men called them. These were sails attached to small spars that were normally stored along the main yard but could be extended to lengthen the spars. The extra sail area let the ship catch additional wind on days when it was nearly calm. We ran out the stuns'l spars on the main course, then on the topsail and topgallant yards above, and we saw crews doing the same on the other masts. Additional sails were rigged between the masts and from the foremast to the bowsprit to catch any puffs of air from the south quarter. The ship was now a billow of white linen, and with all of the sails spread, she moved through the sea a little faster than before, though still at a slow pace. Looking around at the other ships, we saw that extra sails were being spread on all of them.

"He is in a rush, he is," said Billy. "I have rarely seen such sail." We waited as the watch went on, but no ships were seen on the horizon. The fleet crept slowly along. At sunset, the stuns'ls were furled and the yards shortened to avoid the risk of strong winds during the night. But at first light, with the air nearly calm, we extended the yards and spread the sails again. The ship was sailing east toward the coast of Spain, but we saw nothing except low clouds in the distance.

About five o'clock, two bells of the morning watch, the sky was beginning to brighten, and the wind was just enough to fill the sails. Billy and I climbed to the topgallant yard, but nothing was visible in the gloom of early dawn. About an hour later, Billy called out to me in an excited voice, "John, look to the east!" I turned, and at first, I saw only low clouds right at the waterline. Then as I looked closely, the clouds resolved into the sails of an immense armada stretching for miles.

"That's them," said Billy. "That's our target." He called down to the deck that ships were in sight. Shortly, the second lieutenant joined us on the yard to confirm the sighting before reporting to the captain.

"How far away, do you think, Billy?" I asked.

"Nigh onto ten miles from us, hours of sailing at this rate," he said. A few minutes later, we heard the drum sound out "Beat to Quarters," the signal to get the ship ready for battle. At almost the same time, we heard the identical signal from *Victory*, sailing a musket shot ahead of us.

"Time to scamper," called out Billy, and we quickly descended the shrouds to the deck, which was filling up with men from the other watch. The next two hours were a burst of activity. A layer of sand was strewn around the deck to keep it from getting slippery if blood was spilled on it. The sleeping quarters of the captain and officers, which were made of removable wall panels, were taken down and moved into the hold along with the furniture. At each gun position, the sailor's sea chests were moved to the hold, along with anything that might be in the way of loading the cannon. The guns in the captain's and officers' quarters, normally stored parallel to the hull, were manhandled with bars until they pointed at the gunports. Muskets, swords, and pikes were removed from the weapons locker and placed where they could be seized if needed to repel boarders. When breakfast time arrived, the whole crew stopped to eat, then returned to work. The galley fires were extinguished, and all food and cooking vats were moved below. A large net to catch debris was spread above the quarterdeck, where the officers would be stationed during a battle.

By nine o'clock, two bells of the forenoon watch, Billy and I were ordered back to the fighting top, where we were to wait and trim sails as ordered. From there, the enemy fleet was clearly visible. The ships moved slowly through the water with all sails spread. The fleet stretched for miles, and we could not see the last ships in the line. Activity on the deck below us subsided. Our ship was ready for battle.

We saw our ship's boat returning from *Victory* bearing the captain who had met with Lord Nelson. When he reached the deck, he spoke to the first lieutenant, who spoke to the bosun, and shortly a whistle sounded out, along with the order: "All hands assemble on deck." We descended quickly and joined the rest of the crew, who were arrayed by watch and duties. A few minutes later, the captain came to the railing at the edge of the poop deck and spoke in a loud voice.

"Men, we shall be in battle soon. You will fight for England, for your wives and families, for the land that we love. I have just returned from a meeting with Lord Nelson. He is confident that British ships will be victorious today, and he sends this message to you: England expects that every man will do his duty."

There was a cheer from the waiting sailors, not so much at the words, but that Lord Nelson had sent each of them a message, for they held his name in high regard. Some had sailed with him and participated in other battles, and their memories of him were similar. "He never asked a man to take a risk he would not himself take," said one grizzled old sailor. Another man, one of the cook's helpers because of a crippled leg, spoke up, saying, "I would follow that man into hell if that is where he led us." All the men on the ship had heard comments like this, and their respect for Lord Nelson was great.

When the cheering died down, the captain continued, "It will be a long wait until the battle begins. You are to lie down at your stations. The time will come when you play a part in this affray. When that happens, know that you are fighting for more than this ship; you are fighting for our way of life."

The captain turned away and spoke to the first lieutenant, who addressed the crew, saying, "An extra dram of grog will be issued to all men." At this remark, a cheer went up, almost as loud as that for Lord Nelson.

Shortly afterward, Billy and I climbed back up the shrouds to the fighting top with a few other men. Ordered to lie down on the small deck area at the yard, we lay on the rough boards and looked out toward the enemy fleet. They presented a massive wooden wall that the British ships would have to break apart. As we lay there, Billy turned to me and said, "John, if I don't live through this battle, there are a few things in the sea chest I would like to go to my mother in Manchester." I assured him I would take them to her, but joshed him a little, saying likely as not in a few days we would be sitting on the topgallant yard two hundred feet above the bosun's mate, enjoying the sunshine.

"Maybe so," he said, "but when I look at the rows of guns facing us, I believe it will be a long afternoon." I followed his gaze and for the first time, realized how many guns would be firing at us. The French and Spanish ships had opened their gunports to reveal hundreds of cannons. The progress of *Temeraire* through the water was so slow that many minutes would elapse before our cannons could return fire.

The first shot came from the enemy ships just after one bell of the afternoon watch. We saw holes appear in the sails of *Victory*, which was traveling a musket shot's distance ahead of *Temeraire*. We saw other shots striking the ship and sending wooden splinters flying. We heard screams in the distance, indicating that men had been hurt. A short while later, cannonballs began to reach *Temeraire*. Most went wide, splashing harmlessly into the ocean. But occasionally a shot passed through one of our sails. One of the stunsail spars was shot away, and the sail hung limp until Billy went out on the foot rope and cut it loose to drop into the sea. There was little else we or anyone else on the ship could do. Our guns pointed to the side and could not be directed forward. There would be long minutes of enduring enemy gunfire before our guns could come into play.

A scream sounded from the deck below. A cannonball had hit one of the cannons and knocked it over onto a man. Other men were hit by splinters, and bodies lay on the deck. More shots hit *Temeraire* as we crept closer to the line of enemy ships. On the deck below, men threw dead bodies overboard, and we watched in horror as the corpses gradually drifted behind the ship. Ahead of us, *Victory* was struck by shot after

The Battle of Trafalgar[5]

shot. The top mizzenmast was shot away, and its sails hung in tatters. But the ship kept moving forward until at last, it passed through a gap between two French ships. As it did, the *Victory*'s cannons belched forth flame and smoke, pouring cannonballs into the stern of one ship and the bow of the other. Soon afterward, *Temeraire* passed between a massive Spanish man of war on the larboard side and a French man-of-war on the starboard. Our guns fired one after another. The ship shuddered with each blast. This was our chance to return the treatment we had received. We watched as our cannonballs tore into the enemy ships.

Billy and I went out on the yards to cut away the stunsails, and the ship slowed and made only slight headway through the water. Ahead of us, *Victory* was entangled with a French ship, and we saw a crowd of French sailors massed on the main deck, ready to board *Victory*. *Temeraire* eased slowly up on the other side of the French ship and fired a cannonade filled with grapeshot into the crowd of French sailors. The seething mass of attackers was reduced to a deck full of lifeless bodies. I had never seen anything like this: men instantly turned to corpses, and I stared in shock at the carnage.

Across the deck of the French ship, I saw the quarterdeck of *Victory*. Sometimes through the smoke I could make out the slight, uniformed figure of Lord Nelson himself, walking beside the larger figure of Captain Hardy, the commander of *Victory*. Then the smoke obscured them for a moment from my sight, and when it cleared, I saw Nelson lying on the deck with Hardy bending over him. I had no more time to look because a whistle from below called us down to the deck.

Billy and I were sent below to assist gun crews that had lost men. When I descended the ladder onto the gun deck, the scene was something I could not have imagined. The air was filled with smoke so thick I could only see the nearest guns. The men were stripped to the waist and had their shirts tied around their heads to help protect their ears from the deafening noise. Between the explosions of gunfire, I could hear the screams and groans of wounded men. As I walked across the deck to the gun where I was assigned, I had to step over bodies and parts of bodies that had been moved out of the way of the guns.

The next two hours were a chaos of activity. I swabbed out the cannon barrel each time it fired, then packed a cloth sack of gunpowder into it, followed by the twenty-four-pound iron ball and the wadding to hold it in place. After the cannon was levered around with bars to aim it, we backed away as it fired with a noise that was beyond imagining. Then we swabbed out the cannon barrel again and repeated the whole operation, firing every ninety seconds. I had no idea where the shots were going or if they were hitting another ship, and there was no time to look. But screams from around us on the gun deck indicated that enemy shots were killing and wounding our crew.

Each moment seemed to last forever. But eventually we were ordered to stop firing. I looked out through the open gunport and saw the side of a French ship that had been close alongside *Temeraire* but was now slowly swinging away from us. Huge holes had been blown through the side of the ship. No masts remained standing, and the main deck was a shambles with bodies draped everywhere. One of our officers approached and issued orders. I could not hear what he said, but he motioned, and we dragged ourselves up to the main deck. I could not believe what I saw there. Only the lower part of the main mast was standing, with bits of rope and sail remnants hanging from a piece of the main yard that was still attached. The fighting top where Billy and I had lain before the battle was gone. The deck was a mass of debris. Large pieces of the railing were missing, and men were throwing shards of wood scrap over the side, along with the bodies of dead seamen. I had only a moment to look before I felt a shove. Turning around, the officer pointed toward the stern, where the French ship was still entangled with *Temeraire*. Our mizzen mast had fallen onto the other ship, and men were using it as a bridge to cross between the two vessels. The officer motioned again and spoke, and some of his words were clear. "Go over and keep that ship afloat," he said, pointing to the French vessel. "She is our prize and worth money to us."

Crossing the mast to the French ship was entering a nightmare. Bodies lay everywhere, and the deck was covered with blood. The ship was a wreck; no masts were standing, and there were huge holes in her sides. Keeping her afloat meant pumping, so we descended to the lower gun deck to find the pumps. There was more light than usual on that deck because of the holes through the side of the ship. The pumps were sitting idle, and we began to crank on the handles. Amazingly, the pumps were not damaged, so water began flowing out of the ship. I was already exhausted from working on the gun crew, and turning the crank was even more of an ordeal. With four men at a time on each pump, we cranked until we could do no more. Then we moved aside and lay exhausted while others took our place. A few French sailors who were uninjured worked with us. Because of the language barrier, we couldn't talk with them, but we worked side by side trying to save the ship. Daylight faded, and the gun deck grew dark. We pumped in darkness through the night, and the hours were an endless stupor of exhaustion and pain. A storm was brewing outside the ship. It rocked in the waves, and wind howled through the breaches in the hull.

We kept pumping, but by morning we were losing our battle to save the ship. It sat lower in the water, and waves splashed through the ragged voids in the hull. Eventually we were ordered to stop pumping and return to the upper deck. The storm was raging around the ship, which was now separated from *Temeraire* but connected with a long hawser. An officer motioned us to the rail, where we watched as one of the ship's boats from *Temeraire* moved through the water toward us, dancing up and down in the waves. It seemed impossible that the boat could survive in the violence of the sea, but the men kept rowing. It came closer and pulled up next to the French ship. We clambered down a net hung from the rail and fell or leaped into the vessel. When the boat held as many men as was safe to carry, it pushed off, leaving men still hanging on the net of the French ship.

The trip back to *Temeraire* was terrifying. The boat rode low in the water, and waves slopped over the sides. Those of us not rowing bailed as fast as we could, using our caps or cupped hands to frantically throw water over the side, only to have it come back in the next wave. Finally, the great bulk of *Temeraire* loomed above us, and we faced the task of grabbing the net and climbing to the main deck, where we were pulled over the rail by waiting sailors. We lay gasping on the deck while the ship's boat returned for another load of men. After I recovered and stood up, I was ordered to accompany the French sailors to the lower gun deck, where they joined others held prisoner, guarded by a squad of marines.

Meanwhile, a group of seamen carried the walls of the captain's and officers' cabins up from the hold and reinstalled them. All the glass had been broken out of the windows at the stern, but after the walls were installed, the ship had a semblance of normalcy. The debris was cleaned off the main deck, and new shrouds were mounted to the stub of the main mast that still stood. A temporary yard was hung on the mast so a little sail could be spread, although the winds were too strong in the storm to attempt this immediately.

Gradually, the day turned into night and then into day again. We were allowed to hang our hammocks and sleep in them. The gun decks were crowded because a section had been walled off to hold French prisoners. Some of the hammocks were occupied by our men who were wounded in the battle. A few of them were missing arms or legs, while others had masses of bandages covering their wounds. We could do little for them, and groans were heard throughout the dark hours. In the morning, men were found who had died during the night.

The storm raged for four days. We sat helpless, our anchor with a precarious hold on the seabed. The Spanish coast lay only a few miles away, strewn with rocks and violent surf. The French ship we had tried to keep afloat sank during the first night, taking with it the bodies of the French sailors and a few live men who were too badly injured to move.

When I woke on the morning of the second day after the battle, I looked for Billy, whom I had not seen since we descended the mast at the start of the fighting. He had been sent with a group of topmen to another captured French ship to try and sail her away from the rocks. I asked about the fate of that ship every day. Finally, on the fourth day, word came that the ship had wrecked on the rocks and the waves were so rough that no one had been saved. Billy, who taught me most of what I knew about living aboard ship, was gone.

After the storm subsided, *Temeraire,* sporting only a scrap of sails, was towed the few miles to the British base at Gibraltar. The wounded men were taken ashore, and some repairs were made. Crews built temporary masts, installed glass in the windows of the captain's cabin, and replaced railings. The ship was a ship again, but just barely, as we began the slow trip back to England. The crew was shorthanded, having lost almost two hundred men killed or wounded in the battle. The lower gun deck was full of French prisoners of war headed for the prison hulks in Portsmouth harbor. All the British sailors were berthed on the upper gun deck. Although crowded, the air was fresher and there was more light than the lower gun deck, where I had lived for the past two years.

Our mess was quiet on that return trip to England. Big John had been killed while working on a gun crew, and his body was shoved overboard during the battle. One of the lads had been impaled by a wood splinter, and his leg was amputated by the doctor. He was still alive when we reached Gibraltar, but his chance of recovery was poor. The rest of us sat quietly and looked at each other, wondering how it was that we were alive when others were gone.

We finally arrived in Portsmouth, where the ship went into dry-dock for repairs. The sailors were paid off, and I received my wages, so my pocket held silver when the ship's boat landed me at the dock with a group of others. A loud reception was waiting for us. Word had spread about the ship's exploits at the Battle of Trafalgar, in which eighteen French and Spanish ships had been captured or destroyed. Cheers erupted from the throng as we climbed onto the dock. The crowd was filled with young women, some of them wives who had waited months to see their husbands. Other young women were there because they knew that returning sailors had money in their pockets and wanted to spend it. As for me, I just wanted to get home to Falmouth. But I had not been on land for two years, and the dock was moving under me. The street at the end of the pier was not much better.

There was a pub at the nearest corner and I thought a beer would help with my unsteadiness, so I entered and ordered a pint at the bar. This tasted so good after months of drinking the weak beer supplied aboard ship that a second one tasted just as good. I knew I should look for a boat to Falmouth, but I could do that tomorrow. A night's rest was the best thing for today. The pub owner accepted my money and showed me to a shabby room with a bed. The bed felt hard after the comfort of a hammock aboard ship, but I lay down and soon fell asleep. Sometime later, I woke and felt a hand fumbling in my pockets. Still groggy from the beer, I opened my eyes and found a young woman standing beside the bed, leaning over me. "I thought you might like some company, sir, after your long voyage," she said. She protested when I pushed her away from me and out the door. I slammed the door shut and shoved the bed against it, then lay down again and fell back asleep.

The sun was shining when I woke, and the day looked better than the one before. I took my small bundle of possessions, which included a few of Billy's things that I promised to bring to his mother, and began to search for a passage to Falmouth. The ground was not moving under me as it had the day before. At the harbor, I found a coastal vessel that was leaving shortly to sail east and secured passage on it. Two days later, I walked off the boat in Falmouth. I headed along the waterfront of the familiar town, planning to walk to the dock where boats crossed the bay to my home in St. Just.

A few blocks along, I turned a corner, and there in front of me was the Dog and Whistle, the pub where my adventure began two years earlier. A pint would taste good, so I entered. Behind the bar was Betsy. When she looked up and saw me, she cried out, "John Lower himself! There you are, as brown as a nut and just back from the sea, I'll wager."

"Hello, Betsy," I replied with a laugh. "I wanted to find out if the ale is any good here."

She brought me a mug and said, "This one is on the house, John. I expect you need it after the last two years."

"Betsy, I was on *Temeraire,* one of the ships at Trafalgar," I said.

"I don't know much about that," she said. "But James and his friends will want to hear about it. They spend most of their time talking about the war, not like they have seen any of it up close." She called to an old man sitting at a corner table, saying, "James, here is a man for you to talk with. John is just back from Trafalgar."

The old man beckoned me over to an empty seat at his table and called out for two of his friends who were standing at the bar to join us. "Let me buy you a pint, lad," he said. "Please tell me about the battle and the death of Lord Nelson."

I started talking about the battle, and one pint led to another. Friends of the old man stopped in at the pub, and they all wanted to hear about the battle, so I told the story several times. It was past supper time when I got up to leave and found my legs were not as steady as I would have liked. One of the men spoke up, saying, "Lad, let me walk with you down to the dock." I accepted his offer, and he helped me walk the few blocks. There I found a man with a rowboat and negotiated a price for him to row me to St. Just. The light faded as he rowed across the bay, and it was fully dark by the time we reached the landing. A short stroll took me to the end of the lane to the farm. The house looked much the same as it had when I left it two years earlier. Smoke drifted up out of the chimney. The latch on the door stuck a bit, as it had before I left, but I gave a tug and the door flew open. My three children were sitting in front of the fire and looked up at me without recognition. Libby was seated nearby, stitching together squares for a quilt. She raised her head and saw me, looked me up and down for a moment, then spoke.

"Well, John Lower, it is about time that you come back. Children, this is your father, back from the wars and likely just out of the pub. Welcome him now."

I was home.

———◆———

A tap on my shoulder brought me wide awake. There was my granddaughter Mary looking at me. Little John nudged me insistently and said, "Grandpa, you were telling us about the fighting and Lord Nelson, and then you fell asleep. I want to hear the rest of the story."

"So you shall, John. There is much to tell." The little ones came close to me, and I continued on with their story.

Historical Note

The *Temeraire* underwent repairs for sixteen months to repair the battle damage received at Trafalgar. It then returned to the active fleet for four more years. The ship was converted into a hulk to house French prisoners and later into a victualing ship to receive and dispense goods to the British fleet. Her masts and cannons were removed in 1811, when the ship was no longer used as an active warship. However, she remained in steady use until she was broken up in 1838, when metal steamships began to replace wooden sailing ships in the British Navy.

CHAPTER FIVE

The Crossing

England experienced a period of economic hardship following the defeat of Napoleon in 1815. The labor market was saturated with returning sailors and army veterans, and the mechanization of industrial production reduced the amount of labor needed to produce everyday goods. Factories replaced cottage industries, and rural areas suffered. The following decades saw an increase in migration from England to places with more opportunities, including Australia, the colonies that would become Canada, and the United States. Emigration from Great Britain to the British North American Colonies increased from 680 persons in 1815 to 28,808 in 1833. Each family that emigrated had its reason for leaving Great Britain. For some, it was new opportunities in the colonies, while others had lost their livelihood. For many families, the reason for leaving was desperation.

Passenger manifest of the barque *Alchymist*, sailing from Falmouth, Cornwall, to Saint John, New Brunswick, on July 26, 1833.[6] It includes the Scabora family: John, his wife Acadon (Eden), and their three children, Mary, John, and baby Joseph. John Scabora's occupation is listed as a shoemaker.

John Scabora, 1802–1867

August 1833

Ocean swells surged and ebbed around the barque *Alchymist* as it sailed west through the North Atlantic. A man stood at the rail of the ship and looked out at the sea. He was compact in size, with a spare and muscular build, blue eyes, and gray streaks in his brown hair. His trimmed beard was dark, with a noticeable white tuft at his chin. As the ship rocked back and forth, he stood with his feet wide apart for better balance and held onto the rail with one hand. The motion reminded him of when he was a boy and spent long days on the small boat with his father. His job was to bait the hooks and untangle the lines while his father sat at the stern and handlined for mackerel. They didn't talk much during those days, only when his father needed a new bait or decided to put out another line. If the boy saw a line jerk or become taut, he called out to his father and watched as the man pulled in the fish and dispatched it with the fish club that rested at the bottom of the boat.

John Scabora was no longer on a fishing boat, but on a ship sailing to Saint John in the New Brunswick colony of British North America. His wife, Eden, and their three children slept in the steerage area below deck and would soon wake. The weather was good this morning with wind from the southeast, and the sails were drawing well. John envied the sailors who climbed the rigging to adjust the mainsail. He wanted to climb with them to get a better view of the sea around the ship, but the captain had forbidden passengers to go aloft. Instead, he stood at the rail and looked out at the sea. Nothing could be seen except the water, rising and falling again. It was mesmerizing, and as John stood there, his thoughts drifted back to the events that had brought him to this voyage.

It was late afternoon on a spring day, eight years earlier. He had rowed the short distance from his rented rooms in Arwenack to the dock in

Falmouth. In the past, many packet ships departed from Falmouth for British colonies around the world. Now, increasingly, the packet ships sailed out of Plymouth or Southampton. Fewer ships entered the Port of Falmouth each month. Still, John came to the harbormaster's office once a week to check on expected ship arrivals. His future as a harbor pilot did not look good. The senior pilots were men in their sixties, and most of the apprentice pilots were their sons. There was little chance for an outsider to break into this fraternity, but John paid his yearly license fee, checked in regularly at the office, and occasionally went out with a senior pilot to guide a ship into the harbor. This day brought nothing.

Leaving the dock, he walked along the street that fronted the harbor. A pub sign swung back and forth in the breeze. John had not visited this one before. The image on the sign was a dog on the hunt for a bird, its ears pricked up as it waited for a command from its master. The name of the pub was the Dog and Whistle. Opening the front door, John saw a middle-aged woman standing behind the bar polishing beer mugs. She was well-kept, wore an apron, and had a few lines in her face. He entered the pub, ordered a pint, and watched as she drew it with a well-practiced hand. She brought the foaming mug to him and waited until he took a sip and nodded his approval of the ale.

"What brings you to town, young man?" she asked.

John looked up and said, "I am an assistant harbor pilot and stopped at the harbormaster's office to check on ships due next week. Few are expected to enter the harbor, and my future as a pilot does not look good. I decided to have a pint before I row back to my rooms in Arwenack."

The woman smiled at him in a motherly way, then glanced to the side as if someone was approaching. John felt a tap on his shoulder. Turning his head, he saw an older man standing near him. The man was wearing work clothes and looked a little the worse for wear. He was not elderly, just weatherbeaten, as though he had led a hard life. He nodded at John.

"Young man, I have a story that will interest you," he said. "Buy me a pint, and I will tell you about it."

The barmaid spoke up, saying, "John Lower, this young man is not here to spend hours listening to your sea tales. Leave him alone to drink his ale."

"It's all right," said John. "I have a little time, and this man has something he wants to say." He placed a few coins on the bar to buy a pint for the stranger.

"Well," the barmaid replied, "he has told the story so many times in here that I could tell it to you myself. Sits in here all day he does, waiting for someone to enter the pub who has not heard his yarns. If they supply the pints, he will talk for hours. How he gets across the water to his home in St. Just, I don't know. On most nights, he leaves here barely able to walk."

"It is quiet tonight," said John, "and I have no other obligations. We will drink our pints, and then I will row across the bay and make sure he gets home safely."

The stranger took a long draught of his ale. When he finished, he spoke up to the barmaid: "Betsy, if this young man has a boat and the strength to row it to St. Just, he is a fine man. When I was his age, it was nothing at all for me to row across the bay."

The woman gave a little snort and replied, "John Lower, in that case, there must have been a pint waiting for you on the other side of the water."

The man turned away from her and said to John, "Let's sit at a table and enjoy this ale. I will tell you how I fought in the great battle of Trafalgar alongside Admiral Lord Nelson. My story starts in this very pub in 1803. Betsy can verify what I am saying because she stood in that same spot when the press gang entered. They seized me, and I was put aboard the man-of-war, *Temeraire*."

John nodded, and the man continued.

"She was the biggest ship you ever saw, masts the size of mighty tree trunks reaching into the sky and enormous sails that billowed out to catch the wind. I climbed up those masts and set those sails, me and Billy, we did. I saw some of the battle from up there, then I worked with a gun crew for the rest of the fighting. Have you ever heard the sound of cannon fire?" John shook his head, so the man continued, "Each blast shakes the ship, and your eardrums will burst unless you pack them solid. I wrapped a shirt around my head to protect my ears. A bloody time it was. Men around me had their arms and legs ripped off by French cannonballs. It was a terrible sight."

The man continued talking, and John suspected the stories could go on for quite a while. He had nearly finished his ale, so he urged the man to drink up and walk with him down to the dock. They rose to leave, and John steadied the man with his arm. As they reached the door of the pub, Betsy called out, "Thank you for looking after old John. His wife will be grateful that you brought him home."

The two men slowly made their way to the dock where the boat was tied. John helped the older man into the dory, seated him in the stern, unshipped the oars, and began to row across the bay. The dock at St. Just was a four-mile row from Falmouth. For much of the trip, John Lower continued the story of his life aboard His Majesty's Ship *Temeraire*. He talked about his friend Billy, about a man named Big John, about working as the mess cook, and about his life aloft on the yards, helping to set and furl the sails. He described how many men were packed into the ship, a few women as well. Then his voice grew quiet, and John realized John Lower had fallen asleep, only waking when John tied up the boat to the dock at St. Just.

A short walk brought the two men to a lane with a small house at the far end. John knocked at the door, which was opened by a slender young woman. She glanced at John, then gazed longer at the older man. "Father," she said, "it is good to have you home, even if it is hours later than we expected. Come in and have supper, and bring this young man who rowed you here. He deserves supper for his efforts." John tried to thank her and leave, but she would not hear of it.

"There is enough stew for all of us, and I know how long a row it is from Falmouth," the woman said. "I have done it a few times myself when Father has not returned home." She opened the door wide and beckoned the two men into the house. It was not large, a main room with a kitchen alcove in one corner and a table with six chairs in the center. An opening on one wall led to a bedroom, and a fixed ladder led to an opening into a loft above. An older woman sat at the end of the table while two young men filled the seats along one side. The young woman introduced herself as Eden Lower, then identified the others as her two brothers, Robert and George, and her mother, Elizabeth. She made a place for her father at the end of the table opposite her mother and a place for John on the side, next to her.

Meanwhile, she spoke about the events of the day, how well the new lambs were growing, how beautiful was the sunset, and how good was the stew they were about to eat. It was delicious, John agreed when he tasted it, simple but hot and filling. Meanwhile, Eden's mother added little to the conversation, and the brothers ate their stew and said nothing at all. They were sturdy young men dressed in work clothes. Both looked as though they had been in the fields all day, and merely nodded at John when he sat down at the table. When Eden stopped talking in order to eat, her mother, Elizabeth, finally spoke up, asking, "What brought you here tonight, young man, and how did you come to meet my husband?"

John explained he was an apprentice harbor pilot and had made a fruitless visit to the harbormaster's office before stopping at the Dog and Whistle, where he met John Lower. He left out the part about buying him a pint of ale, but related that when they started talking, the older man told him about the time he served aboard the *Temeraire*. John noticed Elizabeth frown and purse her lips at the mention of the ship, so he skipped the rest of the story and finished by saying it was a quiet night, and the trip across the bay from Falmouth to St. Just had been a pleasant row.

"And what do you do the rest of the time," she asked, "since the pilotage has not proved successful?"

"I do a little of everything to pay for my room and board at Arwenack," John said. "I worked at Bluett's Shipyard when they were finishing a packet brig and as a crew member on the brig during sea trials before the owner took her to the Thames. Then I worked as a laborer at the demolition of one of the old mill buildings. There was even a few weeks of work as a helper at a print shop in Falmouth. None of these jobs lasted, but they paid the rent and bought the materials for the dory that brought us to St. Just. I built it last winter, and it takes me around the harbor."

John saw Elizabeth listen intently at his mention of the print shop. "So you can read and write then?" she asked. "Yes," replied John. "My father insisted that all his children learn to read. In our house were a few old books that had been passed down through the years. It meant a lot to him, though he worked as a fisherman, a career where reading and writing have little use."

"Where did he fish?" Elizabeth asked.

"I grew up in St. Columb Minor, on the west side of Cornwall," John said. "My father worked there out of a small boat on the inshore fisheries. As a young man, he fished at the cod banks near Newfoundland, but when children came along, my mother wanted him home in the evening. He has been gone for ten years now, drowned and washed ashore at Tregardock Beach near Tintagel. I was only twelve years old when he died, but I made up my mind then not to be a fisherman. The water calls to me, and I have been on many boats, but I will not spend my life at sea."

At this, John saw Elizabeth nod, then return to her supper. The meal was soon finished, and John got up to leave. He said good night and started for the door when Eden spoke up, saying, "I would like to see the dory you built."

John was startled, but he welcomed the young woman's company, and they left the house, walked down the lane and toward the dock. Eden carried a tin candle lantern in one hand to light their way. During the walk, she told John a little of her story. She had lived on their farm her whole life and had started working at five years old, caring for the chickens and weeding the garden. Then she took over care of the sheep and goats. Eden explained she never learned to read or write because neither of her parents could read, and so could not teach her. Her father was a kind man, she said, but after he returned from the sea, he avoided farm work as much as possible. He went to Falmouth whenever he could get away from the farm and spent his time in one of the pubs. Her brothers ran the farm now, and her father had only small tasks.

When the two of them reached the dock, Eden examined the little dory. She asked John how he had learned to build a boat, and how he knew the boat wouldn't leak. He showed her how the planks overlapped and were fastened together with copper nails clinched over on the inside of the boat to make sure the joints would stay tight. He had carved the oars with a drawknife, he explained, and wrapped the shafts with a strip of leather where they fit into the oarlocks. The boat was painted two colors, green and white, and John said it looked smart in the daylight.

"Well," Eden said, "I hope you will row here in the daytime so I can see how smart it looks, and perhaps you will take me for a ride in it."

John promised her he would return, and the two parted. John started the long haul across the bay in the darkness toward Arwenack. As he rowed, he looked back over the stern of the dory and watched the candle lantern swing back and forth as Eden made her way toward home.

The little dory made the trip from Arwenack to St. Just many times that spring and summer. Sometimes, John helped with work at the Lower farm during the day, and then he and Eden went for a boat ride in the evening. They talked and watched as the sun set over Pendennis Castle while the light slowly faded. At harvest time in the fall, John spent a week at the farm, working alongside Eden's brothers in the fields and sleeping in the barn at night. More than a few times over the months, he and Eden rowed across to Falmouth to find her father and bring him home. Sometimes, the older man was at the Dog and Whistle, but other times they had to search for him at the half dozen other pubs that fronted the harbor.

At the end of the haying, when it neared time for John to return to his rooms at Arwenack, he waited for a quiet moment and then approached Eden's mother.

"Elizabeth, I would like to marry Eden," he said. "But before I ask her, I would like to have your approval."

"You are a good man," Elizabeth replied, "and I can tell that you will look after her. Her brothers will marry soon, and the farm will not have room for all of us. My husband's working days are long over. Perhaps he and I will move into rooms in Falmouth. I can take in laundry to pay for our lodgings, and he can tell his stories at the pubs. It is not the life I imagined when he and I got together, but I could tell even then he would not amount to much. He was good to the children, and that has been a blessing. You and Eden have my approval to wed, and I don't imagine she will turn you down."

That was eight years ago, years of hard work without much to show for it. John was a little heavier now, and his hair was streaked with gray, though he had only turned thirty years old. He still maintained the pilot's license, although there was almost no chance he could become a senior pilot. Over the years, there had been work at the shipyard and at many construction jobs, but also months with no work at all. During those months, there was barely enough money to pay the rent. The two rooms in Arwenack had been enough space for him and Eden, but they were crowded now, with the two of them and three children. Eden was no longer the wiry, light-hearted girl he had met, but a mother with another child on the way. Each fall, John and Eden returned to the Lower farm at St. Just, where they helped with the harvest in exchange for food, which they stored for the winter. Without those supplies, there would have been nights with little to eat. John fished in the bay and brought home a few bottom fish, and that helped put food on the table, but Eden worried that the dory would overturn in rough water and John would drown like his father.

Twice during their marriage, John and Eden made the twenty-four-mile trek to St. Columb Minor to see John's mother. His three older sisters had married and moved away from home. Two of them married men who worked in tin mines, and the other lived with her husband at his family's farm near Mawgan. John's older brother had found work as a gardener at Heligan House, the home of the wealthy Tremayne Family. He liked it there and offered to find John a place on the estate, but the idea of working for a wealthy family did not appeal to him. At the end of their second visit, John asked his mother if he could take the cobbler's tools and lasts that had belonged to his grandfather. Perhaps, he thought, there might be a business repairing boots for the men who worked at the shipyard. Back in Falmouth, he practiced until he felt comfortable with basic shoe repair, and he began to accept boots to fix, but he soon found there was little money in the business. A local dry goods store had started to sell boots made in a huge factory in London, and most men chose to buy new boots rather than pay to repair their old ones.

John and Eden's children were growing fast. Mary was five years old, Johnie four; both of them bright-eyed and active. They loved to spend time with their father, going with him to see ships arrive in the harbor and sitting with him in the evenings while he read stories out loud. Joseph, the baby, was a round little fellow who laughed often and looked out at the world with wide eyes.

A conversation at the Dog and Whistle one day motivated John to leave Falmouth and move his family to British North America. After another fruitless visit to the port office, he had stopped at the pub. At the dock was a three-masted barque being unloaded, and the air was filled with the scent of freshly cut wood from the timbers that were lifted from the hold. *Alchymist* was the name painted on the bow, a ship John had seen before in Falmouth Harbor. At the Dog and Whistle, he looked for John Lower, but the older man was not in sight. Betsy, working behind the bar, said he had not been in recently.

"The regular customers here have heard his story many times," she said. "They won't buy him a pint just to hear it again. He is probably up at one of the pubs by the road to Truro, hoping a traveler will stop in and be interested in his tale."

John sat at the bar and nursed his mug of ale. He had nearly finished when a man sat down next to him and ordered a pint. John glanced at the newcomer. It was clear from the clothes he wore and the calluses on his hands that he was a sailor.

"Stranger, where do you hail from?" John asked.

"Saint John, in the provinces," answered the man. "I crew on the *Alchymist,* moored now at the dock. We brought a load of timber for the shipyard and will leave in a few days with a load of passengers."

"How is it to work aboard the ship?" John asked.

"These commercial vessels are not like navy ships," he said. "The ship owners are too cheap to hire enough crew to man them safely. It is all right on a clear day with steady wind, but during a gale or rough seas, there are only ten men to do the work that should be done by twenty. But the *Alchymist* is a sound ship, and up to now, we have had safe crossings."

"How does it work to carry timber in one direction and passengers the other?" John asked.

"Once the timber is unloaded," the man said, "we quickly refit the cargo hold. We build wide shelves that will serve as beds, each one with a board across the front to make sure that the passengers don't get thrown to the floor when the boat is tossed about in the waves. There is an iron stove on a layer of bricks for them to cook their meals. It is a simple setup. If people want privacy, they hang blankets to wall off their bed from their neighbors. Most don't though. They don't have the blankets to spare."

"How many passengers does the boat carry?" John asked.

"This trip, there will be thirty, although fifty could be crammed into the hold," the man replied. "It is not a fancy accommodation, but the fare is cheap, three pounds for each adult, and there are people willing to endure the discomfort for six weeks or longer to reach Saint John."

"What do they find when they get there?" John asked.

"There is always work in a frontier land like New Brunswick," the man said. "Settlers are pushing the forests back from the town, cutting timber for us to haul to England, then digging out the stumps and making the land ready for crops. Men are always needed to clear land. It is not easy work, and the pay is low, but the landowner provides a place for his workers to live. Otherwise, they won't stay."

"Is the work year-round?" John asked. "I have heard the provinces are very cold in the winter."

"Yes, it gets cold for four months or so, and the ground freezes solid," the man said. "But they build fires to thaw out the soil so it can be worked. You see, the landowner may get the land for free at first, but there is a schedule of payments, and it is a race to get the land into production so that it will pay for itself. Many of the people we carry to Saint John work for a landowner clearing land for a year or two. Then, they strike out on their own, obtain raw land further from town, and begin to cut the forest. It is not an easy life, but there are men willing to try. Most of New Brunswick is forest. It seems as though it never ends."

"Do you make this trip often?" John asked.

"We have been to Falmouth often," the man continued, "but this is the first time we will take on passengers from here for the return trip. There is always timber to bring to England, but most of the time, we carry goods back to the provinces. You see, nothing is made over there. If iron nails or china cups and saucers are needed, they have to be brought from England. It is the same with coffee and tea and other staple items. We only carry passengers when there are enough to make it worthwhile. Passengers make for a lot of extra work. They all get seasick for a few days after we put to sea, and a few of them even die. Most of them get used to the motion of the ship, and for the rest of the voyage, they are underfoot. They want to be up on deck during good weather, and they get in our way. Some of the little boys climb up the shrouds, and we have to bring them down. It is an extra worry when the hold is filled with families. A woman gave birth on a voyage last year, right there in the hold. He was a cute little thing, the baby was, born aboard ship in the middle of the ocean. Two weeks later, the mother carried him ashore in Saint John."

John sat quietly and listened to the man's stories of shipboard life.

He had seen handbills around town advertising for settlers to come to New Brunswick, but it had not seemed real in the way this man was describing it.

"Will you take passengers again after this trip?" John asked.

"We never know for sure, but I heard talk of another run at the end of summer," the man replied. "The weather is better then, and the trip easier than a winter passage. Until then, it will be lumber one way and mixed cargo in the other direction."

John finished his pint of ale and thanked the sailor for his stories. He nodded at Betsy to show he was done, swung off the stool, and left the pub, pondering what the man had said. There was always work in New Brunswick. That would be a change from Falmouth, where his life consisted of one short job after another with nothing saved for the future. What would happen to Eden and their children if he became hurt or sick?

A few days passed before he talked with Eden about moving. She listened to what he had to say and then said, "You have been silent these past few days, John, and I knew that sooner or later, you would tell me what is on your mind. We work every day here, you at your jobs and me taking care of our children, but we will never save the money to have our own place. When you were a single man, the money went far enough, but now there are five of us. Your wages barely pay the rent each month, and there is little left to buy the cheapest food I can find. There is no room at the family farm for us now that my brothers are married and have children of their own. If you think we could do better in the provinces, I will go with you. It must be soon, while our children are small." They talked about the difficulties of moving for a while, then went to bed, and in the darkness, they held each other close, lost in their own thoughts.

The next few months were a time of frantic preparations. John worked as often as he could while Eden gathered warm clothing and extra blankets. They visited Eden's parents to tell them about their decision to leave Cornwall. Eden's mother cried a little when she learned of their plans. Eden's father was quiet while he held the two children on his lap. When he passed them back to their mother, each with a small candy clutched in their fists, she saw his eyes were moist with tears. "It is the last time he will see the little ones," she told John when they left the house. "He was a good father to us when we were small."

Selling the dory was hard for John, but they needed the money to help pay the cost of their passage. He had built the little boat and carved the oars himself, and it had carried him many times to the dock in Falmouth and across the harbor to St. Just. Now he had to part with it, like all of their possessions, except for the small amount that would go with them. He decided to bring the cobbler's tools and lasts in case they might bring in a little work when the family reached Saint John.

John took a final trip to see his mother, who had moved to Mevagissey, near where her oldest son worked at Heligan Estate. She looked tired, and John remembered she had birthed and raised eight children and had been alone for eighteen years since her husband drowned. She wept as she hugged John and asked him to write to her when they reached Saint John. She said she would pray for them to have a safe voyage, and she gave him an old Bible that had been passed down through the family. John remembered that his father had read it out loud to the family many years ago. John was sad when he left her, for he knew he would never see her again.

As departure time approached, they had still not raised enough money to pay for their passage, and John grew desperate to come up with the rest. Besides the cost of the tickets, the family needed to buy food for the long voyage. He had no answer until one afternoon, a chance conversation occurred with Betsy at the Dog and Whistle.

"Enos Dryer owns land in New Brunswick and lives here in Falmouth," she said. "He comes here for supper most evenings. Perhaps he might know of a way to help with your problem."

John waited in town until evening, then returned to the pub. Betsy was not behind the bar, but the young man on duty pointed out Enos Dryer, who was eating dinner at one of the tables. John waited until the man finished, then approached and introduced himself. Enos was a portly man who looked to be in his late fifties, dressed carefully but not ostentatiously. He looked up at John's approach and listened as John explained his predicament. He stopped to light his pipe and think for a minute before he spoke.

"So, you want to travel to Saint John with your family?" he asked. "You know it is a backward place, not like Falmouth. A man must work hard to make his way there."

John answered that he understood, but he knew how to work and could do a good job in the right situation.

"Well, young man, I like to see a man willing to take a chance to better his state in life," Enos said. "I own land in New Brunswick that is being cleared for farmland. It is a two-day walk from Saint John. There is work there for a man and a simple cabin for his family. If you agree to work there for two years, I will provide an advance on your wages. Of course, this agreement must be in writing to make sure we both understand what has been agreed to."

Two years, and far outside of town. John wondered how his family could live there. But he was desperate to raise the money, and this was one way to do it. He agreed to come to the man's office the next day to sign the papers.

Eden was relieved when John reached home that night. "I worry about you, John, for I know how anxious you are about this trip," she said. "I worry also, but for a different reason. I fear the work will be so hard that you will lose your dreams of how our life can be. I have few dreams myself, only a desire to find a safe place for you and me to raise our children. If it means living in a cabin in a lumber camp, so be it. We will find a way."

After John signed the paperwork the next day, Enos advanced the rest of the money to pay for the family's passage on the *Alchymist*, which was scheduled to sail from Falmouth in late July. He also gave John a draft to purchase food and other goods at the store Enos owned in Falmouth. It was not a large amount, so the food would be plain, but it was enough to sustain the family during the long voyage. John built two storage boxes, into which they packed their belongings. It wasn't much, only clothes, blankets, food, and cooking equipment, along with a few tools. Anything else they would need to buy in Saint John.

Eden had been warned about how poor the accommodations would be aboard the *Alchymist*. Still, she was dismayed when she saw where they would live during the voyage. The hold had a low ceiling, barely tall enough for John to stand upright. He and Eden both had to bend down when they passed beneath the beams that held up the deck. There was a wooden shelf to serve as their bed, with a space underneath for their possessions. There was no privacy from the areas allotted to other families. Most of the cargo hold was filled with kegs and barrels, so the space left for passengers was cramped. A small iron stove sat on a brick platform in one corner. Sanitary facilities were a chamber pot curtained off in another corner. The pot would have to be carried up the ladder each day and dumped over the side of the boat. Access to the space was a ladder from the deck above, and the hatch cover would be secured at night and during bad weather. Open flames were strictly prohibited, and only two small tin candle lanterns were allowed. These provided faint light.

Eden hid her disappointment and turned to the children. "We are going to have an exciting adventure!" she said. "This will be our home while we are aboard the ship. Other children will be here, so you will have someone to play with."

The hold filled up as other families descended the ladder and surveyed the dingy area that would be their home for the next six weeks or longer. A farm family from Mylor, James and Grace Gapes, with five children, arrived and moved into their space. They had sold their farm outside Falmouth to pay for the trip, and James hoped they could start again on new land in one of the river valleys. "The soil there has never been worked," he said. "If we can afford enough acres, we can lead a good life." A tin miner from Perran, William Sarah, came with his wife and three children. He described what brought them to the ship. "The mine was played out," he said. "Only a few men are still working, and their pay is based upon the weight of ore they dig daily. There is no money in that. I thought New Brunswick could not be any worse. The forests there are said to be enormous, and I can swing an ax as well as a pick."

One more family arrived, that of Thomas Randall, his wife, Mary, and two children, from Truro, where he had worked as a printer. Other passengers included a married woman, Mary Lewis, and her young son. She was traveling to meet her husband, who had gone to New Brunswick on the *Alchymist* earlier in the year and now had a steady position. Also aboard was a blacksmith, George Martin, who had buried his young wife and stillborn child only two months earlier, and was looking to make a new start in the provinces. There was a boy of sixteen, Andrew Tong, whose mother had died two years ago. His father was a mariner and seldom came home, and the boy could not find steady work in Falmouth.

All in all, the passengers looked like a group who could get along for the duration of the voyage. Each household settled in at their assigned place. The women looked at each other and approved of what they saw, although they were not yet on speaking terms. All were on the ship for the same reason. They were leaving their homes and the lives they knew and going to a strange place to start a new life.

When the ship was ready to sail, the passengers were ordered to stay below deck until it was underway. They heard yelling and footsteps on the deck above, and finally the ship eased away from the dock. Johnie wanted to go up on deck to see what was happening, but John held the boy back. A short while later, the mate came to the top of the ladder and shouted down that passengers could go on deck if they wanted to get a last look at Falmouth. John told Mary and Johnie they must hold onto his hand while they were on deck. They stood at the rail and looked out at the land they were leaving.

The ship passed out of Falmouth Bay and started to toss in the waves of the channel. Gradually, Pendennis Castle shrank until it was only a dot on the shore. As the ship reached open water, the pitching and rolling increased. John was used to this motion from the years he spent with his father while the man was fishing, but it was new to the children. First one, then the other showed signs of distress. Johnie turned to his father, "Daddy, make it stop!" he said, while Mary merely said, "I don't feel so good." John knew there was little he could do to make the children feel better, so he led them down the ladder to the cargo hold where the passengers lived. Most of them were seasick. Some had vomited while others lay groaning in their beds. John turned to their alcove. Eden lay on the wooden shelf, which was softened slightly by a blanket. Her eyes were closed, and she moaned gently. Hearing him come near, she whispered, "John, please take the baby. I cannot manage these sick feelings and take care of him also."

Little Joseph lay beside his mother with his eyes wide open. He smiled at the sight of his father and cooed when he was picked up. John told the two older children to lie on the blanket beside their mother and assured them the queasy feeling would pass. They were unhappy that he did not make them feel better right away, but they climbed onto the shelf and lay down.

Eden lay on the bed and suffered for the next two days, only taking the baby when it was time for him to breastfeed. Mary and Johnie were miserable for a day, but on the second day, they were up and running about. The seas outside remained rough, so John did not allow them to climb the ladder to the deck. Little Joseph remained calm and happy. He seemed to enjoy being held by his father and was not affected by the pitching and rolling of the ship. John looked down at him with some wonder and thought perhaps the motion reminded him of the months he spent in his mother's womb not so long ago.

Most of the passengers were seasick, and the few who felt better cared for those who were miserable. The children were less affected than the adults, and by the second day, they ran around and played hide-and-seek among the barrels and crates. John heated broth on the stove, and Eden drank a little, but she could not eat anything. He made porridge on the morning of the second day, and Mary and Johnie each had a bowlful. When Johnie finished eating, he looked at his father and asked, "Are we almost there? John could not bring himself to tell his four year old son that the voyage had just begun and would last many weeks. He smiled at Johnie and said, "We are getting there, but it will take time."

By the third day, most of the passengers had grown used to the motion of the ship. Still a little shaky, Eden stood up and smiled weakly.

"I can take the baby for a while, John," she said. Somewhat reluctantly, he passed Joseph over to her. Over the two days he had held the baby, John had become used to his warmth and the gentle noises that stopped only when the baby fell asleep in his father's arms.

A pattern developed that would last for the rest of the trip. The women became acquainted, worked out a schedule for using the little stove, and commiserated about the small amount of fresh water they were allowed to use each day. The men shared stories and talked about what they hoped to find in New Brunswick. Smoking was forbidden below deck, and several times each day the men climbed the ladder and smoked their pipes while looking out at the sea. All they saw was water with endless swells on all sides. The wind continued to blow from the south, and the ship made slow but steady progress each day.

Two weeks passed, and each day was much like the one before. Then John woke one morning to an odd feeling. He felt no motion; the ship was still. Curious, he climbed up to the deck. The sails hung limp on the yards as there was no breeze. The ocean was flat like a lake with only slight swells. The sun was just above the horizon, and the shadow of the ship stretched far across the water. It was peaceful. John returned to the hold and woke Eden. "Come up to the deck. It is very quiet," he whispered.

Eden rose and followed him, leaving the little ones sleeping. They stood at the rail and looked out at the sea. John put his arm around Eden, and she rested her head against him.

She spoke softly. "John, are we making the right choice, taking this voyage?"

He thought for a minute before he answered. "It may be years before we know the answer. Life will be hard at first, but we will make a home for our children."

"John, I am scared of the difficulties that lie ahead of us."

"I am scared also, but we will face each problem one at a time, and we will do it together."

They stood at the rail for a little while, holding each other and looking out at the sea. "We had better go down," she said finally. "The children will soon wake up and need our attention." The ship sat becalmed for two days. When the wind returned in the middle of the night, it blew out of the west and pushed the ship back toward England. John heard a commotion on the deck and the stamping of men's feet above his head as the sailors toiled. The next morning, he saw what had been done. The ship had altered course and was sailing north. He asked one of the sailors the reason for the course change.

"The captain wants to use this westerly wind to push us north, where the currents are more favorable. The sea is full of ice up there, and we will have to keep a sharp lookout."

For several days, the ship sailed north, and the air grew colder each day. The sails were reefed at night, and the ship only crept slowly through the water in the darkness. A few days later, John rose in the early morning and went on deck. All around the ship were icebergs, some small and flat, others tall and with odd shapes. The ice extended deep into the water. The ship moved slowly, threading its way through the icefield. John brought Mary and Johnie onto the deck. He tried to persuade Eden to come up to see the icebergs, but she shuddered at his description. "It is cold enough here already," she said. "I don't need to go on deck and get colder."

Sometimes, the ship brushed against small pieces of pancake ice and pushed them aside, but it stayed far away from the larger icebergs. It was not until several more days had passed that open water appeared ahead and the ice was left behind. The wind shifted to the east, once again driving the ship toward its destination.

Days passed uneventfully. One evening, the sun shone red at dusk. John saw the sailors checking the lines to make sure everything was secure. He asked one of them why, and the man replied, "The captain expects a storm during the night. Tie off your belongings. It may get very rough." John passed this along to the other families, and they secured their loose items and cases. Shortly after dark, the wind rose to gale force, pitching and rocking the ship violently in the rough water. Waves covered the deck, and water poured in through the cracks around the hatch cover. The sound of the wind was a high-pitched whine as it passed through the rigging amid great crashes of thunder. John feared that the ship might break apart.

In the middle of the storm, the hatch opened and the mate descended the ladder. He spoke to the group: "I need men to man the pump. The sailors are repairing sails and rigging and cannot be spared. Some of the seams in the hull have opened up, and the ship is taking on water." John and the other men followed the mate into the lower hold. It was dark, with only a candle lantern to show the way. The mate led the group to the pump, which reached down into the bilge of the ship and had a long crank protruding from one side. The mate pointed to the shaft. "Four men are needed to turn this crank to run the pump. It can pump one hundred gallons each minute, although if you can pump even half that much, it may be enough to keep up with the water coming in through the open seams. Don't try to turn it fast, for you will wear out quickly. Establish a steady pace. I will send men to help if the wind lets up."

John and three other men took hold of the crank and began to push and pull it around. It took a tremendous effort, and John knew they would tire soon. The violent rocking of the ship made it difficult for the men to keep their balance and also turn the crank. The work was exciting at first, then it became tedious and repetitive. Fatigue set in. First one man, then a second, had to step away from the crank and drop to the deck, exhausted. The two other men took their places. John was in good shape from all the rowing he had done, and he kept on working alongside the blacksmith, George Martin, who was a heavy-set man with muscular arms. Eventually, even they both tired and had to stop. Their places were taken by the two men who had sat down earlier. John saw they would not last long at the crank. He was about to climb up the ladder to ask the

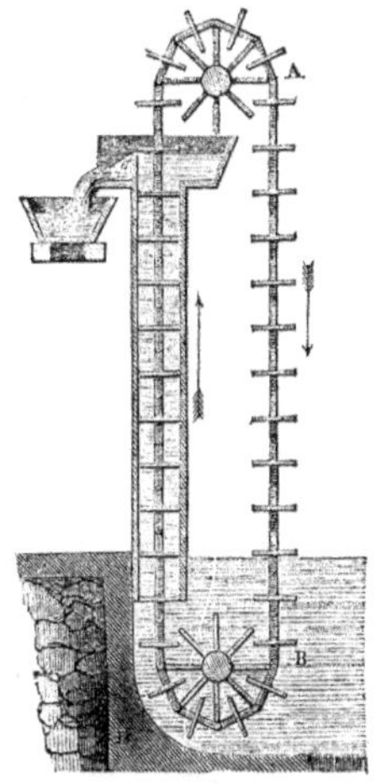

A chain pump[7]

mate to send more men to help when he heard footsteps, and Eden led three women into the hold. John looked at her with surprise.

"What are you doing here?" he asked.

"We decided if our husbands are pumping to save the ship, we should help."

"But what about the children?"

"Grace Gapes is looking after them," Eden answered. "She has five children already, and she said a few more would be no problem."

The women joined in to help at the pump two at a time, working with two men. This kept the pump turning constantly, and the hours went by. It was tiresome work, but all of them were desperate. From time to time, one of the women climbed the ladder to check on the children and reported they were sleeping. Morning came, but it remained dark in the lower hold. One of the older children brought a message that food was ready. The men and women took turns going up the ladder to eat, then returned to continue working. As the day passed, the motion of the ship grew less violent. It was evening when the mate descended the ladder, accompanied by four sailors. He was surprised when he saw women working at the pump alongside the men, but he spoke up. "The storm has passed, and the ship is not taking in as much water as before. "My men can take over the pumping.

Thank you for your efforts. You have helped to keep this ship afloat."

The passengers gratefully gave up their places to the sailors. Exhausted, they climbed up the ladder and returned to the upper hold to rest. John looked at Eden with admiration. She had taken her turn at the pump crank throughout the night and day, and never complained. They reached their bed and quickly fell asleep.

Two more weeks passed without a major problem. The wind blew and the ship rocked in the waves, but it continued to sail west. The passengers took turns at the cooking, and they watched each other's children. They talked about what they would do when they reached New Brunswick. Each man had worked at a trade in Cornwall, but only the farmer thought he would do the same work in the new land. The rest of the men expected to work clearing stumps, or logging, or perhaps hiring out to a farmer. None of them expected life would be easy, but there was a chance they would obtain land of their own. John listened to the talk and told his story, his agreement to work for two years in return for the advance on his wages to help pay for his family's passage on the ship. The men agreed to keep in touch if possible, and to let each other know if they heard of possibilities of obtaining land.

It was a clear morning in late August when excited voices were heard on deck. John climbed the ladder to find out what was going on. Off to the west, a low black coastline could be seen.

"That there is Nova Scotia," said one of the sailors. "We will follow that land south until we reach the Bay of Fundy."

The ship sailed southwest that day and the next. The land remained a distant line on the horizon. Flocks of birds flew overhead, sometimes carrying small fish in their beaks as they returned to the shore. Whales spouted in the sea between the ship and the coast. John took each of his children onto the deck to show them the land. He even took little Joseph into the fresh air and stood at the rail, talking with the baby as he held him in his arms.

"You won't remember this day when you are older, but we will remind you that you first saw the New World today. You will spend the rest of your life here, and you can tell your children you crossed the ocean when you were a baby." Little Joseph looked at his father and smiled.

The ship gradually turned to the west, then to the northwest, and finally due north as it rounded the southern tip of Nova Scotia and began crossing the Bay of Fundy to Saint John. On the last full day of the voyage, the passengers knelt and prayed together, giving thanks to God that they had crossed the ocean and were about to arrive safely in their new home. John read from the old Bible his mother had given him, a familiar passage in English, translated from the handwritten Latin script in which the book was written. He looked around at the others and thought to himself: we might never see each other again, but I will always remember them.

The journey was nearly ended, and John grew anxious about what would happen next in their lives. Had he made a huge mistake, bringing his family to this forested wilderness, leaving behind the well-ordered fields and towns of Cornwall? Should he have stayed in Falmouth, persevered with the pilotage, and tried to get on steady at the shipyard? How would he raise his family in this raw land? He had heard stories of bears and mountain lions that lived in the forests, creatures unknown in Cornwall, but familiar sights in the forests of New Brunswick. Would there be a way to teach his children? Eden could not read or write her name when they met, and she had learned her letters in the years since as her children learned. Still, her knowledge of the world was narrow. She had never traveled far from her home in St. Just. John felt that the next few years, maybe many years, would be hard ones. The ship voyage, despite the dangers and discomfort, would be remembered as a safe interlude before the uncertain times that followed. He was protective of Eden and the children, the little ones who woke up each day with such curiosity about the world around them. Yesterday, his four-year-old son stood on the deck beside him and looked out at the ocean. Dolphins were swimming alongside the ship, and they leaped out of the water as they swam. Johnie watched them for a while, then he turned to his father and asked, "Daddy, why do fish live in water?"

John had no answer to that question, but finally said, "The sea is where they were born, and they stay there because they have learned to swim so well." This did not seem like a complete answer, but it must have been enough, because Johnie nodded his head and continued to watch as the dolphins flashed into the air and splashed back into the black water of the Bay of Fundy.

That night, lying on the bed in the darkness, John's mind raced ahead. The ship would reach Saint John tomorrow, and the next part of their life would begin. He pulled the blanket close around him. He heard soft breathing from Eden, who lay with the baby held close to her body and the two older children next to her. John could feel the warmth radiating off their small shapes. He rested his hand gently on the shoulder of his son, who slept peacefully. John could feel the boy's heartbeat through his fingers. Maybe, he thought, despite his fears, if his wife and children could sleep calmly on this night, then possibly everything would be all right, and perhaps tomorrow will be just another day.

Epilogue

The life of a new immigrant is filled with hope for the future, but lived within the harsh realities of the present. The written record of John and Eden's life in New Brunswick is bookended by the ship's manifest in 1833 and a two-line obituary in the *Saint John Morning News* in 1867. The obituary reads simply:

> d. Sunday 14th inst., Stanley (York Co.) John SCOBORIA, age 67, left widow. The deceased came to (St. John) city from West of England, many years member of the Methodist Church.[8]

John died in a community named Williamsburg in York County, a wilderness area in Central New Brunswick first settled in 1861. How the family arrived there is not clear, but the lack of other documentation tells a great deal. Much as the modern homeless go uncounted in the federal census, the newly arrived, impoverished and landless immigrants of the nineteenth century often fell through the cracks of history. They survived, raised their families, and in some cases eventually reached a level of stability and safety, but it took many years of living in temporary homes, lumber camps, and backwaters.

John and Eden Scoboria made a permanent home in Williamsburg, New Brunswick, thirty years after landing at Saint John. One hundred and seventy years later, Williamsburg is little more than a wide spot in the road, a church, and a scattering of houses along a highway. What land was cleared has mostly reverted to forest. After John died in 1867, his family left Williamsburg and moved to the United States. It was left to his children and grandchildren to reach a more established level of society.

CHAPTER SIX

Finishing the Brass

Joseph Scoboria, 1876

Margaret Scoboria, 1876[9]

Joseph Scoboria, 1832–1905

December 15, 1876

Somerville, Massachusetts, Near Boston

Joseph woke in darkness and lay silently as his thoughts gradually cleared. He had been dreaming, but the substance of the dream was drifting away. It had been about his father, dead these past nine years, but often in his son's thoughts. Joseph's mother, Eden, lived on, a tiny old lady cared for by one of Joseph's sisters at her home in New Hampshire. Eden had always been calm and composed, protective of her children and watchful for anything that might be a danger to them. She made sure they were fed and clothed, bathed at least once a week, and warm at night. In the lumber camp where the family lived when they first arrived in New Brunswick, their home was little more than a shack, and icy winter winds seeped through cracks between the boards. Joseph shared a bed with his older brother and sister. On cold nights, their mother piled her winter coat on top of their blankets for extra warmth. Joseph remembered how heavy were the blankets with the coat piled on top. He had tucked down into the covers with only his nose and forehead exposed to the frigid night air. One night, he dreamed he was falling and woke suddenly to find himself shivering on the floor beside the bed.

Eden had moved with the rest of the family from New Brunswick to New England after her husband John died, worn out by the years of hard work trying to make their homestead farm a success. She missed him and told stories about him to her grandchildren. She recounted how they had lived in Falmouth at the southern tip of Cornwall in southwest England and had met one night when John had rowed her father home across Falmouth Bay after the old man had too much to drink. Years later, they crossed the Atlantic Ocean on a sailing ship with their three children. Both of them had hopes of what they would find in New Brunswick. Joseph did not remember the trip, for he was only a baby at the time, but his father said that he was never seasick and seemed to enjoy the rocking of the ship.

Joseph's first memories were of the logging camp where the family lived during their early years in New Brunswick. His father had signed an agreement with a wealthy landowner to work for two years at the camp in exchange for an advance on his wages to help pay for the trip. The two years had turned into half a dozen. During that time, the family lived in a primitive shack while John worked cutting timber and clearing land to prepare it for farming. There was no school for the children to attend, but Joseph's father read to his family from the Bible on Sunday, and Eden showed the children how to make letters using a lump of charcoal on a flat piece of wood. Life in the camp was simple, their food mostly potatoes, along with greens from the kitchen garden and berries harvested from wild vines. Water came from a pump on the other side of the camp. Joseph remembered walking there and back with his mother. He carried a small bucket full of water, while she carried two large ones. His mother always praised him when they reached the cabin and thanked him for his help.

Joseph and his brother John and sister Mary, and later his brother Peter, born a few months after they reached New Brunswick, spent the summers playing in the dirt outside the shack, making brush forts in the woods, and floating sticks down the nearby creek. Eden insisted that a child never go into the woods or down to the creek all by themselves. Their father, John, went off to work before they rose in the morning and returned after dark, tired and soiled from the day's toil. After washing his hands and face in a basin of water, he sat down with Eden and they talked for a while. The children were expected to be quiet during this time. Sometimes, Joseph's older sister Mary read aloud softly to them while the younger children clustered around her on the floor.

Fully awake, Joseph slipped out from under the covers and tucked them back snugly around his wife Margaret. She stirred in her sleep and murmured softly. Always a restless sleeper, she was troubled by memories she would not disclose. Joseph had learned it was best to listen when she wanted to talk and accept the days when she remained silent.

Wrapping his robe around him, Joseph felt for his slippers on the floor beside the bed and slipped his feet into them. He padded softly to the bedroom door, passed through, and pulled it shut behind him. The match safe sat on a shelf near the door. He withdrew a match, struck it on the rough side of the stove, and lifted the glass chimney of the kerosene lamp. He lit the lamp and replaced the chimney, adjusting the wick to burn with a bright light. Carrying the lamp into the parlor, he glanced at the mantel clock. A few minutes before five o'clock. Joseph was used to rising before light, but it never ceased to amaze him that he woke at nearly the same time each morning.

He dressed quietly in the cold parlor. Chores awaited. He stirred the embers in the stove and added a shovelful of coal, then adjusted the damper for better draft. The embers glowed, and the coal began to burn. Joseph warmed his hands against the cast iron sides of the stove. In a few minutes, he could heat water for his tea. At the back door of the house, Joseph put on a hat and coat before stepping outside. The night was clear, the temperature below freezing, and the tang of coal smoke filled the air. Above his head, the constellations were clearly visible, Orion high in the sky. In the more established neighborhoods of Somerville, gas streetlights reduced the view of the stars, but in this area of modest homes along New Walnut Street, the streets were dark.

Joseph liked this time of day, the darkness and the silence. The glow of a lamp could be seen from inside a nearby house, but most dwellings were still dark. He visited the outhouse, noticing it would soon be time to dig a new hole and move the structure again. The houses on New Walnut Street were built on top of a low area near the river, a marsh that had been covered with construction spoils. An outhouse hole could only be dug two feet deep before it filled with water. The outhouse had to be moved every year. Joseph hoped this chore could wait until the ground thawed in April.

Back in the house, the stove was hot. Joseph drew water from the barrel in the kitchen and filled the teakettle. He opened the breadbox. Two loaves lay inside; one partially used. He cut two thick slices for his lunch and wrapped them in brown paper. A slab of cheese cut from the block would complete the midday meal. He wrapped it and placed both packets in the tin lunch box. In a few minutes, the water for tea was hot, so Joseph added loose tea to the kettle and let it steep for a few minutes, then filled the tin thermos, snugging in the cork stopper and wrapping the thermos with a rag to help retain the heat for a little while. He poured a mug of tea, added sugar, and sat at the table. There was time to start a letter to his mother before he left for work.

Joseph tried to write regularly, for he knew his mother was lonely and still grieved for her husband. They had been a good couple, devoted to each other throughout their married life despite the many hardships the family had faced. Joseph had heard stories of the ocean crossing, about icebergs and fierce storms, and the great relief they felt when the coast of Nova Scotia was seen. But that was only the beginning of years of struggle in the new land. Joseph remembered his father returning from work after dark, his clothes soiled and often wet. The family lived in a drafty shack with only two rooms and a rough wood floor. Joseph watched his mother mix flour and water into a paste, soak pages of newspaper, then spread the pages on the walls to help seal the cracks between the boards. Joseph learned to read by following the newspaper articles plastered on the walls. It was frustrating to begin an article, learn that it was continued on the next page, and the page could not be found.

As the years passed, he saw his older brother leave for work in the morning with his father, and Joseph knew his time would come soon. Maybe his work would be leading the draft horses that dragged logs out of the forest, or maybe it would be piling brush that the men cut from the downed trees. Joseph remember how the piles were burned to help clear the land, but filled the air with smoke. Sometimes, the smoke drifted into the camp and made it hard to breathe. When it was time for him to start working in the woods, his mother took him aside and told him, "This will be hard for you, Joseph, but remember, it is not forever. There is a better life for you than working in a logging camp. When you have a family of your own, you can make a good life for them."

Joseph's father hoped for many years that things would go better for the family. After twenty-five years of laboring for others, the family secured a grant of raw land in a new development in the middle of the New Brunswick colony. Williamsburg, the town was to be named. They traveled there by horse and wagon, cleared a small area of forest, and built a log house. But the land was a disappointment. The soil was shallow and poor, and their garden yielded little. The forest stretched around them on all sides, but it was miles to the nearest mill, and the logs they cut down could only be burned. After a few years, Joseph's younger brother, Peter, left the farm and traveled to Australia to try his luck in the gold fields. When that failed, he returned to the United States and settled in Somerville, a town on the edge of Boston. He wrote that there was plenty of work there, and life was good.

While the family wandered through New Brunswick, for one year they lived in a logging camp near the head of the Bay of Fundy. Joseph was in his early twenties then, doing a man's job but still living with his family. In another shack in the camp was a family with three daughters. Joseph became friends with them, and after a year proposed marriage to the middle daughter. She accepted, and their lives seemed secure when first one son, then a second, was born. The older boy was named Joseph Lower, taking Joseph's name and his mother's maiden name. The younger boy was named Charles after his wife's father. Joseph did not want to raise his sons in a logging camp, so he moved the family to Saint John, rented a house, and took a job at a factory.

A few years later, a smallpox epidemic swept through the city, and Joseph's wife became infected and died. The boys were safe, but Joseph could not raise them alone. He returned to his family and left the boys with their grandparents while he grieved the loss of his wife. Several years went by, years when he didn't know what to do. He traveled to Fredericton, the capital of New Brunswick, and took a job at a brass smelter. The work was hard and dangerous, but Joseph enjoyed creating the brass ingots. There were other positions he could do at the smelter, and over time he worked as a molder and a machinist, turning out milled brass parts, then learned the art of polishing and finishing brass.

Joseph met Margaret at the wedding of his younger brother. She was the bride's sister but was not included among the wedding party. Instead, she sat quietly in a corner during the reception. Joseph introduced himself to her and asked if she would dance with him. She demurred silently, so he asked if it would be all right if he sat at the table and kept her company. She nodded, and they watched as other couples whirled around the floor. Joseph learned from his brother that she was a widow. Her husband had been killed a year earlier in an accident at work, and she had returned home to live with her parents.

A few months after the wedding, he wrote to her, told her about his two young sons, and asked if he might call upon her. She replied in a short letter that it would be better if he waited until spring. Joseph visited her for a year. Sometimes, she did not want to see anyone and stayed in her room, so Joseph sat and talked with her father and mother. Gradually, she became comfortable with his visits and came into the parlor while he was there. Often, she said very little and sat silently while the others talked. During the summer months, she sat with Joseph on the porch and occasionally laughed. But as the winter months approached, she became more guarded, and her eyes had a distant look.

When Joseph's older son turned eight years old, Joseph asked Margaret to marry him. "We have both lost our partners," he said, "and we are both alone. Let us spend our lives together."

Margaret looked at him for a long moment before she answered, "I don't know if I can be a good wife to you. I don't want to have children of my own. The dark winter months each year are difficult for me. I could not care for little ones also. But if you accept me as I am, I will marry you, and I will be what help I can be to raise your boys. They should live with their father."

Joseph and Margaret married in August of 1863, at the time of year when she was the most cheerful. Joseph's parents came from the homestead in Williamsburg and brought the two boys with them. The wedding took place at the Methodist Church in Fredericton. This pleased Joseph's father, who had become a devout Methodist during the years in New Brunswick. John Scoboria looked tired, and his wife, Eden, told Joseph she worried about her husband's health. "He feels the cold much more than when he was a young man, and it is always cold at the homestead."

Joseph had news for his parents. "Margaret and I will move to Boston," he told them. "Peter has done well there, and he says there is plenty of work. I want my sons to have a good education, and they will get that in Boston."

Joseph's father shook his head but said nothing. Eden spoke up, saying, "Your father and I left Cornwall to seek a better life on this side of the ocean, although it has not turned out as well as we hoped. If you feel that your sons will have a better life in the United States, then it makes sense for you to go there. The Civil War is nearly over, and the Union is winning. It would be wise to move to Boston while there are plenty of jobs."

The family left Fredericton and traveled to Saint John, where they boarded a steamer that took them down the coast to Boston. They brought with them little more than their clothes and a few other possessions. Joseph's father gave them the old leather-bound Bible that had been passed down through his family. The ink had faded on some of the pages, and the leather was cracked, but Joseph remembered how his father read passages from it to the family when Joseph was small. He carefully wrapped oiled paper around the book to protect it on the sea voyage to Boston.

Boston was a bustling city, much larger than Fredericton or Saint John. The family rented furnished rooms in Somerville, on the west side of Boston, and Joseph found a job at a brass smelter not far from their rooms. The boys were enrolled in school, and after some initial awkwardness because of their Canadian accents, they prospered and did well. Even Margaret seemed to flourish in the new environment.

There were many women's organizations in Boston, and she became a member of several clubs. The winter was still very difficult for her, but the regular schedule of caring for her husband and the boys kept her life busy. Margaret was as good as her word. She looked after the boys as if they were her own sons, dried their tears when they were hurt, patched their clothes, and lengthened the hems on their trousers as they grew taller. There was always a hot meal on the table at supper time. But Joseph knew that during the hours when the boys were at school, she often went back to bed and stayed there until the boys were due home in the afternoon.

A few years later, Joseph learned that new houses were being constructed near the river on land built up over a marsh that had been filled in. The houses were small, and no city utilities would be installed until years later, but the family would have a home of their own. Joseph rented one of the homes, and the family moved. He walked to the smelter where he worked, and the boys took the horse-drawn streetcar to school.

The years passed quickly. Joseph thought back to the time when they arrived in Boston and the boys were small. Now, they were young men. Joseph Lower, the older boy, attended Tufts College, lived at home, and took the streetcar to the college each day. He was studying divinity and planned to become a Unitarian minister. It was hard for Joseph to understand this choice, for he and Margaret only infrequently attended church. But when the boys lived with their grandparents, Joseph's father read the Bible to them every night. The younger boy, Charles, was more outgoing than his older brother and always ready to take part in games with boys who lived nearby. Joseph was determined that both boys attend college, so he worked extra hours and took extra shifts whenever they were available. He changed jobs a few times over the years but remained a brass finisher. He had learned all the methods of polishing and antiquing, and he could complete complicated brass finishing projects like the bas-relief memorials of Civil War battles that were popular orders in those days.

Despite having a steady job, Joseph was always looking for a better work situation. One day, he heard of an opening at the Nathaniel Tufts Meter Works, which made and distributed gas meters. Joseph thought it a bit ironic that he might work at a factory that made gas meters when his own house was not piped for gas. But he applied for a job and was accepted at a good rate of pay. The factory was near downtown Boston, farther from home than his current job, but a streetcar stopped near the factory gate. It would take nearly an hour to get to work in the morning. He left his old position and began working at the gas meter factory.

Joseph awoke from his reveries and looked down at the letter he had begun to write. There were only a few lines on the page, and he would have to finish it in the evening. The time was 5:45 a.m., a few minutes before he had to leave. He rose from the table, added more coal to the firebox of the stove, and adjusted the damper so the fire would burn slowly until Margaret rose at seven. Wrapping a scarf around his neck, he put on his hat and coat, picked up the tin lunch box, and left the house.

It was still dark outside, and Joseph carefully descended the wooden front steps and walked out to the street. There were no streetlights in this neighborhood, and he walked slowly along the edge of the graveled street, feeling with his feet for the transition between the street and the dirt at the edge of the road. A faint light shone from the front windows of some of the houses he passed. In the distance, a gas streetlight could be seen on Broadway, where New Walnut met the larger street. The houses he passed were like his own, unpainted boxes with dirt front yards and outhouses in the back. He read in the Somerville newspaper that the city had plans to run water and gas lines to this area. Until then, the residents had to use kerosene lamps and haul their own water.

Joseph reached Broadway and crossed the street. It was ten more blocks to Melrose Street, where he would catch the streetcar. The houses on the south side of Broadway were older and larger than the ones in his neighborhood. They were two stories tall, painted, and the steady light from the windows confirmed that gas was piped to each one. He thought back to the shacks where his family had lived in the logging camps of New Brunswick. In the evening, the only illumination was from a candle, and the flickering light reflected off the pages of the book he was reading as he puzzled out the unfamiliar words. His mother sat beside him, quietly knitting, ready to help if a word stumped him. The old Bible was written in longhand script, and sometimes the shapes of the letters confused him. The pages were dog-eared, and the binding was cracked and darkened, but the book held together. His father told him solemnly that he must read every page before he could go on to one of the other books on the shelf. As he sat and read, his mother sitting beside him, they waited for his father to return home.

On winter days, darkness fell early, and the men worked by torch-light for several hours. When his father entered the shack, often wet and muddy from a long day in the woods, his mother put aside her knitting and rose to pour her husband a cup of tea sweetened with sugar. She added milk if there was any in the house. John Scoboria silently rested at the rough table for a while, his hands cupped around the warm mug. Then he talked with Eden, told her some of the events of the day at work, and asked about the children. During the week, Joseph's father was too tired to sit with his children at night. Instead, he went to bed shortly after eating dinner to be ready for an early start the next day. Only on Sunday was there time to sit together, read the Bible aloud, and occasionally play a game with his family.

Joseph reached an area where a ditch had been dug in the center of the street. City workers were installing a sewer line with connections for side sewers extending to each house. Joseph thought what a pleasure it would be to have running water and a bathroom inside the house. He hurried on and reached Melrose Street, crossed over, and stood at the corner. A streetcar could be seen approaching in the distance, stopping every block to pick up passengers. Joseph could hear the clopping of the horse's hoofs on the cobblestones. The car neared him, and the operator pulled back on the reins to halt the horses. Joseph climbed up the steps, deposited six cents in the fare box, walked to the rear of the car and stood, holding onto one of the vertical posts. The operator flicked the reins and spoke to the horses, who surged forward. The car slowly made its way down the street which curved around the base of Prospect Hill. It was a mile to the corner outside the building that housed the meter works. As Joseph stood in the car, he thought about the day ahead. The steam engine would be running when he arrived at the door to the factory, although the belts that drove the equipment would not be engaged until work started at seven o'clock. For the next ten hours, the constant roar of the spinning pulleys and the scream of the belts, mixed with the pounding of the engine, would make it impossible to talk during the workday. Foremen communicated with the workers with a series of hand signals.

The streetcar stopped at the corner near the factory. As Joseph left the car, he could hear the throbbing roar of the steam engine inside the building. It had been left to idle during the night, but early in the morning the firebox had been stoked with fresh coal. Now the engine was up to full power and ready for the start of the workday.

The meter factory occupied a four-story brick complex. The ground floor housed the steam engine and the casting house, where workers melted steel and brass ingots and cast them into meter housings and other parts. At one end of the floor were the stamping machines, which pressed flat sheet metal into the convoluted shapes needed for the different types of meters. All day long, the repetitive thudding of the stamping machines shook the building. As Joseph climbed up the stairs, the pounding of the steam engine reverberated off the brick walls of the stairway.

The second floor of the factory was a wide-open room. A drive shaft spanned the length of the room, suspended from the ceiling. Attached to it were pulleys spaced a few feet apart. The drive line was connected to the main shaft of the steam engine with a heavy, flat belt. At precisely 7 a.m., the belt engaged the shaft, and power was transmitted to the machines standing in long rows on the floor, each connected to the drive line with a flat belt.  When the drive line and belts were all turning, the noise on the floor was deafening. The employees stood at their workstations, each operating a lathe or drill press, turning out the cogs and gears that made up the moving parts of the gas meters.

At the far end of the room were rows of workstations, each equipped with a grinding wheel and sanding disk. This is where Joseph worked for the first six months after he started at the factory. Rough parts were delivered from the casting house and stocked in large bins. All day, he and the other men took parts from the bins, ground off the casting stubs, and sanded the parts smooth, then placed them in a bin of finished parts. The work was monotonous and demanding. Each piece had to be examined closely for defects. During the winter months, the gas lights that hung over the factory floor provided only minimal light, so Joseph used his fingers to find any rough or malformed places on the castings. He had to bend over to see the parts clearly. By the end of the day, his eyes were tired from the strain. The belts never stopped, and the men ate their lunches sitting in front of the whirring machines. Dust and chips from the grinding filled the air, so most of the men wore handkerchiefs over their noses to filter out some of the flying debris.

After six months, a job opened in the finishing department. Joseph had been hired because of his brass finishing experience, so he took the job and moved to the third floor, where the finishing department was located near the room where the meters were assembled and tested.

The finishing department included one room used for spray-painting the steel meter housings. In another, the brass nameplates were engraved with identification numbers then installed onto the painted meter housings. Nearby was a room containing the liquid-filled vats used to finish the brass parts and keep them from tarnishing. This was Joseph's domain. The work was similar to what he had done at other brass finishing plants. Most of the time, the work was routine. He engraved the nameplates, then cleaned and lacquered them to prevent tarnishing. Occasionally, a special order required him to do more complex work.

A mansion had recently been built on Beacon Hill in Boston. The owner's name was Robert Greene, and as part of the home's design, all of the exterior metal railings, door hinges, locks, and other metal parts were to have a distinctive green bronzed finish. This included the gas meter, pipe, and fittings that would be visible on the outside of the house. Greene hired the factory where Joseph worked to provide these special pieces. The project started in the casting house, where workers poured molten brass into molds to make the two halves of the meter housing. After cooling, the parts were sent to the second floor, where the brass stubs from casting and the rough edges were ground off, and the housing halves were lightly sanded. Next they went along with brass pipe and fittings to the third floor, where it was Joseph's job to give everything a finished appearance.

First, he immersed the housing, pipe, and fittings for two hours in a pickling bath composed of nitric acid and oil of vitriol, heated to boiling. It was crucial not to disturb the surface of the bath, as it would release caustic fumes. If any of the liquid splashed onto his clothes, it would burn holes in the fabric and the skin underneath. Joseph opened the windows of the room to help with ventilation, and he tied his handkerchief around his face to filter out some of the acid fumes. Next, he carefully hung the parts in the acid bath.

After the parts had spent two hours in the pickling bath, Joseph removed them, handling them carefully with brass pliers. He placed the parts into a cold-water bath, then rinsed them carefully in boiling water. Joseph was careful not to touch any of the parts with his fingers. Next came the burnishing, the careful rubbing of every surface with chamois leather and a polishing compound, until all the surfaces achieved a uniform high level of gloss. This was the most delicate part of the operation because all surfaces had to be buffed to the same level of finish, or they would not stain uniformly. Joseph was scarcely conscious of the passage of time while he worked. When noon came, Joseph stayed at his station and picked up his lunchbox. He ate the bread and cheese, washing it down with cold tea.

After lunch, he continued the burnishing. When Joseph was satisfied that all faces and parts had been equally buffed, he carefully rinsed each item in cold water, then in boiling water, laying them aside to await the stain and lacquer.

Joseph had to complete the final finishing immediately after burnishing, or the surfaces would quickly tarnish. The bronzing process required that each part be dipped into a bath composed of nitric acid saturated with copper, then heated until the metal turned to the desired shade of green. Then they were placed on a lacquering table, a steel plate mounted above gas jets. The parts were heated until the lacquer sizzled as Joseph carefully brushed two coats of lacquer onto the hot metal. The finished items were then allowed to cool and cure overnight.

The finishing and bronzing of the housing and other parts took the entire day. Only after applying the second coat of lacquer did Joseph stop to rest. Daylight had turned to dusk, and the siren sounded, signaling the end of the ten-hour workday. Joseph looked at the work he had done and was satisfied. The housing halves and other parts had a uniform green hue. The next day, the meter assembly would be installed into the housing, and the two halves would be bolted together to form a finished meter. It was time to return home.

Joseph's throat was raw from breathing the acid fumes. He untied the handkerchief from his face, removed his work apron, and laid them both on the stool in front of his workstation. The noise level in the factory gradually decreased as the drive shaft slowed down and the steam engine was allowed to idle for the night. Joseph descended the stairs, nodding to some of the men he passed. Outside, he waited for a streetcar, boarded, and rode up Melrose Street until it reached his stop. He crossed the street and walked the ten blocks through the neighborhood. During the day, the city crews had made progress on the new sewer line. New pipe had been installed with stubs for side sewers into the adjacent yards. The evening grew completely dark as Joseph crossed Broadway and walked the remaining blocks to the house he shared with Margaret and his two sons. Kerosene lamps were visible through the windows of the houses he passed. A few men were on the street, most returning home from their day jobs, but a few others walked in the opposite direction, going to work as night watchmen or second shift workers in factories.

Joseph reached the house and entered, hung up his coat and hat, and called out. Cooking smells filled the air. He greeted Margaret in the kitchen and sat down at the table. She was lost in her thoughts, and it took a while for her to acknowledge he was home. After a few minutes, she poured a cup of tea for each of them and sat down beside Joseph. She gently took his hand in hers, looked at him quietly, and waited for him to tell her about his day. Joseph talked about his morning walk, the progress on the new sewer line, and people he had seen on the streetcar. He described the parts he had finished and bronzed during the day, and he told her about his thoughts during the walk home, his memories of reading the Bible in the cabin when he was a child. She listened patiently, sitting next to him and holding his hand in hers. Joseph knew she rarely left the house during the winter days and sometimes spent most of the time lying down in the darkened bedroom, rising only to prepare hot food for Joseph and the two boys.

"Joseph Lower will be home late tonight," she said. "He is attending an evening class at the college. Charles is out with friends." Margaret served the food, and the couple sat and ate their supper, as they had done each night since their wedding twelve years earlier. It would be a quiet evening, and Joseph wanted to finish writing the letter to his mother.

December 15, 1901

Twenty-Five Years Later
16 Maple Street, Somerville

Joseph sat in the parlor and smoked his pipe as he reread the letter from his son Charles. The letter was dated a week earlier and sent from upstate Minnesota. Charles recounted the recent events in his busy life. He worked as a doctor and traveled to isolated logging camps, where he treated men injured in logging accidents and vaccinated men against smallpox, which had a recent upsurge in cases. Charles was growing discouraged with the endless crises in his work. A recent article in the newspaper described that in Washington State, areas were opening up for fruit ranches on the east side of the Cascade Mountains, where the soil was fertile and the Columbia River provided water for irrigation. He and his wife had discussed the idea of leaving Minnesota, moving west, and establishing a fruit orchard near Yakima, Washington. Joseph shook his head as he read. He had not seen his son for eighteen years, since the young man left his medical practice in Somerville and moved to Minnesota. Now, he was planning to move a thousand miles farther west. It was a seven-day train trip from Boston to Seattle, and Joseph could not leave his job at the gas meter factory for the three weeks it would take to travel and have a good visit with his son. He sighed, disappointed.

At least he could visit his older son, Joseph Lower. After eighteen years of ministering to small congregations around New England, he had returned to Somerville with his family so his son, Clarence, could attend Tufts College. There had not been an opening for a Unitarian minister at any of the local churches, but Joseph obtained a position for Joseph Lower at the gas meter factory. There he worked on the second floor, operating a lathe and fabricating brass parts for the coin-operated mechanism of the gas meters. After fabrication, the parts were taken to the third floor, where the meters were assembled. That was Joseph's department.

After ten years of working in the brass finishing department, the constant exposure to acid fumes had damaged his lungs, and he requested a transfer. He moved to the assembly room and now, eighteen years later, he was the foreman in that department. At first, the work was intimidating. Most of the gas meters were activated by inserting a token into them, which allowed a fixed amount of gas to be released for use in the house or business. The mechanisms had many moving parts. It was months of assembling meters before Joseph was confident that his assemblies would pass inspection. Now, he could assemble a meter with his eyes closed. As foreman, it was his responsibility that the finished meters passed the performance tests to which each one was subjected. He spent his days solving supply problems, monitoring the quality of the parts that were sent to his area, and making sure the employees stayed focused on their work. He had paperwork to complete at the end of each day and did not arrive home until after six o'clock. However, a new streetcar line had opened on Cross Street, and the walk from there to his house was only a few blocks. The new electric streetcars were much faster than the horse-drawn trolleys they had replaced. Several days ago, he had even seen an electric car purring down Melrose Street while he waited for the streetcar. He watched in amazement until it disappeared down the street.

The house on Maple Street was a good home to come to every evening. Joseph looked around the parlor, taking in the wind-up Victrola standing against the far wall, the hot water register that gave off steady heat, and the photographs of his sons and their wives standing on the mantel. He and Margaret had saved for ten years to accumulate $1,500, which was the 50 percent down payment required by the bank to take out a mortgage and buy the house. Five more anxious years awaited until they paid off the balloon payment and the house became theirs. No more outhouse or heating bathwater on the stove. The coal furnace in the basement had copper coils wrapped around the firebox that ensured a steady supply of hot water during cold weather. The water closet in the bathroom meant no more cold trips to the privy on dark mornings.

Work had changed greatly in the twenty-seven years since Joseph had started at the factory. Electric arc lights were installed last year, and now there was always plenty of light shining on the work. The light made the job safer. There were still occasions when men were caught in the moving belts, but it had been a few years since this had resulted in a death. The quality of the work was higher. Joseph heard a rumor that soon the company would start installing separate electric motors at each workstation and remove the overhead belt system. The new ventilation system, installed a few years ago, exhausted the fumes from the factory high into the air above the building instead of fouling the air in the workrooms.

Joseph leaned back in the overstuffed chair and closed his eyes. It had been a long journey from the crude shack where his family lived during their first years in the logging camp. His boys were doing well, and he and Margaret had everything they needed. It was hard to imagine that life could be any better.

Final Note

Joseph Scoboria suffered a heart attack and died suddenly on January 4, 1905, at the age of seventy-three, after working at the gas meter factory for thirty-two years. He worked at the factory until the time of his death. His wife, Margaret, followed him into death within a few months. Joseph Lower Scoboria and his family moved into the house at 16 Maple Street in Somerville. He continued to work at the gas meter factory for thirty-five more years, retiring at the age of eighty-five as a foreman in 1940, the first year that Social Security monthly payments became available. He occasionally gave sermons as a visiting minister at Unitarian Churches in the Boston Area. In 1939, at the age of eighty-four, he renewed his minister's license to baptize his first great-grandchild. His brother, Dr. Charles Scoboria, left Minnesota in 1903 and moved with his wife to Washington State, where they bought land and planted a peach orchard in the sunny Yakima Valley. They lived there for the rest of their lives.

182

CHAPTER SEVEN

Night Train to Calais, Maine

Clarence Preston Scoboria
(1882–1960)[10]

Sophia Hawes Livingstone Scoboria
(1886–1969)[11]

Clarence Preston Scoboria, 1882–1960

August 1906

Outside the train window could be seen endless stands of scrubby fir and spruce mixed with birch trees, distinguished by their white bark. Occasionally, as the old steam engine chugged along, it passed through an area where the forest had been recently logged, and stumps stretched out into the distance. Then, quickly, the clearing was passed, and forest closed in again on both sides of the tracks.

The early morning was dark enough that individual trees could not be picked out from the forest. Clare shifted in his seat, stiff and sore. It had been a long night. The train left North Station in Boston at 10 p.m. and stopped throughout the night at small towns in New Hampshire and southern Maine. There was a layover in Portland, Maine, for an hour, and Clare got a little sleep as the train sat at the station. He remembered brief stops in Augusta and Waterville. A few passengers got off the train, and a few new ones boarded. It started up again and went on to Bangor, where Clare changed trains. The

train to Calais consisted of a few old cars pulled by a weather-beaten steam engine. The seats in the cars were poorly padded, and the roadbed was rough, so Clare felt every road crossing the train passed over. It was a long trip to Calais.

Clare wished he could have afforded a sleeper, but most of his savings had been used to purchase the new suit he was wearing. He had to keep some money for his expenses once he reached Calais. Perhaps there was a cheap hotel near the train station, where he could have some privacy before the day of his wedding. Wedding! He still could hardly believe what was happening. In a few days he would marry Sophia, and there was a child on the way.

How could this have happened so suddenly? He tossed it over and over in his mind. Two years earlier, the future seemed bright. Clare was a popular boy at Tufts College, athletic and well-liked. He came to the college as a legacy student because his father, Joseph Lower Scoboria, had received a divinity degree years earlier when the college was newly established. Joseph had gone on to work as a Unitarian minister. No one warned the young man that the life of a minister would be a long succession of ministering to tiny congregations of ten to fifteen families in one small town or another in rural New England. There were times when he preached at two or even three churches on Sunday. After a few years in one location, the church administration transferred him to a different parish, and the family moved again. His older son, Clare, was never enrolled long enough in one school to make good friends, so he relied on the friendship of his younger brother, Leon. Together, they started at new schools, made a few friends, then lost them when the family relocated. They sometimes fought, but knew they could always count on each other.

When Clare was fourteen years old, his father was transferred to a small church in Oxford, New York, and there the town was home to a boys college preparatory school called the Clinton Institute. Clare's father performed services at the school in exchange for part of the tuition, and Clare attended the school until he graduated. Many of the boys at the school came from wealthy families, and at first, they looked down on this skinny boy who wore the same worn suit to school every day. The first fall and winter at the school were a miserable time for Clare. But when spring came and the school held a field day with races and field events, the skinny boy turned out to be a fast runner. The longer the race, the more he outran his schoolmates. This small area of excellence was enough to give Clare a bit of prestige, and the other boys accepted and even admired him.

After three years at the school, Clare had established his academic and running accomplishments. Tufts College offered no athletic scholarships, but Clare was one of eight young men awarded a scholarship provided by the wealthy widow of one of the school's founders. The family moved to the Boston area and rented a house in Somerville, just outside the city, so Clare could live at home while attending college. There were no openings for Unitarian ministers at the churches in the Boston area, so reluctantly, Joseph Lower left the ministry and took a position at a factory that manufactured gas meters, the same factory where his father had worked for many years. Strangely enough, this change was an improvement in the financial circumstances of the family, because Joseph's pay at the factory exceeded the meager income he had received as a minister. Clare saw his mother, quiet for so many years, actually smile when Joseph Lower brought his paycheck to her at the end of the month.

The train rocked as it passed over a rough length of track. Clare looked out the window and saw that a sidetrack diverged from the main line and ran parallel to it. A series of empty flatcars sat motionless in the dawn light, some littered with bark and small branches. Clare guessed the cars were used to transport logs to a mill farther along the line. Shortly, the train again passed a rough spot, perhaps where the side-track merged back into the main line, or perhaps at a road crossing. He looked for signs of life in the cutover area alongside the track, but he did not see anything moving. Clare wondered if he might see a deer in the dawn light, so he forced himself to keep looking. He hoped it would help him forget how tired and stiff he felt. He looked for houses or lights but saw nothing. It was still early dawn.

———◆———

The years Clare spent at Tufts College were a glorious time for him, even though he lived at home instead of at the college. As a freshman, he wore a beanie cap and suffered the jibes and japes of the upperclassmen. But there were women students at Tufts in some of his classes, and they were fascinating, with long dresses and elaborate hats pinned to their hair. The classes were hard, but Clare had prepared well at the Clinton Institute. He had no money to spend on outside activities, so night after night he spent at his books, the pages lit by the gas lamp in the dining room. As fall turned to winter, Clare ran on the indoor track with his classmates. This was a hardwood running surface suspended twelve feet above the gymnasium floor around the perimeter of the gym, oval-shaped, with sixteen laps to the mile. Clare learned how to maneuver the tightly banked corners and pass other runners on the short straight sections. He looked forward to the times each week when the freshman boys had the gymnasium to themselves for their athletic practices, and he could still remember the pounding sounds of running shoes on the boards of the track. When spring came, the activity shifted to the outdoor track. Clare felt at home there and quickly proved himself to be the fastest runner in the longer races. The highlight of the year was Field Day, when the frosh boys competed against the sophomores and nearly beat them, anchored by Clare's victories in the half-mile and mile runs, and his anchor leg in the mile relay, while Tufts girls watched and cheered from the stands. The school year ended, and Clare worked during the summer in the gas meter factory with his father and his grandfather.

The years at Tufts passed. After watching his father spend years as a minister with low pay and few benefits, the study of divinity had little appeal for Clare. But mathematics was something he could appreciate. Starting with simple rules of numbers and functions, a person could create a complex system. In geometry, a point, a line, and a space could be used to describe the world. When Clare was introduced to the study of calculus, he realized that mathematics was what he wanted to study. His other focus during college continued to be running. Each winter, he ran on the board track. In the springtime, the most exciting day was when the cinder track was declared firm enough to be used. Clare's running times improved, and the school records, once unreachable, now looked possible for him to attain.

At the start of his junior year, Clare was asked to join the Delta Tau Delta fraternity. A few places at the fraternity were open to boys who could not pay for their room and board. Instead, they worked at the fraternity, serving meals and maintaining the stately old building where the members lived. Clare's father, Joseph, was opposed to Clare joining the fraternity, because he feared that Clare would neglect his schoolwork. But his mother, Anna, spoke up, "The boy needs to be independent," she said. So, Clare became a member of the fraternity. He promised he would not be distracted by the social life, but it was a hard vow to keep. Young ladies were forbidden to enter the fraternity house, but it was not uncommon to see several of them clustered around fraternity boys on the front steps, smiling and laughing.

Clare's senior year arrived, and he would soon graduate with a degree in mathematics, qualifying him to teach at the high school level. That spring was a glorious time. Tufts College competed in track meets against other Boston area colleges, and Clare was a mainstay of his team. In the meet against Brown University, he won both the half-mile and mile runs and established new school record times in both races. No longer a quiet boy wearing an old suit, he proudly wore his letter sweater on campus.

Graduation Day came, and school was done. Some of Clare's classmates planned to attend medical school, and others were joining corporations where their fathers were vice presidents. Clare returned to work at the gas meter factory. But his mathematics professor had referred him to a small coeducational school in Portland, Maine, that needed a math teacher. He took off a day from work and climbed onto a train in Boston. Three hours later, the train arrived in Portland.

Westbrook Seminary was a school with both day and boarding students, including some from small towns in northern Maine. The headmaster interviewed Clare and offered him a position as a mathematics instructor as well as duty as a monitor in one of the boys' dorms. The pay would be meager, but the position came with room and board. Clare accepted the offer.

First, there was another summer assembling gas meters. He hoped his pay as a new teacher would be enough so that this would be his last summer to work at the factory. The summer dragged on without the excitement of looking forward to the fall and returning to Tufts. Clare had to save enough money for his travel to Portland and back, and for the two suits he needed for his teaching job.

The time arrived for him to leave home. He hugged his mother, who cried softly, knowing that her boy was going off into the world. His father shook his hand and reminded him to stay true to his beliefs. His brother, Leon, punched him on the shoulder one last time. Clare boarded the streetcar to Boston and tried not to think about how his life was about to change.

A great change it was. He was responsible for fifteen boys aged twelve to fourteen, as well as his teaching assignments. He seldom had time to write a letter home or prepare for the next day's classes. About 200 students attended Westbrook Seminary, 120 boys and 80 girls in grades 7 through 12. At the entrance to the school, two large brick dormitory buildings were connected by a one-story dining hall. On the campus behind the dormitories, a series of classroom buildings bordered an old apple orchard. A small stream meandered through the property and widened into a pond where a few ducks paddled about. A five-foot-tall fence separated the classroom buildings from the orchard and stream, constructed to make it harder for students to slip away into the orchard during breaks between classes.

During the second week of classes, Clare was walking from his rooms in the boys' dormitory to the classrooms. The route took him close to the orchard fence. He heard subdued laughter from behind the fence and was about to turn and look when an apple hit him on the side of the head. Clare dropped his books in surprise at the blow. There was silence for a moment, then he distinctly heard a girl's voice call out, "Sophia, you hit him with that apple!" By the time he retrieved his books and straightened up, all he could see were the backs of two girls racing off into the orchard. One of them had light blond hair. Clare continued on to class and forgot the incident, but a few days later, he mentioned it to one of the other teachers. The man nodded his head knowingly. "That was Miss Livingstone, without a doubt. She is very blond and uses any excuse not to attend classes. Her family lives in Calais at the Canadian border." Now Clare had a name to put with the blond hair.

Over the course of that busy year, Clare taught his classes and monitored the young boys in his charge. He coached basketball during the winter months, even though he had never played the game in school. It didn't matter much, for all his time was spent keeping the boys in line and stopping them from punching each other. Occasionally they listened to him.

In February, Clare was invited to run in a two-mile race in Boston, to be held indoors on a wood track at Mechanics Hall. Some of the fastest runners in the East were invited. He took the train to Boston in a state of great excitement. On February 5, 1905, nine runners lined up to begin the two-mile race, twenty-four laps on a board track. After a mile and a half, Clare was in fourth place. Then his left shoe came off. Within a few steps, his foot was filled with splinters from the rough board of the track, and he stopped running. The race was eventually won by George Bonhag, the national two-mile champion. Discouraged by the result, Clare decided that this race was the end of his running career.

He saw Miss Livingstone from time to time walking to and from classes. At first, she looked away when he passed, and he thought she must be embarrassed by the incident with the apple. But then she started smiling at him as he neared her, and to his surprise, he smiled back. She had a straightforward way about her. If she was happy about something, she showed it. By springtime, it seemed that wherever Clare went, he noticed Miss Livingstone was nearby.

One of Clare's responsibilities in the spring was to organize Field Day, the track and field meet where the boys in the school competed against each other by grade. He drew up a program listing the events, with running events from the hundred-yard dash up to the mile run, and field events such as the shot put, pole vault, high jump, and others. Each class chose boys to enter the events. Clare listed the names in a printed program for the parents and friends of the school who came to Field Day each year.

The day before Field Day, he was walking across the school campus when Miss Livingstone approached him. She came closer and spoke up. "Mr. Scoboria, I made something for you."

She handed him several sheets of paper. He looked down at the top page. It was a handwritten copy of his program for Field Day with one difference. All the contestants listed were girls.

"What is this?" he asked.

"This is a program for the girls events at Field Day," Miss Livingstone replied.

Clare was puzzled. "But there are no girls events at Field Day," he said.

"Why not?" asked the girl. "We can do all the same things the boys do."

"It wouldn't be right," said Clare. "Girls should not do these things in public."

"Well, I would like to," she said. "You will see I have entered every event."

Clare studied the sheets in his hand. Each track and field event was listed along with the names of the girl contestants for each one. The name Sophia Livingstone was printed for each event, even the shot put and the mile run.

"I don't know what to tell you," Clare said. "This has never been done before, you know."

The girl looked up at him. "Well, keep it in mind for the future, Mr. Scoboria," she said. "Girls like to do active things also, not just flounce around in pretty dresses. I turned eighteen during this year, and I will graduate in two weeks, so I won't be able to compete in a girls race next year. But there are girls who would like to."

"What do you plan to do after graduation?" asked Clare.

"I will return to Calais for the summer," she said. "My family has an old stone house outside of town on the banks of the St. Croix River. We go there each summer. We swim in the river and go out in a rowboat. My father likes to fish in the river, but I like to row. In the fall, I will return in the autumn to teach in a little school about fifty miles from here in a small town in the foothills."

"Well," he said, "I hope you have a good summer and that your teaching job goes well."

"That's just it, Mr. Scoboria," she said. "I am worried about the teaching. I haven't been a good student in school, and soon I will be teaching children. I don't know if I can teach very well."

"I am sure you will do fine, Miss Livingstone. Teaching is not so much about what you know as it is about helping others to learn. Sometimes, you have to teach things you don't even know very well. Last winter, I coached the basketball team, but I cannot shoot or even dribble a basketball."

"Mr. Scoboria, if I have questions when I start teaching, could I write to you and get your advice?" Miss Livingstone asked.

Clare was taken aback but flattered. "Of course you could write to me, and I would be pleased to offer any advice that might help," he said. He wrote down the address of his parents' house in Somerville and gave it to her.

———•———

A loud noise startled Clare from his thoughts. The train was crossing over a small river, and the noise he heard was from the train passing by the steel framework of the bridge. On the far side of the river, Clare could see the houses of a small village. Lights shone from candles or kerosene lamps in some of the windows, and smoke rose from a few chimneys. The village consisted of a dozen houses clustered on both sides of the railroad track. How did people live in this remote area, Clare wondered? Sophia had mentioned in one of her letters that the winter snow in Calais, where she was from, sometimes accumulated into drifts taller than a man could reach. At those times, people dug tunnels from their front doors out into the street. The railroad lines were sometimes blocked for days at a time. Clare thought that life in an isolated village like this one must be a bleak experience. Outside the town were small, cleared fields separated by rock walls and hedgerows consisting of scrub trees and brush. Scattered farmhouses were small, some painted white, others with bare wood siding. Most had simple barns and sheds nearby, with piles of firewood stacked next to each building. The winters were long here, and plenty of firewood was a necessity. After a few miles, the forest closed in again on both sides of the railroad track.

———•———

At Westbrook Seminary, the school year ended, and the students left for their homes. Clare took the train to Boston and the streetcar to his parents' house. He needed to work in the gas meter factory again for the summer. The summer passed. Clare occasionally saw old friends from Tufts, but their affluent worlds seemed different from his now that he was a schoolteacher. Midway through the summer, he received a letter from Miss Livingstone. In it, she described summer activities with her family. They planted a large garden, and she described the vegetables they were harvesting. She talked about swimming in the river and how good it felt. She hoped to swim all the way across it one day. She mentioned her seven brothers and sisters, all of whom came to the stone house for family gatherings. One Sunday, twenty-two people had gathered at the house for dinner. Clare could not imagine that kind of activity. His parents' house was quiet, with only his father and mother, and brother Leon. After each day's work at the factory, Clare read or wrote letters in the evening. It sounded from her letters as though Sophia's life was always busy, either with her brothers and sisters or with friends who came to the stone house to spend time there. Clare wondered what life with a large family would be like.

Summer ended, and Clare once again rode the streetcar into Boston and boarded the train to Portland. He moved back into his dormitory room, and a few days later, the boys began to arrive. Some were new, scared and anxious to be away from their homes. Other boys returned from the previous year and happy to be back at school. Clare welcomed them all. The first day of school came quickly, and it was back to the routine he remembered from last year. It didn't seem as overwhelming as his first year had been. Many of the problems that arose were similar to ones he had faced before. He was more confident, and he communicated that to the boys. They respected him in a way that was different from his first year at the school.

Letters from Miss Livingstone appeared with some regularity. She was living in a small town about fifty miles from Portland, where she taught in a one-room schoolhouse. She had children aged six through twelve in her class. Her letters conveyed some of her discoveries about what it was like to be a teacher.

"Mr. Scoboria," one letter read, "I am surprised every day about what I find out about the children in my classes. Some of them cannot read, and I have to start teaching very basic things, things I learned when I was a little girl. I have them practice the alphabet, count off their numbers, and learn the names of shapes and colors. It is so different from what I expected. The older children can read, and I have them practice by reading to the younger children. Every day is hectic, and I go home to my room in the boarding house tired each night. I miss the girls from the school last year, and some days, I wish I was back at Westbrook."

Clare read each letter several times and thought about what he could write in response. "It sounds like you are doing the right things, Miss Livingstone. Each child will have different skills and different needs, and if you can identify the best approach for each one, then you will become a good teacher. If you can make school something they look forward to each day, your classes will be a success."

"Mr. Scoboria," read another letter, "I have students who come to school with dirty faces, and some of them seem not to have eaten breakfast. Last week, one little boy had bruises on his arm, and it looked like he was in pain, but he did not want to talk about it to me."

"Miss Livingstone," Clare wrote in reply, "there will always be problems that are painful to see, and often little that we can do about them. Some of the boys that I have charge of are enrolled at this school because their parents don't want them at home. The boys know that and feel very lonely. I cannot be a parent to them, so I try to listen and let them know they have a safe place here at the school. Perhaps there are small things you can do at your school. Perhaps you can have short hygiene sessions each day, and perhaps some parents might like to send baked goods to the school from time to time, which could be shared among the students. As for the boy with bruises on his arm, the only suggestion I have is that you might talk with the minister at the local church. You cannot become involved in the lives of the families of the children that you teach."

"Mr. Scoboria," came the response, "thank you for your suggestions. Mrs. Walker, the woman from whom I rent my room, twice has made muffins that I took to school, and they were very much appreciated. We have been practicing hand washing each day. I did talk with the minister. He listened, but he said there was very little he could do. It makes me sad. But some of the children are doing well with their reading. That makes me feel as though I am doing something of value. Thank you." The letter was signed, "Sophia."

School continued. The letters went back and forth every few weeks and became an important part of Clare's life. He was glad each time he saw one in his box at school. Winter came and was cold, and the snow was deep at times. Sophia wrote that when she returned to Calais at Christmas, there were drifts up to the roofs of the houses. She was glad to return to Mrs. Walker's boarding house and get ready for classes to start again.

Winter seemed to drag on forever, but finally a spell of mild weather arrived in mid-March. The snow melted quickly, and by the first of April, a few buds were expanding on the bushes at Westbrook School. Flowers followed, and soon it was time for Clare to plan Field Day. It was only for boys again this year, but he thought about Miss Livingstone's suggestion for a girls' Field Day. He had kept the sheets she had made and carefully pasted them into the scrapbook where he kept the newspaper clippings of his college track meets. He looked at the pages and thought about her, wondering if she was enjoying the mild spring weather.

Then another letter arrived. "Mr. Scoboria," it read, "The end of the school year is approaching, and I feel good about how the year went. Your advice to me has been very helpful. My approach to life has always been to face it straight on, but you have helped me see that there are times when I should stop and think before acting. Not everything has gone well this year, but I feel as though I have made a little difference with the children that I teach. I wondered if you might have time to visit me for a day before the end of the school year. There is a train crossing about three miles from the village, and perhaps a wagon might carry you the rest of the way into the village. We could have a picnic at the park if it is a nice day. Please think about it, Mr. Scoboria; it would be good to see you. Sincerely, Sophia Livingstone."

Clare shook his head at her request, thinking it was out of the question. Take an entire day to ride a slow train out into the foothills, walk three miles just to have a picnic, then return the same way to Portland? But as he considered the idea, he realized it might not be so difficult. The school year was nearly completed. Next week was Field Day, then came a week until final exams. He had little to do until the exams were completed. He wrote back and confirmed he would visit on Saturday, June 2, and arrive in the early afternoon.

———·———

The train shuddered as it crossed another rough piece of track, and it jarred Clare out of his reveries. They had reached the outskirts of a town, and the jolt he felt came where several sidetracks diverged from the main line. Off to one side was a series of large buildings with logs stacked nearby. Flatcars loaded with logs stood near the buildings, and Clare realized this was the lumber mill he had wondered about. A sign loomed: Machias. This was the last town of any size until the train reached Calais, two hours away. People were awake, and wagons moved up and down the main street. Smoke drifted up from chimneys.

The train slowed to a stop at a small station. A few people got off the train, and a few new passengers climbed aboard, then the train started off again. The tracks paralleled a river for a short distance, curving around to the north, then crossing the river on a steel bridge. The houses became spread out on both sides of the track, and the train entered another stretch of unbroken forest. The tracks headed away from the coast. Clare saw on the map that the rails passed through land nearly empty of towns until they reached Calais. He stretched a little in his seat. It had been a long night, and he knew the day ahead would be busy. Sophia had written that her family moved back into town in preparation for his arrival and for the wedding. She and her brothers and sisters would meet him at the train station and take him back to their house to meet their mother and father. Clare thought to himself, how can I face this couple, meeting them for the first time to marry their youngest daughter, now two months pregnant? He felt scared and a little desperate about the future. But the day would go on somehow, and the train had nearly reached Calais.

———•———

June 2 arrived, and it was a sunny day. Clare took the slow train out of Portland, which took almost two hours to reach the crossing nearest to the village where Miss Livingstone lived. He was the only person to get off at the crossing, and the road was empty in both directions, so he started walking toward the village three miles away. Soon, a farm wagon pulled by two draft horses came up behind him, and the farmer stopped the wagon to offer him a lift. Clare climbed up on the seat next to him, and the wagon started off. It traveled only a little faster than Clare had been walking, but he appreciated the ride. The two draft horses pulling the wagon moved at a deliberate pace, their huge hooves clopping on the dirt road.

"You going into the village?" the farmer asked.

"Yes," replied Clare. "One of my students from last year is the schoolteacher there, and she asked me to visit and discuss some school issues with her. She lives at Mrs. Walker's boarding house in the village."

"Well, it is a fine day to visit a young lady," the farmer said. "You must have some feelings for her if you have come so far for a visit."

"I don't know," said Clare. "It seemed like the right thing to do when she asked me to come to see her."

"Then you are doing the right thing, young man. I hope your day goes well." With that remark, the man relapsed into silence for the rest of the trip. After a while, he pulled up the horses at a dirt road crossing and pointed down the road ahead. "It is only half a mile into the village from here. Mrs. Walker's house is on the main street, right side, most of the way through the village."

Clare thanked the farmer for the ride, got down off the wagon, and started walking again. When he reached the edge of the village, he saw two-story framed houses lining both sides of the street. A few people were walking on the wooden sidewalks, and they wished him a good day as he passed. Ahead was the house where Miss Livingstone rented a room, a white-painted home with a large, covered porch in front. A picket fence surrounded a well-kept yard. Clare opened the gate and walked toward the house.

Miss Livingstone must have been watching for him out of a window, for she opened the front door and appeared on the porch as Clare approached the steps. In her right hand was a picnic basket, and in her left was a sunbonnet without ruffles or flowers. She wore a modest sundress and sturdy shoes.

She spoke up. "Mr. Scoboria, it is so good of you to come today. Mrs. Walker prepared a picnic lunch for us, and I hope you don't mind if we walk to the park and have our picnic there. It is lovely out today."

Clare nodded, a bit tongue-tied to meet this young woman outside of school. She seemed different from the student he had last seen almost a year earlier. They had exchanged letters filled with news about their classes during the school year. She had written about the long train trips to and from her home in Calais on holidays and how happy she felt when one of her older brothers visited her at the school where she was teaching. In turn, Clare had written and told her news about Westbrook Seminary, the success of the basketball team he coached, and his decision to stop running in track meets in order to concentrate on teaching. As they walked along, Clare noticed that Miss Living-stone, although much shorter than he was, walked with faster steps and kept up with him. They soon reached the park. It was very crowded. Every picnic table was occupied by families with young children, while young couples filled the park benches.

Miss Livingstone turned to Clare and said, "The park is so busy today, it will be hard to find a place to talk. I know of a place that is much quieter. It is a bit of a walk, but I know you have strong legs. Perhaps we could go there?" She gave Clare a little smile as she said this, and he felt a blush rise to his cheeks.

"That will be fine," he said, "Lead the way."

They walked on and soon reached the end of the village. A few cat-tle grazed on the spring grass of the pastures that lay on both sides of the road. Clare carried the picnic basket, and Miss Livingstone walked beside him. Every now and then, she stopped to point out a spring flower growing at the side of the road. She seemed to know the name of every one they passed, told him about them: how this one could be picked, dried, and used to make tea, and that one could be made into a dye. One particular flower she called a touch-me-not, and as she lightly brushed the leaves, they curled up behind her finger. This was new to Clare. He knew how to calculate the area of an irregular polygonal shape, and he could recite the order of prime numbers well into the hundreds, but natural history was unknown to him. Still, he enjoyed learning what she told him. As they were no longer in town, he took off his jacket and carried it in his free hand.

They walked on the road for a while, then turned off onto a dirt lane. Suddenly, Miss Livingstone turned to Clare and said, "We are nearly there, but there is a path we have to follow." She turned off the lane and entered a field. A faint path could be seen where the grass was a little worn. They walked along the path, climbed over a dry-laid stone wall at the far side of the field, then passed into another field.

"One more field," she said, "and a bit of woods."

Miss Livingstone led the way, and Clare noticed how confidently she climbed over the rock wall and strode along the path. She seemed at home in the country, and Clare supposed this was due to the sum-mers she spent at her family's stone house outside of Calais, Maine. He remembered her stories of living there with her family each sum-mer, planting a garden and swimming in the St. Croix River.

As they neared the end of the second field, Miss Livingstone turned to Clare. "The trail gets a little rough here," she said. " You may want to have a hand free to hold onto bushes in places where the trail is steep." Clare put down the picnic basket and carefully folded his jacket underneath the handles of the basket, leaving his left hand free. Miss Livingston pushed aside a few branches and stepped into the woods. Clare picked up the basket again and followed her. Once inside the woods, he found that the underbrush was thinner than he expected, and they could walk easily on the path. It was shady and cool in the woods. In the distance, Clare heard a slight murmur, perhaps the noise from a small stream. Wildflowers grew beside the path, and Miss Livingstone stopped each time she passed one.

"This flower is a trillium," she said as she pointed to a striking white flower with three petals. The name made sense to Clare. A triangle has three angles, he thought, why shouldn't a trillium flower have three petals and three leaves?

"The flower is beautiful for just a short time, then it dies back and is insignificant until next spring," Miss Livingstone said. "There is a bulb underground, and the plant will appear at the same place next year."

As they walked along, the murmur of the stream grew louder and the path began to descend steeply, turning to the left and then to the right in a series of short switchbacks. At several places, Clare held on to low branches to keep himself from falling, but the girl stepped confidently ahead. She was visibly excited that they were nearing their goal, although what that was, Clare had no idea.

Through the branches of the trees below him, Clare could see the reflection of the sun off of water. He guessed there must be a small pool in the woods fed by the stream he could now easily hear. Two more switchbacks on the trail, and they emerged onto a small rocky beach in front of a pool. The pool was perhaps thirty feet across, shallow at the edge where they were standing but deeper toward the far side, where a steep rocky slope dropped straight into the water.

"Isn't this lovely?" said Miss Livingstone. "I found this during one of my walks, and sometimes I come here on sunny days. There has never been anyone else here. I come and sit and listen to the birds. Sometimes, I write letters."

She stepped to the water's edge, stooped down, and felt the water with her hand.

"Oh, the water has grown much warmer," she said. Glancing shyly at Clare, she added, "Let's swim."

"But how?" he stammered, "We have no bathing costumes, and there is no place to change."

"There is no one here, and no one to see us," Miss Livingstone replied. "It will feel wonderful!" At this remark, she took off her sunhat and placed it on a patch of duff next to the beach. She pulled the combs and pins out of her hair and shook her head until blond tresses cascaded over her shoulders. Then reaching behind, she untied the loops on her sundress and pulled it over her head, folded it, and carefully laid it next to her hat. Clare stood by, astonished at what was happening. Miss Livingstone quickly pulled off her shoes, stockings, and petticoat, laying them beside the dress. Then she turned to Clare. "Mr. Scoboria, won't you join me? The water will feel wonderful on this warm day."

Clare was astounded. This properly dressed young lady had quickly become a lovely young woman. He saw she had a few freckles on her arms, and her legs and shoulders were bare, a little tanned, and looked strong. But he could not think of what to say to her.

Seeing no response from Clare, Miss Livingstone moved closer to him. "Let me help you by taking off this tie," she said as she reached up, loosened the knot, and began unfastening the top buttons of his shirt.

"Miss Livingstone, I can do the rest," he said.

"All right," she said. "But please call me Sophia, and I will call you Clarence."

Fumbling at first, Clare removed his white shirt, shoes, and socks and placed them on a clean spot on the tiny beach where they would not get soiled. "Perhaps I will roll up my trousers and wade," he said.

"Now, Clarence, that won't do," she said. "The pool is deep enough at the far side that we can get beneath the water and even swim a few strokes."

"But Sophia," he protested.

"Oh, don't worry," she said. "I have five brothers. Nothing about you will shock me."

At this last remark, she turned away, unclipped her brassiere, removed her underwear, and placed them with the rest of her clothes. As she stooped down, Clarence could see the curve of her breasts, and he felt the awkward sensation of becoming aroused at the sight of her.

Without looking at him, Sophia stepped out into the water at the edge of the pool. She waded ankle deep, then knee deep, and soon the water covered her thighs. As she reached the far side of the pool, the water reached her waist. She called out to him: "Clarence, it is wonderful; come and join me."

He waited until she turned away to swim a few strokes. Then with much trepidation, he pulled off his pants and underclothes and stepped into the pool. The shallow water was warm, and the flat rocks at the bottom were slimy, so Clare had to pick his way carefully. He realized Sophia would turn to check his progress long before the water reached his waist. That happened quickly. She swam as far as she could in the small pool, turned and swam back, then stood and faced Clare. She shook her head and wrung the water from her hair. Clare dropped his hands to cover his nakedness, and he heard Sophia give a little chuckle.

"I am pleased you admire my looks," she said, as she turned away again to swim a few more strokes.

The water grew deeper as Clare continued walking. As it reached his thighs and waist, he let out a little gasp. The water was much colder there, and his arousal left him quickly. He had to do something to warm up, so he shook his arms and dunked his whole body under the surface. As he emerged, water hit him in the face. Sophia had returned and was splashing him vigorously. This was exactly what he and Leon had spent their time doing whenever they had a chance to swim, so he responded with little splashes at first, then stronger ones, until the whole pool surface was rippled from their game.

"I wonder what the fish are thinking about this activity," asked Sophia when they both stopped to catch their breath.

"Fish? Are there fish in this pool?" asked Clare.

"Oh, yes. A school of trout lives in the deep part of this pool. They are hard to see because their backs are greenish brown, but if I stand still, the water surface becomes clear, and I can see their shapes. Sometimes, I can feel them touching me near my ankles. They are very shy and do not bite."

This was all new to Clare, swimming in a pool with fish. The deep part of the pool was in the shade, and he began to shiver.

"Clarence, let's go to the shore and warm up in the sun," Sophia said. With that, she turned and started toward the small beach where they had left their clothes. As she passed Clare, she reached down with her left hand and took his right hand. Her soft touch felt good to him, and he realized this was the first time he had held her hand.

The water grew shallower and warmer as they walked, and Clare stopped shivering. Sophia seemed completely comfortable with the water temperature. He wondered if this was due to her childhood in northern Maine, where the winters were bitterly cold, and the water scarcely warmed up during the summers.

As they neared the beach, Clare felt some confusion. He was naked, but too wet to put on his clothes. Sophia sensed his discomfort and dropped his hand. She lifted the lid of the picnic basket and removed a towel that had been wrapped around the food to protect it from the sun. She quickly dried herself off, gave the towel to Clare to do the same, then she asked him to spread it on the duff of the small beach. She knelt down on the towel, turned to him, and held out her hand.

Clare could not remember quite what happened next or how long it lasted, but he found himself lying on the towel with his arm around Sophia. Her arm was around his waist, and she held him close to her. Their faces were a few inches apart, and he saw how blue were her eyes and how intently she looked at him, so intently he could not look away. They lay quietly in each other's arms, both a little out of breath. Then Sophia moved her head forward, and he felt her lips brush against his. When she moved back, Clare could see little wrinkles at the corners of her eyes, and he realized she was smiling. They lay quietly for a little while. Clare felt the warmth of the sun on his skin, the softness of Sophia's back, and he heard the murmur of the brook as it passed through the pond.

After a few minutes, Sophia spoke up, "I'm hungry. Let's have our picnic." She pulled away from Clare and rose, stepping into the water to rinse herself off. Clare lay still for a moment, admiring her. She noticed him watching and said, "Clarence, come and rinse off. It is time to eat."

He followed her into the pond and rinsed himself in the warm water. Sophia returned to the beach, shook out the towel, and dried herself off, then held out the towel to Clare. She quickly put on her underclothes and petticoat, pulled her sundress over her head, and fastened the ties at the back. Clarence pulled on his underclothes, shirt, and pants, leaving the shirt collar loose and his feet bare. When the towel was spread on the duff again, they sat, and Sophia opened the picnic basket. "Let's see what Mrs. Walker packed for us," she said. Inside the basket were two fried chicken drumsticks wrapped in brown paper, two thick slices of homemade bread, a small container of homemade apple butter, and a glass jar of lemonade with two mugs. At the bottom of the basket, Sophia found a package wrapped in brown paper. She chuckled. "Mrs. Walker knows I love her cookies!"

They ate lunch sitting next to each other on the towel, and Clare could not remember a time when food had tasted so good. They quickly finished the meal, and it was time to leave. They put on their stockings and shoes and stood up, shaking out the towel before packing it in the basket. Clare started to fumble with his tie, but Sophia stopped him, saying, "Let me do that, Clarence. I have been tying my little brother's ties for many years." She neatly knotted the tie, snugged it up to his throat, and turned down the collar of his shirt. Then she looked at him and said, "We must do something about your hair; you look a little like a wild bear."

Reaching into the picnic basket, Sophia pulled out a hairbrush and motioned for Clare to bend down so she could reach his hair easily. She carefully parted his hair, brushed both sides and the top, then stepped back to admire her work. "Much better," she said. She then quickly parted her own hair in the center and brushed out two loose rolls, which she combed and pinned into place. Finally, she fastened her sun bonnet on top with long pins. Clare could only stand and watch in wonder. Sophia had transformed into the proper young woman he had seen earlier in the day. She looked at him and saw his amazement at how comfortable she was dressing on the beach. "Yes," she said, "I have been here before, and I have swum a few times. But I have always been alone."

Then, with Sophia leading the way, they walked back up the twisty trail through the woods, across the field, over the rock wall, and out to the dirt lane. They continued back into the village past the park, so busy earlier in the day. Now, the picnic tables and park benches were empty. Shadows lengthened as they neared the house. At the front porch, Sophia turned to Clare and said, "Mrs. Walker does not allow men callers to come into the house, so we must say good-bye here." Clare put down the picnic basket and turned to face Sophia.

"Thank you, Miss Livingstone, for a lovely day and a fine picnic," he said.

"Mr. Scoboria, thank you for coming this long way to give me advice about my students," she responded.

Clare turned and descended the stairs. Sophia followed him a few steps behind. At the gate, he turned one last time to look at her. She spoke quietly, "Clarence, thank you for coming to see me."

He answered, "Sophia, thank you for inviting me." Then he turned and started the long walk toward the railroad crossing, where he would meet the train and return to Portland.

———

Clare woke from his memories and looked out the window of the train, which was passing through a marsh. On the right side of the tracks was a large lake with trees growing to the edge and downed trees lying in the water. There were no houses to be seen, only woods. There were two small villages of Marion and Dennysville to pass through before the train reached Calais, and a stop at the Eastpoint Junction, where a sidetrack diverged from the main line and went south toward the seaside village of Eastpoint on the Bay of Fundy. The stops would be brief if the train even stopped at all. Clare's trip was nearly finished.

———

Clare worked the final week of school at Westbrook Seminary, then took the train back to Boston where he returned to work at the gas meter factory. After a few weeks, he received a brief letter from Sophia, back in Calais for the summer. She wrote about the activities of her family and how much she loved being at the stone house on the banks of the St. Croix River. Clare wrote back to tell her a little about his life and the social events of his friends, who were finished with school but had not started upon their adult lives.

One Saturday afternoon, Clare was invited to a garden party with a few of his friends from college. The girls were dressed in white summer dresses, the boys in summer suits. They played croquet on the lawn, drank lemonade, laughed, and teased each other. Several of the young ladies smiled at Clare and made it clear they enjoyed his company, but there was a problem. Clare was a schoolteacher who worked in a factory during the summer. These girls had fathers who were doctors and businessmen and would not approve of one of their daughters being courted by a young man with no money and poor financial prospects. Clare rode home on the streetcar and arrived at the house where his parents and younger brother lived. His mother was in the kitchen preparing dinner. She smiled and asked, "Did you have a good time at the party?" Then, as an afterthought, she added, "A letter arrived for you today."

Clare picked up the envelope, neatly addressed to Mr. Clarence Scoboria. The return address read S. Livingstone, Stone House, Calais, Maine. *Sophia.* He took the letter to the sideboard and slit it open.

"Dear Clarence, I am so very happy. I am going to have a child, your child. I did not want to tell you until I was sure, but in the last two weeks, I have become increasingly certain, and I talked with my mother, who has much experience in these matters. She confirmed that I am carrying a child. Oh, Clarence, I hope you are pleased. My parents look forward to meeting you. We have been staying at the stone house, but we will move back into town if you are able to come to Calais. I hope you will come soon. I am so very happy, and I hope you are also. I love you. Sophia."

Clare stopped reading and stood, stunned. How could life change so quickly? Could he have misread the letter? He read it again, but the words were the same. He realized his mother was standing quietly at the sink, watching him.

The first thing Clare realized was that he would lose his job at Westbrook Seminary. It had been made clear to him when he was hired two years earlier that he was hired as a single man, one who had to serve as an example to the teenage boys that he looked after, and that there was to be no socializing with female students, not even ones who had graduated. Now as a father-to-be, there was no way for him to return to the school. Would he continue to work at the gas meter factory for the rest of his life? Clare could only see years of dreariness ahead.

Clare's mother watched him silently, then asked softly, "Is something wrong?" Clare's first thought was to hide what he had learned and go to be alone. But he knew if there was anyone he could talk to, it was his mother. She was quiet and thoughtful. Clare sat at the kitchen table and began to tell her about the day he had spent with Sophia and of the news in her letter. She listened until he finished, then gave him a gentle look.

"Do you love this girl?" she asked.

"I don't know, Mother, I hardly know her. She was one of the students at the school, and I was her teacher. Then we exchanged letters and spent one day together. She is not like the girls I know from college. She doesn't go to parties or wear fancy dresses. She likes to walk through the fields, and she knows all of the wildflowers. I am not sure what love is."

Clare's mother sat quietly for a few moments, then she spoke to him in a way he had not heard from her before.

"Clare," she said. "I am going to tell you a little about your father and me, about parts of our lives you have not heard about. I grew up in Beverly, a small town not far from here. When I was a young girl, my mother died, and my father took care of our family by himself. He worked in a shoe factory, and we were very poor. I left school after eighth grade and began to clean houses for people who could afford a part-time cleaning woman. When I was sixteen, I moved to Boston and began to work as a servant. Near where I lived was a house where two boys lived, Joseph and Charles Scoboria. They were both a few years older than me. Joseph, the older boy, was quiet. He attended Tufts College and planned to become a Unitarian minister, for he had strong feelings of the spirit. Sometimes, when I walked in the neighborhood, we passed on the sidewalk, and we talked a little with each other. He asked me questions about things I had never thought about before, questions like 'What is the difference between right and wrong?' and 'Can we know the nature of God?' I had few answers to his questions, but he listened to the few things I said, and then I went on my way. We became friends of a sort, although I was only a servant girl.

"Several years passed," she continued. "Charles, the younger boy, entered Harvard College and planned to become a doctor. Joseph continued his studies in Divinity at Tufts College and planned to graduate in June. At his final meeting with the examining board, they congratulated him on the good work he had done at school. They were sure he would qualify for a position as a Unitarian minister at one of the congregations located in small towns around New England. The salary would be very small, and sometimes he would need to take care of two small parishes at a time, but there was always a place for the pastor to live, a small house or furnished rooms. After a few years, if he ministered to his congregations well, he might move to a larger church in one of the towns. These opportunities only occurred when a pastor left due to old age or declining health.

"There was only one obstacle that might be a problem. The lead examiner spoke firmly: 'It is always best for a new minister to be married. That way, the church members will come to know the minister and his wife as part of the community. It does not work to assign a young bachelor to a small community and to expect that problems will not arise. If you have serious thoughts about a young lady, this is the time to move forward.'

"Joseph sat stunned. His life at Tufts had been completely absorbed by his studies, and he had little money to spend on other things. He did not have a social nature. In his spare time, he liked to read and think. His stepmother was a kind woman, but she was not close to him, and his father was busy working extra hours to make the money to send Joseph and Charles to college.

"Joseph had never thought about marriage," she said. "Now he realized that in a few months, he would have to find a young woman willing to share the life of a minister, a vocation with low pay, poor living arrangements, and the chance the church might move them to a different congregation at any time."

Clare sat quietly as his mother talked. He had never heard about how she and his father had decided to marry. While his situation was different, he began to sense some of the same confusion and urgency that he was feeling in their story.

She continued: "For several months after graduating from Tufts, Joseph did nothing about finding a wife. The board notified him that they would like to see him at the end of the summer, and they had good hopes of assigning him to a parish if he could finalize his domestic arrangements. But Joseph felt lost. He sat at his desk for hours and took long walks in the park. His brother Charles was preoccupied with his studies of medicine at Harvard and was rarely home. One day, I was walking through the park, and I saw Joseph sitting on a bench, lost in thought. I said hello to him as I approached, and he looked up and gave me a little smile. 'Are you all right?' I asked.

'I suppose so,' he said. 'I just don't know what to do.'

"Then I did the bravest thing I have ever done," Clare's mother said. "I asked Joseph, 'Would you like to tell me about it?'

"He looked at me for a moment and then said, 'Yes, would you sit with me for a few minutes?' I sat at the far end of the bench, and he began to tell me about the request he had received from the examining board that he marry before his first appointment as a minister. I listened and did not say anything. He talked for a while, and finally, after he had explained the situation and his confusion about what to do, he became silent.

"I spoke up. 'You are a good man, Joseph, and there are young ladies who would be honored to marry you.'

"At this remark, he rose and turned to me. 'How can that be? I have no money and no prospect of any in the future. It might be years, maybe decades, before an opening might arise at a large church. There will be years of living in small towns, small houses, probably moving every few years. What young woman would accept that kind of life?'

"'I would,' I answered, 'as would many other young ladies in my situation. I work as a servant in another family's home. I would like to have a home of my own, even if it is small and plain.'

"Joseph looked at me in astonishment. 'You would leave your home and family and come with me, not knowing where it might lead us?'

"'Yes, I would,' I said.

"We were married in December at a quiet family wedding with only our parents and Joseph's brother in attendance. Joseph was assigned to be the pastor of a congregation in a small town on Cape Cod. We lived there for two years, and it is where you were born. Then Joseph was moved to a small church in New Hampshire and a few years later to another one. This went on for years. Finally, when you were fourteen years old, your father was assigned to the church in Oxford, New York State, and you attended the Clinton Institute there. You did so well that you were accepted at Tufts, and you received a scholarship for school tuition. In order to provide a place for you to live during your college years, we left Oxford and moved to Somerville, near the college. There were no openings for a minister at any of the churches near Boston, so your father left the ministry and began to work at the gas meter factory. You see, Clare, other people have had difficult choices to make and have found ways to resolve them. Your father and I did not love each other when we married, but we have grown to love each other. Perhaps it might happen with this young woman and you."

"But what about Father?" Clare asked. "What will he say?"

"Why don't you talk with him?" his mother said. "He was asked to give a guest sermon this Sunday at a local church where the minister is absent this week. He is in the study, revising one of his old sermons."

Clare left the kitchen, walked through the dining room, and stopped at the door to the study. He tapped lightly and entered the room at his father's reply. The study was a small room that his father had fitted up with a desk and bookshelf. Joseph Lower Scoboria sat at the desk making notes on a yellow tablet. A pile of printed sheets sat in front of him on the desk. These were copies of a sermon he had written years before and printed for his records. On the bookshelf were many folders filled with these sermons, all written to present to his congregations. The families who made up his congregations had few possessions of their own, but they had faith in their church and expected the minister to provide something of value every Sunday. Clare knew that his father never wrote on the old sermons when he wished to edit them. Instead, he carefully wrote out the changes and additions in longhand, then had the revised sermon printed so that a clean copy was waiting on the pulpit before he started to speak.

Joseph Scoboria turned to Clare as he entered the room. "Yes, son?"

"Could I speak with you for a few minutes?" Clare asked.

"Yes, of course," Joseph said, motioning to a smaller chair off to the side of the desk. Clare sat. His father stopped writing and waited quietly.

"I don't know how to start or what to say," Clare finally said.

"That's all right; take your time," his father said.

Clare realized how many times he had heard his father say words like this to members of his congregation who came to see him: people with family problems, broken marriages, sickness or despair; people who did not know what to do but who thought a talk with the minister might help. But Clare had never been in that position before, and he was lost for words at first.

"Is there anything wrong at work?" his father asked.

"No, it is different," Clare said, and at this, the words tumbled out about the letter, the news from Sophia, the fact he would lose his teaching job, and that he didn't know what to do.

Clare's father sat quietly through this outburst, watching Clare closely, the pen still held between the fingers of his right hand, his left hand lying flat on the yellow tablet. When Clare was done speaking and the room was quiet again, Joseph waited a few moments and then spoke softly.

"Well, some of this is a surprise, and your life will change," he said. "But it is not the end of your life. Some of the decisions you have already made, and now it is a matter of finding a way to carry them out. This young lady sounds like a fine young woman from a good family. We have not met her, but I am sure we will grow to care about her. You have made your decision to become a father to a child, and now it is simply a matter of going through with it. Probably the sooner you go to see her will be best. It sounds as though she is very happy you will be the father of her child."

"But father, I hardly know her," Clare said. "She was my student; we exchanged letters, but now this?"

"Life can change very quickly, Clare. Often, we have been looking for an answer and cannot see it, though it is right before us. Your mother and I have watched you since you graduated from Tufts. We are proud of what you accomplished there, but when college ends, life begins, and it is hard to know the decisions that lie ahead. Perhaps it will help you to be with someone who can help you make these decisions."

"In the meantime, there might be something I can do," Joseph continued. "I have an acquaintance who is the head of schools in Merrimack County, New Hampshire. He has told me he has a hard time obtaining qualified teachers for some of the rural school districts. I will write to him and see if there might be an opening for a young teacher and his new wife. If she can teach some of the younger children, it might help."

So it was decided. Two weeks later, Clare was on the train to Calais, due to arrive at ten in the morning. Sophia would meet him at the station and take him to the Livingstone house in town to meet her mother and father. The wedding would be a quiet ceremony in a few days, and Sophia's oldest brother would act as Clare's best man at the service. They would all go out to the Stone house for a few days. Then would come the long train ride back to Boston, this time with Sophia beside him, so she could meet his parents and his brother. What would happen in the fall was still uncertain. Clare's father had received an encouraging letter about a possible teaching job in New Hampshire, but Clare would have to go there by train, interview for the job, and find a place for them to live. Meanwhile, Sophia would return to Calais until there was a place for her to stay. Clare's brain whirled with the decisions he would need to make and the changes he and Sophia would face.

He told a few of his college friends about the change in his situation. The boys slapped him on the back and said, "Well, you are in for it now, Clare; no more good times!" The girls were different. Several wished him well and expressed their approval of what he was doing. But several seemed disappointed, and he realized their friendship with him must have been deeper than he had known. But it didn't matter. That part of his life was finished now.

———◆———

Clare looked up. Outside the train windows, he could see breaks in the forest, scattered houses, and signs that they were entering a town. Off to the left side, he could see the glint of the sun reflecting off the surface of a large body of water. Clare wondered if this might be the St. Croix River, the border between the United States and Canada.

The train conductor entered through the door at the end of the car. He called out, "Five minutes to Calais, Maine, with transfers to St. Stephens and points north."

The Rest of the Story

Clarence Scoboria, age twenty-four, and Sophia Livingstone, age nineteen, were married by the Baptist minister in Calais, Maine, on August 6, 1906. They moved to Hopkinton, New Hampshire, in September of that year and began teaching at a small school. They were the only teachers at the school. Clarence taught the older children, and Sophia the younger ones. Halfway through the school year, they stopped teaching. Perhaps some parents were concerned about the date of their marriage and the imminent birth of their child. Their daughter was born on March 13th and was named after Clarence's mother. Through a school friend, Clarence learned about an opening for a mathematics teacher at Poly Prep Country Day School in Brooklyn, New York. He traveled there by train, interviewed for the job, and was hired. For the next forty-four years, he instructed boys in algebra and geometry at Poly Prep, while serving as the faculty advisor and later the coach of the track and field team. He attended every major track meet held in New York City and saw all the famous long distance runners up through the 1950s. When he retired in 1952, he was honored by the school for his many years of dedicated teaching and coaching.

Starting in 1908, Clarence and Sophia lived in rented flats in Brooklyn, and Sophia soon gave birth to two more children. During the summers, Clarence worked as a camp counselor in Maine to make a little extra money while Sophia took care of the children. One day in the early summer of 1922, she walked into the office of the chairman of the board of Poly Prep School, a man who was a wealthy financier. She explained to him she needed to get her children out of the city during the summers while Clarence worked at the summer camp, and he agreed to loan her $1,000. This was enough to buy a small house on one acre of land in the rural countryside outside Bedford Village, New York, about forty miles north of the city. During the school year, the family continued to live in rented apartments in Brooklyn, but weekends, holidays, and summers were spent at their real home in Bedford. Sophia planted flower gardens and pried up stones from the rocky ground to build a patio. One year, she decided the house was too small. She dug underneath the house and carried out the dirt in buckets, which she dumped into the woods. Eventually, this became a modest basement.

When women were granted the right to vote in 1920, Sophia became a dedicated voter. Clarence was a staunch Republican, but Sophia came from a Democratic family. Each Election Day, when Clarence returned home from school in the evening, Sophia was dressed and waiting to go to the polls. "Clarence," she said to him each year, "Take me down to the polls so I can cancel out your vote."

There were walking races for women in Brooklyn, and Sophia competed in some of them, although she never won a race.

Clarence and Sophia lived together for fifty-three years until Clarence died of cancer in 1960. After his death, Sophia sold the house in Bedford and moved to a small house in Pennsylvania, built for her on the farm where her son and his family lived. Under a cedar tree, she made a small stone patio, and she planted wildflowers in a little garden. On summer evenings, she sat on the patio among her flowers.

Her son's family dug a small swimming pool at the farm. Sometimes, on warm evenings, when she heard the family swimming, Sophia went to join them, walking along a path through the field. Under her robe, she wore an old-fashioned bathing costume with a skirt. She sat on the pool edge for a few moments, cooling her feet in the water, then pushed off and swam through the cool water with a slow breaststroke. Sophia loved many things in life, but she especially loved to swim.

Sophia in her garden and in the pool, 1967[12]

CHAPTER EIGHT

Darling Girl

C. Preston Scoboria,
"Scibby," age 23[13]

Gloria Van Wart, age 22[14]

World War II began in September 1939 when Germany invaded Poland. In response, Britain and France declared war on Germany. For fifteen months, battles raged in Europe while the United States remained officially neutral in the conflict. During this time, German U-boat submarines roamed the Atlantic Ocean, and American merchant vessels were targeted because the United States shipped critical food supplies and other necessities to Great Britain. Before the United States entered the war in December 1941 following the attack on Pearl Harbor, twenty-three American merchant vessels were sunk or damaged by submarines in the Atlantic Ocean. This led to the creation of the Armed Guard, Navy personnel stationed aboard merchant ships to provide protection.

An Armed Guard contingent might be as large as twenty-seven enlisted men and one officer, manning antiaircraft and anti-ship weapons. The most common guns included the 20-mm Oerlikon Autocannon and 3"/50, 4"/50, and 5"/50 deck guns. During the war, Armed Guard contingents were placed on 6,236 American and Allied merchant ships. To provide enough officers to oversee the enlisted crew on these ships, men from civilian life were given a three-month training course, then commissioned as lieutenant junior grade in the Navy. These officers became known as "90-Day Wonders." In civilian life, they might have been farmers, bankers, teachers, doctors, or engineers, none of them with any prior experience at sea. Suddenly, they were thrust into war.

C. Preston Scoboria, Jr., 1912–1993

December 17, 1944, Entry from the log of Navy Lieutenant JG C. Preston Scoboria, officer in command of the Armed Guard contingent on the merchant tanker SS *Chapultepec* en route from the Port of New York to Aruba in the Caribbean Sea:

17 Dec. 1944—Weather cold, clear—*Chapultepec* cleared Pier 13 at 1200—anchored out in mid stream—Sea watches took over at 1700, all squared away and underway. Bon voyage—Good sailing and what have you.—General quarters and 5/38 gun drill held—all secure[15]

December 18, 1944

Darling girl,

We are finally away. The ship pulled away from the harbor yesterday, and we began the run down to Aruba. It is cold out, and spray sometimes blows over the deck as the ship plows through the waves. The ship is a good one, though, Darling, and a better gun crew never shipped out of the Port of New York. The captain is a good man. We talked today and the trip will go well. I am still recovering from the cold that I had, but the hot weather in the Caribbean should take care of it. Darling, it may seem like a long time that I will be away, but weeks will turn into months, and then I will be home again.

All my love to you, Darling.   *Love Scibby[16]*

October 1932

Thirteen Years Earlier

The presidential election between President Herbert Hoover and New York Governor Franklin Delano Roosevelt is in full swing. Unemployment in the United States is nearly 25 percent, and camps of homeless men and women have sprung up on the outskirts of many cities. The newspapers have come up with a name for them—Hoovervilles.

At Tufts College in Medford, Massachusetts, on the outskirts of Boston, the Freshman Dance is about to start. Sophomore boys dressed in formal attire stand inside the door of the hall watching as freshman girls enter, each one wearing a nametag. One boy excitedly approaches a young lady as she enters. "I have been looking for you all week. Our trunks traveled on the train together from Stamford, Connecticut, but I could not find you at the Capen House."

"That's because I don't live at the Capen House. I live at my uncle's house on Capen Street. I heard that a group of older boys kept asking for me at the Capen House all week, but I could not understand why."

"Let's move out to the patio, and I will introduce myself properly," he said.

The next day, the boy was walking across the campus when he saw the young lady approaching on the same path. Years later, he wrote about that moment:

> It was a crisp fall morning. She was as pretty as a picture, heading across the campus from the Chapel to Braker Hall. Her cheeks were rosy, and her steps were purposeful. She was heading someplace, and I knew right then and there it had to be with me.

Scibby was twenty years old when they met. Gloria was seventeen.

C. Preston Scoboria, Jr., was named after his father, Clarence Scoboria, a mathematics teacher at a Poly Prep Academy in Brooklyn, but no one ever called him Clarence. His mother called him Preston, but everyone else knew him as Scibby. Although he spent his childhood in rented apartments in Brooklyn, on weekends the family traveled to their small house in Bedford, New York, forty miles north of the city. Scibby spent his summers at a camp in Maine where his father worked as a camp counselor. He attended the prep school where his father taught and distinguished himself as an outstanding wrestler and runner. After graduation from high school in 1930, his family had no money for him to attend college, so he worked for a year as a junior reporter for the *Brooklyn Daily Eagle,* where he wrote articles about prep school and college athletics. The following year, Scibby started at Tufts College, his tuition paid by a wrestling scholarship.

Gloria Van Wart was born in Brooklyn, New York. During the boom years of the 1920s, her father and two partners opened a store in Manhattan to sell radios. Commercial radio stations had begun broadcasting in 1919, and radios were the latest fad. The store prospered for half a dozen years, and the family bought a house in Darien, Connecticut. When the economy collapsed in the late 1920s, the store failed, and Gloria's father could not find employment. The family managed to remain in their home because her mother found work as a private duty nurse, and the children made small amounts of money to help out. In 1932, Gloria was awarded a scholarship from the local chapter of the Daughters of the American Revolution, which paid her tuition at Tufts College. Gloria would live at the home of her uncle in Boston and share a room and bed with her first cousin, Shirley. Gloria said later that Shirley only tolerated the arrangement because it gave her access to Gloria's wardrobe.

On March 20, 1933, Franklin Roosevelt was inaugurated president in the midst of a disastrous run of bank failures. Half of the banks in the United States failed during the Depression. The first week he was in office, President Roosevelt declared a bank holiday, which closed all the banks in the country for a week to help stabilize the economy. A few months later, Roosevelt signed into law the 1933 Banking Act, which established the Federal Deposit Insurance Corporation (FDIC). This insured the deposits of bank customers. It was one of many acts passed by Congress to stabilize the national economy and return the country to prosperity.

A young person in college had more important things to focus on than bank failures. The friendship grew between Gloria and Scibby. They both loved to dance, and weekends found them gliding across the floor to the music of one of the big bands that played in Boston: the Dorsey Brothers, Bennie Goodman, and others. At the end of the school year in 1933, Scibby returned to the apartment in Brooklyn, and Gloria to her family home in Darien. He wrote to her shortly after the summer began.

June 26, 1933

— Gloria Darling —

What's the story on your coming down to the big city some time next week. Course I know it will feel strange, the high buildings and all, but we could have some fun. My Mother, father and sister will be here. I have been look-ing for a job, sleeping, reading, and the movies on Sunday.

Now I'm serious about your coming down. I figured you could come down some morning with your Daddy, and I would meet you wherever its conve-nient for you. Maybe your Mother would like my Mother to write to ask you. If so just write and say so. Maybe you have a job, maybe your away, maybe your in love, how am I to know. Dear, write and tell me what's what, and until I hear from you —

Love, Scibby

During the summer of 1933, Scibby found work digging ditches for a plumbing company. A crisis occurred during his sophomore year in 1933–1934 when his grades plummeted and he lost his wrestling scholarship. He was not allowed to wrestle until his grades recovered. Meanwhile, Gloria and Scibby's lives went on.

After the 1933–1934 school year, Gloria and Scibby returned to their homes and wrote to each other many times that summer. Scibby found part-time work at Sears, Roebuck & Co., but earned only enough to pay some of his expenses. In the fall, school began, and Scibby was reinstated on the wrestling team for his junior year. He did well. The next year was Scibby's final year at Tufts. In the New England Wrestling Championships, he finished in third place, los-ing in overtime to a wrestler from Harvard who went on to take the bronze medal at the National Tournament. Gloria acted in plays and wrote articles for the journalism society at Tufts.

Finally, in June 1935, Scibby graduated from Tufts. Gloria had one more year at Tufts, but a problem arose. Her uncle's family moved away from Boston, and she had no place to live. She found a room at a sorority but had little money to buy food. Every day, she and a friend went to the lunch counter at Woolworth's and ordered the least expen-sive meal on the menu, a grilled cheese sandwich and bowl of tomato soup. She was hungry most of the time. Sometimes she accepted a date request from a young man because she knew he would buy them something to eat. Scibby spent the year in Brooklyn trying to find work. He took on a position at Woolworth's as an assistant manager, hired because a college friend was the son of a Woolworth's executive. Scibby took the train to Boston many weekends to see Gloria. He bought a large breakfast for them on Sunday morning, then raced back to Brooklyn to be ready for work. Occasionally, he drove his old car. A letter tells of one trip.

My Darling Girl

I can't think straight somehow, so I am not going to say too much. We managed to reach Bedford about five o'clock in the morning after running out of gas between Hartford and Danbury and draining all of the hoses at gas stations for about thirty miles. We slept for about two hours then continued on to the city. I bought a toothbrush and razor and performed the necessary functions at the store. This morning has been a hazy one, and luckily we have not been very busy. I guess I can manage this afternoon all right.

Dearest girl, it was a weekend just pack full of interest, fun, and pleasure. It seems that the next two weeks will be long ones, but before either of us realize it, we will be together again. Enjoy yourself my Gloria. I wish I could make the next two weeks as happy as the past two days have been. Take care of yourself dear, take care of our love. You know I am cheering for you. [Gloria had the lead role in a play, and it was about to open.]

Love, Your Scibby

December 1944

Aboard the *Chapultepec*

December 30, 1944, Entry from the log of Navy Lieutenant JG C. Preston Scoboria on the merchant tanker SS *Chapultepec* en route from Panama to Hollandia, New Guinea:

30 Dec. 1944
Pulled out at 0800—Went through the canal—Set out to sea at 1700—Sea watch put on—General quarters held.—Passed between Coral and Cocos Islands—Course 240°—We are on our way—The run is going to be a long one.

Darling Girl, we are in the Pacific now and the weather is warm, with a light breeze. We passed through the Canal earlier today. It is an astonishing place. I want to show it to you someday, when this war is over, and we are together again. Maybe we could travel there with our children so they could see it also. I thought about them often, especially when I saw the little children in Aruba, where the ship was loaded with oil. Darling, keep our little ones safe, and I will be home to you as soon as I can be there. It has been a long day so I will say goodnight to you. Hug the little ones for me.

Love, Scibby

Back in 1936

The American economy slowly improved, although the unemployment rate remained above 15 percent. At the Olympics in Berlin, American runner Jesse Owens won four gold medals. Hoover Dam was completed on the Colorado River. The first issue of *Life* magazine appeared in stores, and the Civil War epic *Gone with the Wind* was published. In November 1936, Franklin Roosevelt won a second presidential term, beating Kansas Governor Alf Landon. Gloria and Scibby voted for Landon, but he won the electoral votes from only Maine and Vermont.

In June, Gloria graduated from Tufts with a major in history and French, and she was hired as a preschool teacher at a small school in Connecticut. Scibby continued working for Woolworth's in New York, but he grew frustrated with the job. At the end of each work shift, he was required to check the shoes of each of the female salesclerks to make sure they had not secreted coins in them. The experience was demeaning. He tried selling insurance but had no success. Finally, in late 1936, he quit Woolworth's and borrowed $100 from his brother-in-law. This was enough money to rent a storefront in Springdale,

Scibby's 5¢ to 50¢ & Fountain in Springdale, Connecticut

Connecticut, and to purchase a small stock of goods to sell.

"Scibby's 5¢ to 50¢ & Fountain" was the name of the store, and Scibby dreamed that this would be the first of many similar stores. His sister came to Springdale and managed the store during the day, while Scibby took a job in a local steel plant and worked at the store in the evenings. There was an ice cream counter in the store, and much of the business came from couples who attended the movie theater next door and stopped in for a cone after the show.

As 1937 arrived, the economy fell back into recession. Unemployment shot up to nearly 20 percent. Over the five years that Roosevelt had been President, Congress passed many new laws that were then ruled unconstitutional by the Supreme Court, which had a majority of conservative justices. In February 1937, Roosevelt supported the introduction of a bill in Congress that would allow him to appoint additional justices to the Court. This controversial proposal was disputed for months before it was tabled in July 1937. However, within a short time, several of the older justices of the court retired, and Roosevelt was able to appoint justices more to his political persuasion. During 1937 three cases came before the Court that remain important eighty years later: the establishment of a national minimum wage, the establishment of the Labor Relations Board, and the establishment of the Social Security system. Each was narrowly approved by the court.

Throughout the ups and downs of the economy and the momentous issues being decided in Washington, D.C., the little store in Springdale managed to stay open. A few miles away, Gloria continued to teach preschool. In the spring of 1938, a notice appeared in the *Brooklyn Citizen* newspaper.

> Announcement has been made of the engagement of Miss Gloria Van Wart, daughter of Mr. and Mrs. Irving Van Wart of Darien, Conn. to Clarence Preston Scoboria, Jr. of this borough and Bedford, New York.
>
> Miss Van Wart is a graduate of Tufts College. Mr. Scoboria is a graduate of Poly Prep Country Day School in Brooklyn, where his father has been a member of the faculty for the last thirty years. Mr. Scoboria graduated from Tufts in 1935.
>
> The wedding will take place in the spring.[17]

January–February 1945

Aboard the *Chapultepec*

SS *Chapultepec* reached Hollandia, New Guinea, after a twenty-five-day voyage across the Pacific Ocean. The stay in Hollandia lasted only four hours, as the ship was assigned to join a thirty-ship convoy heading toward the Philippines, which had been liberated from the Japanese only two months earlier. En route, the ship dropped out of the convoy because of an engine problem. It was a tense time because the ship sat motionless for five hours until repairs were completed. The ship then traveled alone for nearly a day until it caught up with the convoy. Scibby wrote in the log that it was a happy ship when they were back in the midst of the other ships. Four days later, the convoy reached its destination at Leyte Bay, Philippines.

January 31,1945, Entry from the log of Navy Lieutenant JG C. Preston Scoboria, Leyte Bay, Philippines:

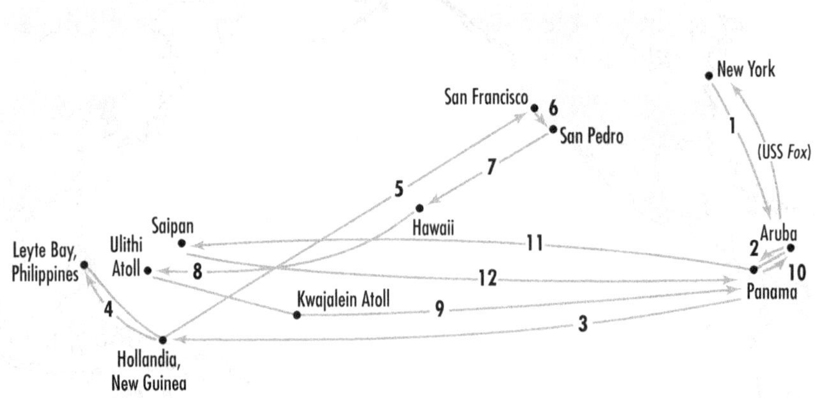

1945 voyages of SS *Chapultepec.* December 17, 1944: left New York; (1) Aruba to load oil, twice; (2) the Panama Canal; (3) Hollandia, New Guinea; (4) Leyte Bay, Philippines; (5) San Francisco; (6) San Pedro, California, to load oil, twice; (7) Hawaii; (8) Ulithi Atoll to deliver oil, twice; (9) passing Kwajalein Atoll, to Panama for a month of maintenance; (10) to Aruba; (11) to Saipan; (12) return to Panama. Scibby traveled to New York via the USS *Fox* on November 8, 1945.

31 Jan 1945—General quarters morning—Sighted Samar Island 0800—Convoy broke formation at 1100—Arrived in Leyte Bay 1300 and anchored.—Activity amazing.—Hundreds of planes move overhead at all times. Must be 1000 ships here.—Remained on ship all day. Air raid alert at 2000. Men manned their guns. Alert over at 2020. All secure 2400—Port watch on.

Chapultepec spent fourteen days in Leyte Bay, discharged oil into a Liberty ship, a Navy oiler, and other vessels, and had two large crash boats unloaded from the main deck. Several nights there were air raids. The island of Leyte had been liberated from Japanese occupation for about three months, but vessels damaged by kamikaze attacks were still in the bay. Lieutenant Scoboria was able to go ashore at Tacloban on Leyte Island, and he wrote about his time there.

Feb 14, 1945

My Darling Girl,

We haven't moved for days and probably will remain motionless for days to come. It is beautiful here, and except for the fact that the boys cannot get ashore, I wouldn't mind staying here indefinitely. I had a trying day last Sunday, but all is peace and quiet again. Gloria, I have had a chance to see the children around here, and they are little darlings, especially the little boys. I have reached down and picked up one of the wide-eyed youngsters more than once and given him a hug. They look me in the eye and laugh and say "Tank you."

The days go by and soon three months will be crossed off the worn calendar on my headwall. Three down and four to go. Of course, don't count too much on this seven month business for it could easily be longer. Keep those letters coming, Dear, for I am looking forward with great anticipation for the next batch. Hug our little boys for me and especially our baby daughter.

Love to all of you.

Scibby

Gloria wrote regularly, although letters often took a month to go each way. She had no idea where Scibby was or where the ship would go next, so she simply hoped that her letters would reach him.

Feb 16, 1945

Dearest Boy,

I haven't been looking for mail from you lately, because I did not know if any would be sent from where you are, and I might have to wait a month or more. It has been a long winter here, and it is too early for spring to start. We had a little snow this week, and today is cold rain, really quite miserable. The boys are inside and racing about, shouting as loud as they can. They are quite comical, really, hugging each other one moment and battling with each other the next. Our baby is adorable, dear. She can turn over as many times as she wants. She crawls to reach her toys, and she stretches up her arms to be picked up when she sees me come into the room. She holds her bottle, then takes it out and bangs it against the crib, then puts it back in her mouth. I wish that you could see her.

Darling, I must get to bed, so will stop and only want you to know how much we love you all of the time.

Your loving wife, Gloria

Gloria did not reveal in her letter that the baby girl had contracted chickenpox from the boys. After recovering, she developed a high fever. The doctor diagnosed pneumonia and prescribed total isolation in a warm room with constant use of a steam lamp. He prescribed a new medicine, sulfa, and said that the other children must not come near the baby until the fever subsided. Gloria's maiden aunt, Mignon, had been helping her with the children. Mignon moved into a closed room with the baby, where she fed and cared for her while Gloria kept the two boys away from the room. After three weeks, the fever let up, and the baby began to recover. Gloria did not mention the illness to Scibby as he could do nothing to help.

After fourteen days anchored in Leyte Bay, the *Chapultepec* steamed out as part of a seventy-ship convoy, returned to New Guinea, then made the long crossing to the West Coast of the United States, where it was loaded with oil and headed out to sea again.

1938, 1939, 1940

War Begins—Scibby and Gloria Wed

Germany occupied Austria and threatened Czechoslovakia. Benito Mussolini was named First Marshall of the Italian Empire. Howard Hughes completed a record breaking flight around the world in ninety-one hours. Superman first appeared in Action Comics No. 1. A fish thought to be extinct, the coelacanth, was caught in deep water off the coast of South Africa. Otto Hahn discovered the fission of uranium, marking the beginning of the nuclear age.

In Connecticut on April 23, 1938, C. Preston Scoboria and Gloria Van Wart were married at the home of her parents. The house was decorated with masses of palms and ferns, combined with smilax, jonquils, daffodils, and snapdragons. The couple drove to Washington, D.C., for their honeymoon. On the return trip, Scibby stopped in Philadelphia, and they attended the Penn Relays, the largest track and field meet in the country. Scibby's prep school, Poly Prep of Brooklyn, won the Prep School mile relay at the meet. Gloria realized that watching track and field meets was going to be a significant part of her married life. The couple returned to live in a small rental house in Springdale.

Six months later, Gloria's family had a financial crisis, lost their home, and moved into the house with Gloria and Scibby. This proved to be an impossible situation for the young couple as they had no privacy after Gloria's parents and little sister moved in. They moved into a tiny apartment above the store, and it was their home for the next two years. A baby was born to them in January of 1939 and named Preston, after Scibby's father and grandmother. When the weather was pleasant, Gloria sat outside the store with the baby in a stroller. People stopped to admire the baby and occasionally bought something at the store.

The war in Europe began in September 1939. In May of 1940, Germany invaded France, defeated the French and British armies and occupied Paris. France was split into a northern half occupied by German troops and a southern half ruled by a puppet French government. German air forces extensively bombed England in preparation for an invasion of the island, but were held off by the Royal Air Force and British air defenses. America was not actively involved in the war, but came under pressure to support the Allied countries.

In the United States, the economy still suffered from high unemployment and low corporate earnings. Among the businesses to close in 1940 was the movie theater in Springdale next to Scibby's 5¢ to 50¢ store. When this happened, the little store could not survive. In spring of 1941, Scibby sold the remaining inventory, and he and Gloria moved to his parents' house in Bedford along with baby Preston. It was a tough choice to give up on the little store they had worked so hard to make a success, but at least they had a place to go. Scibby wrote to his mother just after they reached Bedford.

April 29, 1941

Dear Mother

For four and a half years I have been closing the little store and going upstairs to our little apartment. Habit is a powerful influence, and home is where the heart is, so they say. But Sunday midnight when we piled the old car with belongings, with the baby and dog in the front seat between us, left Springdale and turned into the driveway at Bedford, I had for the first time in four and a half years, that honest to goodness feeling that I was home.

I don't know how long we will be in Bedford. It may be for the summer or maybe just for a month. But wherever we go and whatever we do, when we return to this house, we will have that feeling of coming home. Love, Preston

April 1945

The *Chapultepec*—A Load of Oil

On April 12,1945, news came on the ship's radio that President Roosevelt had suffered a heart attack and died. Vice President Truman was sworn in as president.

April 13,1945

Darling Girl,

Another day is passing and soon it will be another week. The sad news yesterday reached us about eleven right after we had finished firing the guns. It is a great blow to the country and a great loss to the whole world. He gave his life just as any soldier in the battle for a better world of tomorrow.

Dear girl, the war in Europe is just about over. It is a tired world that finally sees the end of the bloody, needless struggle. Over here it is hard to tell how long it will all last. We hope and pray that it will all be over very soon.

We are going to get busy as soon as I get home and find ourselves a piece of land and build ourselves a dream house. It will be so much fun working on it. I can hardly wait until that day comes when Preston and I take our shovels and turn the first spade full of earth.

I am hoping to get off after this trip, but I don't think that I have a chance. No matter, just one more trip will do it.

Everything is going fine, and we are moving right along toward our destination. Another week will find us looking for land.

Take care of your precious self and watch over those wonderful children. I love you all.

Scibby

Gloria also heard of the President's death, and she wrote to Scibby about how deeply she felt. Their letters crossed in the mail and arrived a month after they were written. Gloria was desperate about her husband's absence, and sometimes she cried at night when the babies were in bed.

April 12, 1945

Darling boy,

Today has been a very momentous day in history and a very sad one. Today President Franklin Roosevelt died. It is such a great loss to this country, especially at this particular time, when he will not be able to take part in forming the peace which we all feel to be in the not too far distant future. How sad that he could not have lived to see the end of this dreadful war. I have been listening to very beautiful music in honor of the President. I only hope, as I know you do too, that his passing won't prolong the war in any way.

Do you get my mail regularly? I send at least a letter a day. I know you can't tell us where you are, but you should see Preston and I poring over the map of those thousands of islands, wishing we had some idea of where you were. Is there any chance you might get home before August? I suppose you don't know, but we would like to hope. Answer me some questions, will you dear. It seems that we never get answers, we just send letters.

Love Gloria

April 1945

Somewhere in the Pacific Ocean

April 16, 1945, entry from the log of Navy Lieutenant JG C. Preston Scoboria, on the merchant tanker SS *Chapultepec* in the Pacific, en route from San Pedro, California, to Ulithi Atoll in the Carolina Islands:

16 April 1945—General quarters morning and evening—Temp 90°—weather clear and hot—sea quiet—speed 13½ knots—Position at 1500—11°09′N, 175°29′E—all secure at 2400—Passed 15 ships

April 16, 1945

Darling girl,

The sun is shining, and the heat is giving us a going over. It feels like the summer season out here. Darling don't worry about storms out here for all you have to do is look up in your geography and you will find out that the monsoon winds don't blow until September, October, and November. We have not seen any weather as yet. Fingers crossed and all that sort of thing.

Yesterday, we saw our first atoll, a group of tiny islands resting precariously out in the middle of nowhere. It must be a quiet life for the men who are based on this isolated atoll. The water is clear, and the sand is white, and I saw boys laying around on the beach. They don't go swimming because sharks are reported in these waters.

The sea was so quiet this morning that it was like glass. The only ripple in it was made by the wake of the ship.

I try to play a little chess, do a little reading, check on the boys, try to settle arguments, censor letters, and do my daily dozen exercises.

I hope all the darling children are well and happy. It seems like forever, but in a matter of months I will be coming home to you. I love you all very much.

Love, Scibby

Gloria's next letter was written on yellow lined paper instead of her usual writing paper. The big news was that her younger sister Ruth was planning to marry a sailor who was scheduled to go overseas. The family had not even met him yet. The young couple was borrowing Scibby and Gloria's old car for their honeymoon.

April 15, 1945

My darling boy,

As you can imagine, this is some of our boy Preston's paper, as I am out of my own & had to use something. This is Monday, tho' I put yesterday's date up top. I worked yesterday and Saturday. It was a busy weekend and especially Sunday. I served about thirty dinners besides ala carte orders + I managed fine—no mistakes—no dissatisfied customers—in fact I felt I had done all right because it's the busiest day since I've been there. Everything went very smoothly. It is kind of fun working, and I am sure it is good for me. It gives me something else to think about besides the children.

Well Darling, we are all well + I don't like to keep repeating myself too much, but I yearn for the day when you come home to us. I miss your dear self.

Your loving wife, Gloria

A few days later, a letter arrived written on writing paper, but it was oddly stained.

Thursday, April 19, 1945

My Darling boy

Wait till you hear about what happened to my nice new box of writing paper. I left it on the couch when I came home yesterday, and after I put Raymond to bed, I closed the kitchen door to keep the heat in there. I thought I heard a funny noise, but I opened the door to listen + all was quiet. A little while later I went up with Preston. I went to tuck Ray in. I was horrified to find him snowed under with envelopes, and not only that but the whole package of paper was under him and wet. I took them out and dried them, but they still have a tired, wilted look. Then tonight, after he'd been in bed an hour, I heard weird noises from the front room. All lights on and Raymond doing his best to coax music out of the old organ. He certainly did tear upstairs when he saw the fire in my eyes.

I just heard on the radio that an announcement would be made in the morning. Here's hoping!!

I've just finished struggling through the monthly accounts. More fun! Poppa, you can have the job when you return. The school sent a nice letter which I sent on to you. They are eager to get you back. How do you feel about it?

I am very sleepy, so I'll get to bed—loads of love to you from all of us.

Your loving wife, Gloria

1941

Scibby and Gloria Begin Teaching School—United States Enters the War

Gloria and little Preston stayed in the house in Bedford for four months, while Scibby traveled to Maine and managed the summer camp where his father worked as a counselor. He hated being away from his wife and baby son and wrote to them nearly every day. In the fall, the couple traveled to Pennsylvania and started teaching at Meadowbrook School, a private school for children from kindergarten through eighth grade. Scibby received a salary of $1,000 for teaching eighth grade and coaching sports. Gloria received $600 for teaching kindergarten.

In December 1941, in the middle of their first school year at Meadowbrook, America entered World War II after the attack on Pearl Harbor. Scibby wanted to volunteer right away, but Gloria persuaded him to wait. The couple lived in rented rooms during the school year, but in the summer, they looked for a house to rent. They traveled by train to stations near Meadowbrook. When they reached Yardley, they learned that nearby Castanea Farm had several empty houses. They walked there from the train station and arranged to rent a large older house for $25 per month. Moving in was easy because the couple owned only their clothes, a folding card table, and four folding chairs. Apple boxes in the barn became bookshelves. A fruit orchard supplied apples and pears, and Gloria canned applesauce for the winter. This old house was their home for the next eight years.

When the next school year began, Gloria was pregnant again, and gave birth to their second child in January 1943. They named him Raymond after Scibby's college roommate. Meanwhile, Scibby applied for a position in the United States Navy, but months went by without an acceptance of his application.

In the Pacific War, Japanese forces seized the Philippine Islands and a wide swath of islands in the Pacific. Numerous sea battles were fought, climaxed by the Battle of Midway, in which American planes sank four Japanese aircraft carriers. By the end of 1942, the United States and its allies began to recover islands that had been occupied by Japanese forces. Fierce fighting occurred on the island of Guadalcanal in the Solomon Islands before the U.S. Marines occupied it in early 1943.

May 1945

A Second Load of Oil to Ulithi

May 27, 1945, Entry from the log of Navy Lieutenant JG C. Preston Scoboria, on the merchant tanker SS *Chapultepec* in the Pacific, en route from San Pedro, California, to Ulithi Atoll in the Carolina Islands with a second load of oil and barrels of aviation fuel.

27 May, 1945

0500 General quarters

1000 Inspection of ready boxes and magazines

1300 Fire and boat drills

1400 Sighted object apparently moving at surface of water

1410 Rang general quarters

1420 Trained all guns on object which proved to be dead whale

1425 Fired aft + forward guns and port side 20 m/m—several hits

1500 Position 179°59′E 17°30′N

1730 Radio report from a merchant vessel—Submarine surfaced and submerged at 134°18′E 12°38′N

1930 General quarters

2400 All secure 21.

Soon after the ship left San Pedro, a stowaway was discovered aboard. No explanation was given as to why a person would stow aboard a merchant tanker heading across the Pacific Ocean, but the ship detoured to Pearl Harbor and transferred the stowaway ashore.

The days passed slowly aboard ship. The sun rose, it grew hot, and men stood watch twenty-four hours a day, looking out for submarines and other hazards. Days went by, and they saw nothing. The seventeen young men Scibby had in his charge grew bored and fought with each other. He felt that he wasn't doing much to help the war effort. Men were fighting and dying on Iwo Jima and Okinawa, while he and his crew were doing nothing on a tanker slowly crossing the Pacific Ocean. Scibby had to keep his men busy, so he found work for them to do, gave them tests to see if they

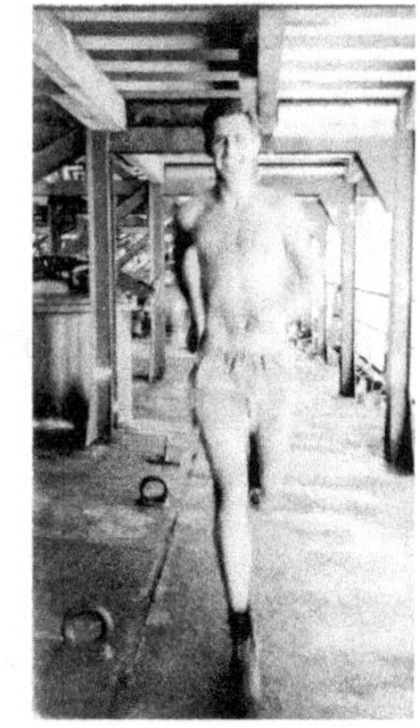

Scibby running laps aboard ship

could progress to the next level of their specialty, and encouraged them to stay physically active. He ran around the ship many times to get exercise, and he encouraged the men to join him.

Most of the time, Scibby maintained the daily routine, wrote letters, filled out the log, went to chow, and kept his men as busy as possible. The days passed.

May 27, 1945

My Darling Girl,

Another day has passed and although I had a little trouble, no matter, it is gone. The trouble I suppose keeps us in better condition. Tomorrow morning, we will pass through the [Hawaiian] Islands and then the long stretch across. I hope that this is my last trip this way. All the time though Darling, the time is sliding by and the war moving closer and closer to the end. It will be some months anyway before the boys from Europe will come over here and when that time comes all will move ahead more rapidly.

There is not a lot to do aboard, and I guess the extra time weighs heavy on my hands. I am used to a great deal of activity and not days of inactivity. The ship is in the best of condition, so there is not a lot for the men to do. I will put on a heavier watch tomorrow, and that should keep the boys a little more tired. They are all young men and full of pep. There's just a couple of men who have been around too long.

These letters are not exactly the kind you are looking for, but they are all that I can turn out right now. I love you all so very much and was so happy to hear that you were all well at home. I wish I could talk with you about the children and other things.

Another twelve days and we will be just around the corner, then unload and turn back. Rest assured tho' Darling that I think of you a good bit of the time out here and that I am as eager to get home as you are to have me. I want to hold each one of those children and hug them and most of all I want to hold you something fierce. Love, Scibby

Gloria wrote regularly, and her letters were many pages long. She related news of her family and described the children, their dog and cat, and people she met in the town. Her youngest sister had married, her middle sister was expecting her first child, and Scibby's sister recently had a baby. Gloria also wrote intimately of how much she missed her husband, and how she longed for his touch and his gentle ways.

May 22, 1945 Tuesday

Dearest Boy,

Today was a very lovely day. Preston is looking very mumpy + rather comical, but not feeling badly at all. He seems to throw off illness quite quickly. We had some fun today—it must have hurt him to laugh, yet everything struck us as funny—the way he looked, the scarf we tied around his chin looked like bunny ears up on top and so we couldn't stop laughing until we agreed it was funny, but we wouldn't laugh about it. I made some new curtains for our room—very simple but kind of pretty. I think you will like them. Just for a bit of privacy—good idea?

Well, Darling, I guess I will go to bed this time. It was wonderful to hear your voice from the West Coast while your ship was there—for a little while you were right here with me. I got the money—thank you—I can manage fine. Darling, I love you so much I just melt to think of it.   Gloria

The *Chapultepec* pulled into Ulithi Atoll on June 6, 1945, and left five days later after unloading oil and barrels of aviation fuel. The ship was directed to Panama for maintenance. By now, the Pacific Islands were familiar to Scibby, and he wrote in the log about passing Kwajalein and Eniwetok. The ship reached Panama on July 5 after twenty-five days at sea. It spent a month in Panama, and most of the time, Scibby and the crew had nothing to do. It was a long month.

July 6, 1945, Entry from the log of Navy Lieutenant JG C. Preston Scoboria, on the merchant tanker SS *Chapultepec,* anchored in the harbor of Panama City in preparation for maintenance at a floating drydock:

6 July 1945 Anchored in harbor—port watches on—General inspection, then men granted liberty—waiting for the scheduled time in the drydock.—All secure

Darling Gloria,

We are in now and will be here for some time. I want to get this letter off to you today when I go ashore. I won't be home for some time now so you just got to make up your mind, Dearest Girl, to hang on for about three more months and then I will be walking up the lane. I received all your good letters and was relieved to know that all at home is fine.

> *They have made it a year on all the ships now and so being just a cog in the wheel I will have to wait my turn along with the others.*
>
> *I love you with all my heart, take care of yourselves and remember I am going to do my best to have Christmas at home this year.* Love, Scibby

The following is a short excerpt of one of Gloria's long letters. While the ship was in Panama, it only took a week for their letters to be delivered. Servicemen were not allowed to call on the phone to the United States, so letters were their only communication.

June 24, 1945

My Darling,

Today was a real scorcher. I guess compared to some of the heat you've felt it wasn't much, but it surely felt hot here. I sleep late every Monday to rest up after a strenuous weekend at the restaurant, but the sun got me up earlier than normal. I gathered up the boys and took them down for a haircut. Raymond is resigned to the barber now (he likes the blond one), while Preston will have only the dark one. After a milkshake at Pryors—we met Neal Nolan's wife in front of the store. She is a nice blond girl whom I meant to introduce myself to since she was pointed out to me on the bus. Her husband is now on an LST at Okinawa + since she hasn't heard from him for some time, she has a swell case of jitters. She has two small daughters. I'm going to stop in and visit her some time soon and we can commiserate with each other....

Darling, your letters were so inspiring. When you come home, do you know what I want? To see you put the boys to bed—to bring you a bottle of beer + a cigarette on the front porch after working in the garden—to have a late supper in the cool of the evening and then to take a walk in the dark + watch a planet go overhead—for you to kiss me and make me feel wonderful. I think of all the times I've wanted to do other things, but what really counts most to me are the nice little things we do at home together. When we're able to laugh at things together again, I know I'll never want anything more.

Your loving wife, Gloria

Back in 1943

Castanea Farm in Pennsylvania

Gloria and Scibby had a four-year-old boy and a new baby. The rented house was solid but not fancy, with a coal furnace in the basement and a coal-fired range in the kitchen. During the school year, Scibby drove the old car to the train station, then took the train to Meadowbrook, where he taught eighth-grade classes and coached football as well as track and field. He worked during the summer at a factory that made balsa wood boats for the Navy. The factory was across the Delaware River in New Jersey, too far to drive the old car because of gas rationing, so Scibby walked to the river and crossed over it on a railroad trestle. The trestle had two sets of tracks, and if a train came along while Scibby was on the trestle, he crossed to the other track. One night, on the way home from the factory, he was in the middle of the river when a train appeared. He crossed to the other track and kept walking. A few minutes later, a train appeared on the other track approaching from the opposite direction. Scibby had no time to get off the trestle before the train reached him, so he quickly moved between the two sets of tracks and flattened himself on the gravel. He lay still as the two trains thundered past, the railroad cars passing inches above his body. After the trains passed, he rose and continued his walk home.

Late in 1943, the U.S. Navy accepted Scibby into the officer training program. He was instructed to appear in February 1944 for three months of training, after which he would then receive the rank of Lieutenant JG (Junior Grade). Additional training would take place later that year, and he would become the officer in charge of the Armed Guard contingent on a merchant ship carrying war supplies. He might serve in either the Atlantic or Pacific.

About the same time, in December of 1943, the German U-boat *U-530* was prowling about in the Caribbean looking for targets when it spotted a U.S. flagged oil tanker. It was the SS *Chapultepec*, a 10,000-gross-ton ship, 550 feet long, with a top speed of 16 knots. The sub fired torpedoes, one of which slammed into the bow of the tanker and ripped a gaping hole in the hull. The ship managed to limp back to port and spent the first half of 1944 in a repair yard, where the bow was replaced.

SS *Chapultepec*, damaged by U-boat torpedo attack, December 27, 1943[18]

By the end of 1944, SS *Chapultepec* reached the Port of New York, where it was fitted with deck guns and awaited the arrival of an Armed Guard contingent. The vessel would travel to Aruba in the Caribbean to load oil and then deliver it to Navy ships in the Pacific fleet.

In the Pacific, Allied troops leapfrogged across chains of islands, attacking and seizing strategic islands and bypassing others. In the Battle of Leyte Gulf, fought in the Philippines in October 1944, an American fleet effectively destroyed the remainder of the Japanese fighting ships. This was followed by Marine landings on the island of Leyte, and Leyte Bay became a vital staging area for the U.S. Navy.

July 1945

Meanwhile, in Panama

July 1945 stretched on slowly in Panama, as the *Chapultepec* waited for scheduled maintenance in the drydock. Scibby sometimes wrote two or three letters a day. Gloria pressed him to find a way to arrange a week's liberty and come home, but most days, he could not even leave the base. Liberty was out of the question. He explained this in one of his letters, unable to say where he was because of war censorship.

21, July 1945

My Darling Gloria

Just received your lovely letter of the 12th and it was very nice to hear from you and home. I know by now you must have a good idea where I am, and if you wonder why I can't get home my dear why the main reason is they just won't let me off. We are in drydock now and will be for a few days and then we will lay around for another week or so....

That beautiful letter came last night. I found it waiting here when I returned to the ship this evening about eight thirty. I have read it over many times already and my darling girl, I just woke to find it clutched in my hand. I place my hand on my heart and find it beating steadily only for you....

I just had dinner, boiled beef and mashed potatoes. It is too darn warm to eat very much so I just peck away a little bit at a time. Darling, I really haven't changed much this year, my hair is quite a bit more gray, but you expect that. Physically I am about the same.... It is not much of a life without a wife. I listen to the men around me boasting of their nightly conquests. It just plain disgusts me. I want to get moving and get home to you, dearest....

From here on the ship, I can look all around here at the harbor. It is not very large, and it is crowded with ships, most of them just like ours. I suspect I will be back here again, and I hope that I will on my way home.

The buildings down here are all set eight to ten feet off the ground. I suspect the dampness is a problem, for it rains hard every day and it is overcast a good bit of the time if it isn't raining. I can see for about fifteen miles along the west bank which is dotted from one end to the other with buildings of all kinds. On the east bank are hundreds upon hundreds of neat American dwellings. But off to the right are some of the decrepit buildings of the native population. Most of the little boats in the harbor are operated by natives, and they move about the harbor day and night. They move slowly, but I can hardly blame them for being uninterested in their work, for the native is paid 17¢ to 25¢ an hour, while the white worker is paid $400 to $600 a month. Quite a difference....

Scibby

Gloria wrote many letters during July, often five or more pages long. She wrote about the children and how she was feeling. She sensed how frustrated Scibby felt having to wait with little to do.

July 12, 1945

Dearest,

I know that you get blue and homesick, and I wish that I could get my arms around you and remind you how wonderful you really are, and to reassure you that everything is all right at home. Dear, for the past ten years you and I have grown to need each other more and more. Together we are a team, a defense against anything outside of us in the world. But apart, we are both vulnerable to various kinds of hurts and troubles. As separate people, which we must be for a while longer, we must keep our minds alert and our bodies active and just make ourselves keep up our morale for us and those who depend upon us, you—your crew, me—the children. Don't worry about writing whiny letters—I've written some too....

We had a terrific thunderstorm today. It's been dreadfully hot and humid all week, and we were looking for rain. I went out with Raymond and the two McCutcheon children and as we walked, we watched a long white cloud on the north part of the sky. Suddenly it leaped toward us, and we could hear a dull roaring noise and saw that behind the white cloud it was all black. We ran for the porch and reached it just as the rain started + it blew from the north at first. Before I could get the windows closed it rained in all over the floor. Suddenly the wind shifted and came in from the south side. It poured, hailed, and blew. The thunder was terrific, and the lightning crackled, and everything electrical in the house clicked and snapped. In a couple of minutes, it was completely dark, and it stayed that way for an hour. The lights went out, and so we sat the children on our laps and sang silly songs for awhile. Finally, after three quarters of an hour, the storm blew over and the lights came back on....

Lynn is a lovely baby. She adores the boys, and they play with her all the time. She could walk alone if she wanted to but she's taking her time, and as yet she has no teeth at one year old. I wish you could see her.

I love you to pieces,

Gloria

Toward the end of the month in Panama, the typewriter broke, and Scibby wrote his letters in longhand. He tried to keep busy, but there was little to do until the ship was ready to depart.

July 28, 1945

Darling,

The mail was really good to me last night. Five letters and a home planning magazine. Three letters from my darling wife and two letters from Pres-ton. As far as money goes, don't worry about it. I will send you whatever I have left from now on after my bills are paid and I am sure that will cover expenses.... The war is winding down now, and Daddy may be home for good in a matter of months. Don't forget to have the coal man go over the furnace before you light it in the fall. I will tell you our destination as soon as I learn what it is, but remember that it is subject to change at any time. I expect that we will have a short trip and that means there will probably be two trips before I get home. I dream of you and the children all the time,

Will write again tonight.

All my love. —

Scibby

Finally, on August 5, the ship left Panama City, passed through the Canal, traveled to Aruba, and loaded oil. The first atomic bomb was dropped on Hiroshima on August 6, followed by a second bomb on Nagasaki on August 9. A few weeks earlier, the heavy cruiser USS *Indianapolis,* the ship that carried vital components of the bombs to the Far East, was torpedoed in the Philippine Sea and sank. The Navy was not aware of the sinking, and for four days, the survivors floated in the ocean, suffering from exposure and shark attacks. Finally, a plane noticed the survivors in the water. Only 316 men survived out of the crew of 1,195.

On *Chapultepec*, Scibby fixed the typewriter and rewrote all the entries in his log because he had not followed the correct format on his earlier entries. The ship traveled back to Panama, passed through the Canal again, and put to sea on August 12. Scibby wrote a letter on August 14, although it was not received until six weeks later.

August 14, 1945

My Very Dearest Wife

We are at sea again but even tho' we have been sliding along for hours, I can still take the glasses and gaze at the horizon on the starboard side and pick out the hills of the coast. This is going to be the shortest trip we have had as yet and I am almost glad to be out again.

I haven't written you often in the past week, but Darling I had so much work to do that I was completely over my head. What kind of work you say? Well, I found out that I had made out my log wrong, so I had to do it over. I guess I must have typed 200 pages and each page required a certain amount of work.   *Love, Scibby*

A few hours later, the Japanese surrender was announced, and he wrote another letter.

14 August, 1945

My Darling Wife

The war is over. Yes, I know that you know it and I would love to be home and say a little prayer with you tonight. I will say one here in my quarters and I know that you will be saying one at home with the children all around you. Dearest, the bad dream is over. The heavy hearts, the long waits, the worry, those depressed periods they are all past now. We have so much to be thankful for. We have so much to live for and remember, we are both living to enjoy those joys that mean so much to both of us.

I can hardly believe that as I sit here tonight in the same quarters that I have sat in for over eight months, worried so many times, a little bit frightened once in a while, and always lonely, and now the war is over. We will be on our way home soon, …

The ship has quieted down. Somehow a large quantity of liquor appeared tonight. There were a number of fights brewing. I have been busy keeping my boys on the job and in line. It is twelve o'clock now and all is quiet. I hope that it stays that way....

It is a wonderful night. I have to check the boys for the last time and also get to bed. So until tomorrow, My Darling THE WAR IS OVER. I love you so very much, Take care of yourself.   *All my love, Your Scibby*

Gloria also learned of the end of the war on August 14 and wrote to Scibby, but because of mix-ups, he did not receive her letter for six weeks.

Wednesday, August 15th

Dearest,

VJ Day—what a wonderful relief to all of us at home to know the war is finally over, and no more of our boys will have to die for peace. We must do all in our little power for the rest of our lives to see that this never happens again. If only enough Americans try to prevent another war, maybe it can be done.... ...

This morning, Preston and I cleaned the attic. If there is any chance of your coming home soon, we want it to be a clean house, as far as we are able. The trouble is I can't even guess when you'll be coming home + I keep fearing the worst, that it will still be months. Relieve my mind if you can + give me some idea, will you? ... ... Today we celebrated by making gingerbread cookies—each boy cut out his own and put his raisins in—only Raymond's was covered with raisins and Preston's was so neat it looked impossible—but they both softened up + got fat in the oven and looked so cute—the children loved them and ate every crumb. Preston keeps saying "The war isn't over until Daddy comes home"—so true—I feel the same way, so how about it Pop—we've got lots of time to make up + things to do my love —

I love you so very much.   *Your Gloria*

1944

Preparing for Service in the Navy

In April 1944, Scibby left for three months of officer training at Fort Schuyler, New York. Then in September, he traveled to Gulfport, Mississippi, for additional training. Gloria took the long trip to the South by train with five-year-old Preston and baby Lynn. Scibby rented a home in Wiggins, Mississippi, thirty miles from the Naval Training Base, and each day he traveled to the base and back to Wiggins to be with his family. Two-year-old Raymond stayed with Gloria's parents for two months while the family was in the South. In November, Gloria and Scibby with the two children took the train back to Pennsylvania. In a short time, Scibby left for duty in Brooklyn. He wrote to Gloria from the Brooklyn Naval Yard.

Lt. JG Scoboria at an antiaircraft gun[19]

Darling,

You should have seen the case we just ran into. Drunken sailors cursing civilians and all kinds of trouble. This has been a real watch with plenty of action. Things are really happening around this base. They sent 1000 men on leave today with orders to report to the nearest naval base to their home. The Armed Guard is getting smaller. When I do get a ship, which I hope will be soon, I will only have about ten men in my unit. It must mean that things are getting safer for the Armed Guard.

Beside me at the desk is the corporal of the guard. He is busy on a case of a drunken sailor who was picked up in Bronxville. He is assigned to a ship but claims to be attached to this base. We are checking now to see if he has jumped ship. If so it will mean a job for the Bronxville police and a court martial. But no, his ship is in Yonkers, and after a good night's sleep in jail, he will be sent back to his ship tomorrow....

I have really been coughing tonight. A little cold and the smoky atmosphere.

Time to close for now.   *Love Scibby*

Within a few weeks, Scibby was assigned to the SS *Chapultepec,* merchant tanker anchored in New York Harbor.

August 1945

The War Is Over

When the *Chapultepec* received news of the war's end in August 1945, it was en route to Hawaii to deliver a load of oil. New orders arrived two weeks later, shortly before the ship reached the islands. The ship was diverted, first to Ulithi and then to Saipan in the Northern Mariana Islands. Because of the confusion about where the ship was heading, its mail was delivered to Ulithi. Scibby wrote letters while the ship was crossing the Pacific, but was unable to mail them until it docked in Saipan on September 8. The stay in Saipan lasted a week, while the ship pumped oil into numerous Navy ships so they could return to the States. During that time, Scibby wrote letters, picked up seashells from the beach, and anxiously waited until it was time to depart. The following letter, written before the ship reached Saipan, is the first time during the war he could tell Gloria where he was.

Written August 24, received Sept. 29, 1945

My Darling Girl,

I heard last night over the radio that they had eliminated the censor, so I can give you the whole story. It is a shame that we diverted here, for we are over in the Far East. If we had unloaded in Pearl Harbor, we would be pulling into the States today. Now I don't know when we will be back, but I hope that it will not be more than two months. Being out here when the war is over is a pretty tough deal, but after all I guess these fellows over here need a little oil to get home, too.

Get your map and I will tell you where we are. Tonight, we will pass close by Eniwetok in the Marshall Islands and in three more days we will arrive at Saipan. There is no telling how long we will be there but let's hope we unload in a hurry. Then of course there is the long trip back. If we go to Panama, it will take 25 days. I will hurry home as fast as I possibly can.

I hope that you have gotten the furnace fixed, for it doesn't look like we will be back before cold weather sets in. Better plan on sometime in November. I think of you and the children all the time now and look forward to just one thing, getting home….

But there are so many bright sides to the picture now there is no reason for us to be blue. I am actually coming home for good. The world is at peace and most of the men should be home for Christmas.

All my love to my wonderful family. *Love, Scibby*

It was five weeks before this letter reached Gloria. During that time, she had no word of where her husband was. She kept writing and sending letters, not knowing when or if Scibby would receive them.

Friday, August 24th

Darling,

No mail for over a week + I keep thinking, foolish optimist that I am that you will come walking in one of these days. It certainly helps to keep me in an optimistic frame of mind-not to say in a dither.

A week later:

Sunday night, Sept. 2, 1945

Darling,

Here it is September, really and truly the summer is over, and I can find something to make me hopeful. Tuesday will be three weeks since your ship must have sailed + you must know I haven't heard a word from you in all that time.

People keep asking—Have you heard when your husband's coming home—and it makes me feel all strange inside. I know it must be soon, but I don't know when—oh Darling, I'm really tired and can't think of anything much to say. We are all well at home—just waiting for you. When you get home and spend a few days with the children, then you and I can take a few days and go somewhere and get acquainted again.—that is what I am looking forward to....

Dearest, for now, all my love to my darling boy.   Gloria

Gloria grew desperate about not hearing from Scibby.

Wednesday, Sept 19, 1945

Dearest,

It's been so long since I've heard from you,—and honestly, I get so I can hardly bear to write, but I know it's not fair for you expect to hear from me + you must wonder why there are so few letters. Everyone has been well lately except me—I haven't been ill, but just sick at heart from not hearing from you for so long. I kept hoping that you'd be able to phone me—then I began to think maybe you were on your way home—then I began to think your ship must have sailed before peace was declared. Now I know it did, or I would have heard from you—but I don't know where you are or where you are going or when you are coming home.

We all love you so much. Just come home soon.

Your loving wife, Gloria

There was little she could do, so she stayed busy caring for the boys and the baby, talked with Aunt Mignon, worked a few shifts at the restaurant each week, and tried not to think too much about the future. Finally, on September 29, letters arrived:

Sept. 29, 1945

My Darling,

Your wonderful letters arrived today. One came last Friday, so I knew that a batch would be on the way, that's how they always come. Darling, my heart aches for you when I think of your ship diverted this last time. It seems people are sort of straggling home in no great numbers + a great many in the remote future. So many people like me have no definite news of when their men are coming home.

Dear, if it's true you really are coming home in November, it does seem too good to be true. I'm worried about the new points system, that may mean an additional six months. I won't let my hopes get up too high just in case of another disappointment. It would be wonderful to just count on you coming November 1st, but do I dare to really hope?

I want to warn you about something that will be our first problem when you get back. It's money, of course. Don't get worried—I don't owe any money and bills are all paid up to date, but I haven't saved any money either, no war bonds except the few we had left. The money you bring home will seem like a lot, and we may start spending it too fast. Money goes so fast these days, I guess it is inflation or something. Let's start out being really careful and use it for our permanent plans. We may find it impossible to buy our land for a while. We have such wonderful years ahead of us we want to make the most of them. I'm really warning you because of my own weakness for spending money. Let's be careful, O.K.? ...

I didn't want to worry you while it was going on, but now the worst is over, I can tell you. There was quite a polio epidemic around here this summer. Several children in Morrisville died + there were a great many cases in Trenton. Children were not allowed in any stores or in public gatherings. Sunday schools and playgrounds were closed. I never took the children off the farm all summer, but the only thing we missed was the barber. I finally cut Raymond's hair, but I didn't want to tackle Preston's. Finally, the barber began to put a chair out on the sidewalk, and I took Preston, and he had his hair cut out in front of the store. He looks so much nicer with it cut, not too short, and straight across in front.

Darling, this is all for now—it's late—tired gal—clean house—get some sleep, poppa coming home.
Love, Gloria

When the letters reached Gloria, the *Chapultepec* was steaming slowly toward Panama at thirteen knots. Now that the war was over, the ship no longer needed to zigzag, and watches were a formality. Everyone just wanted to get home.

15 September 1945 (received October 11)

Darling Girl,

About 19 more long days before we hit Panama again. Oh boy, what will the future bring. When I think of walking up the lane, I get excited all over....

I have a lot of little shells that I picked up on the beaches of Saipan that I will bring home.... Today was just the same as the day before except I won five dollars in the poker session. That makes $16.00 in the hole. I will keep you posted on the day to day results....

I guess I told you that I didn't get any mail at all in Saipan. I know that everything is fine at home, but what a letter would do for the old morale at this point. The next nineteen days will sure drag. As soon as I can get a call through to you from Panama, I will make it....

Please don't plan anything for when I come home. I only want to be with my family. We can make a run up to the city and say hello to all. I hope I can get back before the leaves fall. Pennsylvania is so very beautiful in the fall. We might even be able to take a little trip, just you and I....

That's all for tonight, Sweetheart. I will write again tomorrow. Love you all the time.... Be good and take care of yourself and the children.
Your Scibby

Years later, Scibby wrote about the last few months he was overseas. The Japanese surrender announcement was issued August 14, 1945, but the official end of the war was September 2, when the peace agreement was signed.

The war was over.

August 14, 1945, the radio brought the good news. The men on board celebrated the end of the long war, and all expected to go home. But our ship, the Chapultepec, had just loaded with oil in Aruba, and the word came: "Leave for Pacific Islands" immediately. So off we steamed across the wide ocean. After unloading our oil into many ships full of young men anxious to see home, we came slowly back to Panama.

I was able to get two weeks' leave. I phoned Gloria and said I'd come home as soon as I could find transportation. Luckily, the destroyer USS Fox was leaving, and I found a berth on the crowded little ship. A rough trip up the Atlantic Coast in early November. Happy to see New York. A subway to Grand Central Station. The first train to Trenton. Grabbed a taxi at the station and rode eagerly across the Delaware River, up the road to the farm, into the lane at the big oak tree and up the rocky hill to the house. All the lights were on.

The family was waiting in the driveway. As I climbed down, two little boys jumped into my arms. Over their heads I saw my dear Gloria holding the baby Lynn, smiling, with tears running down her cheeks. The taxi driver waited patiently while we hugged, and then I remembered to pay him. The kind man drove off to tell his wife about our happy reunion. Next day was Veteran's Day, and we all stood on the lawn as I raised the flag in celebration.[20]

Final Note

During World War II, 6,236 merchant ships had Armed Guard contingents aboard. These ships endured 1,966 air attacks and 1,024 submarine attacks. A total of 733 ships were sunk. The Armed Guard is credited with 792 enemy planes destroyed or damaged. A total of 144,970 men served on the Armed Guard, and 1,810 were reported killed or missing.[21] At the end of the war, the Armed Guard was disbanded. Scibby's time on the SS *Chapultepec* was quiet, and the ship never faced gunfire or torpedoes. The greatest challenge was months of boredom and loneliness, together with the threat of torpedoes, mines, or kamikaze attacks when the ship was in the Philippines. The men assigned to guard ships in the Atlantic Ocean had a far more hazardous experience, as German U-boats roamed the entire ocean as well as the Caribbean Sea and the Gulf of Mexico.

Five years after the war ended, Gloria and Scibby borrowed money for a down payment and bought forty acres of Pennsylvania farmland. In

1952, Scibby, with help from Preston and Raymond, built a house for the family. It was their home for twenty-four years. Gloria and Scibby's love for each other never wavered. Their arms were often around each other, and when a band started to play, they were the first couple on the dance floor. In retirement, they traveled up and down the East Coast for a decade, selling dried flower arrangements at arts and crafts shows. They lived in a small house on the Gulf Coast of Florida, where Gloria walked the white sandy beaches and collected shark's teeth, while Scibby built a guest house where visitors could stay. They were never apart again.

Gloria and Scibby with Preston, Raymond, and Lynn in 1947[22]

CHAPTER NINE

State Line

The country of Vietnam is a thousand-mile strip on the coast of Southeast Asia, bordered by China, Laos, and Cambodia. Coastal lowland extends along the South China Sea with extensive forested mountains inland. The south of the country contains the prominent Mekong River delta. Rice farming is the dominant agriculture in Vietnam.

Vietnam developed a culture distinct from the Chinese civilization to the north. The Chinese Han Dynasty ruled Vietnam from AD 100 to 900, followed by five hundred years of independent Vietnamese rule. Intermittent civil wars and colonizing efforts by European nations ended with the conquest of Vietnam by France in the 1880s. French rule lasted until the Japanese occupation of Vietnam during World War II. At the end of the war, French rule was restored but faced a rebellion by the Vietnamese people, who were determined to achieve an independent Vietnam. This led to the first Indochina War from 1945 to 1954.

The battle of Dien Bien Phu in 1954 resulted in the defeat of the French army and the end of French domination of Vietnam. The country was partitioned into two administrative regions: the northern half ruled by a communist government led by Ho Chi Minh, the southern half by a government ruled by Emperor Bao Dai. Bao

Dai was replaced by Ngo Dinh Diem in 1955. Soon afterward, a guerrilla campaign to topple the Diem government was begun by the Viet Cong, a South Vietnamese militant group supported by North Vietnam. The North Vietnamese government was supported by the Soviet Union, which sent arms and military aid. Meanwhile, the United States supported the government of South Vietnam and sent military advisors to help train South Vietnamese troops in their fight against the Viet Cong. By 1963, there were 15,000 American advisors in South Vietnam.

David Scoboria, 1950–

January 6, 1973

Eastern South Dakota

"Would you let me out at this exit?"

The driver was startled by the request. "That exit only leads to a farm road. There is no traffic at all."

"That's all right. I will be fine."

The driver pulled the car onto the freeway shoulder, stopping just past the exit ramp. The young man opened the door, climbed out, and reached back to pick up his pack from the floor. "Thanks for the ride," he said.

"Yeah, good luck to you, kid," the driver said.

The young man closed the passenger door and stepped back. The car accelerated onto the freeway, passed beneath the overpass, and diminished in the distance. The young man walked up the exit ramp. At the top, he looked each way down a two-lane paved road. Nothing could be seen in either direction. No houses or trees broke up the flat expanse of the prairie. At the top of the entrance ramp in front of him was a sign marked with bold lettering:

NO HITCHHIKING PERMITTED PAST THIS POINT.

He looked back at the freeway. An occasional car sped by, but minutes passed before the next one came into view. It was early January, and there were no tourists. The day was coming to an end. Dark clouds drifted overhead, and a chill wind blew. Snow might fall in the night. It was time to get ready for darkness. Checking to see that no cars were visible on the side road, the young man slipped back down the grassy slope to the freeway and walked under the cover of the overpass. A rough concrete berm stretched up at a 45-degree angle. He scrambled up the berm. Near the top, just below the concrete slab, the berm flattened out, and a horizontal ledge stretched back three feet. The concrete girders supporting the overpass extended down nearly to the ledge, but between the girders was a sheltered niche. The young man slung his pack down on the ledge, reached inside to pull out a flashlight, then swept the beam across the ledge. The light revealed only a few scattered pebbles, no trash from previous visitors. This isolated farm road exit was an unlikely place for a hitchhiker to stop. The ledge would be a good place to spend the night.

He swept the pebbles off an area big enough for his sleeping bag. Reaching into the pack, he pulled out a chunk of Visqueen, six feet square, left it folded in half and laid out the three-foot width on the ledge. Next came the foam sleeping pad, unrolled and spread out, followed by the sleeping bag, pulled out of the stuff sack and shaken a few times to fluff up the down insulation. Occasionally, a car passed by on the freeway below, but it was dark at the ledge, and the young man was nearly invisible to anyone passing by.

Sitting on the sleeping bag, he removed his hiking boots and placed them at the open end of the bag. When padded with his shirt, they would be his pillow. Inside the pack was a glass fruit juice bottle filled with water. He placed it on the concrete away from the edge. Next came a brown bag with a partially eaten loaf of homemade bread and a chunk of hard cheese. He cut rough wedges off the cheese block with his pocketknife, tore off chunks of the bread, and washed the food down with water from the bottle. Nearly a third of the loaf remained, enough to last until he reached Pennsylvania.

The young man thought back on the past two and a half days since he walked onto the freeway twenty miles east of Portland, Oregon. Few hitchhikers were on the highways in January, and he had only waited a short time between rides. Last evening, darkness found him standing on the outskirts of Twin Falls, Idaho. A semi pulled over and stopped. The driver was hauling a load of mixed freight to Gillette, Wyoming, and planned to drive all night. It had been a long night sitting in the cab of the truck, talking over the roar of the engine. The young man grew tired, but the driver had picked him up to have some company, so he forced himself to stay awake. The miles and the towns went by: Cody, Sheridan, Buffalo. The driver complained about the government and talked about college football games. The young man talked about growing up on the farm in Pennsylvania and about his brother in the army. From time to time, the driver picked up his CB microphone and talked with other truck drivers on the road.

It was early morning when they reached the exit outside Gillette. The driver pulled the truck over, and the young man climbed out. It was nearly daylight, so he kept going, caught rides from men going to work, crossed into South Dakota, then picked up a series of long rides that took him across the state, sometimes from a salesman, a man going to a convention or heading home, always a single man, usually middle-aged. Now the young man was tired. Sleep would feel good tonight.

The cars passing beneath him on the freeway had their lights on. Daylight had faded to darkness, although it was only about six in the evening. A long night was coming. If he stayed warm, it would be all right. He slipped his legs into the sleeping bag, took off his coat and wool shirt, folded the shirt, and laid it on his boots. He eased his body down into the bag, spreading the coat on top of him. The lower half of his body slowly became warm. He laid his head back on the boots and closed his eyes.

It was totally dark when the young man woke, and the freeway was quiet. Once in a while, a car or truck passed by, and the noise reverberated off the concrete slab of the overpass, then silence quickly returned. A bit of moisture dampened his forehead. Looking up, he saw the expansion joint where the slab met the concrete abutment, and the two interlocked in a series of fingerlike steel projections. A small gap allowed the fingers to slip back and forth when the slab expanded or contracted as the temperature changed, or when a heavy truck passed over. A flake of snow drifted through the gap and onto his face. Another landed on his cheek. The rest of him was warm inside the sleeping bag. This was a good place to pass the night.

He wondered what time it was. Probably nearly midnight, only a guess since he did not wear a watch. He wouldn't know the night was over until the sky began to grow light at dawn, hours away. It was odd to make this trip in the middle of winter. Other trips had been during the summer, when the days were long, the nights warm, and cars crowded the roads. He wouldn't have made this trip at all except for the notice he received last month from the draft board. It directed him to appear at the Selective Service office in Doylestown, Pennsylvania, at 10 a.m. on January 10, 1973. At that time he could appeal the rejection of his application for conscientious objector status. The young man knew the appeal would be rejected. His draft status would revert to 1-A, and soon he would be called up for induction into the Army. What then? There was no point in worrying about that now.

His thoughts drifted back to the farm in Pennsylvania where he had grown up. It wasn't a real farm, just forty acres of mixed fields and woods in eastern Pennsylvania, a few miles from the Delaware River near the border of New Jersey. It was the only home he knew. He was a toddler when his parents borrowed the money for a down payment on the land, and his father built a house for the family to live in. His parents were schoolteachers, born in Brooklyn, met at Tufts College in Boston, and married during the Depression. During World War II, his father served in the Pacific for the Navy. There was a photo in the family album of the young man as a little tyke, with his father's lieutenant hat on his head and the Navy dress coat draped around him, the hem nearly touching the floor. He had two older brothers and an older sister. A rural dirt road bordered the farm, and it was miles to the nearest village, so the family did most things together. They swam in a shallow pool in a nearby stream, played hearts and poker on the dining room table, and worked at landscaping jobs the father picked up in the summers to augment his meager teaching income.

The oldest brother, Preston, went away to college on a Navy scholarship and returned years later with short hair, a college degree, and wearing a Navy lieutenant's uniform much like his father's. The middle brother, Ray, fixed up a series of old cars, which he drove to college and back. He did the wiring and plumbing at the farm and practiced honkytonk tunes on the old piano that sat in the living room. Lynn, the boy's sister, loved animals and kept pets in her bedroom. The boy watched the rest of the family, took part in the card games, and helped with projects when he could. Gradually, everyone left. One brother in the Navy, one at college, and his sister training for a career in nursing.

The year turned to 1963. The house was quiet in the evenings with everyone gone. My parents and I watched TV in the living room, our dinners on metal tray tables in front of us. The nightly news was Chet Huntley and David Brinkley, the old black-and-white TV picture peppered with static. Among the news stories were newsreels about riots in a place called South Vietnam. We watched scenes of crowds and noise, puffs of tear gas, and people fleeing.

One day, a very different event appeared on the screen. The camera showed an old man with a shaven head. He wore a robe, but its color could not be distinguished on the black-and-white TV. The man carried a can in one hand. He picked a spot and sat on the ground, then upended the can and poured liquid over his head and body, drenching his clothes. He lit a match, and his clothing and body were instantly engulfed in flames while he sat quietly. The commentator explained that the man was a Buddhist monk in South Vietnam who was sacrificing himself as a protest against the policies of the government and its leader, Ngo Dinh Diem. I watched the scene but found it hard to understand. A tiny burn hurt a lot when you touched a hot pan on the stove. How could this man carry out an act he knew would kill him while he suffered excruciating pain? The news moved on to other stories, accounts of the freedom riders demonstrating for Black rights in the South. Then it flashed to a commercial of a man wearing western clothing and cowboy boots, smoking a Marlboro cigarette.

Within a week, the news showed a second monk in a robe, calmly pouring liquid on himself, then sitting motionless as he died a fiery death. I wondered, how could a person believe in something so strongly that he would sacrifice himself in horrible pain? The two scenes remained in the back of my mind. Much of the time, I was busy with schoolwork, wrestling practice, and singing in the school choir in preparation for the spring concert. Most memories faded away, but a few, like those of the Buddhist monks, remained beneath the surface, engraved on my memory.

A few months later, the news reported that a revolt of army officers toppled the South Vietnamese government and killed the leader, Diem. A series of short-lived governments followed. A year passed. The United States provided advisors to the Vietnamese army to prepare them to fight against an adversary known as the Viet Cong. Vicious battles occurred, and a few of the advisors were killed. It seemed as though the United States had taken sides in a war, but our soldiers were not allowed to fight. It was strange. Meanwhile, I had a crush on a girl in one of my classes and sat near her whenever possible. I was fourteen years old and lived miles from her house, so I only saw her at school. I ran on the cross-country team, although that year I always finished near the back of the pack.

One night, the news announced that North Vietnamese patrol boats had attacked an American destroyer in the Gulf of Tonkin. President Lyndon Johnson called upon Congress to authorize our troops to respond. This made sense to me. The situation in Vietnam had been confusing for years. Congress agreed that the president could authorize whatever force he felt appropriate in Vietnam. Soon afterward, marines splashed ashore at Da Nang. American troops became entangled in battles in the jungle. Along with the arrival of troops came casualties. Every night on the news, a segment showed photographs of young men who had been killed in Vietnam, men whose ages ranged from eighteen to twenty-two years old. A moment of silence followed the photos.

Then it was 1966, and I was a junior in high school. My oldest brother, Preston, had married. His wife had given birth to a baby boy and was expecting a second baby. My brother, Ray, had graduated from college and was stationed at an Army base in Alabama. I flew there to visit him, and he showed me around the base. We ate hamburgers at fast food joints in the nearby town. On the flight home, I saw a tornado in the distance out of the window of the airplane. My sister Lynn worked as a practical nurse. When I turned sixteen, I passed the driver's license test and started driving to school and back in an old Rambler Metropolitan that Ray had fixed up for me. Meanwhile, the number of American troops in South Vietnam exceeded 400,000 men.

In November, the school principal made an announcement in our school assembly. The school would sponsor two students to attend a weeklong conference hosted by the American Friends Service Committee, a Quaker-affiliated organization. The subject of the conference would be the war in Vietnam. I applied and was accepted as one of the students. It was a long bus ride to Washington, D.C., where the conference was held. There were twenty-five participants, high school students from schools scattered around the East Coast. At the first meeting, we sat in a circle, introduced ourselves, and voiced our opinions about the war in Vietnam. A few students supported the United States' position, a few were adamantly opposed, but most had mixed feelings or no opinion at all. I was in the last group. I supported the United States but knew little about what was happening in Vietnam, and I wanted to know more.

We toured Washington, D.C., visited the Capitol Building, ate our meals together, and met with a variety of officials. A representative from the U.S. State Department spoke to us. He explained that South Vietnam was being invaded by North Vietnam, and the United States was helping South Vietnam protect itself. I came away from this briefing confused. Why were both countries named Vietnam? Why was such a large group of South Vietnamese, the Viet Cong, fighting against the government? The next day, we visited the Embassy of Thailand. Our group was shown into an ornate meeting room where we sat in a circle around the ambassador from Thailand, a distinguished older man. When he spoke, he did not criticize the United States or its actions in Vietnam. Instead, he said something that stayed with me for a long time. He said governments have difficulty admitting they have made a mistake. He did not say this specifically about the United States' involvement in the war in Vietnam, but that is what I understood his statement to mean.

The school year ended, summer passed, and my senior year in high school began. Scenes of the war in Vietnam appeared on the news every night. The Viet Cong staged attacks on cities and government facilities. Also shown every night were scenes of protests taking place in our country against American involvement in the war. The war casualty figures steeply increased. By spring of 1968, American troop levels in South Vietnam exceeded a half million men. One of them was my brother Ray, who was stationed in the city of Hue, in charge of a large supply depot. My life was busy with school, spending time with my girlfriend, competing in wrestling meets, and deciding what to do after high school. My high school years had been focused on getting good grades, but something did not feel right. The grades seemed to have little importance. I knew nothing about the world except what I had learned in school, and it was time to look in other places. Against my father's wishes, I decided to not go to college for a year.

School ended, I spent my last summer at home, worked for my father again, grew a beard as a teenage protest. In the fall, my friends left for college. My summer girlfriend wrote several times from college, then stopped writing. Had I made a big mistake in choosing not to go to school? Then, in late September, I received a job offer from the United States Geological Survey to work as a technician at a research station in the Arctic. I had applied at numerous government agencies during the summer with little hope of actually getting a job. But here it was. In my brother Ray's bedroom, I found an old army duffel bag and packed a few clothes in it. My mother made up a bedroll with two army blankets held together by safety pins, and I stuffed it into the bag. One more thing had to be done before I could go anywhere. I turned eighteen years old, so I went to the local draft office in Doylestown, Pennsylvania, and registered.

A few days later, I left, hitchhiking to California where the USGS office was located. It took thirteen days to get there. During that time, I met people and saw parts of this country that I didn't know existed. A few nights I slept on the floor of college dormitory rooms of friends from high school, but most of the time I was somewhere on the road, usually a little scared.

Each mile passed brought new sights. Ohio and Indiana were flat and open with an endless succession of farms, each with a huge barn. The crops had been harvested, and empty fields stretched out on both sides of the freeway. As I neared Chicago, the roadside was lined with stores and warehouses. At the end of the fourth day, I was dropped off on the outskirts of the city. The sky was clear, but it was cold and dark. A motel loomed just off the freeway exit. I entered the motel office and asked about the cost of a room for the night. Fifty-five dollars came the answer. I only had seventy dollars in my wallet, so that was too much money. I left the office and walked into the parking lot. Beyond the asphalt lot stretched a wasteland, grass and weeds three feet tall. In the dark field past where the parking lot lights shone, I laid the duffel bag in the grass and pulled out the bedroll. It was the first of numerous nights spent outside on the trip.

In central Iowa, with cornfields on both sides of the road, an Allied Moving Van pulled over on the gravel in front of me, and the driver said, "Hop in." He introduced himself as Maynard Haskins, a big man, three hundred pounds or more. He told me he lived in his truck and only visited his home in Minnesota once or twice a year. I rode with him for two days and helped to unload furniture at several houses. We drove through Iowa farm country and through open prairie in South Dakota, where grass-covered hills stretched into the distance. He talked constantly, paid for my meals and gave me twenty dollars when he dropped me off outside of Rapid City.

The next ride left me on the edge of the Black Hills. I started walking through the hilly country, and for several hours, there was nothing but forest on both sides of the road. Then, an old station wagon pulled over. The middle-aged man inside the car looked at me and said, "I will give you a ride and a place to stay for the night if you will go to church with me."

"All right," I said. The man was surprised, but motioned me into the car. He introduced himself as Les. We drove on the winding road through the Black Hills for several hours before crossing into Wyoming, flat and featureless. A half hour of driving took us to a crossroads, where one choice led east into Nebraska. Twenty miles later we reached Harrison, Nebraska. A tall grain elevator towered over the small town.

Les turned a corner onto a side street and stopped in front of a small house trailer. He opened the trailer door and called out, "Mary, we have company tonight." A woman came from the back room, simply clad in a house dress. She nodded and shyly said hello to me. We ate a modest meal sitting at the small table in the trailer. I told the couple where I was from and about my goal to reach California.

After dinner, we walked several blocks to a brick building with a neon sign in front that read "Church." The inside was plain, an open room with rows of folding chairs, mostly filled. We found seats and the service began. It was not too different from the Lutheran services I was familiar with until the end, when the minister asked for people to give testimony. People stood and told stories of how God had impacted their lives, from success in farming to curing them of health problems. Mary talked about how she had suffered from back pain for many years, but had prayed to God, and just the day before, Les had put his arms around her, and she felt no pain. The scene became animated. Some people spoke in a language I could not understand. Others moved to the front of the room near the pulpit, got down on their knees and wailed. Les and I moved to the back of the room. The minister joined us, and we chatted quietly for a while. When the activity in the front diminished, the minister returned to the pulpit, gave a benediction, and ended the service. We walked back to the trailer. That night, I slept on the sofa in the tiny living room of the trailer. Mary cooked breakfast for us in the morning, and Les drove me across the state line back to the intersection with the main highway. When we parted, he shook my hand and wished me good luck. I was moved by the kindness of this gentle couple, who did not know me at all. They took in a bearded stranger, fed him, and gave him a safe place to sleep.

That evening in the darkness outside of Cheyenne, Wyoming, I stopped at a diner for a cup of coffee. When I got up to leave, a young man approached me. He and four others were ferrying yellow school buses to Reno, Nevada. They saw my sign, knew I was hitchhiking, and wanted me to help them drive the buses. What I didn't know was that one of the young men was a drug user, and he needed his fix from time to time. For several days, I took a turn at the wheel of the bus he was driving, while he moved to the back of the bus, shot up and lay motionless on the back seat for hours. The miles rolled by, three buses in front of the one I drove and one behind me. The bus was easy to drive since it had an automatic transmission, power steering and air brakes, but on the long downhill stretches through Utah and Nevada, the air pressure went down each time I pressed the brake. I grew terrified that the brakes would give out, and the bus would careen into a canyon. It was a relief each time the slope bottomed out, and we started up the next rise. On both sides of the freeway was a wasteland with little visible besides sagebrush. We passed miles of sandy barrens where nothing was growing. Once, I saw a herd of antelope running in the distance. At night, we slept for a few hours on the hard seats of the bus. After two days, the convoy arrived at the outskirts of Reno, Nevada. The young men headed off to deliver the buses, and I continued to California. My arrival in Menlo Park at the Geological Survey office, a few miles south of San Francisco, seemed almost a letdown after the trip to get there.

The year at the Arctic research station was a good change from school. Most of the job went well. It was fascinating to live in the Arctic, darkness that lasted for months in the winter, endless sun during the summer. There were no newspapers or TV, just a dozen men living in battered house trailers on an ice island in the middle of the Arctic Ocean. I screwed up a few times, so failure was part of the year's lesson.

Although I didn't hear much about it, the world kept turning during those twelve months. Richard Nixon was elected President, the first moon landing occurred, and a giant rock and roll festival took place at Woodstock, New York. The war continued in Vietnam, and young men died. My brother Ray returned safely to the United States and started attending graduate school. My brother Preston and his wife added a third child to their family. I didn't think about these things. My life consisted of taking mud cores of the ocean floor and getting along with the crew on the ice base. I read *War and Peace,* took walks on the ice wearing insulated pants and a heavy parka, and sat in my trailer to read the letters that came from my family.

At the end of the summer, the ice froze strong enough that a Navy C-130 was able to land at the base, and I left the Arctic. After stopping in Barrow, Alaska, a series of flights took me to Fairbanks, Anchorage, and San Francisco, where I ended my employment with the U.S. Geological Survey. Another flight took me to Portland, Oregon, and the start of college. It was hard to return to school. Classes didn't seem to matter much. For two years I got by while doing as little schoolwork as possible. My draft status was 2-S, which guaranteed I would not be drafted as long as I stayed in college. One notable event occurred on December 1,1969, the first draft lottery. The guys who lived on my dormitory floor clustered around a transistor radio to listen to the sequence of dates as they were called out. We joked about whose birthdate would be the first chosen. I was the loser; my birth date was the 18th date selected in the lottery. If I left school, I would be drafted right away.

That school year was disrupted by protests against America's involvement in the Vietnam War. Classes at the college were canceled for a week, and during that time, there were speeches, discussion groups, and rallies. I was amazed that young men only a year or two older than me could speak with such clarity and fervor about why the United States should stop sending young men to fight in Vietnam. Gradually, I came to believe that my country's involvement in the war was wrong, although I did not know what to do about it. I didn't know how to speak in public, and I didn't believe that violent protests were the answer.

However, student protests were occurring on many college campuses in the United States, and some became violent. At a protest rally in Ohio, four students of Kent State University were shot and killed by National Guardsmen. A few weeks later, a protest at Jackson State University resulted in the shooting deaths of two students.

Spring break approached, and a friend and I decided to visit Vancouver, Canada. Shortly before we left, a young man approached me.

He had received a notice to appear for induction into the army, but had decided to go to Canada instead. Could he travel with us? The three of us left a few days later, drove north through Washington State, and stopped at the Canadian border. We were anxious, but crossing the border was uneventful. We dropped the young man off in Vancouver, and never heard of him again.

After two years, I decided to leave school. The only reason I had for staying in college would have been to avoid the draft, and that wasn't good enough. It was better to face the issue. School had been all right, and I had learned a few things, but the most memorable event was the night a young lady slipped into my bed in the darkness. Life was more interesting than I expected.

In August 1971, a few months after I left college, a notice from the draft board arrived, changing my draft status to 1-A. After much thought, I sat down and filled out an application to become a conscientious objector. Although I had no religious affiliation, I believed the war was wrong, and this seemed like the best way to make a statement about it. It was not like the Second World War when America and the free world were threatened. In the Vietnam War, both sides claimed to represent the people of Vietnam, but the people of that country bore the brunt of the suffering. Many thousands of South Vietnamese were fighting against the American troops. Our presence did not seem to help matters. I finished the application, added the required references, and mailed it off.

Months passed. I didn't look for a permanent job because I didn't know what was going to happen with the draft. The war was always in the back of my mind. In Vietnam, the fighting continued. Governments changed. The United States and North Vietnam conducted peace talks, but they dragged on and on with few results. In the United States, protests against American involvement in the war intensified. President Nixon began to withdraw American troops from Vietnam, and they were replaced in the field with South Vietnamese troops, a process described as Vietnamization. The court martial of Sergeant William Calley and other soldiers for the massacre of Vietnamese civilians in the hamlet of My Lai was major news on nightly TV. I wasn't aware of these events. A friend and I lived in a cabin twenty miles outside of Portland. The cabin lacked electricity, and we did not subscribe to a newspaper, so only rarely did I learn about national news.

Months later, I was called for a draft physical. This was a day of standing in long lines with other young men, all of us stripped to our underwear. We were poked and prodded, measured and weighed. A month or so later, a letter arrived, rejecting my conscientious objector application. I could appeal this rejection, and I did.

The year 1972 was a presidential election year, and the Democratic candidate was Senator George McGovern, who ran on a platform to end the United States' involvement in Vietnam. I moved into Portland and worked on his campaign for two months, coordinating volunteers to send out bulk mailings to voters in Oregon. Election day arrived, and McGovern was badly defeated by President Nixon. I moved back to the cabin and returned to the temporary jobs I had before the campaign, pruning trees in a local orchard and digging plants for a landscape company. In late November, a notice arrived from the Selective Service office. My appeal was scheduled for January 10, 1973, at the Draft Board office in Doylestown, Pennsylvania.

Christmas came, and I prepared to head back to Pennsylvania. It was not clear to me what would happen after the appeal, but I assumed it would be turned down. There might be weeks or months until I was ordered to report for induction. I had no idea. I put my gear together, walked down the hill from the cabin, hopped the fence at the edge of the freeway, and stuck out my thumb.

———•———

In the darkness beneath the overpass, a new sound could be heard: a large truck driving up the exit from the freeway. It stopped at the top of the ramp, then with a series of gear changes, accelerated, approached, then rolled onto the overpass. The expansion joint flexed a little as the truck passed above my head. Perhaps it contained bales of hay for one of the local farms, or maybe a load of cattle. When the noise of the truck receded into the background, silence returned. Only an occasional vehicle passed by on the freeway below. There was no point in getting up. Sleep returned.

———•———

It was early morning when the young man woke up again. Traffic had picked up on the interstate. He rolled onto his side and opened the pack, took out bread and cheese and ate breakfast, washing it down with water from the jar. He slid out of the sleeping bag, put on his shirt, coat, and shoes, and stuffed the sleeping bag back into the sack, rolled up the pad, folded up the Visqueen, and loaded it in the pack. Finally, he picked up the pack and clambered down the concrete berm to the shoulder of the freeway. Outside the shadow of the overpass, the ground was white with a dusting of snow. One hundred yards to the east was a large road sign. As he walked toward it, the words became clear in the early morning light:

YOU ARE LEAVING THE STATE OF SOUTH DAKOTA

One hundred feet farther east was another sign:

WELCOME TO MINNESOTA

The young man walked to a point midway between the two signs, turned around to face traffic and put down the pack, leaning it against his legs. A car approached rapidly on the freeway. He held out his arm with thumb outstretched. The car passed by without slowing. More cars passed. Back at the overpass he had just left, a South Dakota state police car crossed over the interstate, turned back west and entered the highway, heading in the opposite direction. The young man chuckled a little. No state policeman would harass him in this no man's land between the two states. In the next half hour, two cars stopped to offer him a ride, but they were only going to the next exit. He thanked the drivers but passed up their offers. A few minutes later, a large sedan with a Montana license plate pulled over. "I'm going as far as Chicago," the driver said. "You are welcome to ride along."

The young man slid into the passenger seat and leaned his pack against his legs.

"Thanks," he said, "I am heading to Pennsylvania."

Epilogue

For the first two hundred years after the founding of the United States republic, a military leader from a previous war had a good chance of winning the presidential election. Starting with George Washington, the commander during the Revolutionary War, the trend continued with Andrew Jackson, the general at the battle of New Orleans in the War of 1812, followed by William Henry Harrison, general during the Blackhawk War of 1832, and Zachary Taylor, the leading general during the Mexican War. The Civil War furthered the careers of numerous presidents, including Andrew Johnson, Ulysses S. Grant, Rutherford Hayes, James Garfield, Chester Arthur, Benjamin Harrison, and William McKinley. Teddy Roosevelt was widely known for his exploits at the Battle of San Juan Hill in the Spanish-American War. Every president from Dwight Eisenhower to George H. W. Bush served in the Second World War in some capacity.

Beginning in 1992, a new trend emerged. Bill Clinton, who remained in college during the Vietnam War, bested George H. W. Bush, who had served as a Navy pilot during the Second World War. In 1996, Clinton won re-election over Bob Dole, who was seriously injured in Italy during the Second World War. In 2004, George W. Bush defeated John Kerry, who was wounded in combat in the Vietnam War. This trend continued in 2008, when John McCain, a true hero and prisoner of war during the Vietnam era, was defeated by Barack Obama. Finally, in 2016, Donald Trump, who had a medical deferment from serving in the army,[23] defeated a host of other Republican candidates during the primaries, none of whom were veterans. Trump went on to win the presidential election. In 2020, Trump lost the presidential election to Joe Biden, who also had medical deferments during the Vietnam War.

From 1954 through 1973, 3.4 million Americans served in Vietnam. American involvement reached its peak in 1968, when there were 536,000 military personnel in the country. This number was gradually reduced over the next five years until the final pullout of American troops in March of 1973. The number of men who were drafted into the army fell from a high of 382,000 in 1966 to 49,000 in 1972, and down to 646 in 1973.[24] In Vietnam, after the evacuation of the American troops, the South Vietnamese army continued to fight, but they gradually lost ground to the Viet Cong and North Vietnamese soldiers until their final defeat in 1975.

What about the young men who, in one way or another, chose not to be part of the United States military effort in Vietnam? Was there any difference between a man who stayed in college, a man who received a medical deferment, or a man who applied to be a conscientious objector? After all, the result was the same: one less person eligible to be drafted and serve in Vietnam. None of them were heroes. The heroes were the men who went to Vietnam and served in a war that sometimes made little sense to them. 58,200 American servicemen died in Vietnam, and several hundred thousand returned to the United States damaged in body or mind. Did the war check the spread of communism in Southeast Asia, or was it a losing fight against the desire of the Vietnamese people for independence?

The young men who served in Vietnam, those who stayed in college, the ones who fled to Canada or received medical or other deferments, are now old men, if they are still alive. They receive Social Security and Medicare. The signs held by men at freeway entrances and outside of shopping malls no longer read "Vietnam Vet." In 1994, the United States established normal diplomatic relations with the government of Vietnam. Fifty years after the end of the war, Vietnam is an important trading partner to the United States, and it acts as a check on Chinese expansion in Southeast Asia.

What about the young man who was heading to Pennsylvania to appeal the rejection of his conscientious objector application? He reached Pennsylvania after five days on the road. The next morning, he called the draft board to check on his appointment. To his surprise, he was told he had been reclassified 1-H. He had served his year of eligibility and was no longer subject to the draft. This was stunning news, an outcome he had never considered. Almost all American troops had returned home from Vietnam. No more soldiers were needed for the war. He stayed in Pennsylvania for a few days, then loaded his pack and headed back to Oregon. He didn't know what he was going to do, but it was time to make new plans.

I remember that trip, still feel the cold winter wind on my face, and hear the roar of a truck passing by on the freeway. Vaguely, I remember the anxiety I felt about my decision to file as a conscientious objector during the Vietnam War. But fifty years have passed, and after raising a family, working at a career, and experiencing hopes and disappointments, that image is far away. It is like the vision that I saw as a small boy when I looked at the world through an empty toilet paper tube. Off in the distance, I see that young man and watch what he is doing. But can that faint, distant image actually be me?

Final Notes

I began this project several years ago with no idea if there was anything to discover about my ancestors. Much of what I found was a surprise to me. In chapter 1, there is no way to know if the Scobaria mentioned in Foxe's *Book of Martyrs* from 1563 describes a person who was one of my ancestors. However, I come from a family of teachers, and that man was a teacher. Perhaps it was only a coincidence that the name is similar to mine.

Chapter 2: The photo at the start of the story is a real barn, located on Skyburriowe Farm in South Cornwall. The photo was taken by my mother in 1971 on a trip she and my father made to England. They only found Skyburriowe Farm because my father became bored with the museum in Falmouth where my mother was looking at Cornwall Parish records. He left the museum and stepped into a nearby pub. As he drank a pint, he struck up a conversation with another man in the pub and described what brought him to Falmouth. "Scoboria!" the man exclaimed. "I live just up the road from Scoboria Farm." Dad quickly retrieved Mom from the museum, and they followed the man from the pub along country roads for a dozen miles, until they reached a lane with a signpost at the end that read "Skyburriowe." My parents drove in the lane. The farm was owned by a family who were no relation to Skyburriowe, and they knew of no one by that name. But there were two old barns on the farm, and it was said that the farm was named after them. My mother took a photo of the barns and sent a copy to each of her children. The barns were old, but no one knew when they were built.

Chapter 3: There are no records of a Scoboria fighting for the king in the British Civil Wars, but Cornwall did muster out for the king, and there was likely great pressure for local men to join one of the bands. Barbados was the most successful of the early British colonies in the New World, and it was not unusual for men to become bound workers in order to make their way overseas. We know that family members lived in Cornwall at the time because a man named John Skebyrryow was listed on the muster rolls in 1569, and he owned a bow and armor.[25]

My wife was born Linda Potter. When she was a girl, her grandmother told her that the Potters "had left England in a fat hurry, and when they got to the American colonies, they wanted to change their name because of the bad association with the name Potter." It made sense to incorporate Vincent Potter's story into that of my ancestor in chapter 3.

Chapter 4: By the time of the Battle of Trafalgar in 1805, the parish records are extensive. While John Lower is not listed on the HMS *Temeraire* in 1805, a man named James Scoborya was listed as a landsman aboard HMS *Conqueror* in the battle. He is described as a volunteer, but perhaps he too was a pressed man.[26]

Chapter 5: The parish records of the wedding of John Scobora and Eden Lower in 1828 note that John signed his name but Eden made her mark, indicating that she did not read or write.[27] John was the son of James Scobora, and in 1815, a man named James Scobora was found drowned on a beach in West Cornwall.[28] If this was John's father, he left behind a wife and eight children. My grandmother told a story that her husband's ancestor had been a ship's pilot in Falmouth, Cornwall. The Falmouth pilot records from 1815 revealed that all the senior pilots were men in their sixties and seventies. The apprentice pilots were men in their thirties and all had the same last name as the senior pilots. If John Scobora was a pilot, it was only as an apprentice, and it would have been hard to break into a profession where fathers passed along their knowledge and their position to their sons.

The passenger manifest of the barque *Alchymist* lists the Scabora family among the passengers on the voyage to Saint John, New Brunswick, in 1833. Most of the old records from New Brunswick were destroyed in a fire in the late 1800s, so it was only by chance that this manifest survived. The lack of other records about the Scoboria family after their arrival in New Brunswick is as telling in their absence as records would be.

Chapter 6: It was a surprise to learn that my great-great-grandfather and my great-grandfather worked for over seventy years in the same factory near Boston. U.S. Census records list their occupations as brass finisher and machinist, so it is clear they worked with their hands. I will always wonder if my great-grandfather left the ministry for financial reasons, or because he had a change in his beliefs.

Chapter 7: My grandfather was a fine runner in college, and he did participate in a famous two-mile invitational race in 1905. His best time in the two-mile was not even close to the winning time in that race, which was won by George Bonhag, a man who won several gold medals in the 1908 Olympics. The loss of a shoe made no difference to the results, but I am proud that my grandfather was invited to participate.

Chapter 8: During World War II, both my mother and father saved the letters they received from each other. Documenting their experiences required choosing a few excerpts from hundreds of pages of very personal writing. The story includes only a small fraction of what they wrote to each other during the year that Dad was away. Their dedication to each other lasted for the rest of their lives.

Chapter 9: The Vietnam War occupied the lives and the thoughts of young men during the 1960s, both the men who went to Vietnam, and the men who opposed the war. I felt great relief that our nation was at peace when my son turned eighteen years old in 1999. Fifty years after the end of the Vietnam War, a land war is being fought in Eastern Europe with no end in sight. It makes me wonder if our species can learn to live in peace?

What did I learn about about the family stories that I heard as a boy? There was a particle of truth in each one, though perhaps not the story told at our dinner table. While I will never know if my stories approximate the experiences of my fathers, I learned that each of them faced difficult times in their lives and had to decide what to do. Whether it was to cross the Atlantic Ocean to an unknown land, to leave the ministry and work in a factory, or to marry a young woman because of an unplanned pregnancy, each of them had hard choices to make. I respect their decisions.

Evolution of a Name

1500–1600: Cornwall Parish Records

Skebereow

Skeberyow

Skeberrow

Skeberoon

Skeboriowe

Scoberrian

Scrarraborow

1600–1700: Cornwall Parish Records

Skaberie

Scaberio

Scibberio

Sciberio

Skibberow

Skeberrioe

Skeberriow

Skeberrio

Skeberyowe

Skeberio

Skeberioe

Skyburio

1700–1800: Cornwall Parish Records

Scoboryo

Scoborye

Scoberya

Scoborio (1788)

Scoberrian

Scaborio

Scabery

Scaberya

Scaberrio

Scaberiah

Skeboryar

Sciborio

Sciborier

Scraberrian

Skyberio

1800–1900: Cornwall Parish Records, Newspapers, Passenger Manifests

Scoboria (1822)
Scobery
Scoborio
  (Australia)

Scoborie
Scoboryo
Scoberia
Scoborier

Scaboria
Scaboyer
Scabora
Scibboyer

1900–2000: Newspapers

Scoboria
  (United States)

Scoborio
  (Australia)

Scaboria
Scorboria

Internet, with Misspellings

Scoboria
Scoborio
Scaboria
Scoborie

Scorboria
Scorborio
Scoberia
Seoboria

Soboria
Skoboria

Acknowledgments

Genealogical material in these stories come from a variety of sources. Most of it derives from research done by William Tregonning Hooper, the borough librarian of Falmouth, Cornwall, 1935 to 1941. This information was requested by Dr. Arthur Scoboria (1872–1950), the first cousin of my great-grandfather. His interest in family genealogy descended to his daughter Marjorie Scoboria (1906–2010), who completed a family genealogy of the Scoboria family in the United States and Canada from 1833 to 1970.

My mother Gloria Scoboria spent time at Falmouth in 1971 looking into the parish records. Her research confirmed and added to the information provided by Tregonning Hooper.

Modern sources of family information include the Cornwall OPC Database and Ancestry.com. Other sources are listed in the bibliography for each chapter.

Many people have read and provided helpful comments on the rough draft. These include my brothers Preston Scoboria and Raymond Scoboria, my son Evan Scoboria, my niece Francine Scoboria, and my stepdaughter Mindy Styczynski. Judy Klayman and Karen Reed read the rough draft and made many useful suggestions.

Michael Heatherly did a line by line edit of the rough draft and his suggestions improved the document a great deal.

Finally, this book would not have been completed without the tremendous support and encouragement given by my wife, Linda. She listened to each story and gave helpful suggestions, did a line-by-line edit of the early rough draft, and was an unceasing source of help.

Skyburriowe Farm is a family-run Cornish dairy farm set in the gorgeous surroundings of the Lizard Peninsula and makes an ideal base for a holiday or weekend break in Cornwall.

Notes

1. John Foxe, *Foxe's Book of Martyrs,* 1563. Chapter V, "The Persecution of Dr. Constantine," https://www.ccel.org/f/foxe/martyrs/fox105.htm; https://bibletruthpublishers.com/foxes-book-of-martyrs/john-foxe/lbd22649.

2. Unpublished photograph, taken by Gloria Scoboria at Skyburriowe Farm, Cornwall, England, 1971.

3. William French, *Oliver Cromwell at Marston Moor,* painting by Ernest Croft, 1860.

4. J. L. Comstock, *A System of Natural Philosophy: Principles of Mechanics* (Pratt, Woodford, and Co., 1850), 79.

5. Erica Guilane-Nachez, *Naval Battle: Trafalgar.*

6. Passenger Manifest of the barque *Alchymist,* taking passengers from Falmouth, England to Saint John, New Brunswick Colony, July 1833, New Brunswick Provincial Archives.

7. David A. Wells, *The Science of Common Things: A Familiar Explanation of the First Principles of Physical Science,* 1873, https://etc.usf.edu/clipart.

8. Obituary for John Scoboria, *Saint John Morning News,* April 22, 1867, Provincial Archives of New Brunswick.

9. Unpublished family photos, Joseph and Margaret Scoboria, by Edward S. Dunshee and Son, artist photographer, Boston, 1876.

10. Photo of Clarence Preston Scoboria, Tufts College Yearbook, 1904.

11. Unpublished family photo of Sophia Hawes Livingstone, photographer unknown, 1904.

12. Unpublished family photos of Sophia Scoboria, photographed by Raymond Scoboria, 1967.

13. Unpublished family photo of Clarence Preston Scoboria, Jr., photographer unknown, 1935.

14. Unpublished family photo of Gloria Van Wart, photographer unknown, 1936.

15. Unpublished unofficial log of the Armed Guard officer, Lt. JG C. P. Scoboria Jr., on the SS *Chapultepec*, 1945.

16. Unpublished letters of C. P. Scoboria Jr., 1944–1945.

17. Engagement announcement of C. P. Scoboria Jr. and Gloria Van Wart, *Brooklyn Citizen*, November 27, 1937.

18. "German U-boat attacks, 1943," photo of the damaged U.S. tanker SS *Chapultepec*, December 27, 1943. Document no. 80-G-207601, National Museum of the U.S. Navy, www.history.navy.mil.

19. Unpublished photo of Lt. JG C. P. Scoboria, photographer unknown, 1945.

20. Newspaper column written by C. P. Scoboria Jr. and published in the *Venice* [Fla.] *Gondolier*, November 11, 1992.

21. "Naval Armed Guard Service in World War II," Naval History and Heritage Command, June 1, 2022, www.history.navy.mil.

22. Unpublished family photo of the Scoboria family, photographer unknown, 1947.

23. Dave Roos, "7 Ways Americans Avoided the Draft During the Vietnam War," History.com, May 27, 2025, www.history.com/articles/vietnam-war-draft-avoiding; Leo Shane III, "Trump Made up Injury to Dodge Military Service, His Former Lawyer Testifies," *Military Times*, February 27, 2019, www.militarytimes.com/news/pentagon-congress/2019/02/27/trumps-lawyer-no-basis-for-presidents-medical-deferment-from-vietnam.

24. "Vietnam War U.S. Military Fatal Casualty Statistics," National Archives, 2018, www.archives.gov/research/military/vietnam-war/casualty-statistics.

25. Cornwall OPC Database, record no. 10727 in the Muster Database, transcriber Louise Haywood, www.cornwall-opc-database.org.

26. The [UK] National Archives, "Nelson, Trafalgar, and Those Who Served," s.v. Thomas Scobouja (Scoboryo), www.nationalarchives.gov.uk/trafalgarancestors.

27. Cornwall OPC Database, record no. 1675191 in the Marriage Database, transcriber Nanct Dunstan, www.cornwall-opc-database.org.

28. Cornwall OPC Database, record no. 772581 in the Burials Database, transcriber Philippa Stout, www.cornwall-opc-database.org.

Bibliography

1. The Boat

Foxe, John. *Foxe's Book of Martyrs.* John Day, 1563. www.gutenberg
.org/ebooks/22400.

2. Building the Barns

Barrat, John. *Armada 1588: The Spanish Assault on England.* Pen and
Sword Books, 2005.

Brigden, Susan. *New Worlds, Lost Worlds: The Rule of the Tudors, 1485–
1603.* Viking Penguin, 2001.

Bryant, Arthur. *The Elizabethan Deliverance.* St. Martin's Press, 1981.

Erickson, Carolly. *The First Elizabeth.* St. Martin's Griffin, 1983.

Hanson, Neil. *In Confident Hope of a Miracle: The True History of the
Spanish Armada.* Alfred A. Knopf, 2005.

Morgan, Kenneth, ed. *History of Britain, 1485–1789.*, Sphere Books,
1985.

Usherwood, Stephen, ed. *The Great Enterprise: The History of the Spanish Armada.* Bell & Hyman, 1982.

Websites

History Stack Exchange. "How Long did it Take to Get News of the
Sighting of the Spanish Armada from Land's End to London?"
March 10, 2018.

Strangers Guide.com. "Signal Fires." 2016.

The Year of Living Englishly, "Beacons Across Britain," June 5, 2012.

Wikipedia. "Dissolution of the Monasteries."

Wikipedia. "Prayer Book Rebellion."

Wikipedia. "The House of Tudor."

Woodbury, Sarah. "What Did Medieval People Drink?" Blog post. February 15, 2018.

World History Encyclopedia, "Food and Drink in the Elizabethan Era."

3. Fighting for the King

Abram, Andrew. *Dragoons and Dragoon Operations in the British Civil Wars, 1638–1653.* Helion & Co., 2023.

Barratt, John. *The Civil War in the South-West.* Pen & Sword, 2005.

Brown, H. Miles. *Battles Royal: Charles I and the Civil War in Cornwall & the West.* Libra Books, 1982.

Royle, Trevor. *Civil War: The War of the Three Kingdoms 1638–1660.* Abascus, 2005.

Websites

Gentles, Ian. "The Impact of the Sales of Confiscated Land on English Society During the Revolution 1647–1660." *Social History* 13:26 (1980).

The History of Parliament. "Bevil Grenville (1596–1643)." www .historyofparliamentonline.org/volume/1604-1629/member/ grenville-bevill-1596-1643.

Wikipedia. "Bevil Grenville."

Wikipedia. "John Grenville, 1st Earl of Bath."

4. Trafalgar

Bennett, Geoffrey. *The Battle of Trafalgar.* Naval Institute Press, 1977.

Cornwell, Bernard. *Sharpe's Trafalgar: Spain 1805.* Harper Collins, 2000.

Nicolson, Adam. *Seize the Fire: Heroism, Duty, and the Battle of Trafalgar.* Harper Collins, 2004.

Nordhoff, Charles. *Man-of-War Life.* Pen & Sword, 2013.

Pope, Dudley. *Life in Nelson's Navy.* Naval Institute Press, 1981.

Rodger, N. A. M. *The Wooden World: An Anatomy of the Georgian Navy.* William Collins, 1986.

Schom, Alan. *Trafalgar: Countdown to Battle 1803–1805.* Athenium, 1990.

Willis, Sam. *The Fighting Temeraire: The Battle of Trafalgar and the Ship that Inspired J. M. Turner's Most Famous Painting.* Pegasus Books, 2010.

Websites

Animagraffs. "How an 18th Century Sailing Ship Works." YouTube video. March 10, 2023. https://youtu.be/4Nr1AgIfajI.

Britannica. "Battle of Trafalgar."

Christy, Gabe. "A Day in the Life of a Royal Navy Sailor from 1806." War History Online, March 7, 2017. www.warhistoryonline.com/instant-articles/sailors-life-day-life-royal-navy-sailor-1806.html.

History Detectives, "British Navy Impressment." www.pbs.org/opb/historydetectives/feature/british-navy-impressment.

Lampert, Andrew. "Life at Sea in the Royal Navy in the 18th Century." BBC History, February 17, 2011.

UK Parliament, "Press Gangs." www.parliament.uk/about/living-heritage/transformingsociety/private-lives/yourcountry/overview/pressgangs-.

Wikipedia. "Battle of Trafalgar."

5. The Crossing

Campey, Lucille H. *Planters, Paupers, and Pioneers: English Settlers in Atlantic Canada.* Natural Heritage Books, 2010.

Harper, Marjory, and Stephen Constantine. *Migration and Empire.* Oxford University Press, 2010.

Wilson, D. G. *Falmouth Haven: The Maritime History of a Great West Country Port.* Tempus, 2007.

Websites

Cornwall Parish Records, Cornwall OPC Database, www.cornwall-opc-database.org.

Lavorgna, Karol. "New Brunswick as a Home for Immigrants." New Brunswick Provincial Archives. https://archives2.gnb.ca/Irish/Databases/ImmigrationRecords/text/en-CA/Immigrants.pdf.

6. Finishing the Brass

Brown, William Norman. *The Principles of Dipping, Burnishing, Lacquering and Bronzing Brassware.* Scott, Greenwood & Co, 1900.

Kimball, George A. *Map of the City of Somerville, Massachusetts.* Greenough, Jones, and Co, 1874.

Map of the City of Somerville, 1895. Greenough & Co, 1895.

Somerville Journal, 1872–1929.

Somerville, Massachusetts. *Annual Report of the City of Somerville.* 1876, 1901.

United States Census. 1870, 1900. www.census.gov.

7. Night Train to Calais, Maine

Maine Marriage Records. 1906.

Timetable of the Maine Central Railroad Company. 1905.

Tufts University Yearbook. 1904.

United States Census. 1900–1950. www.census.gov.

8. Darling Girl

Partial Daily log of the Armed Guard officer for the SS *Chapultepec.* December 8, 1944–July 3, 1945.

Scoboria, Gloria. *The Good Life of C. P. Scoboria Jr.* Unpublished manuscript, 1995.

Websites

Britton, Beverly L., Lieutenant Commander. *Navy Stepchildren: The Armed Guard.* U.S. Naval Institute, 1947.

National Museum of the United States Navy. "1943: December 26, Damage to SS *Chapultepec*."

Naval History and Heritage Command. "Naval Armed Guard Service in World War II." June 1, 2022. www.history.navy.mil.

Wikipedia. "United States Navy Armed Guard."

9. State Line

Karnow, Stanley. *Vietnam: A History. The First Complete Account of Vietnam at War.* Viking Press, 1983.

Websites

Brittanica. "Vietnam War 1954–1975." https://www.britannica.com/event/Vietnam-War.

National Archives. "Vietnam War U.S. Military Fatal Casualty Statistics." 2018. https://www.archives.gov/research/military/vietnam-war/casualty-statistics.

Roos, Dave. "7 Ways Americans Avoided the Draft During the Vietnam War." History.com. May 27, 2025. www.history.com/articles/vietnam-war-draft-avoiding.

Shane, Leo III. "Trump Made up Injury to Dodge Military Service, His Former Lawyer Testifies." *Military Times.* February 27, 2019. www.militarytimes.com/news/pentagon-congress/2019/02/27/trumps-lawyer-no-basis-for-presidents-medical-deferment-from-vietnam.

Statista. "Annual Number of United States Military Personnel Conscripted Via the Draft from 1964–1973." https://www.statista.com/statistics/1336037/vietnam-war-us-military-draft.

Wikipedia. "Vietnam War Casualties."

www.ingramcontent.com/pod-product-compliance
Lightning Source LLC
Chambersburg PA
CBHW070459010826
48976CB00021B/1457

9 798889 195082 5